THE LAST SPIRITS OF MANHATTAN

THE LAST SPIRITS OF MANHATTAN

A NOVEL

John A. McDermott

ATRIA BOOKS
New York Amsterdam/Antwerp London
Toronto Sydney/Melbourne New Delhi

An Imprint of Simon & Schuster, LLC
1230 Avenue of the Americas
New York, NY 10020

For more than 100 years, Simon & Schuster has championed authors and the stories they create. By respecting the copyright of an author's intellectual property, you enable Simon & Schuster and the author to continue publishing exceptional books for years to come. We thank you for supporting the author's copyright by purchasing an authorized edition of this book.

No amount of this book may be reproduced or stored in any format, nor may it be uploaded to any website, database, language-learning model, or other repository, retrieval, or artificial intelligence system without express permission. All rights reserved. Inquiries may be directed to Simon & Schuster, 1230 Avenue of the Americas, New York, NY 10020 or permissions@simonandschuster.com.

This book is a work of fiction. Any references to historical events, real people, or real places are used fictitiously. Other names, characters, places, and events are products of the author's imagination, and any resemblance to actual events or places or persons, living or dead, is entirely coincidental.

Copyright © 2025 by John A. McDermott

All rights reserved, including the right to reproduce this book or portions thereof in any form whatsoever. For information, address Atria Books Subsidiary Rights Department, 1230 Avenue of the Americas, New York, NY 10020.

First Atria Books hardcover edition October 2025

ATRIA B O O K S and colophon are trademarks of Simon & Schuster, LLC

Simon & Schuster strongly believes in freedom of expression and stands against censorship in all its forms. For more information, visit BooksBelong.com.

For information about special discounts for bulk purchases, please contact Simon & Schuster Special Sales at 1-866-506-1949 or business@simonandschuster.com.

The Simon & Schuster Speakers Bureau can bring authors to your live event. For more information or to book an event, contact the Simon & Schuster Speakers Bureau at 1-866-248-3049 or visit our website at www.simonspeakers.com.

Interior design by Davina Mock-Maniscalco

Manufactured in the United States of America

1 3 5 7 9 10 8 6 4 2

Library of Congress Control Number: 2025001329

ISBN 978-1-6680-5873-2
ISBN 978-1-6680-5875-6 (ebook)

For Cornelia Banks McDermott,
who taught her children many vital lessons,
chief among them—
never leave the house without a book

Odd things happen to all of us on our way through life without our noticing for a time that they have happened.
J.M. Barrie, *Peter and Wendy*

◆

I like large parties. They're so intimate.
At small parties, there isn't any privacy.
F. Scott Fitzgerald, *The Great Gatsby*

◆

I lived in that house for twenty years.
Never saw a ghost.
Curzon Taylor

THE LAST SPIRITS OF MANHATTAN

The Blue Girl

The blue girl was dead. Her name was Isabella, but everyone she remembered called her Snug. That was years ago. What remained of her body lay in a coffin in Woodlawn, a train ride away in the Bronx. She was something else lingering here. A ghost, she supposed, that was it. Other words she'd considered: apparition, phantom, vision. Revenant, spirit, spook. She had a lot of time to think on East Eightieth Street.

Snug spent most of her days in the basement, in the coal room of No. 7, its walls stained by decades of deliveries, mounds and mounds of fuel long since burned. The history of the house clung to the plaster in dirty shadows. The furnace was an octopus with a great wide belly and tentacle pipes thrust and intersecting through the five floors above. It had a creaky hinged door Snug liked to open when she was alive, careful not to singe herself on the sturdy metal handle. With tedious practice, she had learned to open it again, wrap her hand—the energy of her hand rather, if not the actual flesh—around the bar and tug. There was the fire, still raging, like Snug had in the early days of her afterlife. Oh, such anger. Rage, rage, but the furnace had a purpose. Rage with intention: heat the home, keep the occupants alive. Snug's rage had served no one, least of all herself, so it was rarer these days, if not altogether gone.

Lately the house had fallen silent, grown cold. For most of the years after her death, No. 7 thrummed with a sturdy pulse. Her aunt and uncle, her mother, and her younger brother were seldom still, the servants galloping up and down the narrow staircase. Snug had felt the beat of life and it roused her on days even when she didn't want to stir.

Now, with their absence, she sensed a warning of another waning—this time, perhaps, of her surprising second existence.

BEFORE THE PARTY

1

February 11, 1956

WHITE LIGHTS SPARKLED AGAINST the restaurant's broad windows. Across the harbor, the neighborhoods of Superior, Wisconsin, glowed. If she looked through her reflection to what lay beyond the glass, Carolyn Banks saw long ships in the dark water, ore boats going out to the Great Lakes. Behind the restaurant loomed the hills of Duluth. The Flame had the best view of both cities. Look up and there were the ice-gleaming streets. Look across, there was the frigid lake. Between them was Malcolm, preparing his marriage proposal.

It wasn't unexpected. Malcolm fondly reminisced about their yearlong courtship as opening argument. He was good at laying things out, but Carolyn found herself listening vaguely, weighing the moment when the house photographer would stroll by to capture her ambivalent mood. The languid notes of the piano in the next room, the candle flickering in the opaque red centerpiece jar, neither made her feel less divided.

Usually when the Flame's cameraman captured a moment, her older sisters, the twins, Helen and Maud, would laugh and say, "Another toothpaste advertisement!" Carolyn did have a fantastic smile and she dated handsome men. But the twins vetoed boy after boy with extraordinary teeth. "Look at the two of you," they'd sneered, tossing aside the glossy photo in its thick paper folder. "You'd have monstrous babies."

Her sisters hadn't thought anyone was good enough—until Malcolm. Helen and Maud *liked* him. He was loyal and smart, they were right to point out. That fella's okay, they chimed. Sure, he had glorious teeth, but it worked. Malcolm looked like Laurence Olivier, and everyone said Carolyn favored Joan Fontaine.

"You make a matching set," they'd said.

"An imposter pair," Carolyn countered. "And if we're playing *Rebecca*, there has to be a dead wife."

They laughed. They always laughed. It was a wonderful way to dismiss her. "But he's one of us," they insisted.

There it was: Her sisters approved of Malcolm Tower because he fit the family. He had graduated Exeter and then Yale, just like their father and their older brother, Andrew. Malcolm worked at the bank, which their father captained. His job at First National made it cozy. Yet for all their fawning over him, Carolyn waffled. Perhaps that was unwise, but she couldn't shake her hesitation.

If only her mother were here to tell Carolyn what to do. Her mother, her closest confidante, her sweetest advisor, her best friend, six months dead and forever silent on every matter that confused Carolyn. She would never benefit from her direction or hear her voice again.

And here came the cameraman.

"Smile, lovebirds!" He was older, jovial, a little drunk. An occupational hazard. How else to bear the boredom? This guy had shot every young person in the port cities at least once, twice, maybe more depending on their dating life. Carolyn had half a dozen Flame photos in her scrapbook. This time he lurched before setting the shot and caught himself on the edge of the table, rattling the ice in their cocktails.

"Whoa there," Malcolm cautioned and slid closer to her, squeaking across the red leather booth, hips touching. He slung one arm around her shoulders and squeezed too tightly. She resisted the fleeting impulse to shake it off, because . . . why? Malcolm was the real deal, he was. No dead wives in his past, no shadowy children lurking in some forlorn country house. She wasn't going to do better, and she could have done much, much worse.

Pop! The birth of one more portrait, this one titled *Banks in Limbo*.

After the war, when the boys came back—except for Andrew, who'd died on Normandy Beach—the twins had gathered handfuls of proposals. Some of those guys would have married any breathing body. Her sisters, far better than merely breathing, had both hitched young. Carolyn was only thirteen on V-E Day, but now at twenty-four, she knew what those fellas wanted: a darling miss; the house with the sugar-scented kitchen; the well-tended children. Safety. Her mother had offered the same a generation earlier (not that it saved her from grief or cancer). Carolyn found her sisters' beaux from those years too intense, so dedicated to doing well in school, landing a spouse, getting ahead in a career. And here was Malcolm, too young to have been called up for Europe or Japan, and lucky to have missed Korea, but still gung-ho to settle down. He was college-educated, able-bodied, and gainfully employed, dating an intelligent, attractive woman who supposedly loved him. He wouldn't expect anything but affirmation.

Where *did* her diffidence come from? Her father would call it dithering. Malcolm was offering her everything her sisters had. Here was security and happiness on a clean and sturdy plate. Take it, her mother might have said, and Andrew, sweet dead Andy, what would he have given for that sort of life?

The strand of electric lights blocking the full view of the lake didn't feel romantic; they were tired remnants from holidays past. Leftovers. Malcolm had come back to Superior after New Haven and had met Carolyn while she was helping her mother bear the indignities of her last months. The twins, busy with their own small children, had helped, but Carolyn was the most attentive nurse. It was a string of hazy days, of baths and bedpans, pills for her swelling, pills for her pain. Dates with Malcolm were an escape from her mother's illness. With her mother gone, Carolyn felt elbowed into marrying a boy who treated her well. She couldn't stay on the market forever, her sisters warned. This time, with this boy, she should say yes.

The bulb flashed again. Malcolm beamed his matinee-idol smile; he could turn the charm off and on at will. She imagined what the photographer saw, their grinning, not-entirely-sober faces. Pretty people in a pretty place by pretty plates. Her mind flashed to her work at Sutter's, the store where she clerked, here on the Minnesota side of the bridge. Carolyn appreciated the store's ordered beauty, the delicate bone china in tasteful patterns, the gleaming silverware, or silver plate if you were on a budget. Place settings, wineglasses, water goblets, demitasse cups. It was frivolous and functional and really meant nothing, but everything, at once. Carolyn had worked at the shop in Duluth all through high school and then again after she'd dropped out of the university in Madison. She dealt with nervous brides all the time, all day long. She didn't relish being one.

And after the vows, she'd probably have to give up her job: Betty, her last single friend from high school, had just gotten married and promptly canned from the phone company because the boss didn't think married women needed the work. "You've got a husband now," he told her as he handed her the pink slip. "Relax. Let him bring home the bacon. You have a baby."

Would Mr. Sutter fire her if she went from Carolyn Banks to Carolyn Tower? Worse, Malcolm would expect her to quit. He'd want a wife just like his mother. Just like her sisters. How her aunts, back East—well, *great*-aunts—had counseled Maud and Helen when they were teenagers and Carolyn, still a child, her mouth full of angel cake, had squirmed at their advice for women of means.

"If you play with pigs," Great-Aunt Isabella had pronounced in the ornate parlor of her Manhattan home, "you are going to get dirty."

She'd steadied her gaze at the girls, first the twins, then at little Carolyn, who wasn't so young as to escape her line of fire. Great-Aunt Mariah sat next to her sister, a mountain of iron-gray hair piled on her head in outdated Victorian fashion, hands folded in her lap. The twins, wearing penny loafers and rolled socks, their legs crossed at the ankles, sat silently, while Carolyn stared at her Mary Janes. Her mother had listened from the threshold of the room. Later Carolyn would admit to her mother she *liked* getting dirty and her mother had laughed. Years later, Carolyn loved work, the glass display cases, spotless every morning, the gleaming knives on green velvet, the plates and platters, Wedgwood and Spode, delicate and smooth, she loved it all.

Candlelight cast tiny stars on the side of her glass. The trio of whiskey and water and the late hour, amplified by Malcolm's baritone, made her head wobble. Carolyn was not a wobbly sort.

"So," Malcolm said, "in summation, gentlewoman of the jury: do you think you—"

Pop! Carolyn thought the man with the camera was back, but the lights went out all around the room. All that remained were dancing wicks on tabletops. Superior burned even brighter across the water.

The maître d' soothed the crowd—"Stay calm, everyone! No need to get ruffled!"—but no one was panicking. Except for Carolyn, who could anticipate Malcolm's next sentence without hearing it. Laughter rolled from the kitchen, across the long bar, and Malcolm's easy chuckle made her feel simultaneously lighter and excruciatingly heavy with awareness of every moment. In the corner of the room, someone inhaled on a cigarette and its orange end flared. Malcolm found her hands again on the tabletop and laid his fingers across hers, poised to finish his thought. She was primed: a deer waiting for the crack of broken twigs that meant danger in the shadows.

Then, in the quiet dark, she heard a voice by her ear, as clear as a radio. Her mother's voice, hushed but strong, urging, "Go." Carolyn's fingers brushed at her hair, grazed her earrings. "Go," her mother insisted.

Could no one else hear her? She glanced at Malcolm and felt his steady gaze, eyes alight like a cat at night, some trick of the wick and the flame.

A lumbering shadow jostled the table and a man grunted "Excuse me." Carolyn watched as the photographer stuck out his hand for balance and dipped the cuff of his sleeve over the dancing flame. It caught, a bright blur at his wrist, brilliant in the black room, and before the fire could eat more man or material, she doused it with the remains of her highball, mostly melted ice, a quick flick and a splash. A bitter scent—scorched cloth, burned hair—wafted over the table. The man patted his arm and staggered away with a mumbled *thank you, thank you.* Then they were sitting in the dark again.

"That was—" Malcolm said, surprised admiration in his tone, "efficient."

"Thank you," she answered, still trying to tally the swift jumble of fire and water, stunned by the speed of it all.

"You could have kept him burning," he snickered. "A light in the dark." Carolyn winced, but Malcolm couldn't see that. He plowed on. "So, I was interrupted."

"Wait," she blurted, sitting up straighter. Never meet a challenge with poor posture, her mother always said. "I have to go somewhere."

Malcolm swiveled to take stock of the restaurant. "Can you find the ladies' room without light?"

"No," she said, "not that."

"Then what do you mean?" His voice grew firm.

What did *go* mean? Carolyn had heard her mother in the dark, but that wasn't possible. Where? she wanted to ask. *Go where?* And she felt a gentle brush on her cheek, a kindness. "New York," she said, testing the words. She nodded. "Yes, New York." Carolyn was surprisingly certain that was what her mother meant. But where did that certainty come from? She had no clue. And now that she'd said it, she felt adrift again.

"What?" His tone was confused and angry.

She wasn't surprised by that. She was more concerned with feeling her way along the conversation from here, her hands patting a damp cave wall. Where was she going with this? "I need to go to New York."

"That was sudden." His expression shifted in the shadows, difficult to read, but she knew he wasn't smiling.

"Yes, I suppose so," she agreed. He wasn't wrong.

"And you'll come back when, exactly?"

"Soon," she said. "Sooner rather—"

"Than later," he finished. "I *was* going to ask you something important." He tapped a cigarette from his familiar pack of Pall Malls.

"I know." She flinched. "I mean, I'm pretty sure."

Malcolm raised his lighter and it sparked with a metallic click. He took a drag, held it, then let the smoke drift from his slightly parted lips. She looked away and imagined his initials engraved on the lighter, *MAT*, behind his firm grip, a memory of other evenings. "But are you sure you know what I was going to say?" His voice was edged with amusement.

"I think so," she said. She kept her spine straight. "Yes, I do know what you were going to say."

Malcolm laughed. Then she joined him. They were the only table laughing.

"I need a little time," she offered weakly. Carolyn wondered why she couldn't simply say yes, why she couldn't say yes and they'd get it over with and everyone would be happy and her life would move forward. That was a sort of *Go, Go*, wasn't it? Perhaps she was imagining her mother's resistance. Maybe it was her own convenient hallucination.

"I can wait," he said. She sensed a flicker of something hard dart across his eyes. "But not forever."

"Thank you," she said, though she doubted that was the proper response. "Thank you, Malcolm."

"I want to offer the right thing at the right time." He glanced out to the icy lake. "And I want you to respond in the way I want for the right reasons."

There was commotion across the building and electric lights burst on all over, to strangers' cheers and a neighboring couple's surprised "Oh!" There was the gleaming lighter and their glasses of melting ice. There was the wet tablecloth and the soggy wick on the white candle in the red jar, water pooling on the wax. Carolyn looked at Malcolm, his attention on the glittering windows. Her mother's voice seemed a phantasm, a trick of the air. No. She wanted to believe what she'd heard and still, it left her so unsure of what was next, sitting on the shoreline, waiting for a recognizable horizon to come into view.

2

February 13, 1956

PUDDING. TIRES. POTATO CHIPS. These were the stuff of legend at Young & Rubicam. Breakfast cereal. Popsicles. But it was pain reliever that made the agency run. Y&R sold an avalanche of Bufferin to relieve America's throbbing headaches, and Pete Donoff aspired to compose copy that could sell even more, whatever the client wanted to pitch. He knew he could write as well as anyone on Madison Avenue, though he'd only moved up from glorified gopher after the New Year. He'd been given a chance and Pete was going to grab the moment, toss them his shiniest ideas, and relish the cavalcade to come: the corner office, his own secretary, a brilliant team of artists to launch fresh campaigns, land ever bigger accounts. Cars. He wanted to sell cars. And airlines. Those were only going to get ritzier.

But before all that, he had to do one simple thing: find a haunted house.

Of course, it wouldn't be a problem, they told him. This is the city that never sleeps—somebody was bound to have come across a ghost or two in Manhattan, and surely, on this crowded island, everything shoulder to shoulder, there were dozens, if not hundreds, of spooked spots. Easy-peasy, The Duck had assured him—Bob Buck, his immediate boss, the link between Pete, minor leaguer, and the rest of the company's creative management, a man nobody ever called anything but Mr. Buck to his face. In the break rooms, in the bars at happy hour, it was Buck or Lucky Buck or Lucky Duck or simply, The Duck. Everything the man touched turned other agencies green. Do this for The Duck—on paper, for Bristol-Myers, which was the account—and maybe some of that luck would come Pete's way.

And really, he thought in moments of awe, he was doing it for Mr. Hitchcock, who ran the show, literally, the eponymous *Alfred Hitchcock Presents*. It was Mr. Hitchcock's dream to have his cocktail party in a verified haunted house. The famous director had visited the agency after the first of the year, and though Pete wasn't invited to the war room while the honored delegation got the grand tour—Hitchcock had come with an entourage—he had spied the famous silhouette. He'd also been given a firm directive: Don't let the big fellow down.

No problem, Pete had convinced himself three weeks ago, I'll find one in a jiffy. The glittering new aluminum ball had barely descended to welcome 1956 and Pete held a residue of joy from the holidays and his measly-but-still-a-raise promotion. He was always a glass-half-full-of-wine kind of guy, and his nonna and ma, his brothers and sister, zias and zios, cousins and nephews and nieces in Red Hook, they were all rooting for him. Sure, Ma would have preferred he brought a nice girl home for Christmas, not news of more work in Manhattan. He was single and liked it that way. Maybe someday that would change but today wasn't someday. Someday, when he'd made something of himself. Someday, after he tackled this pressing request. Make the most of the ghosts, he'd told himself. He didn't need to believe in spooks—he didn't, he was a practical guy—but if the Important People wanted cocktails with Casper, he'd get him. What he needed to believe in was *himself*.

But there were the stipulations. *Stipulations*, the *Roget's Thesaurus* on his desk told him, was a fancy word for *catch*.

The Duck told him there were just three.

"First, kid, the place has got to be eerie. Gothic. Think Edgar Allan Poe. Think cobwebs and creaking doors and rattling chains."

"Jacob Marley," Pete offered, scribbling *Poe*. He drew a blotchy spider. It looked like a tiny black sun.

The Duck guffawed. "That's the spirit." He snubbed out one of his ubiquitous Luckies in an already-crowded ashtray. "Think: a creepy Charles Addams drawing in *The New Yorker*."

Pete jotted on a legal pad: *Creepy, New Yorker, Charles Addams*.

"It's all about ambiance," The Duck said.

Ambiance, Pete scrawled and underlined twice.

"Second, it has to be on the island. Not Brooklyn." At that, The Duck raised an eyebrow, aware of Pete's home turf. "Not the Bronx, not Queens, definitely not Jersey. This is a Hollywood party, right. They aren't going to haul out to Hoboken for any shindig, not even for the Headless Horseman himself."

Pete's note: *Nothing but Manhattan*.

"And lastly, most importantly, it needs plumbing. Bathrooms worthy of the smart set. No loos, no ladies, got it? The women are going to be in heels."

He stood above Pete, looking for confirmation: Yes, Pete understood women wore heels. He wasn't an idiot. "I knew you'd be the right guy for this task. Consider the toilets a key element to a successful evening."

Decent plumbing, he wrote. *Decent loos.* Then he added an exclamation mark. *Decent loos, The Duck insists!*

He reread the trio of stipulations.

"Sure," Pete said. "No problem, Mr. Buck."

"And the party's in March. March seventh. Hitchcock's already set the date."

"Two months," Pete said. "Consider it done, sir."

With a little of Duck—or dumb—luck, of course, he'd find the perfect place.

Easy-peasy, right? Except now there was less than a month to go and *Nothing but Manhattan* was starting to look simply, frighteningly, like *Nothing* and the famous silhouette was shadowing him, cast in strange corners, in automats and laundromats, in his apartment kitchen, down Midtown avenues and Greenwich Village side streets, trailing him like an ominous bird.

Snug didn't need heat. She didn't need shelter. She could go where she chose and live—no, not live, *exist*—where she wanted. For all these years, she *wanted* to be here, near her mother and her brother and her aunt, even her uncle, who had long been like her but nothing like her, too. His spirit seemed further reduced. He never ventured; she supposed he had nowhere else to go. Oh, the hospital, he could go there, or the medical college, but he kept to his bedroom, the library, the parlor, his faint gray presence resting in an armchair. He never spoke, gave no more than a nod of good morning or wave of good night. He had learned to pick up books. Snug, however, went all over: the gallery, the rooftop, every bedroom, every balcony, and, weather permitting, the walled back garden. She roamed while he stayed put. Some days she went farther: to the lawns of Central Park, the Metropolitan Museum, mere blocks away, to one river's edge and then the other. Oh, what would become of her in cold, cold water? She restricted herself from touching that. And every day she returned to the lowest place, and turned the latch, and dirtied her hands, and watched the furnace fire glow.

Her diaphanous blue hands turned black, her cheeks soot-streaked; that was the catch to time in the coal room, where she first taught herself to move things. She ran her fingers along the filthy walls and specks of dirt stuck one day, after weeks, or months, or years. Time was a soup. In those early years, and sometimes later, she wept, imagining all the things she would never do: marry, birth a child, labor for husband and house. She had always been something of a homebody. Her aunt Isabella and uncle Thomas encouraged that in a girl. Girls served boys, not themselves. Everything Aunt Isabella did was for the Doctor. "The Doctor needs his rest." "The Doctor needs his tea." "The Doctor won't be here this evening. He's lecturing." Perhaps her aunt chaffed at the boundaries of her intellectual life. Maybe she wanted more. Snug couldn't tell. Aunt Isabella was as involved as a woman of her status could be, charities for the indigent, even the board for the Babies Hospital, despite her own inability to have children. Oh, that, too, Snug shared with her aunt. Neither would ever be a mother.

And her own mother? From Mariah, Snug learned what it meant to have a husband, raise children, tend a home. It meant the man could leave at any moment, the children could die, the home could turn as sour and fatal as a crudely jarred preserve. Mariah was humiliated by what Snug's father had done. A public shame, trumpeted by no less than *The New York Times*. It was a town crier heralding her heartbreak. "Taylor Wedding a Surprise," her mother whispered the headline, how many times over how many years? "Certainly it was a surprise," she spat, holding in a curse that could have been forgiven given the circumstances. What man deserved curses more? What sort of man leaves his wife and children for a colleague's widow, then claims to be a widower himself at a clandestine Canadian marriage? "It wasn't lawful," her mother had said. "Though he contended we were already divorced. It wasn't right by the state. And certainly not right in the eyes of God, Snug, surely not there."

Her father had coined her nickname, for the little girl who liked to cuddle more than anyone else, who took every opportunity to curl herself in his lap. "Snug as a bug," he'd said. It stuck and she adored it. Otherwise, she was simply another Isabella. There was a troop of them—a pair of her great-grandmothers, her grandmother, her aunt, her younger cousin off in the Middle West—as if it were a law to have one or more in every generation.

Just another Isabella she would have been, but he had made her Snug.

She was still able to curl up wherever she desired. No longer her father's lap, but the dim place where only the servants ventured. She was snug there, in that necessary and grimy room at the bottom of No. 7.

No matter the grime, she learned. It fell from her hands and she was clean again. Matter slipped from her not-quite-skin, her outer layer something electrical (was this celestial light, her shell, she wondered), and *voilà*, her palms were spotless. Spirits, she discovered, don't stay dirty. If only the living worked like that. Her father could have gleamed again. No one would have seen him as a philanderer, as a faithless husband and neglectful father, as the ruined broker, as the man who—no, she didn't like to dwell on the gun, that other Taylor surprise.

Something *was* different lately. Since her mother and Aunt Isabella died, the house had hushed. Snug could only watch her mother's pale figure from a distance; even after death a wall existed between them, while Aunt Isabella happily reunited with the Doctor.

The maids and the nurse were gone, those old Irish women; the driver, a Swede—once a liveryman, so long had he been employed at No. 7—dismissed as well. She knew what was going to happen to the tall and narrow house. Eavesdropping was any ghost's keenest talent. It would be sold, possibly turned into apartments for other families, perhaps razed. She had listened to the strange visitors. She would leave then, she supposed, banished. They would tear the old furnace out, like uprooting the base of a massive tree, and replace it with something modern, something new and efficient, something fit for an era where Snug didn't belong.

3

February 17, 1956

CAROLYN'S FATHER SUMMONED HER to the First National Bank. Even expected, his beckoning felt ominous, and the frigid wind off Lake Superior had turned everything to glassy iron: the streets, the trees, her hands, her feet. She used to love seeing her father at his office, the wood-paneled room with the tall windows looking over wide Tower Avenue. Once upon a time there were regular visits with her mother. Arm in arm they walked through the solemn lobby with the cashiers' desks, then up a story to the president's aerie. Since her mother's illness and death, these had been infrequent solo flights, heels clacking across the white marble floor. Agnes, her father's longtime secretary, was still there, slower, grayer, but always with a ready smile, always with a candy dish on her desk. Carolyn hadn't been by the bank in weeks—perhaps to avoid Malcolm at the teller's window, even before their outing last Saturday—but she wouldn't admit it. She told herself she was busy, *so very busy*, at the shop.

Though he'd been in surprisingly fine humor through Christmas and the New Year, her father was a stern man and losing his wife hadn't made him lighter. For this conversation, she hoped he might invite her to the cabin in Solon Springs. The twins refused to spend time in the wild, while Carolyn was always game. Andy had been their father's boon companion and Carolyn had felt a responsibility to fill in, where Maud and Helen did not, and there was a benefit. Her father was gentler in the woods. The bank seemed less welcoming than a wintery stand of birch.

When Agnes ushered her in, her father was at his gleaming desk reading a leather-bound portfolio. They embraced before he led her to a pair of armchairs by the windows overlooking the blustery street. Carolyn had slipped off her long wool coat, but there was still snow in her hair and she rubbed her cold pink hands. Agnes gave a little *good luck* wave as she shut the door on her way out.

"Thank you for coming, Carolyn," her father said. "I know leaving the shop isn't easy."

"Tammy can help if there's a sudden rush, which there won't be. It's wicked out there." She straightened her spine and lifted her chin. She, too, could be all business. "You seem nervous, Daddy," she said, to mask her own anxiety.

"No, not nervous." He shook his head and cleared his throat. "I do have a question."

Perhaps he had heard her mother's voice as well? She stifled an urge to laugh, imagining *her* question. *Have you heard from Mother?*

"Why do you want to go to New York?"

Carolyn came back to the real world. This was the work of her spying sisters. Helen and Maud should stay out of her business, but that would be like the lake giving up its tide.

"I want to visit Aunt Bella," she said, an excuse that felt immediately reasonable, though she'd decided it at that moment. Her mother had loved her sister-in-law. This, too, felt like her mother's prodding.

"You think Bella needs company?" he scoffed. "She's perfectly fine left to her own devices. Always has been." He shook his head, Carolyn knew, at Bella's bohemian bent.

What would her father say if she told him Mother had spoken to her at the restaurant? He would think she'd lost her mind. At the least, call her ridiculous.

"It's just a feeling I have." She shrugged. "Maybe she can give me direction. Mother always admired Aunt Bella. And you admit yourself she's been very successful . . . both in love and work."

They studied each other, then he gave a rare chuckle. "You're wily, Carolyn. You know how to get your way. There's a brain behind that beautiful face."

"Hmph," she said. His compliments too often sounded like insults.

"It's a shame you can't come work here." He always changed the subject when he was uncomfortable.

"Really?" Carolyn leaned forward and tapped the brass brads of the armrest. "That's your highest praise." She settled back. "But you're not serious. You wouldn't have a woman here."

"I have Agnes—"

"You know that's not what I mean." She didn't want to fight him. That wasn't her intent. "Besides, I like my job at Sutter's."

"You run that place for him. It should be Sutter and Banks." He tidied his lapels. "Banks and Sutter." He, too, was trying to avoid a quarrel. She could give him credit when it was due, but then why doesn't he offer something real?

Go. Oh, what had gotten into her?

"You could help me," she said, fingers lingering on a side table's clean glass ashtray emblazoned with the bank's name. Her father hated it, called it a gimmick, but the younger fellows were charmed by the novelty. He had listened to them. "Give me a loan and I'll buy Sutter's." She picked up the ashtray. "I'll put Banks and Sutter on one of these. Customers will love it."

Too far. He put his hand up like a traffic cop, then lowered it. "This isn't about work," he said. "It's about you. And Malcolm."

She returned the ashtray to the table and laced her fingers in her lap. "Of course." She swallowed and forced herself to stay put.

"He's a fine man. From a fine family."

"He is." She looked up at the familiar white ceiling, as if she'd find an answer hovering there, then steadied her gaze on her father. "What do you think Mother would have thought?"

A flitter of pain crossed his gray eyes. "That's an impossible question. And it doesn't matter. I want to know what *you* think, Carolyn." She bit the inside of her mouth. If she were honest with him, he'd call her crazy. There was more than merely a question of marriage, but she couldn't name it, so she named her crisis Malcolm.

Her father shifted. He was a presence, broad and tall, with a full head of gleaming white hair, accustomed to attention and impatient when he didn't get prompt answers. "I know what he's proposed," he said, stepping into her silence.

"That's nearly the right word," Carolyn said. "But he didn't. Not yet. Not technically."

Her father looked confused. "He asked me at the holidays."

"He asked *you*? I stopped him when he tried to ask *me*. I knew where the conversation was going." She wanted to squelch this conversation, too, and felt her frustration flare. "The twins have already told you about Saturday night."

He leaned toward her and took her still-pink hands. "No, it was Malcolm, but he can't have told me everything." Of course it was Malcolm. And her father was right. Malcolm couldn't tell him everything. She glanced down at his hands—the age spots, the sinews—not those of a deskbound clerk, but a fisherman, a hunter, all the things he did in the woods he had taught her to do.

Carolyn was a fair shot with a rifle and could pole up rapids with gusto. Her father was a surprising man among his peers.

She wanted to trust him, and his instincts, on so many things. Just not this.

"Go to the city if you need to," he said gently. "Chat with Bella. Consider your life."

"But then I'll just have to come back. And I can't come work at the bank. You don't really want me intruding." She steadied her gaze. "Neither would Malcolm."

"No, that's true." Her father glanced at his pocket watch. "But think of it. Your husband working here. Solidity. Security. A life that's familiar to you."

What had she expected him to say? That she could buy Sutter's store when the old boy retired, that he'd have the bank give her a loan and make it hers?

No, that's not what he suggested. He suggested marrying a man because he offered her a life she'd recognize.

He peered out the leaded windows. "You can continue on with the shop until you start a family, while Malcolm progresses here." The sky was like wet gray felt, but at least the snow had stopped. "You know, Andy would have followed me, if it hadn't been for the Germans." He turned back to her and gave a sad smile. "It would all be familiar and safe for you. There's nothing wrong with either condition."

He strolled back around the imposing desk. It was a signal that it was time for him to return to business. She collected her purse from the small table by the door, then kissed him on his clean-shaven cheek. She didn't know how he did it, every thread in place, dapper from the minute he finished dressing in the morning until he retired at nine every evening. Not a hair out of place, never a crease in his suit. Her brother hadn't inherited his unflappable glamor. Andy had always been on the goofy side, a lovable puppy. Her sisters were easily flustered. It was Carolyn who inherited his grace and gravity—though she wasn't sure what good it did her. Oh, it had made her a better nurse. There was that.

He gave her hands a quick, gentle squeeze. "I know you miss your mother."

"I know you do, too." They held each other's hands for a beat, then he released her.

"Say hello to Uncle James for me," he jested.

She laughed, genuinely, remembering the family joke. "Of course." James Lenox—father's great-great-something or uncle, the crazy book collector.

Long dead, but years ago he'd helped establish the New York Public Library. Her father's ridiculous insistence on waving to Uncle James every time they passed the stone lions on Fifth Avenue and her mother's playing along . . . her mother's healthy stride in those years, her pretty complexion. Those trips east were always joyful. Maybe that's why New York seemed an answer on Saturday night, and even more so this afternoon. "I'll give him your regards." She pecked her father again on the cheek.

Agnes appeared at his door as if by magic and took Carolyn away like a visiting dignitary. She placed a caramel in Carolyn's palm.

"I miss your mother, dear," Agnes whispered. "You so remind me of her."

"Thank you," Carolyn said. "We all miss her."

There, with the clatter of business below them, with Malcolm at his desk, Carolyn began to confess. Agnes's sympathetic eyes glistened. "Do you think Mother—"

"Yes?" Agnes touched Carolyn's bare wrist. Her fingers were warm.

But Carolyn felt herself a coward. "Do you think it's safe to drive?" She lowered her eyes. Driving never scared her.

Agnes gave a little good-natured snort. "Of course, dear. You are steadier than anyone I know." She paused. "Your mother thought so, too."

The words were sweet as candy, but just as fleeting.

Five minutes later it wasn't only the fresh dusting of snow that made Carolyn sit stiffly in the driver's seat of the dark sedan as she prepared to drive over the bridge, back to Duluth. The questions roiling around her head weighed heavily. Everyone was simply trying to secure her future and she was fighting it. Was she acting ungrateful? If only she could ask her mother. Aunt Bella would have to do; Aunt Bella, always her own woman.

The radio played Nelson Riddle's orchestra over the gruff engine and Carolyn pulled the Ford onto the icy road. Its tires rolled tentatively over the slick asphalt of Tower Avenue and the sedan shimmied. She straightened it out, grasping the steering wheel like a captain at the helm, and considered her destination in the gauzy white distance.

4

February 22, 1956

PETE STILL DIDN'T HAVE bupkis. He and The Duck had cabbed around the island, checking spots the locals (and the tour guides) called haunted. They liked the Merchant's House in the East Village, once owned by a family named Tredwell, but when the current owners found out it was a party for Hitchcock, they'd nixed it. No actresses, no ad men. Not respectable, you know? They tried the wine caverns under the Brooklyn Bridge, but there were no decent loos and no running water, and it would cost five hundred dollars just to jerry-rig something for one night. That got the kibosh quick.

The Duck complained Hitchcock pooh-poohed every conventional spot—*no hotels, please, of course they're haunted*—and pulled their leg harder every time he asked for an update: "But does it really have ghosts, gentlemen?" When Pete mentioned that ghosts didn't exist, he riled The Duck's feathers. "The customer is always right. Even when you think they're nuts. It's our job to give them what they want. If Hitchcock wants ghosts, he's going to know we looked for ghosts." But then he laughed and added an amendment: "And then we're going to give him something he thinks he wants because that's the business we're really in. But I bet he knows that, too."

So, with straight faces, they turned to the research department—fellows capable of in-depth reports on everything from canned peas to hosiery—and they turned, perhaps with less-than-straight faces, to self-proclaimed spectral experts, the American Psychical Research Institute. "Get them to tell us where the *real* ghosts are," The Duck said. "Hitchcock will like that. Not that I think he believes in ghosts. I sure as hell don't." He clapped Pete's back. "But I do believe in billable hours."

What did Hitchcock believe? Pete wondered. He knew what he saw on TV, what Jim Allardice upstairs wrote in the quippy moments before the episodes began. Everyone thought that was Hitchcock, but it was Hitchcock distilled. "Allardice knows Hitchcock better than Hitchcock's mother," The Duck said. Pete didn't ask if anyone at Y&R could fact-check with the elder Mrs. Hitchcock. It didn't seem prudent. Then Pete read she was dead. She'd be no help at all.

On Wednesday they'd heard the bad news. The ghosts of New York were gone, the expert told them flatly. There *had* been spectral activity in Manhattan until about a decade ago, right after the second war, but they seem to have fled. "There's no fertile ground left for them," the APRI researcher relayed over the phone, then laughed. "There's hardly ground left at all, except for Central Park. Maybe the ghosts still cavort there, but you can't pitch a party in the Sheep Meadow at midnight, can you?"

The Duck was agitated, as if he expected something different. He told Pete to get APRI to visit the agency, explain it in person. Pronto.

"Did you think they'd tell us there were ghosts available?"

The Duck guffawed. "Of course not. But when I ask for a rundown of my options, I need more than a simple no. I want to hear all of it. He might have a list of spooky spots, places with stories. I'm not looking for the real deal. Remember—it's ambiance we're hunting. Consider all the angles, son." He smiled. "Even if the other angles seem like bunk."

He waved Pete away with the brush of his hand. "Get them here tomorrow. Tell them we'll have Danishes," he said. "And coffee. But keep it under budget. Then they can tell me what I need to hear."

Seymour Barnes, the sole member of the APRI staff willing to speak in public, was tall and gaunt in his pale gray, faintly lavender suit. Pete had imagined what he'd look like and this was pretty darn close. Slender, a little cadaverous, but ageless in a wrinkle-free way. Likely under thirty, handsome in the right light, and the late winter sun streaming through the fourteenth-floor windows was incongruously joyous, more Christmas morning than February dreary. And when Seymour Barnes spoke, it wasn't with Vincent Price menace. He smiled and Pete watched the guy's aura go from a sedate dusk to a caffeinated dawn. Wait, why was he evaluating his aura? He had a silly cousin in Boston who read palms and horoscopes. That was enough to make Pete skeptical of it all. But Seymour Barnes seemed sane, with, what was it—authority? Trustworthiness? That couldn't be it. The man believed in spirits.

"I thoroughly enjoyed gathering these numbers for you," Seymour said. His voice was a song. "No one in your industry has asked the Institute for help in ages." He paused in laying out a dozen graphs on the wide conference table. There were, as The Duck promised, sweet rolls and a pot of coffee. Seymour pushed those gently to the side to make way for his diagrams, awash in black and orange ink, like Halloween decorations on graph paper. The Duck had been waylaid by a quick phone call, but Seymour Barnes was getting right to business, Pete his sole audience. "We were a well-respected organization fifty years ago, long before I arrived," he sniffed. "That may be overstating it. Some people have always thought we were quacks. You may be among them, Mr. D'Onofrio."

Pete blinked. "It's Donoff."

Seymour stopped and looked at Pete with a steady hazel-eyed gaze. "D'Onofrio is so melodic. A shame to give it up."

"My father wanted something simpler."

"Your grandfather wasn't pleased," Seymour said.

"No, he wasn't." Pete felt a chill at the back of his neck. "Wait, how do you know that?"

Seymour grinned. "We talk to lots of people in my line of work."

"My grandfather and father have both been dead for—"

The Duck barreled through the glass door, a stenographer following with her notebook and pen already poised. Pete thought her name was Anne, but he wasn't sure and felt a tug of guilt.

"Sorry for the delay, Barnes. I'm eager to hear what you've got." The Duck gave Pete a nudge.

"I'm afraid it's not entirely the news you wanted," Seymour said, continuing to pull folders out of his seemingly infinite briefcase. "It isn't a picnic to find ghosts anymore."

"Let's see." The Duck motioned for the stenographer to sit. Anne glanced at Pete and her face soured. He wasn't sure if that grimace was meant for him, The Duck, or Seymour Barnes. Maybe it was simply the subject. Half his family rolled their eyes when he mentioned the quest for the right party spot. The other half spit to ward off evil and fingered their rosary beads. "Don't mess with that, sonny," his nonna had said. "Not even for mister big-shot director."

"There is a remnant of a silver lining." Seymour hustled about the table, flattening fold-creased charts and linking up corners. "Which do you want first—gleaming border or the clouds?"

The Duck frowned. "Hit me with the clouds. I'm a believer in take your medicine first."

"I knew that, I knew that," Seymour sang. "The bad news, from our observations and calculations, gathered through decades of legwork, contact with residents, interviews with volunteers, charting radio waves and temperature levels, and—you can't skip this step—countless hours walking the streets of Manhattan, peering into every neighborhood: there is scant spectral activity left on the island."

"Scant," The Duck repeated with a smile.

"To be blunt," Seymour spoke with an undertaker's gravity, "none."

"None?" The Duck tucked his chin. "Who'd a thunk? A town this size."

"None." Seymour bent toward him. "The Institute hasn't recorded a legitimately proven contact with the Other Side since the war."

"Since the . . . war?" The Duck looked confused.

"The second one," Pete suggested.

The Duck glanced at Pete and shook his head, clearing it of a sudden fog. "Yeah, right, of course." He rubbed his forehead. "Sorry. Not sure where my brain went just now."

"That's not uncommon, Mr. Buck," Seymour said in a fatherly tone. "Talk of spirits makes a cloud in some minds. It's a phenomenon we've studied. A residual effect, we imagine, akin to shock. Simple conversation can create a mental vapor." He lowered his voice. "Actual sightings can spur memory loss, fatigue, a sudden bout of short-lived drunkenness, even madness."

The Duck turned his back to Seymour, smirked at Pete, then went back to business. "What happened to all the phantoms?" He paused. "Not that I really believe in them. No brain fog here. Just not enough stimulation this morning." He lit a Lucky Strike.

"That's part of the problem, Mr. Buck," Seymour lamented. "No one believes in ghosts in the middle of the twentieth century."

The Duck bent to study the charts, cigarette smoke drifting over the table. Pete sat at the edge, taking notes despite Anne's busily scratching pen, musing over the neat reports with the APRI logo on the top of each page. Graph paper and hash marks, all those little boxes, reminded him of windows of the Manhattan skyline. He absently drew a small square on his legal pad. Then another. He filled in the boxes with little faces, all smiling. Then one not: not quite a frown, but not entirely passive. The little face was listening, just like Pete in the room, in the skyscraper right then. Anyone outside the actual window would see them just so, four little faces in a skyscraper diorama.

"Ghosts are like Santa Claus? Peter Pan?" The Duck raised an eyebrow. "You have to believe in them for them to exist."

"No," Seymour said. "No, no, I didn't mean that. They exist whether we believe or not. But the environment needs to be conducive to their thriving.

Like any entity, they need the right conditions. Fish live in the sea, birds in the sky."

"And ghosts live in—?" Pete prodded.

"Ghosts don't *live*, Mr. D'Onof—Mr. Donoff. They inhabit. Sometimes they incorporate. But they can't do that in a place with no history."

"Every place has history." The Duck snubbed out the butt. "This ashtray has a history."

"Not quite true," Seymour Barnes countered, treating The Duck like a schoolboy. Pete held his breath, but The Duck listened. "New York is a city that has been very busy reducing the past. We aim toward the future. Once we were an island of natives, then small farming villages, then a booming shipping center. Now—well, here we are in gleaming Midtown. We are glass and steel. Once we were wood. Wood is a particularly suitable conductor for the spirit world. Glass, not so much."

"You're saying this is a problem with *architecture*?"

"Modern buildings are not inviting."

"So if I die tomorrow, I won't be forced to haunt Madison Avenue? Skyscrapers don't do it for ghosts?" The Duck laughed. "I thought every New Yorker dreamt of a gleaming penthouse."

Seymour was serious. "Would you float around the halls of a forty-story building where every floor is a window? Every evening the janitor comes to spray the desks with disinfectant?"

"Cleanliness is a problem, too? Bauhaus and Lysol." The Duck nudged Pete. "There are your culprits."

"Not so much cleanliness as erasure," Seymour said. "We erase yesterday in Manhattan. March into tomorrow! Your industry is on the vanguard of this philosophy. You can't sell aspirin to the dead. No one from yesterday needs a new car. Tomorrow? Yes! We all have needs *tomorrow*. But yesterday is gone and nothing more can be sold there."

"You're not wrong," The Duck said, his voice louder than before, reenergized with talk of sales. "We like to think of ourselves as a wave of the future."

"And you are! You are! But that is not the best way to find haunted spots. The future is only haunted if we let the past remain." He held a finger to his lips, then moved it up as if gauging the wind. "How old is this building?"

The Duck shrugged. "Not a clue."

"Nineteen twenty-six," Anne said. They all looked at her. She sat up proudly. "The girls in the pool are required to memorize the company's history."

"But it doesn't feel like an old building," Seymour prodded, "does it?"

"No," Pete said. "It feels pretty new."

"Because you update it all the time," Seymour said.

"Nobody wants old," The Duck proclaimed. "New is what we sell."

Seymour snapped a finger. "Exactly!"

"Wait, wait," The Duck argued. "Sure, Midtown is growing, but look at the rest of the island."

"The rest of the island is filling with transistors. Television tubes. Movie projectors. Cars and cars and more cars. Appliances of every sort. Electricity roars through a hundred million wires. All of that is contrary to the natural habitat of an apparition."

"Why?" Pete felt himself grow defensive. He might not believe in ghosts, but he couldn't believe they wouldn't find Hitchcock the perfect place. Nothing was impossible with the right information, right? If he failed at this task, he'd clean coffee cups for other copywriters for the rest of his life. The dream of a corner office wobbled.

"We're not exactly sure. Too much noise? Too much information? The past is squeezed by the present in a terrible bear hug and has no room to breathe. You tell me. Where does the past fit into the Young and Rubicam vision of today, much less tomorrow?"

"Today we're looking for the past," Pete spoke up, "so Mr. Hitchcock gets what he wants."

"Mr. Hitchcock's own industry is part of the problem. Televisions are too much, too much for spirits."

The Duck chuckled. "We could sell a lot of spirits on television, Mr. Barnes. They just don't let us."

"Clever wordplay, yes. But the Other World is not enticed by cleverness. We believe it may even be *repelled* by it."

Pete held up a hand, like a diligent student. "So, say there's nothing doing in Manhattan. Okay. We're out of luck. But what's the good news? That silver lining?"

"The good news is the other boroughs are still active. Havens, we call them. The Bronx, Queens, Brooklyn." Seymour glanced at Pete. Did he have I'M FROM RED HOOK stenciled on his forehead? "Staten Island. Go farther. Connecticut, New Jersey, you'll find a host of possibilities."

"Yeah, not the sort of possibilities Hitchcock wants," The Duck bucked. "He's set on a spooky old place on the island of Manhattan."

"Then I'd say he's about ten years too late. Look at these charts." Seymour waved at the neatly displayed sheets. "There are no ghosts left active in Manhattan."

The Duck picked up a sheet, read it, set it down. "I thought this place was crawling with weird stuff. I've been to the Village, you know what I mean?"

"There's no more activity in the Village than on the Upper East Side, Mr. Buck. There is no *weird* left here."

There was a brief rap on the door and another of the girls poked her head in the room. "Mr. Buck?" she said. "Mr. Wilcox wants you on line two." Anne and the girl exchanged a knowing nod. Pete didn't recognize her. He really needed to pay attention.

"Thanks, Bev," The Duck said. He turned to Seymour. "And thank you for your time, Mr. Barnes. I was hoping to hear Manhattan was rife with possibilities, but, hey, we'll make do. Mr. Hitchcock might have to settle for less than the haunt he wanted." He stepped out and closed the door behind him.

Pete sagged.

Anne looked at him. "Do you need me?"

He was startled out of his thoughts. No one had ever offered to stay for him before.

"No," he said. "Thank you, Anne."

If he could only find the place, he might be seen as a leader. Then he'd remember all their names.

"But thank you for asking."

She smiled and left the room. The air changed, a shift in the ozone. Seymour gathered his pages and tucked them with a rustle into his faded briefcase. "I'm sorry I couldn't be more helpful, Mr. Donoff. I would love to have a house that gave you all sorts of opportunities to celebrate with those who came before us."

"Me, too," said Pete. "But like Mr. Buck said, we'll make do." He paused. "Hey . . . how *did* you know about my name?"

"I'd tell you the white pages, but that would be a lie." He gave him a sly smile. "Your grandparents lived in Brooklyn?"

"Yeah. I mean, they did. My grandpa died when I was a kid. My nonna lives with my mother now."

"The outer boroughs are not quite so busy erasing the past. Your grandfather says it's time to take the name back."

"You talk to my grandfather?" Pete said with a nervous laugh.

"I wouldn't call it talking, Pete," Seymour said. "I've had *communication*."

The Duck stepped back into the room with a waft of cool air and the tickety-tick chorus of an army of Underwoods.

"That's what Hitchcock wants," he said, freshly invigorated team spirit in his voice. "Some communication!"

Pete held his breath. What had The Duck heard? Whatever Seymour Barnes believed, it wouldn't spell promotion.

"At the party," The Duck added. "That's all we want. Communication!" He turned to the sideboard to top off his coffee.

"You can breathe now," Seymour whispered to Pete. "May you find some representative of the afterlife dancing at your party." He gave a small bow. "I sincerely wish you the best of luck." He shook hands with both men. "Let me know if you need anything."

Need Seymour Barnes? A guy who thinks he's talking with his nonno? Pshaw. Not likely.

"Thank you," Pete said, and he showed him to the elevator, happy to see the strange man disappear. Seymour Barnes had set his nerves jangling.

He returned to The Duck's office and found his boss annoyed by the briefing.

"That," The Duck growled, "was a bust. No ghosts in the city? Not even for one night? I do not want to tell that to Mr. Hitchcock. You, Donoff?"

Pete had no intention of telling the famous director anything but good news.

"We'll find a place in Manhattan, Mr. Buck." He leveled his gaze at him. "You'll see. There's more to this city than meets the eye—or the graph."

He strode back to his desk, feigning confidence, Seymour Barnes and doubt be damned.

✦ ✧ ✦

"We need to do what we do best," Pete said when he returned to The Duck on Thursday afternoon. "We need an advertisement."

"An ad for a haunted house?" The Duck took the unlit cigar out of his mouth and set it in an oversize glass ashtray. His desktop was spotless and roughly the diameter of Delaware.

"Yes," Pete said, moving closer, hands behind his back. "Plus, it'll be swell publicity. We'll put it in the *Times*. The real estate section. We'll get Hitchcock himself to sign it."

The Duck hesitated. "And Jim Allardice will write it? The same tone as the bits for the show?" He cocked his head, then smacked the desk with glee. "Yes! Jim will come up with the right quips."

Allardice always did. Pete wanted to get into that ring, too—snag credit for coming up with the plan. He'd come prepared and slipped a sheet of typed copy on the Duck's blotter.

The Duck looked over his glasses at Pete and picked it up.

He read it silently. Read it again. He raised his eyes. "Good work here, kid." He nodded. "We'll find our place yet."

There it was: the mock-up for the ad—with his words—on Pete's cramped desk Friday morning. It would run on Sunday in the *Times*' real estate pages, but everyone would talk about it, realtor or not.

Real Estate Wanted

NEED TO RENT REVENANTS FOR ONE NIGHT

For an evening of spirited festivities in Manhattan. Desired: a home with good old-fashioned gloom in which to fete my television collaborators and assorted ghouls. The living guests are ours, the delightful dead ones may be yours. Prefer home in frightful condition. Please call Murray Hill 9-5000, ext. 423, weekdays.

ALFRED HITCHCOCK

Snug died in the spring of 1919, yet, gift or curse, she lingered. She had seen avenues once bisected by streetcars crowded with sleek automobiles. Witnessed electric toasters and telephones and radios, yes, the radios, so many voices, another set of spirits trapped in a box. Snug was trapped, too, though she couldn't say why or how or by whom. Her afterlife, her second act, her days as a specter, or more accurately, a spectator, were not her doing, but were they done *to* her? She could not say.

Snug still dreamt of the Witching Waves scenes in the Fatty Arbuckle film, the last film she'd seen. She had gone to the theater with her friends—against her mother's command, her mother who thought the movies were crass, the crowds and their coughs a dangerous miasma—but Snug laughed, belly laughs, so hard she had tears in her eyes. The scenes at Coney Island and the pretty actress's nausea made her want to return to the amusement park all the more. She hadn't gotten sick when *she* rode the Witching Waves. Snug had strong nerves and a steel stomach. She knew she could handle it.

Of course, that had meant defying a previous decree from her mother: Coney Island was on her list of Loathsome Modern Things. Snug had snuck out, as always with Meredith and Phoebe, and rode the Witching Waves herself. The rollicking metal course shifted up and down, up and down, and around, until she roared with glee. Her friends turned various shades of green, but no one upchucked and Snug rode it twice. The momentum was delicious, the track just the right amount of topsy-turvy. She loved the anticipation of being jostled and the uncertainty of how her body would respond. Would she giggle or tremble, shake or shout?

For the length of the ride, Snug was an adventurer in a whirling world. The Witching Waves let her lose herself for the duration of the journey. It lasted only a few minutes, but she would have ridden it for hours. Seeing it again at the pictures was a thrill and a torture. To ride it again, she would have to defy her mother once more, yet, had she lived, she would have done it without hesitation.

How she missed the physical fact of her body, the blood and flesh and bone, her toes and her fingers and her heart. It was impossible to jostle spirit. She could drift through walls, float downstairs, zoom up the dumbwaiter, fly to the rooftop, soar over all Manhattan when she cared or dared, but she never *felt* anything. No wind on her cheeks. No pressure on her feet. Nothing pushing at her spine or her stomach. She never felt a breath or an ache. She came and went as she wished, and even if she disappeared—and she could, though only for a little while, always called back by something not of her own will—even when others couldn't see her, she still existed. She was there and not, not and there.

It was a knot.

There she was, a doomed and insubstantial girl.

5

February 27, 1956

PETE THANKED THE ELEVATOR operator and stepped out onto the fourteenth floor, briefcase in one hand, folded overcoat in the other. He strode into the open space, aiming for his desk, the last in a line of six in the center of the brightly lit, enormous room, and stopped short. A strange man loomed over his station. Simultaneously, he felt a presence behind him and heard a startled "Oh!" Anne, again, the girl from the typing pool, mamboed past gracefully and tapped him on the arm. "Be careful there!" and click-clacked down the hall in her black heels. Pete stood and studied the life-size cardboard man propped next to his desk. It was yellow with age, but still sturdy. A grocery store prop of a cartoon villain: top-hatted, a thin mustache curling menacingly above his nasty sneer. He was lean and white—an outline more than a full presence. On his shirt, in script, *Mr. Coffee Nerves.*

"Mr. Coffee Nerves?" Pete spoke aloud.

The Duck stepped out of his corner office with a laugh. "We thought you needed some help."

"From him?"

"So far the only ghost we've got." The Duck looked dapper; his gray hair combed neatly, his tie a vibrant green. He handed Pete a cup of black coffee. That was odd. Bob Buck wasn't known to wait on his staff. Pete couldn't remember ever receiving anything from The Duck but orders or advice. Morning coffee? Relics of past campaigns? These were new days.

"He's a ghost? He looks like a villain from *The Perils of Pauline*." Pete walked around the cutout, as if he were inspecting a car. "Who was the client?"

"Postum." The Duck grinned. "See, coffee is evil." He nodded at Pete's cup. "Postum is for the good folks."

"My cousin used to drink that stuff. During the war."

"Lots of us did. And it made Post a lot of money. But it's tough to dismiss the glory of actual java."

Pete hung his hat and coat on a rack along the wall and sat at his desk. The Sunday *Times* was folded, open to the real estate section, and there was his ad. NEED TO RENT REVENANTS. Just as he'd written. He wanted to frame it, talk about how great it looked, but the Duck was enamored with the cardboard man. What a pair. "He doesn't look like a ghost."

The Duck put one arm around Mr. Coffee Nerves's shoulder. "There's your mistake. You never know what a ghost looks like! This fella was potent. He urged coffee drinkers to do *terrible* things. Ignore their children, divorce their spouses, kill the neighbors' chickens."

Pete choked on his drink. "This campaign worked?"

The Duck picked up the cutout and adjusted him behind Pete. Mr. Coffee Nerves watched over his shoulders.

"Like gangbusters." He patted the cardboard man with a pair of *thud*s. "There. Now he can edit all your copy. He's got an excellent eye, I hear."

Pete swiveled around. He was face-to-face with Mr. Coffee Nerves's whiskers, but he looked up at his boss.

"I can write more?"

"First, let's see the response to your ad. Find the right house and who knows what you'll be writing down the line."

The Duck strolled back to his office. "If Mr. Coffee Nerves can't help find a ghost for you, nobody can." He shut his door. *Robert Buck*, in silver sans serif font, gleamed on the polished wood.

Pete raised his cup. "Here's to you, Mr. Coffee Nerves."

The Duck's door popped open and his head crested the threshold. "And if you get uptight, just go find a chicken and wring its neck." He shut the door again.

You can find anything in New York if you just know the right people, his nonna always said.

The right people. Who were they? Seymour Barnes. Alfred Hitchcock. Mr. Coffee Nerves. Pete willed his phone to ring: Ring. Ring.

And it did.

✦ ✧ ✦

That call was a dud. As were the dozen that followed. A woman in Queens swore her basement was infested with spirits. Dead milkmen, dead meter readers. Peter thanked her, but apologized and explained Queens was too far away. Two more calls followed, equally as unhelpful. An old man in New Jersey with an unruly presence (his wife) and a couple in Washington Heights with bumps in the night, but bumps that were probably rats. By ten he was out of coffee and out of patience. The next call was a columnist, Mike Berger, from the *Times*. He'd been covering the city for thirty years and knew it better than any cop or cabbie. He'd seen the ad and wanted to know how the hunt was progressing.

"It's not," Pete admitted. "You got anything for me?"

"Maybe. I did a piece on a lady last year. December. An artist. She's a fixture at Ten Gracie Square."

"Gracie Square has ghosts? Ha. That'd be a coup."

"Ah, heck, it's got Picassos—but this lady said her elderly aunts lived in a big old place on the Upper East Side. The last sister just died. When I was interviewing her, she complained—well, not complained, but griped mildly—about the house. It's a headache, it's empty, it's up for sale. Blah blah blah. But in the meantime, might have the right touch of decrepitude, if you know what I mean. The old ladies couldn't keep the place up so well. Expect lots of cobwebs."

"Tell me more."

"I can't, not much. That's all I got. Her name's Isabella Markell. Classy dame. She's a painter but was married to some fella in finance. Money that married money. Fiorello was a friend of hers, you know? Give her a call. You might be in luck."

"Can you send me a copy of your article?"

Within the hour a courier delivered a mimeograph of Berger's piece. Pete put his feet up and read. The columnist knew how to write a portrait; a genteel lady painting tugboats on the river from her view in one of the ritziest addresses in town and he made it interesting. And if she knew where to find ghosts? Pete finished it and took a deep breath. He had a good feeling.

After lunch, a grilled cheese and a glass of Coke from an automat on Fortieth, it didn't take ten minutes to find Isabella Markell in the phone book. Mrs. Markell was as gracious and frank as Berger suggested.

"My aunt Isabella was ninety-seven when she passed last year. Aunt Mariah was younger, but went first, a few years ago. The house was Isabella and her husband's, Dr. Thomas Satterthwaite. Brilliant medical man. Aunt Mariah had lived with them for decades. The good doctor died ages ago, in the thirties. Since then, it's just been the two women and their house staff. Oh, and my cousin Curzon, but he moved out of the house long ago. He's still in the city, if you want to chat with him."

"Any chance of our renting it for just a night? For a cocktail party? We wouldn't make a mess of the place, wouldn't hurt it. No matter what you've heard about advertising people, we're mostly civilized."

She chortled. "I'm sure you are. But that wouldn't be up to me, entirely. There's a realty company involved. And my brother. Aunt Isabella and Dr. Satterthwaite bought it, goodness, at the turn of the century, I think—it was paid off—but the women had debts. It's being sold, our lawyers advised, probably turned into apartments. A tragedy. It's a handsome old place, five stories, a block from the museum. I used to visit often, but I've been neglectful these last few years. I feel terribly. I should have been more attentive."

Pete wasn't sure how to console Mrs. Markell or if consoling was even what she wanted, but he needed to take a look at the place.

"I'm sorry for your loss, Mrs. Markell. I know what it's like to want to visit elderly relatives and not getting the chance"—he felt a swift jab under his ribs, a poke from his grandfather, or his father, then he was fine again—"but maybe we could take a tour? See if it's what we need?"

"Let me discuss it with my brother. He's not here, he's in Wisconsin, but I'm sure he'll want some say. A party? For actors? I don't want it to grow . . . unseemly." She giggled. "Honestly, if it were up to me, I'd say go ahead, enjoy the place. If you spent any time with Aunt Mariah, she *did* have a sense of humor. Life simply handed her some terrible cards." She paused. "It's not like they'd be there. I'm afraid they aren't the ghosts your ad requests."

"You've read the ad?" Pete flushed with pride. What, was he ten? He shook it off, but still grinned. It's not like she could see him.

"Of course. It was charming. Everyone saw it. But I'm afraid it would have to be a bring-your-own-spirits event." Her laugh was light for a woman her age. Pete figured she had to be in her sixties, at least.

He thanked her for her time, reiterated the agency's interest in the place, hoped to hear from her soon—he was as pushy as he felt he could be and still call it polite. Maybe he could peek in the windows on his own? He couldn't wait by the phone anymore. "Oh, what's the address, Mrs. Markell? Of your aunts' place?"

"Seven East Eightieth Street. It's a Beaux Arts limestone. Take a walk in the neighborhood. It's lovely." She paused again. "Mr. Berger visited me not long ago . . . and I'm not far from my aunts' home. Come chat. I would welcome the company."

Pete nodded. "Thank you, Mrs. Markell. That's a kind invitation. And if the place is what we're looking for, perhaps we can meet at the party."

"If you do visit the property, you'll see it's still partially furnished. No one's been up to take out the last of their belongings. I really should go myself one of these days. Happy hunting, Mr. Donoff."

Pete listened to the click at the end of the call and set the receiver back in its cradle. He really, really hoped the hunt was over. *7 East 80th*, he'd written across a sheet of Y&R stationery.

He stood at the threshold of The Duck's door and knocked. A low voice called, "Come in."

Pete popped Mr. Coffee Nerves's cardboard head across the jamb and waved him.

"Time to take a trip uptown?" Pete said.

The Duck's face lit up. "You find the place?"

Pete slung an arm over the caffeine villain's shoulder. "I believe the stipulations have been met."

Snug was on the ride again, around and around. Then her mother reprimanded: She wasn't supposed to go to the movies, but how could a girl resist? Meredith was going, Phoebe was going. She couldn't say no.

"You don't know what you'll catch, Snug," her mother warned. "The air in crowds is not healthy. The city shouldn't allow picture shows, not with sickness still in our midst. You know that. It's foolish to even consider."

Memory was like the Witching Waves: spinning, jolting, it could have made her queasy, but never Snug. She had a strong stomach, her father always said. Of course, he was never around to praise her—now that he was off with his new family—but Snug was sure he would have let her go with her friends. It wasn't like they were at Coney Island now, not in March, but the movie was funny, everyone said so, and only cost fifteen cents. She had that and more in her coin purse upstairs and she would take Curzon if she must; a little brother is a tagalong but if it meant her mother's approval, she'd do it. Meredith and Phoebe wouldn't mind. They had little brothers of their own.

So, of course, she went. Not with Curzon, he stayed home, and at the last minute she was glad he did. What if there *were* some danger in the crowd? Everyone knew about the flu. But things were getting better. It wasn't like the wintertime. As they rode the streetcar downtown, Snug lost the last of her hesitation. Meredith and Phoebe were always gay girls, and this would be one of the final outings when Meredith was still truly one of them. Her marriage in June was mere months away. Who knew how long it would be before both of her best friends were off running their own households, someday with children of their own?

Snug still felt like a child, though she was nearly twenty when she died. Her parents' turmoil forced her to recognize the pain and ridiculousness of adulthood from an early age. Her father was a brilliant, stupid man and her mother was simultaneously joyous and bitter. Naturally full of life, Mariah loved things passionately—books and art and food and travel—yet her husband's abandonment had stripped her of so much verve. She was just starting to find her way back to some happiness; she helped Aunt Isabella with the Babies Hospital, where Uncle Thomas worked, and she was contemplating a trip to Italy, where Grandmother spent so much time. There was hope, for the first time since Father had left them.

Snug had been an adolescent then, but once her father chose Mrs. Morgan over them, the second Mrs. Taylor, or maybe not, depending on whom one believed—there were those who said he was simply a bigamist—Snug's interest in boys went dormant. Young men had come calling for her, there was talk of certain boys, but that disappeared in the intervening years. Snug knew she had reverted to avoid the next stage. Then the next stage came anyway: it was here. Meredith and Phoebe would be gone, and Snug would have to choose to metamorphose into a woman of her own or retreat, back to her room with the decade-old dolls and the books and games. She still played gin rummy with Curzon—but time was moving for him as well. He'd be a young man soon and brothers don't stay behind for lonely sisters. Curzon would go off to college, marry, raise a family. And Snug would continue to sit with her mother and Aunt Isabella and Uncle Thomas in the quiet, narrow house.

Flickering images of Coney Island, like echoes of the previous June, made summer feel like the day before and a million years earlier. After, the girls left the theater and stopped at a bakery. There were crowds everywhere. The war was over, the flu was fading, everyone was certain. It had been bad for weeks and weeks, but not tonight. A warm night, spring was tugging at everything, every branch and blossom waited. It wouldn't be long.

Snug tiptoed back into her bedroom and slipped off her pale yellow dress. She put on her nightgown and washed her face. In bed, she thought about the picture show: the men sneaking into the park, Buster Keaton's long face, Fatty in an enormous bathing suit, and yet, there was love, too. Maybe she would run away and become an actress? Oh, wouldn't that surprise her family! They would be horrified. She would enjoy playing the ingenue in a movie even better than in real life. Romances made for a lively plot, but so did terrible marriages.

Snug had seen both in film and real life. Her aunt and uncle had a strong marriage, if a bit work-like. They never had children, though her mother confided they had wanted them. That was a heartbreak no one ever spoke aloud. Aunt Isabella and Uncle Thomas doted on each other and though he worked long hours—he was one of the city's most important doctors, Mother said—Aunt Isabella was hardly alone. She had her organizations, the church and the Women's Aid Society, and, always, the Babies Hospital. There was the Metropolitan Museum a block away. Both her mother and her aunt volunteered there and took classes.

In the last year, the museum had acquired a little blue hippo for their ancient Egyptian collection and there was a contest to name it. Snug entered but didn't win. No matter: the little blue hippo—freshly christened William—was among Snug's favorites. So cute and so old. He was new to New York, but not to the world. Snug felt the same way; new, perhaps to this life, but not to life itself. Maybe she had been an Egyptian lady, a lady-in-waiting, of course, even then waiting on someone or something else, but alive, long ago. Those were her last thoughts that March night: Egypt. William. Playing pretend for a camera. The Witching Waves. It left her breathless. Maybe that's how riding *time*—the years of her life to come—would feel. Up and down days, up and down years, laughing and queasy all at once.

She woke with a cough. A fever. A strange heaviness in her limbs. She stood and caught a glimpse of herself in the dresser mirror. There was . . . not Snug, but someone else. Someone tinted faintly *blue*. Like William and his hard blue body. The surprise made her stagger, and she stumbled at her bedside. Then she thought, I'm going to fall, and fall she did. She collapsed to the cold wood floor, her nightgown gathered around her shins.

Her mother found her, called for the maids, had her hoisted back into bed. The weight of wool blankets and the scent of camphor. They summoned the doctor, who dragged her mother from her room. Curzon, forbidden from visiting, lingered at the doorway and witnessed the commotion, then ran off to hide.

This was what her mother had prophesied, this was the calamity so many had faced. Here was Snug fulfilling a trite fate. She'd been warned: stay away from people, as if that were possible in Manhattan. Snug was tired of hiding. She'd been hiding from so much. It was the cusp of a new decade, and she was ready to get out again. Both she and her mother would get out, she had vowed, move on from her father's betrayal.

Snug clutched a small doll at her chest, a worn little woman in a faded blue dress. Her father had given it to her on her last birthday with him, eight years ago. She didn't know it then, but it would be his final gift. Snug supposed he still gave gifts, to his new wife and her children. He certainly didn't pay any attention to her or her brother.

She was sweating and there was an even greater weight in her lungs. It was work, this business of breathing, as if she'd been running for days. Running from what? Better, she thought, as she turned in the wet sheets, to head somewhere than to flee blindly. She was going somewhere, yes, toward something.

Then she was dead.

That was Sunday evening. Monday morning, Snug's body stiff and cold, the house was struck with strangled grief, too much despair for weeping out loud, the silence a suffocating gravity. Poor Snug, poor sad Snug, they whispered in the corridors, the maids and the cook, the liveryman and the postman. Poor Snug, moaned her brother and her aunts, she would never see another day. Poor Snug, cried her mother. Oh, Isabella! She is gone, she is gone.

And then she returned.

6

February 29, 1956

THE CABBIE WHISTLED WHEN they pulled to the curb. "Here you go. Ten Gracie Square. Nice digs."

Carolyn glanced at the posh apartment building's looming entrance, over to the dark East River, then back to the driver in his newsboy's cap and his genuine awe. "It's—it's not as intimidating as you'd think," she said, with false breeziness.

"You a Vanderbilt or something?" He smiled around a smoldering cigarette.

"Or something." She handed him a dollar. "Keep the change!"

"Thanks," he laughed. "I'm saving for the penthouse."

The yellow Checker squawked its horn in farewell, a short sharp burst, and disappeared down Eighty-Fourth Street. One small brown suitcase sat at Carolyn's heels, like her loyal terrier, Nip, back home. She'd filled her valise with everything she'd need for a week in the city—a pair of skirts, a pair of blouses, a simple black pencil dress, a cardigan and capris, underclothes, a warm nightie, and an extra pair of pumps. Everything but answers about Malcolm. She'd find those here, though, she was certain. Manhattan had everything.

Okay, she was only sort of certain. But sort of certain was better than doing nothing and she needed to climb out of limbo. Afternoons wandering museums and crowded sidewalks, bookended by a round-trip cross-country train ride on the *Lake Shore Limited*, had to shake loose the thing stuck inside her. With a little topsy-turvy to her life, she'd find her answers like she'd find a nickel in the pocket of last season's sweater. Her mother had sent her for a reason.

She reviewed the outfit she'd worn for the days on the train: only mild wrinkles and no stray coffee stains. Her shoes were damp with exhaust-filthy snow melting in untidy piles along the curb. Those she could slip off in the foyer: she wouldn't make tracks on Aunt Bella's rugs.

◆ ◇ ◆

Carolyn had stayed at Gracie Square years before, visiting with her father. That had been in 1950, the summer after high school. While he socialized with old Yale chums, Carolyn roamed with her aunt and dreamt of her own tiny apartment in some nearby neighborhood. Aunt Bella had succeeded in New York, why couldn't she?

Bella was her father's older sister, a woman who'd made the journey from the Northwoods decades earlier. She'd studied at the Sorbonne before she married a jovial and successful businessman who worked in international trade. They'd traveled widely and often, but sometimes while he was journeying across the globe she stayed behind and painted. After his death, she made a name for herself with cityscapes. While the second war raged, Bella had befriended Mayor La Guardia. He decreed she was the only artist allowed to document the East River's shipping life. Alone in her high rise, Bella painted the harbor and the tugs. The mayor adored her work, displayed it in city hall, and feted her with a showing of two hundred of her river paintings in Gracie Mansion.

Bella wasn't immune to the lure of glamorous society, but she was weary of it. Still quick and gracious, she preferred canvases to cocktails. When she wasn't at the easel in her paint-smeared smock, she hosted discreet gatherings. She was even known to invite dockworkers up for luncheons to critique the authenticity of her sketches. They all knew Bella, treated her like the mother she was, to three grown sons who were off with their own families. The laborers waved while the gray-haired lady worked on the balcony. When Carolyn first stood on that balcony, not yet out of her teens, Bella had to remind her of sailors' specific interests in young women.

"Sit while you're out there, dear," Carolyn remembered her aunt telling her one gorgeous June morning. "The men will try to look up your skirt. And don't stand backlit unless you're wearing a slip."

"They can see us up here?" Carolyn eyed the boats churning in the distance.

"If you can see them, they can see you," she'd said. "Also, they have binoculars."

It wasn't long after returning from that trip that Carolyn took the job at Sutter's and learned the particulars of silver patterns and high-strung brides.

She wondered what her life would have been like if she'd told her father she wanted to stay with Aunt Bella. Not that it had been a real option—no one had invited her.

She considered the river from Bella's balcony again. It hadn't changed. She had. On a gray spring day, the bridges in the distance felt familiar, and not only because she crossed one every day between Superior and Duluth. She seemed always between states.

◆ ◇ ◆

The next morning, Carolyn joined her aunt in the sunny living room adjacent to the spacious balcony. It was temperate, nearing fifty, but still too chilly for Bella to attend the small easel by the wrought iron furniture. Later, it would be warm enough. Before then, Aunt Bella learned her niece's story, prodding Carolyn with direct questions over cups of coffee.

"I'm a late bloomer, that's all." Carolyn held her hands aloft, drying her freshly painted nails. "And honestly, what kind of flower do I even want to be?"

Bella sat with one leg tucked under her rear, a cigarette burning between her long fingers. Her skirt, a bold floral print, made Carolyn think of Madrid. Around her neck hung turquoise beads. No one up north dressed like her aunt. "Your parents had a lovely marriage. Helen and Maud have made good matches."

"It's not that I've had poor role models." Carolyn blew on the wet red polish.

"Truth is," Bella said, like a detective revealing a motive, "you enjoy your independence and love your job. This Malcolm gives you a different vision, more like your mother's life—babies who turn into toddlers who need to be fed and who get colds and need round-the-clock care. And, of course, there's hospitality for your husband's colleagues. It's not appalling, but it's not appealing, is it?"

"I do love my nephews and nieces, I do," Carolyn protested, "but—"

"It's that *but* that brought you back to me."

"Yes."

Bella strolled to her Hepplewhite desk, directing the conversation in just the way Carolyn's father would. Carolyn momentarily missed him. Bella's voice snapped her back. "While you're here, you can do this for me." She handed Carolyn an ivory envelope, flap torn open. "It's not my sort of thing anymore. But you're the right woman."

Carolyn took the invitation, a single sheet of heavy stock shaped like a tombstone. "A costume party?"

"Not quite. You can wear a pretty dress. It is, however, a theme party. Spooks and ghouls."

"They do know Halloween's not in March?" She read aloud, "*Mr. and Mrs. Hitchcock invite you—* Wait. *The* Mr. Hitchcock?"

"I suppose. The one named Alfred." Bella blew a dragon trail of smoke from her thin lips. "You know his work?"

"Auntie, everyone knows his work. Yes," Carolyn said, "even in Superior. Alfred Hitchcock invited *you* to a party? Has he seen your paintings?"

Bella took another long drag. "I'd doubt that. He invited me because he's using your grandaunts' house." She pointed. "Check the address."

Carolyn read the rest of the card. "Grandaunt Isabella's house? He's using *her* house? Oh, I can't imagine what she'd say!"

"I'm sure you can." Bella smiled. "But she can't complain, can she? There's a young man from an advertising agency arranging the party. Pete something. The boy wants to see the place again. They only found it on Monday—visited it twice—and immediately rented it. Really, they've been in a frenzy! Sending out invitations *special delivery*. Now they want to take stock of any last-minute particulars they need to get the place properly outfitted. That gives them, what, a week?" She looked at Carolyn. "You should go with him. Give him a tour. I've spoken with him twice now. He's pleasant."

Carolyn sensed there was more behind Bella's word than *pleasant*, but she ignored it. "When's he going over?"

"Tomorrow afternoon. The realtor has the key, but you could meet them there."

"Why don't you want to go?"

Bella scowled. "I prefer to paint."

Carolyn laughed. "I do love that old place. A haunted party? It has the right . . . ambiance." She chose the word carefully.

"That's a word for it. *Dusty* and *neglected* are others." Bella retrieved the invitation, glanced at it once more, then dropped it atop a tidy pile of envelopes. "They've been planning the party for weeks, but couldn't find the right spot. They wanted ghosts. Or someplace that looked ghost friendly. Isabella would be appalled. The hoi polloi in the parlor! Actresses! Journalists! Ghastly!" Bella snubbed out her butt in a ceramic bowl on a small side table. "The old sisters were stern. Snug and I used to laugh at it all."

Carolyn frowned. "Who's Snug?"

Bella paused and tilted her head, listening to ships in the distance. Tug whistles and boat horns.

"I've never told you? Your mother never told you?"

Carolyn shook her head. "Never."

"Well," Bella said, and returned to her seat. She tapped out a fresh cigarette and plucked a stray bit of tobacco off her tongue, then smiled dreamily. "Snug was my cousin. Yet another Isabella."

"Of course," Carolyn said. "Not confusing at all."

Bella chuckled. "Yes, the grand tradition. There we were, Isabella and Isabella. She grew up here, I grew up in Superior. We saw each other once a year, sometimes twice, then less. But we adored each other. Snug and Bella. Two peas in a pod."

"What happened to her?" Carolyn slipped a cigarette from her own pack.

Bella's face fell, only a little, but enough for Carolyn to note. "She died. A long, long time ago. The flu. When we were young."

A boat on the river bleated again, a greeting, a warning.

"What was she like?" Carolyn felt she was intruding but couldn't help asking. There would come a day when no one asked about her mother anymore. Or Andy. Even now he seemed a relic. It was so long ago. Perhaps this was why she was in New York, talking to Bella. There were stories to hear, things her mother wanted her to know. "Would you tell me about her?"

Bella gave a gentle smile and began.

T he youngest Isabellas sat on the Persian rug while the adults gathered in an arc behind them, along the wall of the crowded parlor. Snug and Bella loved the commotion. It was a sunny winter day and Bella was thrilled by her cousin's companionship. Snug, however, complained about the cramped space. She wanted freedom to run across the snowy lawn.

Gilt-edged paintings hung on every available inch of wall and a battalion of statues, small white ones on tabletops, knee-high marble alongside the armchairs and ottomans, made for ornate claustrophobia, like a dragon's cave stuffed with treasure. This was The Cedars, their grandmother's estate on the Hudson River, north of the city.

Their grandmother held court at the center of the arc, the oldest living Isabella, doted on by her sons and their wives. Snug visited with her aunt Isabella every six months or so. Her mother stayed away from The Cedars, avoiding Grandmother's caustic assessment of Mariah's domestic tribulations. This afternoon was different: Mariah was there, but Aunt Isabella and the Doctor were not. They had stayed behind in the city. He had too much work, an article due for a medical journal, and where the doctor labored, Aunt Isabella was at his elbow.

William, Bella's father, was grim-faced behind his thick mustache. Perhaps he smiled on occasion, but who could tell with such drapery, whispered Snug. Bella giggled. She knew her papa smiled often. "At least to me," she said.

The photographer had set his camera on a heavy black tripod. "It looks like a tall insect." Snug's voice was solemn. "Have you ever thought of a photograph? What it means?"

"It means we better stay still until Grandmama says 'shoo.'"

They watched the photographer bend and peer through the lens. He straightened, fiddled with a knob, then bent to look at them again.

"A photograph is forever," Snug said. "I read that the Indians think it will capture their souls. They don't like to get their pictures taken. It's a sort of theft to them."

Bella rubbed her knee, then tidied up her skirt and looked back at the adults. "I like the idea of forever," she said.

"I don't know," Snug said. "Maybe we *do* lose something?"

"Like what?"

Snug eyed Bella. "A piece of who we are? Or maybe there's a clock somewhere, and every time we get a picture taken, the picture steals some of our lifetime. The more pictures you get, the more you pay."

"That's ridiculous!"

Snug laughed. "It is! It all is. Clocks and photographs and worrying about eternity. There's no such thing—"

"Shh," Bella hissed, clutching Snug's wrist. "That's blasphemy!"

Snug wrestled her wrist free. "I don't mean it like that. I can believe in lots of things and let other people believe whatever they want. It's no skin off my nose if someone wants to go to heaven and I don't think it exists."

The photographer called their attention. The adults stilled. The leather-bound books and oil-painted portraits of earlier generations waited quietly in the background. The fire crackled on the great hearth. The photographer held up a hand while he ducked behind the black curtain attached to the camera.

The flashbulb illuminated the room like a burst of lightning and the air went *pop*, an uncorked bottle, something unsettled and free and ready to spill everywhere. The adults all exhaled.

"I hope he takes another," Bella whispered. "It's like a promise we'll get to the future."

"You just want to live forever," said Snug. "Who wants to do that?"

Bella squinted at her cousin. "Who doesn't?"

The photographer told them to get ready.

The girls held hands and squeezed.

7

March 1, 1956

THURSDAY MORNING, SIX DAYS before the party, Bella stood behind Carolyn as they tended their outfits in front of a long mirror in the master bath. Her taste was elegant but ran to silk scarves and flamboyant prints. Carolyn was more subdued. She was trying to choose the right earrings for the day: silver . . . or silver. Her jewelry packing had been ridiculously spare, her head elsewhere. Bella fiddled with a strand of Venetian glass beads. "The woman from the realty company is going to meet you and the young man from the advertising agency at the house this afternoon. I told them you would act as the family agent."

"And that means?"

"Not much of anything. Keep an eye out they don't pocket the valuables? They couldn't march away with the battered Chesterfields. There's still some furniture to move out. Watch that they don't make off with the light fixtures?" She chuckled. "I don't know. Act as if we care."

"I do care," Carolyn insisted. "But from what you've said, it's worse for wear already. Aren't the buyers going to raze it anyway? Hitchcock could burn the place down and do them a favor."

Bella centered the colorful necklace, yellows and blues and pinks. "I don't think the neighbors would agree." She studied her profile, first one direction, then the other. "But I understand the allure of torching the past. If Isabella and Mariah aren't there, then, really, why should it remain?" She flinched and held one hand still at her long neck. "That was stupid of me. Just because they aren't there doesn't mean it's empty."

Carolyn glanced at her aunt. Bella, uncharacteristically, looked away, as if hiding her emotions. Carolyn followed her gaze out to the bedroom, out the broad four-over-four paned windows, over the rumbling streets, over the busy river. Both women faced the white clouds, the hints of blue sky, both breathing more carefully than a moment before. Carolyn wasn't sure if she should ask what her aunt was thinking.

"Snug will always be there." Bella spoke quietly. "To me, at least."

"Of course." Carolyn led her aunt from the bathroom to the four-poster bed and sat beside her on the ivory coverlet. She felt impertinent giving this sophisticated woman advice, but kindness compelled her. "Of course she's there. And if the building is gone, the memories aren't."

"I'm too old for this sort of sentimentality, Carolyn. Yet with Aunt Mariah—her mother—dead, and Aunt Isabella dead, all of the servants gone, it's only me." Bella inhaled, her chest rising, then shook her head and collapsed into herself a tad, but enough for Carolyn to read it as defeat. "When your father married your mother, I felt very fortunate to gain a sister. She was a gift. You know that?" She squeezed her niece's hand.

"Yes, I do. I know you loved her."

"I still do."

Carolyn didn't want to cry, so she blinked back her tears and sat up straighter. "Didn't you say Snug had a brother?"

"Curzon," Bella laughed. "He's still here in the city, an architect." Bella glanced at the telephone on the nightstand, as if expecting it to ring. "He never cared much for the house. It was stately in its day, the old place. Past its prime now." She patted her gray hair. "Oh, aren't we all?" She glanced at Carolyn. "Not you, dear. You are lovely."

Carolyn felt a blush rise in her cheeks. "Thank you."

"It will be your job to secure the key after the party. We're renting it to them for a single day—twenty-four hours. They come in, they set up, they have their gathering, they clean up, they leave. Like good campers, they leave the place as they found it. No mess, no disrepair."

"I can do that," Carolyn agreed.

Bella patted her arm and thanked her. "And the woman's name is Dolores. I've never met her, but she seemed competent over the telephone. I admire a woman in business." She nudged her niece's shoulder. "Like you."

✦ ✧ ✦

The turn off Fifth Avenue onto East Eightieth Street led to a staid, tree-lined block of town houses. No. 7 stood in the middle of the block, a white limestone with a wrought iron terrace balustrade and a short flight of steps down to its front entrance, a bright red door behind an ornate gate. The man waiting by the door was short and thick, his gray overcoat a bit too tight, his hat with a longish brim casting a shadow over his face, looking very much like a character in a Hitchcock movie. Carolyn paid the elderly cabbie and watched him go, reading the sign on the roof of his taxi: *Don't be a duck!* It was meant to discourage the constantly honking traffic but wasn't working. A chorus of horns punctuated Fifth Avenue's multitudes. Only boy ducks honked—girl ducks quacked, of course—so it wasn't her problem. She doubted the city boy who wrote that sign considered it. Well, maybe honking boys were her problem, at least the one named Malcolm. She crossed the street and introduced herself.

"You aren't a Dolores," she said pleasantly to the wide fellow.

"Dolores is my mother," he answered, an unlit cigarette between his teeth. "Vincent Valiano." He leered—Carolyn considered *maybe* he just had an unfortunate face—and stuck out a big bare hand. She took it, then regretted the choice because Vincent was the sort that tried to crush fingers. She didn't give him the pleasure of a grimace and he let go first. "Nice to meet you, Miss Banks." He motioned to the house behind them. "This is some address. A baby like this doesn't come on the market often." He cupped his hand to shield his lighter from the breeze.

Drawn curtains on every floor gave the place a disdainful air and Carolyn recalled the last time she was at this door, fifteen years earlier. It felt like a century. "My grandaunts lived here."

A young man in a gray suit strode toward them, waving his hand. His gait was bouncy, his neat dark hair jostling where a front curl had come loose. "Hello!"

Vincent's faint sneer slid into an annoyed smile. He tapped ash onto the sidewalk and turned to Carolyn. "Now you got two guys who aren't my mother."

The men shook hands and Vincent harrumphed. "I don't run into folks from Madison Avenue much."

"I don't have much experience with realtors. My first time renting a haunted house." He had a big grin. Nice teeth. Her sisters would have opinions.

"It's just another lease to me," Vincent said. "The ghosts are your business." He turned to unlock the front door.

"Pete Donoff," the young man introduced himself.

"Carolyn Banks." His grip was firm, but he wasn't trying to prove anything.

"I'm in charge of finding the right venue. Or since we have it, my job—" he hesitated as if a better word was scurrying to catch up, "my job changed. Now I'm in charge of making sure all the details are correct. For Mr. Hitchcock." He gave a nervous shrug. "For the agency's higher-ups, really. If they like what I do, I'll be happy. I'm not sure we can predict what Mr. Hitchcock admires."

The front door opened into a dim foyer. Carolyn realized she was holding her breath at the threshold.

"I've been here before," Pete said, breaking the silence. "Twice actually, but briefly. Enough for my boss to fall in love with it. We found it in the nick of time." He turned to her. "I've spoken to your aunt. Right?"

"Yes." She smiled. "Aunt Bella."

"How many aunts you got?" Vincent reappeared and tapped a fresh cigarette out of his pack. He patted his pockets, searching, while the cigarette draped from his mouth.

"Bella is my father's sister. The women here were my grandfather's siblings." Carolyn watched Pete digging in his jacket. She took a lighter from her purse and offered the flame to Vincent. He was reluctant but took a draw. Pete was entertained.

"Thanks," Vincent said, but he didn't sound like he meant it. He wasn't the kind of man who wanted to owe a woman anything.

She tucked the lighter away as swiftly as she'd retrieved it.

Before he led them further, Vincent turned to Carolyn. "I'm supposed to give you the keys. Consider this my formal transition. We give you the keys, you hand 'em to Donoff here." He seemed to linger on the last name, making sure he'd gotten it right. "And Mr. *Donoff* gives 'em back to you at the end of the night. Party's over, keys back where they belong. Until we hand 'em over to the folks that are gonna buy the place at the end of the month."

"That soon?" Carolyn touched the red door.

"That soon," Vincent echoed.

They entered.

No. 7 was narrow and tall and, after a short entryway, opened into a long gallery, still partially furnished, though cloaked in heavy cloth. The air was stale and their shoes made footprints in light dust, mussing earlier footprints, evidence of prior visits.

"We're not going to need much by the way of furniture." Pete rested a hand on the back of a tarp-covered couch. "Or art. Look at that."

Vincent and Carolyn turned to the portrait of a grim-faced woman in a black dress.

"She's a battle-axe," Vincent guffawed.

"That," Carolyn said, "is my great-grandmother." She brushed a thin layer of grime from the gold frame. "I've seen other pictures. Not quite so grouchy, but she *was* a battle-axe. From what I've been told."

Pete walked up from behind. "You never know what happened to her before she had to sit. For hours. A hot day. A bug in her shoe. Maybe the painter was a jerk."

She turned to him. "Do you always look for reasons? For why people are—who they are?"

"I guess so." He really looked at her. "I hadn't thought of it that way."

Vincent wandered from the gallery to the back of the first floor. "There's a kitchen back here," he called.

"That's where we'll set up the main food," Pete said. "According to the information Dolores sent over, there's another smaller one on the third floor and a butler's pantry on the fifth."

"Two and a half kitchens?" Carolyn said.

"I thought you'd been here before." Pete tossed back the cover of one chair to reveal faded red upholstery.

"I have. I've sat in that very spot." She drifted to the staircase with its heavy carved banister. "But I only got as far as this room and a parlor up a flight. Oh, and there's a library. I remember that. But I didn't go exploring. Aunt Isabella and Aunt Mariah weren't the kind to encourage it."

Pete followed her. "And what would they think of this plan?"

"They'd hate it. Absolutely."

He stopped. "Do you?"

She looked down at him. His brown eyes were sincere. "I mean, it's not hallowed ground, but I hope you treat the place with respect. They lived here for years."

"We'll be careful. You're coming with your aunt?"

"In her place. I'm her second, I guess."

"Swell," he said simply, then added, "but it's not a duel. It's a party." When he smiled, he had dimples.

Two floors up and they counted a fireplace in nearly every room. Miles of mantel space and ample nooks for covering every surface with knickknacks. The house felt vulnerable and abandoned yet simultaneously crowded with enough candlesticks to light a small city. A chorus of varied statuettes—dancing couples and shepherd girls and ugly dogs—along with empty vases, Chinese and Persian and Greek, lingered in shadowed corners.

"And what are those?" Pete pointed at yet another mantel, this one with a squat pair of tarnished copper bowls commandeering the center. The taller of the two—more of a pitcher, really—had a serpentine snout that wound its way to the shorter. "It looks like something a mad scientist would use."

"An alembic," Carolyn said, walking toward Pete. "It's very old."

"An alem-what?"

"Alembic," she teased. "You never had a chemistry class?"

"Not that used ancient teapots."

"It's not a teapot."

"That grew an appendage."

"It's for distilling."

"Handy. We'll make the house drinks from scratch."

They inspected the two halves. The larger bowl had a crown like an onion dome, a miniature Russian church, and its spout snaked to the side like a plague doctor's mask. Beneath the tarnish, it was copper, as she'd suspected, and crusted with a seal of dust. No one had touched them in a very long time. Pete ran his finger along the smaller of the pair, looked at the grit on his hand, and tried to blow it off his fingertips. "Aladdin's lamp? Not the thing I'd expect from a pair of spinsters."

Carolyn hummed. "They weren't spinsters. One of them married a doctor. Maybe he used it?" She turned the smaller bowl and squinted at its blackened stand.

"He was an alchemist? If it can make gold, we're in luck."

"Doubtful. It's held together by luck and rust as it is."

He patted a tarpaulin-covered couch and dust shot up like flour. "So, the party needs to be a big hit or I'll lose my job and no alchemy can save me."

She rubbed the pot's face. "You could take up moonshining. Alchemy and alcohol aren't that far apart."

Pete took the whole kit from her and set it gently back on the mantel. "I haven't a chemist's bone in my body. But I do like an old-fashioned."

Vincent returned, footsteps echoing with unexpected cracks. "Anybody ever die here?" Carolyn and Pete turned to him slowly. "I mean, if you want ghosts and all."

"We're not *really* expecting anything," Pete said.

"Maybe?" Carolyn was thinking aloud. "I don't know."

"For your sake," Vincent said to Pete, "morbidity all around." He winked at Carolyn and jogged up the steep staircase, hand casually skimming Carolyn's back before he let it run up the banister's dark wood. Little puffs of dust fell in his wake.

Pete watched him disappear. "Sorry about that."

"Don't worry," she said. "Forget it."

"You don't like winkers," he added.

"You can tell?" She let herself laugh. "No, I don't like winkers."

"Noted," he said. "That guy—he's something. Reminds me of guys I grew up with."

"Don't worry about me, Mr. Donoff. I'm very capable."

Up the stairs they went, Vincent loud above them, exclaiming over each room with a whistle of delight.

It was all as she remembered or imagined; on the second floor, a large parlor spanned the width of the building—maybe sixteen or seventeen feet across. Beyond that, a narrow dining room, crowded with a long table and eight chairs. The third floor had the library, bedrooms, a terrace with a view to a private backyard, its walls overgrown with winter-gray vines starting to bud. Above that, a floor with a quartet of bedrooms and a balcony, and above that an enormous nursery and living quarters for at least two servants, each with its own small bath. There was the door for rooftop access. Nothing above—no modern garden—but a clear view of the street below and in the distance, she could see the Metropolitan Museum and the green edge of Central Park.

Pete was impressed. "Nice," he said.

"Isn't it," Carolyn agreed.

"It's a great view from any angle," Vincent said, and when Carolyn turned he was eyeing her legs. "No complaints here."

"Excuse me," she said.

"It's just—I've seen a lot . . . of houses. I know a good view when I spot one."

"You're an expert?"

He smirked. "You could say so."

"But I wouldn't," she sniffed, and headed down the narrow stairs. Pete followed. He stopped her at the third floor. He lingered by the doorway of the largest room. Carolyn watched him survey a stately four-poster bed and the tall built-in bookshelves, some empty, some crowded with old volumes.

"This is where we'll put the old man."

"What?"

"We've got a mannequin," he explained. "We're going to put him here in the bed. Party guests can wander this way. He'll make them jump. Hitchcock insisted on a corpse or two."

"Or two?" Carolyn wondered what Aunt Bella would say about that.

Pete laughed. "You don't have a poker face, Miss Banks. Too gauche for you?"

She bit her lip. "Maybe. But it's not my party."

"There's more. We've got a full-size lady in aspic. Going to put her by the grub."

She frowned. "Delightful."

"De-lovely. Jell-O's a client, so we got her on the cheap. Another order from the director. Go figure. He thought it would be creepy."

She shivered. "Guess that's why he's a success."

"Hey," Pete beamed. "You want to help me set up? Wednesday morning? I mean, you're going to have to police me anyway, make sure we're not running off with the china—which, by the way, we aren't because the caterer's bringing his own plates—but it might be fun."

"What does *set up* mean?"

"Decorate. I mean, after the place is cleaned. Then we'll come in and make it look ramshackle again."

"Like Christmas decorations?" The white lights in the Flame floated around her. Malcolm and the stale dazzle of spent holidays. No, that's not what this boy meant. Why this sudden queasiness about Christmas lights? She used to love them. She wanted to again.

"Right," Pete said. "Like that. Only . . . spooky."

Vincent found them again. "I knew the morbid stuff was gonna be big."

"Morbid is Hitchcock's game," Pete said. "We're all just playing it for a night."

Vincent held a yellowed issue of *LIFE*, curled in his big hand like a baton. "Think it'll be in here?"

"It better be," Pete said. "He's not doing this for anonymity. That's the whole point. Make people talk."

"I'm sure they will," said Carolyn. She handed him the keys and it felt strangely monumental, as if she'd surrendered something important.

"Thank you." Pete jiggled the ring. "What do you say? You'll help?"

She'd just met him, yet the answer was easy. "Certainly," she said. "I'll help."

The trio stepped out of the shadowy house and into the Technicolor

Manhattan afternoon. Vincent gave her one last unwelcome once-over before he hustled off, leaving a wake of tobacco and musky cologne.

Pete walked her back to Gracie Square, like a boy carrying her books after school, and thanked her for the tour. As she watched him amble away down Eighty-Fourth—bouncing with every step—Carolyn felt sure-footed for the first time in weeks.

◆ ◇ ◆

That evening, Carolyn sat in Bella's living room and spoke too much about Pete Donoff. She heard herself say his name for the sixth time since returning from No. 7 and she didn't miss her aunt's arched eyebrow, Bella's face reflected in the broad riverside windows. The glass was dusk-dimmed and dotted with lights coming on for the night in the buildings across the water.

"They want people to have died there? They have choices." Bella disappeared into her bedroom, then returned and handed Carolyn a yellowed newspaper. It was folded into a sheaf, an obituary circled in red ink on the top page. "They complain it's not spooky enough, show them that."

Carolyn read aloud as Bella wandered into the kitchen.

Mrs. Isabella Banks Satterthwaite, widow of Dr. Thomas E. Satterthwaite, a founder and former president of the Babies Hospital, died yesterday at her home, 7 East Eightieth Street. She was 97 years old. Her husband, a prominent doctor in the city for many decades, died in the Eightieth Street residence in 1933 at the age of 91.

"Your young man at Y and R might find it useful," Bella said as she returned and handed Carolyn a highball. "Whiskey and water. It's five o'clock."

"He's not my young man." Carolyn flushed.

"Regardless," Bella chided. "His bosses will be impressed. Mr. Hitchcock will be thrilled, I'm sure."

Carolyn grimaced. "I keep telling you, he's not my young man."

Bella laughed, her voice light. "That's right. You have a young man back in Superior. You can have two, you know. At least this side of the altar."

"Not when I don't want either," Carolyn snipped.

Bella folded the newspaper in her lap and leaned forward. "That's an answer right there, Carolyn." She touched her hand. "Don't say *yes* to anything you aren't certain about. Life is long, much longer than a young person can imagine, and a bad match would make it an eternity."

WESTERN UNION
TELEGRAM

```
CAROLYN BANKS C/O ISABELLA MARKELL
10 GRACIE SQUARE
NEW YORK NEW YORK

MARCH 2 1956

DARLING
I HEAR THERE IS A PARTY. NEED A DATE? CAN BE
THERE IN A JIFFY.

MALCOLM
```

The telegram tucked in its envelope smoldered in Carolyn's purse while she kept thoughts of Malcolm at bay with shopping—Bella insisted on buying her party clothes at Bonwit Teller—and museum trips. And eating New York food. So much pasta, so little time, Carolyn bemoaned, but not to Bella. She'd done that instead with Pete Donoff, who was definitely not *her young man*, but with whom she found she could spend an easy hour or two. A day after the house tour, he had called and asked if she wanted to have coffee. She'd turned him down, but only because he'd caught her off guard. The audacity, she complained to her aunt. When Carolyn was finished acting shocked, Bella pushed her to a telephone tucked in a hallway alcove. Carolyn felt forward returning Pete's call after her quick refusal, but there she was, the receiver's cord dangling by her stockinged leg. And there was no hiding who was pushing her; Pete even said, loudly, "Hello, Mrs. Markell!" keen to Bella's eavesdropping. That call led to coffee at a diner on Sixth, then dinner the next night at a place called Napoli's in Little Italy; they were so smitten—only with the food, of course—they went back two days later.

They'd gone for strolls, they'd window-shopped. She'd taught Pete to wave as they passed the public library. "Hello, Uncle James!" he called, game to play along. She had a flash of how much her sisters would enjoy him (or not, given his perfect teeth) and then wondered what she was thinking.

This was not why she'd come to Manhattan.

But it wasn't *not* why she'd come to Manhattan either.

Malcolm and marriage seemed a million miles away, not the twelve hundred on the map. What she was doing with Pete, that was vacation.

Why shouldn't she have some fun? Talk of the hunt for the house—the stipulations!—and stories of his life at the agency, discussions of Bella's art, explaining her sisters and her father, even, briefly, Andrew's and her mother's deaths, none of it had the heaviness of conversations with Malcolm. Pete was a sharp observer who asked the right questions and made her laugh. Maybe that *was* why she had come to New York.

WESTERN UNION TELEGRAM

```
MALCOLM TOWER C/O
FIRST NATIONAL BANK
SUPERIOR WISCONSIN

MARCH 4 1956

NO BUT THANK YOU. PARTY NOT YOUR SPEED. THERE
WILL BE COSTUMES. STAY PUT.

CAROLYN
```

Now it was the day before the party—March 6—and right after dinner Carolyn chose two outfits: 1) for the morning, capris and flats to help set up the decorations, and 2) for the party itself, a green shantung dress, a gift from Bella. The black pumps she'd packed would work. The jewelry she'd borrow from Bella's impressive collection.

While she was in the bath, she missed another phone call from Malcolm. Bella asked if she wanted to call him back. "No," Carolyn had said, still wrapped in a towel, "I don't want to run up your bill," and felt fortunate for the excuse. She had avoided two phone calls from him in as many days and this felt like a hat trick. A letter from her father had arrived the day before and he had asked how she felt about "her big decision." She ignored it. The less she pondered, the better she felt. She knew she couldn't play ostrich forever, but the end of forever wasn't here yet.

Bella entered Carolyn's room with a handful of onyx and jade earrings. Carolyn chose one set, then another, then returned to the first. She checked her profile in the mirror. The earrings were nice, but overdone paired with her nightgown. Carolyn turned to joke with her aunt but Bella's face was stern.

"There's something we need to discuss," she began.

Carolyn knew what was coming: She would tell her she was acting the fool. Bella would speak with her mother's voice. Malcolm was a known quantity. This was all a distraction, all this socializing, a way to avoid real life. She turned to see the actual woman, not merely the reflection. "Yes?"

"I believe Snug is still in the house."

Carolyn hadn't expected that. Her breath caught with compassion. Not everything on Bella's mind was about Carolyn's dilemma. "Of course she is."

"No," Bella said, "you misunderstand me." They sat together on the edge of the bed. "I believe she's *still* there."

Carolyn tried to focus, as if she were deciphering hazy words on a distant page.

"Her ghost," Bella said.

Carolyn laughed, a quick inadvertent hiccup, then stifled it. Her aunt wasn't joking. "You believe in ghosts?" She reached for her cigarettes on the nightstand and lit one with surprising speed.

The older woman shook her head and a strand of gray hair fell across her eyes. She tucked it back into place. "I didn't quite say that." The mantel clock kept time in the living room, a decibel louder than it seemed the second before. How could she hear it across the apartment? *Tick, tock.* "But Mr. Hitchcock may have rented the right home."

Carolyn held an ashtray in one hand and tapped her cigarette with the other. Smoke rose in a thin tendril. "You think she'll make an appearance at the party?" Would Pete love that? Hate it? Had Bella lost her mind? "That would be—an event."

"There's no guaranteeing she won't." Bella shrugged, her lips pursed.

Carolyn snubbed out her half-finished cigarette. "Wait . . . have you *seen* her?"

"You're going to think your old aunt mad."

An autumn Sunday afternoon before the war. Bella was visiting her aunts on a chilly, wet day. The doctor had been dead, what, six years? She went to fetch a cup of tea for Aunt Mariah—Snug's mother, that would be, she reminded Carolyn—and felt a cold draft blow through the small room. Then, there she was, floating just as you'd expect a spirit to float. That was Snug's premiere.

"And since then?" The mantel clock kept its pace.

"Once or twice a year."

"Since before the war?" The sudden lump in Carolyn's throat felt like a marble, a big cat's eye she'd rather not swallow.

"Every year since then. Every year I visited. I've been neglectful lately."

"Every year!" Carolyn stood and paced beside the dresser. She absently picked up the alternate earrings. She put them back. What was she going to tell Pete?

"I haven't told anyone this. Not my husband, not your father. Not even Curzon. I nearly told your mother once, but I stopped and I'm not sure why. *You* are the first person to whom I have confessed." Her eyes shone with tears. "I am not mad."

Carolyn returned and sat knee to knee with the older woman, so much like the first night when Bella consoled her about Malcolm's pressure. Aunt Bella's hands were strong, conditioned from years at an easel, but her skin was beginning to loosen, brown age spots speckling the backs. Time was relentless. Carolyn thought of her father's hands in his office, her mother's surprising grip as she lay dying.

"Did she ever speak?" Carolyn whispered.

"She did." Bella trembled. "At first, just a word or two. Later—and it's been years since I've been to the house—later, the last times, she seemed angry with me. That's why I didn't visit Mariah and Isabella. I was afraid. Now I'm ashamed."

Bella stood abruptly and strode down the hall to the bedroom-turned-studio, the only room free of antique chairs and polished side tables. Within the first day of her visit, Carolyn knew it was Bella's sanctuary. Carolyn followed and stood in the doorway. Her aunt perched at a sturdy easel by a table cluttered with brushes and tubes of paint. A palette knife. Gesso-covered canvases stretched across wooden frames, short and squat, long and lean, lounging like soldiers against one wall. A pair of finished landscapes tilted against each other. The air was pungent with linseed oil.

"Don't be ashamed," Carolyn said. "You believed a ghost was speaking to you. That's reason enough to stay away."

Yet she believed her mother had spoken to her and had the opposite response. She ran to it. She wanted to believe the voice was guiding her. But she didn't expect *this*, not from her sturdy, independent aunt.

"It's not that she's a ghost. She was sad. So terribly sad."

None of this was what Carolyn had expected Bella to say. She didn't know how to console her.

Bella filled the gap with motion, swift strokes on a blue-gray canvas. The whisper of horsehair. "And what happens when Mr. Hitchcock's guests run shrieking down Eightieth?"

"He'd enjoy that, wouldn't he?" Carolyn smiled weakly. "Pete might panic, but I think it's exactly what Mr. Hitchcock would want."

Bella tried to relax. "If she does appear, play it off as a parlor game. It's a haunted party. With decorations. She's just one more."

"I can do that," Carolyn said. "They are planning a few surprises."

"More than a few, I'm sure. There won't be any subtlety. They'll make it look like a Charles Addams drawing before they're done."

"He'll probably be there. Pete said he and Hitchcock are chums."

"Really?" Bella kept at the canvas: tugboat and bridge, building and sky. "Perhaps I'm being silly."

"I don't think so," Carolyn said.

"She might not show up at all. In which case you may forget all I've said." She swirled the brush in a jar of gray water.

Carolyn took a breath. "What if I *want* her to show up?"

They exchanged glances, then Bella smiled. She continued at her painting, making the waves around the tugboat crest against the small hull. "I'd say be careful what you wish for."

If the dead could come back, as Bella had said . . . if the dead could speak, as Carolyn suspected . . . and if Snug could do more than speak, if she could *appear*, then why not her mother?

What wouldn't Carolyn give for five more minutes with her?

Her aunt made waves where before there were none and Carolyn marveled at the trick. A little paint turned canvas into water beneath air above boat guided by men. Everything changed form in the most mundane way and then transformed again. Carolyn put her hand on her aunt's arm as if to say, *wait* or *go on* or *I don't understand* or, simply, *lovely*. Where there was nothing before, there was life.

"And be careful," Bella said, pausing midair with a sky-tipped brush, which she plunged into the muddy water in the glass jar by her elbow. The blue was swallowed by dirty brown, dirty brown turned to black. "Snug might not be alone."

THE DAY OF THE PARTY

March 7, 1956

Another dawn in a litany of afterdays, the house dark. Isabella Satterthwaite sat in the library of No. 7 with her husband, Thomas. Her hands darted as if she were knitting, but there was no yarn in her lap, no needles in her grasp. Anyone watching her go through the motions would have thought it a graceful pantomime. There was no one watching. The couple glowed a faint gray in the unlit room. The fireplace was cold, the furnace in the cellar barely burning. There was a distinct chill in the air, but they didn't mind. They were both dead, he for decades, she for months. They were happy to share existence again on the same plane, their domestic routines resumed.

"Mr. Hitchcock is throwing a party, dear."

"And who is Mr. Hitchcock?" Dr. Satterthwaite dipped the edge of the *Times* so he could peer at his wife.

"A motion picture director from England."

"I haven't seen a motion picture in so long. What sort of pictures does he make?"

"I believe he likes to frighten people. Bloody things. Murderers and such."

"I have no interest in that sort of story." Dr. S. went back to reading. People had often called him Dr. S.—Satterthwaite was such a mouthful— and he still thought of himself as such. Thomas to his wife, Uncle Thomas to Curzon and Snug, Dr. S. to everyone else: a trio of roles. "There's nothing frightening about death and even less about bleeding." He spoke from behind the curtain of rattling paper. "We all have bodies, doesn't he know?"

"Perhaps that's what makes his films effective. We all have bodies. Bad things happen to the bodies in his stories. Audiences remember bad things can happen to their bodies."

Dr. S. scoffed. "Good things can happen to bodies as well. Unexpected things. Maybe he should focus on that." Even now, years after his own decline, he perused the news every morning. He liked to stay informed. Though some mornings he sensed it was the same paper he had read the day before. And the day before. His memory wasn't what it used to be. Thankfully, repetition seldom bored him. Repetition, he recently reminded Isabella, was better than nothing at all.

Mrs. Satterthwaite often chatted with her husband, but usually not when her sister Mariah was about. She didn't want to flaunt her long and loving marriage. Walter, Mariah's husband, was dead, too, dead longer than anyone but Snug. Mariah said of Walter, "He was fine until he was not." That had been a reference to his qualities as a husband, not as a breathing human being, but it applied to either circumstance.

Isabella considered her grandniece, Carolyn. She had been on her brain since the afternoon a week earlier when the girl visited the house with the pair of strange men. Many years ago, Carolyn had visited the aunts at No. 7 and sipped tea in the second-floor parlor. The second-floor parlor was for family. It was less formal than the first-floor gallery. The girl seemed the relaxed sort, an exemplar of modern American girlhood. Isabella was uncertain if she admired this generation or was appalled by it. Perhaps a little of both.

"Do you ever imagine married life, Carolyn?" Aunt Isabella had prodded the child that winter Sunday.

"Yes, I suppose so. A house filled with commotion. Redbrick and lots of windows." Carolyn bit her lip. "But not for a long time."

"And when *a long time* arrives, may you live there a long time. It is good to live a long time in one place."

"Until it's not," Mariah had quipped.

Isabella ignored her sister. "I have been in this home since before the first war. We intended on filling it with family. I wanted children. Dr. S. wanted children. But we couldn't have them. It was a mystery that foiled us our entire lives. Yet he was a happy man. He had the hospital and his students. He was a loving husband."

Mariah touched Isabella's arm. "You *did* fill it with family. Not the family you expected, but I will remain forever grateful for how you took us in."

Isabella and Thomas had welcomed Mariah and her children when their bodies needed shelter and their spirits needed care, though Isabella could do nothing to ease her sister's troubles or the terrible toll the children had paid. What a cur Mariah's husband Walter was, slave to his body and its desires. He had ruined everything.

Oh, what a fool. He was a memory she tried to ignore.

Isabella shook her vaporous head, made a little eddy in the air that no one was present to sense. Dr. S. still had his nose in the news. So what if the house was soon to be filled with strangers? It would be full again with living bodies, warm bodies, bodies eager to satisfy needs—food and drink and whatever other needs a party fulfills. Society? Camaraderie? Even love? Dr. S. had a view of the human body. Mariah had a view of the human body. Walter and Snug and Isabella herself, all the dead and the living and even the living-once-again. Who didn't have an opinion about what a body wants? The care and tending of the human body had been her husband's passion, and hers as well.

They were past that.

There was no body anymore.

If she had the chance to have hers back, would she take it?

Isabella wasn't certain.

"Unexpected things," Dr. S. repeated.

"Perhaps that's what the party will bring," she said, ever the optimist to Thomas's pragmatism. "The fun of a party is the unexpected."

Dr. S. folded the newspaper. "I always thought the fun of a party was the food."

"Do you miss it? I don't, not yet anyway."

He touched his wife's hand. Someday she would develop the power to reciprocate.

"What might the director discover this evening?" She gazed at her husband. "You are a man of science. What is your hypothesis?"

"I have always believed there is much to discover in the mundane. Let him come into our home, let them all come, and see what they can find of our average existence."

He raised the paper high before his face with atypical panache, as if to sail with pride into the prosaic, a commonplace spirit catching up with the times.

8

WHEN PETE AND CAROLYN arrived at No. 7 at nine a.m., a truck from the caterers was already at the curb, another double-parked and idling beside it. A pair of stocky deliverymen were carrying boxes into the mansion. They followed them in, unburdened by anything but Pete's anxiety over impressing his bosses and Carolyn's fresh fear of an actual apparition—or apparitions, plural. She was looking for anything odd the moment she stepped into the foyer. Had Bella lost her mind? Dwelled too long in the imaginary, alone with her canvases?

Carolyn's instincts told her Aunt Bella wasn't mad, not mad at all.

In the morning sun, the house struck her as worn down, cleaner, yes, but creakier than even a week earlier. One improvement: the first thing the boys from Y&R did was throw open the sash windows to flush out the still, stale air. Light was helping, too, nearly made the place cheery, but it couldn't stay that way. Their goal was to make it unsettling. Come nightfall, the rooms would be shadowy, the damask curtains pulled closed to create inky corners. Waiters in dastardly apparel would ooze helpfulness in oily tones.

"Fake cobwebs?" Carolyn laughed as Pete spread a thin veil across one of the narrow doorways. "My aunts would be appalled."

"Appalled at the price of this stuff," he said. "We're hemorrhaging cash to mess up their house."

She stood on tiptoes to drape a strand along a transom. "You'd think it would be dirt cheap."

"Ouch," Pete grimaced, laying another pattern. "Everything about this guy's night is pricey. Good thing the show's a hit. Lots of Bufferin moves out the door because of him."

"Well, you can't have a haunted house without cobwebs," she consoled.

"No cobwebs, no ghosts," Pete spoke with the confidence of a Toastmaster's MC.

"That so?" Her voice came out shakier than she anticipated. She added a chuckle to cover her nerves. "Always?"

He grinned. "Since right now. Making pronouncements is going to be my duty today. I feel it. Dictating where the cobwebs go."

"King Spider," she said, nodding.

He christened her shoulders with a mock benediction. "Saint Carolyn of the Dusty Coves."

"Dusty coves? But you just had—"

"Fake dust is better than real dust! Sprinkle it like powdered sugar." He flipped open the top of a cardboard box left on a short curio cabinet and pulled out a heavy piece of card stock. "The menus!"

She plucked it from his grasp.

Carte de Mort was stamped at the top. The appetizers were listed first.

Morbid Morgue Morsels

Suicide Suzette (avec crêpe)

Consommé de Cobra Vicious-Soisse

"Goodness," Carolyn said. "How unappetizing."

"That's what we were going for!"

Next came the entrées. She drew a polished nail down one column, then the other.

Home-fried Homicide	*Stuffed Stiffs with Hard Sauce*
Ragout of Reptile	*Gibbeted Giblets*
Charcoal-broiled Same Witch-legs	*Mobster Thermidor*
Corpse Croquettes	*Tormented Tortillas*
Barbecued Banshee au gratin	*Ghoulish Goulash*
Opium Omelette en Brochette	*Blind Bats en casserole*

She gave a belly laugh. "Did you write this?"

Pete grinned. "Only a couple. I'm proud of Vicious-Soisse. Barbecued Banshee is mine, too."

On the bottom of the page were the desserts: *Fromage d'Abbatoir, Python Pudding, Morphine Meringue Glacé,* and *Fresh-cut Lady Fingers (in season).*

"Who's got a thing against snakes?"

"The Duck. They creep him out."

"Fitting. What's really on the menu?"

"You don't think we can get lady fingers?"

"Not these." She wiggled her free hand. Pete snatched it. She was surprised she didn't mind and surprised she was disappointed when he let go. Her sisters would ask what had gotten into her. What *had* gotten into her?

"Actually, it's all chicken. And some beef. No snakes or women will be harmed."

"Good to hear."

"Also, there will be booze—"

"Also good to hear."

"Flip over the card."

"Bloody Marys," she read aloud. "Anisette d'Arsenic. Hennessey's Heroin, Dead Granddad, Formaldehyde Frappe." She dropped the menu back in the box, on a stack of dozens. "Heroin always makes for a lively party."

"We're rather hoping for a deadly one," he said.

"Touché," she said.

"Dead Granddad is mine."

"That's my favorite."

"Thanks," he said. "Bloody Marys felt too obvious."

"Obvious," Carolyn said, "but delicious. Oh, you missed a rhyme. *Delicious* and *malicious*."

He gave her an approving nod. "Watch out. You get good at this and we might try to hire you."

"Tell that to my father," she scoffed.

He raised an eyebrow.

"Long story." She tapped the menus. "You know, get the guests to drink too much, they'll need more Bufferin."

"You saw right through our ruse."

"It wasn't difficult," she said. "Everything is sales to a salesman, right?"

"Maybe not *everything*," he said and grinned.

He really did have nice teeth.

✦ ✧ ✦

The last chore before lunch was putting that corpse in the bedroom on the third floor, the one with the solid four-poster. Carolyn at the mannequin's arms, Pete holding the feet, they hoisted the uncooperative model (hard plastic dressed in a fresh blue-and-white-striped nightshirt) up the narrow flights and dropped it unceremoniously on the mattress. Someone had put on new sheets and turned them down, as if the house were a fine hotel. Carolyn looked for a foil-wrapped chocolate on the pillow. If there'd been one, it was lost now in the wrestling match between the copywriter and the cadaver. Pete yanked the stiff arms into a pose beneath the blankets and tilted the geriatric-looking head just so on the pillow. He patted the man's thatchy wig. "If we need more bodies," he said, swiping his hands like a satisfied baker, "we can go to Frank E. Campbell's."

"Who's Frankie Campbell?" She fluffed the adjacent pillow.

"Not who, what. It's New York's most famous mortuary. And it's right around the corner."

"I didn't know you could have a *famous* and *convenient* mortuary."

"In New York," he proclaimed, "we have famous and convenient everything."

He caught his breath, studying the bookshelves, thick with actual dust the service had missed and empty save stacks of yellowing medical journals and a long set of heavy encyclopedias gathering Upper East Side grime on their faded red bindings. She stood beside him and bent to read the titles on a quartet of unmatched books: *Manual of Histology, Practical Bacteriology, Diseases of the Heart and Aorta, Diseases of the Heart and Blood Vessels.* All of them had the same author: Satterthwaite.

"Famous ballplayers, famous pizza, famous mortuaries. Frank E. Campbell's are the folks who threw Rudolph Valentino's funeral. It was a riot. An actual one. Weeping women standing in the rain for hours just to see his body. Which may or may not have been his." He glanced at their own imposter. "And Mussolini sent an honor guard, four guys in uniforms, except they were actors. Made Valentino look like Italy's second-favorite son."

"Your agency would never do anything like that."

"Guys in outfits pretending to be what they're not? Absolutely. That's what our spooky waiters are. But fascists. I draw the line at fascists."

"Shouldn't we all?" Her voice was unexpectedly serious.

A photo of Andy, smiling in his dress uniform, flitted through her mind. Pete touched her hand and she could swear he understood. They exchanged a swift sober glance, then the gloom subsided.

They stood beside the bed and admired the scenario. It was tidy and disturbing. Exactly what Hitchcock wanted.

"It's good to know you have limits," she said. She punched him lightly on the arm.

They bounced out of the bedroom, leaving their new old friend to molder for the evening in someone else's bed. Carolyn looked back into the dim room and thought she saw, for a moment, a pale gray figure at the far end. She blinked and it moved toward her. She blinked again and it was gone. She tripped over her own feet.

"Whoa," Pete said, catching her elbow. "Look out for loose boards."

"Did you see—?"

Pete waited.

The air seemed frozen, the calm before disaster, and she tapped her toe on the floor. "Loose boards," she agreed, and stamped her ballerina flats in a little flurry. "Safety first!" She linked her arm with Pete's and hurried him down the hall, resisting one last look behind her.

✦ ✧ ✦

It was noon and they needed a break. With a pair of wrapped sandwiches and bottled Coca-Colas pilfered from the caterer-frenzied kitchen, they snuck out the service door. The air was fresh after the musty confines of the shuttered upper floors and Pete suggested the park behind the Met as a place for lunch. Even with the unseasonable temperature—fifty by midday and sunny—they would need to find a brighter place than a tree-shaded bench.

"I know a hot spot," he promised.

They crossed Fifth Avenue and headed north, past the museum's broad steps. The tourist crowds were thin on a Wednesday afternoon; a huddle of uniformed students followed a pair of teachers up to the great doors, but mostly they watched the taxis crawl in a steady parade. They kept north and turned in to Central Park and Pete pointed. There was Cleopatra's Needle, the ancient Egyptian obelisk sticking up like a pin to poke the blue spring sky. They found a welcoming spot on the lawn, as he guaranteed, and Carolyn sat as elegantly as she could, given her capris and the soft breeze ruffling the paper napkin spread across her lap like a tiny tablecloth.

"That is remarkable," she said, gazing at the monument.

"Maybe designed by the same guy who made your aunts' alembic." Pete sat cross-legged beside her.

Carolyn nodded. "At least neighbors."

He unwrapped a sandwich—"Ham and cheese!" he said, as if discovering a new constellation, and Carolyn laughed. He was enthusiastic about everything. She imagined men in New York would be overbearing or overconfident or both, too cool for outbursts of glee, except perhaps about the Yankees or their own careers. In one morning, Pete had found pleasure in the plastic eyeballs stacked in boxes on the makeshift bar counter, the view from the fourth-floor bedroom ("Look at all the trees! You can hardly tell it's a city street!"), the fireplace screen in the library, a meshwork of metal owls. He got a genuine kick out of decorating for the party and his attitude was a happy kind of contagious.

"So, Carolyn, really, why are you here? In the city? You didn't just miss your aunt." He took her Coke, slipped a bottle opener from inside his sport coat, and popped off the top with a swift yank.

"You carry one of those everywhere?"

"I liberated it from the kitchen. But I'm not a habitual thief." He held up three fingers. "Scout's honor."

"Larceny and oaths. Nice combo."

"The motto is *Be Prepared*." He flipped the top off his own soda and it twirled to the early green grass. "Cheers," he toasted. They tapped bottle lips and took sips. "You ignored my question."

The pop was sweet, but she had trouble swallowing. Truth tightened her throat. "Does there need to be a reason?" What would Pete think about Malcolm, the hemming and hawing, her hanging a guy out to dry? One more look in his honest eyes and she would confess it all. Instead, she gathered the pair of bottle caps, digging a little among the blades and dirt.

Pete watched her as she carefully unfolded the wax paper around her sandwich. "You just seem like a woman who would need a reason. For everything." He took a big bite.

"Actually, I'm famously spontaneous."

"Not," he held up a hand and chewed, and chewed, and swallowed, "at all. And I've known you for, what, five days?"

"Six. You're confident of that from our brief meetings?"

"An afternoon, an evening, an evening, another evening." He was counting on his fingers. "And a morning." He held up his spread hand. "But who's keeping track? And yes. I can tell."

She bit her lower lip and stared at the fluffy clouds. The sun *was* warm. The first scent of spring—or something other than winter—was tantalizing. Not quite there yet, but almost. It was a postcard: the park, the obelisk, the tourists, the boy.

"You're not wrong. I'm a pros and cons gal. I'm here to think about . . ."

"About?"

"Nosy, aren't you?" She bit into her sandwich, surprised how hungry she'd grown.

"Research is how copywriters get their best material. I need to know about a topic for inspiration."

"You're going to write an advertisement about me?"

"No." He looked sheepish.

"It's a great way to avoid talking about yourself," she countered. "Always ask the questions and no one ever gets a chance to ask you anything. Like, are you nervous? What do you think Hitchcock will be like?"

"The Duck tells me what he wants, what he's vetoed, and then I act accordingly. He's picky. I suppose he'll be demanding. But charming? I don't know." He took a great gulp, swallowed, and wiped the back of his mouth. "Yes, I'm nervous."

He told her about the bills he had worked up for the evening's props, a rundown of the gags they'd supplied for the party, how they sat pinned on his desk on Madison Avenue. Sixteen pairs of luminescent footprints from Tannen's Magic shop in Midtown, the very ones he and Carolyn had glued to the walls that morning. A pair of coffins they'd rented from a place in Hoboken, set to arrive around two. (He checked his watch. An hour and a half to go.) The life-size doll from NBC was cheap, but putting her in gelatin was, strangely, expensive, even with Jell-O supplying the goo. Getting her to the party without jiggling her right out of the truck would be tricky. The pair of wax dummies, one of which napped where they'd tucked him that morning. The other? Pete had yet to decide his fate. And lastly, seven hundred and twelve plastic eyeballs, which the bartending waiters, Joe and Ray—rather, Igor and Renfro, as they'd been rechristened by Pete, with The Duck's approval—would deftly place, one apiece, in each guest's cocktail. It was a hefty tab. And Pete had directed it all.

"That's a job," she said, looking at his furrowed eyebrows. She wanted to reach out to calm his tapping fingers.

His hand stilled and he looked straight into her eyes. "Whatever your reason for visiting your aunt," he said, standing, flicking crumbs off his khaki pants, "I feel like you had to come for the party. Fate brought you."

"Fate's a mighty big word," Carolyn said, tidying up, too. "I'd settle for a little weird fun."

"Did you know *weird* originally meant fate? Who says fate can't be fun?" Pete swung out to touch her hand, then seemed to remember something. He stopped himself. She would have let him take it. She wanted him to take it. "This is your chance to have weird fun, Carolyn."

She didn't doubt him. By the time they'd thrown away their empty wrappers and the bottle caps in a city trash can and strolled back to No. 7, she was only thinking about the next chores on their to-do list. Two more delivery trucks had double-parked up the street.

"The neighbors are loving you," she said.

"We've hardly begun." He ushered her through the front door, still propped open, this time with a short gargoyle. "We haven't even started on the music and the sound effects yet." He waved his arms, a circus ringmaster standing at the gate. "Of course, every holiday has its favorite melodies. 'Jingle Bells' and ho, ho, ho. But this isn't Christmas." He shook his head dramatically.

"No, no, no," she sang.

He wagged a finger. "This isn't Halloween."

"Not in March," she agreed.

"This is far better!" He took her by the arm and they faced the open door. "This is Hitchcock Eve."

And as if by command, the bay of a howling wolf welcomed them inside.

The blue girl didn't sleep. There was no comfort on a soft blanket or curling up under a duvet. Yet there were times when the train of her brain paused its endless spool of ticker-tape thoughts. For moments, maybe minutes, maybe months, it was hard for her to gauge or predict, she simply disappeared. She was like a cloud in the sky, shaping and reshaping, continually coming back to herself. Look! A girl! Then the wind blew and the girl dissipated. The wind shifted again and the stratus reformed, and she returned, her silhouette straining across the sky.

She was. And she wasn't. There was no napping in between.

That morning, she was aware: of the men in the house, the bustle and the rustling, the currents racing between the floors, through open windows and open doors. Voices called for help or called, Hello! There were handshakes and hauled boxes, and one boy, one boy went to the basement and readied the coal room. There were people coming to the house. They would make it warmer, body heat and breath, all that living amongst them, standing and talking and breathing in the same space, but they would need help with the heat as well, and the old furnace would kick to life, back up to full power if only for one more evening.

Snug anticipated the change, waited for it, the way she did when she was young, for her birthday, for a cousin's visit, for Curzon and her mother to go to the shore.

She envied them, the living, and yet, she discovered, her jealousy didn't make her resent the party: she wanted it all the more.

It was time for guests.

9

THE YOUNG MAN HIRED to supply the soundtrack knelt by the far wall of the first-floor gallery. The cuffs of his chinos were rolled and his sneakers scuffed, the sleeves of his blue chambray shirt pushed above his elbows. Locks of dark hair fell over his brow as he bent spooling wire along the baseboard, a speaker tucked in the corner hidden by a chaise lounge.

Fainting couch, Carolyn thought from across the room. The grandaunts had called it that, but she couldn't imagine either sturdy woman ever having fainted. She watched the man work. There was the distinctive shake of his head, the duck of his chin. She had seen him do it hundreds of times in Wisconsin, huddled over piano keys, the latest popular song hurtling out of his fingers. Jostling kids crowded around him every time he sat at the upright in Camp Nebagamon's lunchroom turned makeshift dance hall. She skittered in her flats across the Persian rug.

"Johnny?" Oh, what a welcome sight he was! "Johnny Kander, what in the world are you doing here?"

Johnny stood, untangling his lean limbs from the wires, and grinned. "Carolyn Banks! I could ask you the same question!" They hugged, then he stopped and held her at arm's length to take in her face. "Boy, growing up has been good to you!"

"You, too—you're not a pound heavier than you were a decade ago."

"It's all about swimming. But I traded lakes for the Y."

"At least not the rivers! Swimming's what you do here, not making brilliant music?"

Like a stream of boys from St. Louis and Chicago, Johnny went to the Jewish boys' summer camp outside Superior. Carolyn's family had a place in the country and every summer of her teen years she would get to know the counselors and, if they were particularly witty and talented, like Johnny, she'd spend a few months canoeing and building campfires with them. She and Johnny didn't date—it was one of those immediate friendships that leapt right over romance—but they had been good pals. He could play anything, just name the tune—"*Don't Fence Me In!*" the kids shouted, "*Swinging on a Star!*"—and he'd have it figured out in a jiffy. They'd all sing along (even Carolyn, though she could barely keep *Happy Birthday* in tune). Then he'd surprise them and play Mozart or Chopin. She always thought he'd write a hit tune and she'd hear him on every radio.

"I'm doing rehearsal piano for a musical, writing some stuff. Side jobs like this, but it pays the bills." He shook his head. "Okay, not normally like this. This is different. They hired me for *ambiance*."

Carolyn giggled. "Everyone uses that word!"

She couldn't believe she was a thousand miles from home and here was Johnny.

He nodded at the reel-to-reel case by his snake coil of cords. "They didn't want much actual music, a few creaky piano bits and some distant, eerie choirs. The rest are sound effects. Creepy wind, knocking doors, squeaking floors."

"This place already creaks." She pressed a floorboard and it groaned cooperatively.

He wiped a strand of hair from his eyes. "And what are *you* doing here?"

"This is my grandaunts' house," Carolyn said. "Was. Is?"

Johnny frowned. "What?"

"*Was*," she decided. "They're dead." She didn't mean to sound callous. "Everyone's dead who lived here. That was related to me, I mean. It was my father's aunts' house. I've been here a few times, back when Aunt Isabella and Aunt Mariah were alive." She couldn't stop babbling.

"Did they rent it because of your aunts? I mean . . . are they still here?"

Carolyn brushed away his question with a flap of her hands. "Ha ha, no," she insisted. "No! This isn't one of our fireside ghost stories. It's a party, not a séance. Don't believe anything these guys tell you." She glanced at Pete across the room, directing the waiters by the staircase. "They just wanted that mood. Old place filled with old stuff." Shakespeare sounded in her head, *the lady doth protest too much, methinks*. She bit her tongue, really bit it. Johnny would be able to tell if she was lying. Sure enough, he looked suspicious. Or maybe just confused.

"Lots of potential for Victorian hijinks," she rolled on. "I bet you have screams up your sleeves."

"Screams. And hoots. Owls."

"Owls in New York?"

He spied a springing wire and knelt to tape it to a tall baseboard. "You're doubtful? Go listen in Central Park."

"We were just there." She nodded at Pete. "I heard nothing." There was a memory of Johnny and a clutch of boys making a ruckus at the end of a dock one long-ago August night, hooting with a parliament, back and forth, a call-and-response. Johnny was a magnet for everything.

"Try *later*, Banks," he laughed. "I guarantee night owls in this city."

"Har de har har," she said. "You're a card."

He stood and gripped the tape case by the sturdy handle. "They've got me stashing this stuff in closets—like Oz behind the curtain."

Pete came hurrying over, an unreadable expression clouding his handsome face. When he gave Johnny the once-over, Carolyn introduced them. Pete nodded but didn't move to shake hands.

"You're the fellow Mr. Buck spoke about," Pete said, his arms unnaturally tucked behind his back. Carolyn tried to peer around him. He turned to face her, dancing a stiff minuet, and said to Johnny, "I'm sure you'll do a bang-up job!"

Johnny gave Carolyn a quizzical look, then loped off with his equipment. Pete swung his arms around and presented Carolyn with an enormous black cat with wide green eyes. Its long tail, draped over his arm, flicked like a furry rope.

"Oh, a kitty!" Carolyn cooed, reaching out to stroke its sleek fur.

"More like a miniature panther," Pete joked. "His name is Oscar."

"Where'd you get him?" She pressed her nose to the cat's. He tolerated the intimacy.

"Rented," he said smugly. "Just for the night."

"You didn't mention that in the expenses." Her attention was still firmly on the cat.

Johnny announced his return with a sneeze. "Count that among the sound effects for tonight," he said, keeping his distance. "I can't be in a room with one of those things and not—" as if to prove a point, he sneezed again, "and not do that." He shook his head to clear it. "The first scary thing of the evening for me." He dug in his pants for a handkerchief, picked up a last loop of wire, and strode off in the other direction.

Pete frowned. "I hadn't thought of that."

Carolyn was still stroking the cat. "Most people aren't allergic."

"I should have done a guest survey first." His voice was glum.

"Tell everyone it was The Duck's idea."

"It was The Duck's idea."

"Then you're in the clear. They'll blame him." She baby-talked the cat. "Who's a handsome boy? Who's so handsome?"

"Thank you," Pete said.

She looked up and gave him an assessing glance. "You're not bad either."

Pete blushed. Carolyn liked the ping in her chest. He pulled Oscar out of her reach and sauntered backward to the hallway, the cat his bait. She followed.

"Who would think you'd know the sound guy?" he told her.

"It's a small world," she answered, "after all." She'd caught up with him and nuzzled Oscar.

"Brave new world," he corrected. "That has such people in it."

She studied him.

"I just had Shakespeare on my brain," she said. "How'd you know?"

"Great minds think alike and all that," he said. He set the cat down and it darted back from where they'd come. "He's gonna go annoy your friend."

"Johnny can protect himself," she said.

From across the house they heard an *ah-choo*. Pete grimaced. "This is gonna be a test."

"Don't worry so much," she said.

They trooped past the pantry and the atmosphere was festive, a holiday in the making, even with the cooks in the kitchen clanking pots like heavy chains. A man with deep crow's-feet and slicked hair was stocking the makeshift bar, the ring of a glass pealing like an occasional bell. The food was on schedule—all the giblets and goulashes—so Carolyn caught Pete's attention and nodded to the staircase. They scurried up a flight like naughty children to the parlor. More heavy furniture, another tarnished gold chandelier. Someone had draped a heavy black sheet from its curved lamps.

"Fire hazard?" Carolyn pointed.

"Nah," Pete said. "I got a plan."

Carolyn arched a brow.

"Maybe," he admitted.

"This place is a tinderbox. You'll get Barbecued Businessmen."

"Fricassee of Film Auteur."

"Distillation of Director."

"Ooh, you win," he said.

A pair of ornate couches squatted in the center of the room. "Chaise lounge," Carolyn said, "or davenport—"

"—is everybody else's sofa," added Pete. "Different words, same thing."

Behind the parlor was the dining room with a heavy-legged table soon to be laden with hors d'oeuvres, gothic tchotchkes and half-burned candelabras, yet to be lit, arranged around it like an audience.

"Some of this stuff was the aunts'." Carolyn strolled, doing an inventory. "But some of these nasty bits are definitely not." She pointed to a taxidermied boar's head mounted on a wall plaque above one of the house's countless fireplaces. "Not my aunts'." She turned on her heels, careful to avoid Oscar threading his way around her ankles, and stopped short at a side desk. She bent to the glassy eyes of a stuffed white owl. "Not my aunts'." She pursed her lips and studied yet another frozen creature, set like a footstool by a heavy rosewood armchair: a badger trapped mid-growl. "Definitely not my aunts'."

"Props," Pete explained. With a silver Zippo from his jacket and a practiced flick, he lit four of the candles. "The number of dead animals in warehouses across the tri-state area would astound you."

"And they're all here. Goody." She flopped on the couch. "This was here before. I sat and listened to my aunts give me worldly advice."

"Like . . . ?" He perched in a wingback chair tucked in a corner, his face half-masked in shadow. The cat stood like a small sentinel at his feet.

"Mostly, it was *don't work*. Don't get a job. Find a man to marry and avoid sullying yourself with the *hoi polloi*." She ran her hand along the polished wood. "They preached it, but did they really believe it? They were smart women and completely underutilized. I'd like to think they didn't want me to wallow in boredom or idleness. It was just the only world they knew."

"And you ignored them?"

"Every word." She patted the badger. "Don't get me wrong—I liked them. But they were from another planet. Long skirts and piled hair. My mother kept her hair short since the twenties. Aunt Isabella and Aunt Mariah had hair the weight of a steam engine."

"Heavy." He blew out the candles.

"No kidding. I saw Mariah's hair down once, out of her bun. It fell all the way down her back, a massive waterfall. It was beautiful, but she never showed it off. And never cut it. Some Victorian pride."

"Hair as one more way to keep them from working?"

Carolyn shrugged. "Something like that." She thought of Betty and her pink slip from the phone company. Her short hair hadn't saved her job. She ran her hand through her own curls and knew a hairstyle wouldn't change her father's mind. Or Malcolm's.

The Duck came to inspect the house midafternoon and declared it horror-ready, though he wasn't impressed with Pete's fire marshal instincts. On his own initiative, Pete had a solution for any conflagration: bags of sand, bought from a company in Queens. Carolyn and he and a pair from the catering crew had filled twenty metal pails to the brim and hid them strategically behind the damask curtains, four to a floor, skipping the basement. Walking up flight by flight with a handle in each hand was an athlete's task. Carolyn's legs were burning by the last trip, but she was a trooper. No guests would see the buckets, but the staff would know where they were. Honestly, the old house was a deathtrap, a deathtrap dressed up for a drink. Lipstick on a pig and all that. Freshly glamorous, still flammable.

She rested on the parlor couch with her shoes kicked off while Pete explained it all to The Duck. It was like watching a tennis match.

The Duck was confused. "Pails of sand?"

"In case," Pete explained, "one of these hundred-year-old owls combusts."

Carolyn snickered, but The Duck bit his cheek, unimpressed.

"Or if somebody gets casual and flicks their ash willy-nilly," Pete said, miming negligence.

"Or a drip from a candlestick," Carolyn added. He looked at her appreciatively.

"That can't happen, Pete," The Duck warned.

"Now we can stop it if it does," Pete said.

"There isn't going to be any *if*. No disasters." He put a hand on Pete's shoulder. "Do you want to know the secret to my success, son? What you all call my luck?"

Pete paled like a kid whose teacher had caught him with a note. "Oh, we don't think it's luck, sir."

The Duck ignored him. "There's no such thing as luck." Pete waited. The Duck obliged. "Dwell on disaster, you create disaster." His voice was firm. "Keep your eyes to the sky and you soar."

Carolyn perked up on the couch. "That's the way these things work?" She tried valiantly to keep skepticism out of her voice, but it was a fight.

The Duck looked back at her. "That's the way these things work for me. I think something into happening. And I'm thinking," he poked Pete in the chest with a stiff finger, "I'm *thinking*," he tapped his temples, "this shindig is going to be a huge hit."

"That's a gift," Carolyn said.

"It is." The Duck nodded at her. "Plus, these folks will flick where they want to flick. You're going to tell young Balaban what to do?"

"Who's *young Balaban*?" Pete stammered. "A knight of the Round Table?"

"The daughter of the president of Paramount Pictures. And she's married to Grace Kelly's agent, a fellow named Jay Kanter. All of them, Friends of Hitch. F.O.H."

"Pronounced 'foe'?" said Carolyn. Pete's eyebrows shot up.

"Not any he'd want," The Duck warned. "And they're all F.O.G.: Friends of Grace. Balaban's daughter is set to be a bridesmaid in Monaco."

"I read about that in the papers," said Pete.

"You bet you did," said The Duck. "Monte Carlo is the place to be."

"Even more than here, tonight?" Carolyn was feeling feisty.

"Even more than here, tonight." The Duck checked his pockets, like a man looking for tickets. "You know, Pete, Grace sent her regrets, but she's probably busy packing." He found his Lucky Strikes.

"She was invited?" Carolyn heard the awe in her voice. She felt indiscreet, but at least she'd kept her jaw from dropping.

"She was invited." The Duck lit a cigarette. "She's practically Hitch's second daughter." He waved his match dead and held it aloft, looking for an ashtray.

Pete pulled the alembic from the mantel, popped off its cap, and offered it to The Duck, who dropped the dead match in it. He glanced at the candles and the buckets. "We need ashtrays, that's what we need."

"Yes, sir!" Pete said.

The Duck held Pete's shoulder and his gaze. "Of course, we'll put out the fires. That's what a good agency does." He turned to exit, then looked back. "We won't burn down the house, Miss Banks. As per the rental agreement, I'm sure." He winked at Carolyn and jogged down the stairs.

Pete collapsed on the couch next to her. "That was exhausting," he sighed. He still held the alembic, forgotten in his grip. Carolyn took it from him, rested it on her lap, then patted his hand.

"You're sweating. And I need to go back to Bella's and change anyways."

Pete glanced at his damp, stained shirt. "I was thinking—"

—and the room went *pop* like a champagne bottle. Pete scrambled to his feet and held up a hand. Stopping traffic? Carolyn's brain flittered. Stopping what?

A shimmering girl appeared in a brilliant blue burst. Pete gasped and threw an arm over his face, as if blinded by lightning, and Carolyn hunched like a turtle. The cat by Pete's feet bolted, shot from a circus cannon, one quick strangled yowl, then a furious zipping black blur across the parquet floor.

Carolyn held her breath and listened to the phantom's electric hum. The blue girl had settled into a rich buzz, arms spread like an angel. She wore a long skirt, which eddied around her dark lace-up ankle boots. Her blouse had a high collar and a thin ribbon that dangled when she turned. Her figure was hourglass, cinched in the middle with a wide belt. Her hair was piled in a thick bun. She was, perhaps, twenty, maybe younger.

Carolyn blinked. Could she hear Pete blink beside her? A faint *phip phip*. That was impossible, but the room was a vacuum, nothing but the glowing girl drifting by the chandelier. Whatever she was—vapor or smoke or delusion—made the draped cloth sway. She inspired a breeze. Pete was a statue. Carolyn waited. His stillness had an anticipation to it: a glass suspended above a hard floor, a hand on the volume dial of a silent radio. She could have reached out and touched him, a boy caught in a moment, this frozen moment, the only thing moving in the room was the girl aloft. But he clearly saw the girl. The girl who must be Snug.

Pete cracked the frost with a slow and audible "No." He turned abruptly, an affronted man leaving an insult, and marched out of the room to the staircase, turning once, twice, nearly spinning, to check to see if the ghost—that's what she was, Carolyn was certain, a ghost—remained. She bobbed. An inch or so higher, then lower. Was she playful? Or a fish on a string? Pete stayed at the top of the stairs, his hand on the banister.

The ghost spoke, her voice clear and calm: "Wait," and Pete did the opposite: He ran down three steps, back two, down three, then barreled back to Carolyn and grabbed her hand. She still sat staring at the blue girl.

"Come on," he cried. "Come on!" He pulled.

She resisted, yanked free from his grip, and clutched the alembic in both hands like a treasure. He lunged at her elbow as if she were drowning.

"Pete," Carolyn said, shaking him off in protest, attention stuck on the girl, who watched them. Carolyn was determined to stare back. "She's looking at us," Carolyn whispered, uncertain if she spoke aloud or not. She said it louder. "She's looking at us."

"Nope," Pete said. "Nope, nope, nope." He yanked with more force this time, tried to get her to stand.

"Ouch. Don't." He dropped his arm and stood, wavering a bit, like a man about to faint. "Don't you see," Carolyn said quietly, "she's real."

Pete groaned and scurried back to the stairs. He turned, dropped to the top step, and flattened on his belly, a soldier in a trench, ready to duck when the sniper fires.

"Carolyn," he hissed. "This is not a game."

She shook her head, clearing fog from her brain. "I know."

"I didn't do this! I didn't *hire* anyone to do this."

The blue girl glanced at Pete, her head cocked like a curious dog, then swerved to Carolyn, back to Pete, then back to Carolyn. "He didn't." Her voice was soft, polite, young but not girlish. "He didn't make me. No one made me," she said. "Oh, He who makes the lion and the lamb, little lamb, made me, but not . . . thee." She pointed at him and giggled.

"Ah," Pete cried and down the stairs he went, scampering.

The girl studied Carolyn.

Carolyn held her gaze. "Blake," she said. "Little lamb who made thee."

"You know his poetry?" The ghost swooped down to face her, still ten feet between them. A cold wind rushed over Carolyn's cheeks, then faded, quickly, like a fleeting thought.

"From school," she said. What a strange conversation to have with a ghost. Small talk be damned. "You're Snug," she blurted.

The girl nodded. "I am." She looked back to the staircase. Pete was gone. "How do you know my name?" Her light grew brighter. "What are you doing in my house?"

"I'm Bella's niece. Your cousin Bella. Bella Banks." Carolyn felt herself blabbing. "Which means, I guess, I'm your cousin, too."

Snug extended her hand, a graceful move, a dancer's arm, her shadowy form undulating. She was never completely still. There was always an ebb and flow to her silhouette, like water in a pool brushed by a soft breeze.

"A pleasure to meet you," she said. "I am Isabella. Well, Snug. And you are?"

"Carolyn," she said. "Just Carolyn."

They held hands and Carolyn swore she felt a resistance, a pressure, and a softness, the faint but familiar weight of human flesh. "Your young man is gone," she said. "You better get him back."

And then Carolyn was alone in an empty room, quieter than any quiet she remembered, wanting to correct Snug—"He's not my young man!"—but more importantly, wondering if it had all been a dream.

Pete's footsteps on the staircase clattered like a herd of small dogs. He held a fireplace poker in his hands, a nervous cricket player who'd lost his teammates.

"She's see-through," Carolyn stated, as if she were still looking at the girl, her long skirt, her glinting eyes. "She has hair like my aunts'." She cocked her head. "Wait—what are you going to do with that?"

He collapsed into the wingback and balanced the poker across his bouncing knees.

"Okay, not quite see-through, but she wasn't really solid either," Carolyn continued. "Nothing you could smack."

"At first I thought maybe she was a projection."

Carolyn snorted. Then remembered the blue girl waver. "I thought she'd be less—corporeal."

"You *thought*?" He shifted to stare at her.

From the moment Snug appeared, she knew this confession would have to come. To avoid his gaze, she crossed the room and set the alembic on the mantel. "Aunt Bella," she began, "told me this was a possibility."

"She told you this—a ghost—was a possibility? Like rain? Drizzle? Hey, by the way, there's a chance of ghost tonight."

Carolyn winced and returned to her seat. "Not quite like that, but sort of."

"Why didn't you warn me?" He stood. He paced. He pivoted. He sat down next to her on the couch, leg by leg. "You should have warned me."

They were quiet, but with a different weight than before. The crew in the kitchen was making normal noise, not spectral, and Pete took Carolyn's hand.

"Whatever we just saw," he said. "We can't tell anyone. The ghosts tonight are supposed to be *pretend*. I can't control the real thing! This could—she could ruin—this would not be good."

"But maybe this is just what your bosses wanted? You found a haunted house." She was trying to make Pete feel better, but what would Bella say? Don't let them onto her. He wasn't wrong.

His grip tightened. "The Duck doesn't want real. He wants *pretend* real. He wants what we concoct, not . . . surprises."

"Okay," Carolyn agreed. She focused on his brown eyes. "We won't tell anyone." She *would* have to tell Bella.

The men below laughed, the front door opened and closed with a clatter, and the clock on the parlor mantel ticked with the casual relentlessness that clocks did in rooms all across the world, from Superior to New York to Istanbul. The alembic shone in the dim room, as if the sunlight sneaking through the curtains was there solely to highlight its gleaming surface, all the more charming for its spots of tarnish and wear.

10

SIX THIRTY AND ALREADY dark, lights burned on bishop's crook lampposts: it was just another Wednesday in Manhattan. Taxis blurted their urban frog song and the chatter of a million voices bobbed along the avenues. The network boys, burdened with heavy cameras, stood in clutches on the sidewalk. Orlando Fernandez, nimble with his Leica, had already scouted the best angles inside the house. Now he assessed the scene from the sidewalk, the house starting to bustle with early guests, everyone waiting on the man of the hour. One of the waiters with the ghoulish makeup smoked by the front door and waved Orlando over. "Who you with?" He flicked ash from a cigarillo.

"*New York World-Telegram and The Sun*," Orlando said.

"That's a mouthful." The guy watched a cab roll down Eightieth without stopping. There had already been a half dozen couples who arrived by Checker. No one thought Hitchcock would descend by taxi, but every car that pulled to the curb had the potential for some surprise.

"Normally I just say *Telegram and Sun*. Keep it simple. A nice duo."

"Abbott and Costello are a nice duo. *Telegram and Sun* is weird."

Orlando looked at the waiter through his viewfinder. "You'd prefer *Telephone and Moon*?" With the streetlight behind him, the shot was aptly moody. The waiter posed nonchalantly and the camera whirred.

"*Telephone and Moon*," Orlando echoed. "I like it. You be *Telephone and Moon*, I'll be *Telegram and Sun*, and we'll see who breaks a story faster."

"Or who gets paid for this gig first." The waiter snubbed the butt under his shiny spat-covered black shoe.

Spats. Orlando hadn't seen those in a while. His camera was pointed down anyway. He raised it an inch and clicked. Something would develop later. "You're an actor, right?"

"What gave it away?"

"I don't think real waiters look so vibrantly dead."

"Last week I was doing a show off-off Broadway. Tonight, I'm serving drinks for Hitchcock. Seems a step up."

"Maybe he'll put you in one of his pictures," Orlando said.

"That'd be a start. But I really want his job." He jabbed his thumb at his chest. "I wanna direct."

So what's your name?"

"Jo—" the waiter said. "No, not tonight—tonight it's Igor. Igor." He laughed. "I gotta remember that. Yours?"

"Orlando. My actual name." They shook hands, Orlando balancing the camera on his other forearm. "You met him yet?"

"Nope. But I've heard stories."

"He's a piece. Fat and smug. Kinda charming. I've covered him a few times."

"Stunts like this?"

"Not quite like *this*."

They stood at the door listening to the hubbub in the house behind them. A glass shattered and then a curse, followed by laughter. "That would be Renfro," Igor said. "Another actor."

"You know each other?"

"Auditions. Never in the same show."

A young man bounced out of the house, dressed in identical garb: morning coat, slicked hair, pancake pallor. "Speak of the devil."

"Renfro, Orlando. Orlando, Renfro."

"Did you hear my attempt at losing this job before it began?" Renfro glanced back through the open door. "Broke two glasses, but I'm too snazzy to fire." He snapped his lapels. "And no way they can find another fella to fit this monkey suit on short notice."

Orlando raised his camera, twisted the lens to focus on the men's made-up faces, shadowed angles in the twilight. "Let's get this before the mayhem begins."

"*Wellkommen*," Igor said, spreading his arms.

"*Bienvenue*," Renfro added.

"Howdy," Orlando chorused. A pop and a flash and then behind them the sound of a procession churning up the quiet street. A pair of sedans and in the rear, a hearse.

The men gawked.

"Of course," Orlando said aloud. "What else?"

The guys from the ad agency who'd been organizing things came hustling out like a battery of servants at a manor house. The boys from ink all over town, and Los Angeles as well, readied their equipment. The early guests peered out the front windows and some passersby on the other side of the street paused at the parade. Every bit of metal and glass on the hearse was polished. The driver, dressed in formal livery, hurried to the back door and opened it with flair. First came a middle-aged woman, hair slicked high in a modified bride of Frankenstein, wearing a burgundy polka dot cocktail dress and low black heels. Orlando recognized Alma Hitchcock: wife, partner, editor, friend, defender. Next came another woman, decidedly taller and younger. Her white skin was sepulchral, and her black hair made the contrast even stronger. Her dress was tight in all the right places. *And some of the wrong ones*, Orlando heard his mother's voice in his head. Her heels were high and her legs were long. Yowza. Definitely not Hitchcock's daughter. Next came a very tall man with a slight stoop. His suit was a nondescript gray, his features common, but his eyes twinkled like a well-fed satyr.

"Charles Addams," one of the other photographers whispered, to no one in particular.

Lastly, a familiar figure emerged, bulkier than his celebrated silhouette. He was shorter than Orlando remembered, and balder, too, and, as always, a little jarring in the flesh. He was such a figure of the collective imagination, seeing Hitchcock in person was—despite how many starlets and politicians Orlando photographed on a regular basis—a reminder that this particular celebrity was body and blood and not just another creation of his storytelling. As the stout director stepped onto the sidewalk and began his stroll up to the house, flashbulbs popped steadily. The radio microphones set up at the gated door crackled and one brave reporter shadowed him. Hitchcock's mouth twitched—amused, annoyed, both, Orlando couldn't tell. He lifted his Leica and watched through the viewfinder.

A man who announced he was from Bristol-Myers handed Hitchcock a silver whistle. The Englishman beamed like a smug, rotund lighthouse, like a cartoon from a kid's book.

"Acme," he said, delighted, as he read the name on its small metal casing. "Bobbies use these back home and Wile E. Coyote uses them here in the American desert. And ringmasters, of course! A perfect match of the utilitarian and the dreadful."

He raised it to his lips and blew a shrill blast. A camera flashed and flashed again as the whistle kept screaming. One of the admen watched from the doorway and Hitchcock stopped, his cheeks red. The sound of ice already clattering in metal shakers spilled to the sidewalk. Hitchcock blew a second short tweet and then smiled.

"That should wake the dead," he said with a smirk and open arms.

Orlando held his breath through the scattered crowd's burst of applause. Why did that silly sentence jar him? *Don't speak ill*, came in his mother's voice again.

A gaggle of reporters, with pens and notebooks ready, surrounded the Englishman.

"Mr. Hitchcock, what's the purpose of the party tonight?"

The director stopped before he reached the front door. "I didn't realize a party needed a purpose. Who sent that memo?"

The reporter snickered. "So, no real aim for tonight? Just letting off some steam?"

"I'm not holding any steam in, contrary to my appearance. There's no hot air in here. Just my brilliant wife's superb cooking. Letting off steam? No. We're celebrating. With spirits." Hitchcock looked around, grandly, a silent-movie pantomime. "Where are the waiters? Where is the bar? I do need spirits for a ghost party!"

The reporter jotted in his notebook. "What's your next film?"

"The wrong man," Hitch said dryly.

"*The Wrong Man*," the reporter echoed.

"No, you're asking the wrong man."

"What do you mean?"

"I never title my own films. You'll have to ask one of the gentlemen from the studio here this evening. They have all the answers." Hitchcock waved an arm. "You have your pick. They're crowded here like ants at a picnic. Eating my food, drinking my liquor. They have the answers you seek."

"You don't name your films?"

Orlando took it all in with his head down, his eyes on the shot, trying to frame it. Hitchcock was accustomed to posing when he made hokey pronouncements. It made Orlando's job easy.

"Never. I wanted *Front Window*. A terrible crime to rename that one. *The Man Who Knew Too Much*? Ridiculous phrase. Never. I've never met a man like that. Men who know too little? I'm surrounded by them. Again, I direct you to the studio chiefs."

The reporter hung at his elbow. "Sounds like you've got a grudge with the big guys."

"Have you looked at me?" Hitchcock deadpanned. "I never have a grudge against larger fellows. It's the lean and hungry types will be my undoing." He gave a little bow. "Excuse me. I have to attend to my guests."

"Testy," the reporter mumbled.

"Tested," Hitchcock corrected, raising a finger. "Tested in so many ways."

Alma sidled over to his shoulder, they exchanged a knowing glance, and she took his arm. They waltzed past the camera boys and the crowd shuffled and shoved in their wake. Orlando put up a hand to protect his gear. Renfro had retreated inside, but Igor was still there.

"Fasten your seat belts, *Telegram and Sun*," he said, watching the entourage enter the house. "It's going to be a bumpy night."

11

CAROLYN STOOD AT A third-floor window and watched as a hearse pulled to the curb. Hitchcock had arrived. She needed to go downstairs to Pete and the others waiting in the foyer, but everything was unsteady, like the first steps from a Ferris wheel's carriage.

The note that Bella had left on the living room desk in Gracie Square was cryptic, but not impolite. *Last-minute errand. Enjoy yourself tonight! We'll catch up later! Love B.* Gorgeous penmanship, the sort you'd expect from an artist. Carolyn could have stared at the graceful loop of the *L* all night in her dazed state. Yet, she was surprised. Why had her aunt ducked out? Carolyn didn't need her help—she had her outfit, she had her accessories, she knew where she was going, she'd been there all day—but surely Bella understood she'd want an encouraging word. She'd thought Bella would want to hear about the preparations, wish her a good time, but maybe that was exactly it. She hadn't wanted to hear about the house. That was why she'd given Carolyn her invitation after all.

Why was she realizing this just now?

Carolyn needed to tell Bella about Snug's appearance. She'd walked the mile from No. 7 to Gracie Square in a haze, the automobiles and buses, the dog walkers and the nannies, all of them beyond a new bridge built across her foggy brain. She was on one side and everything and everyone else was obscured on the other.

She couldn't have really seen a ghost. Pete had returned to his office for a clean shirt and a fresh suit, not even back to his apartment, and neither mentioned Snug when they parted at the front door. Thank goodness Johnny wasn't around. He would have been able to tell she was a mess. An hour later, sitting on the sofa in her new dress, staring out at Bella's balcony, she was still quiet, nearly meditative, but her brain was flitting like an absurd bird.

She hadn't seen a ghost. She had seen a ghost. She hadn't. What did the

Cowardly Lion mutter in desperation? *I do believe in spooks, I do believe in spooks.* But did she? *IdoIdoIdoIdo.* She did. She didn't. Carolyn didn't know, but Snug *hadn't* been a figment of her imagination. Perhaps The Duck was pulling one over on them, cameras and lights he hadn't revealed. Advertising was a game, after all, and it was best played on an unsuspecting audience. Maybe she had been a test run. Maybe it had been Pete's idea?

No, he was even more rattled by it than she was and he wasn't that clever an actor.

She returned to Eightieth Street, the cabbie lost in a world of his own, so they rode in a convenient silence, and then she escaped up the stairs, undisturbed, and lurked alone among the bedrooms. She wasn't quite ready to talk to Pete again. Perhaps she was waiting for the house to explain itself, but there was only silence. Nothing spoke to her; no cold drafts brushed her skin. She peered out at the growing commotion from behind a curtain. Maybe Snug had slept here? There were still faded dresses in some of the closets, but nothing for a girl. She tallied all the props and decorations from that afternoon. It seemed a lifetime ago. What was this place? Just a musty space in an old house filled with fake stuff for people who did fake jobs. They didn't work in banks. They weren't selling anything solid. It was pretend. They peddled in make-believe and why should she think any of it was real?

The guests were arriving, a steady stream of cabs at the curb like a caravan of camels. Pete came in behind her. He looked handsome in his dark suit, his hair neatly brushed, his cheeks flushed with excitement. Or maybe he was already a cocktail into the evening.

"You look great," he said, and she was about to say "Thank you," or "You, too," or "What the heck happened this afternoon?" when she remembered the hearse.

"He's here," she said.

They leaned closer against the glass and their breath fogged the pane. Pete touched her shoulder. She felt the energy from his fingers through the fabric of her dress, a current strong enough to light a lamp, and felt her mouth *O* in surprise—though really it wasn't a surprise at all, it was the purpose of this entire silly night—and she turned to Pete's bright nervous eyes and said, "Are you ready?"

12

THE GUEST BOOK RESTED on a walnut lectern in a corner of the cramped foyer. A large leather-bound volume, a black prop revolver weighed open its first pages. A dun-colored quill and a squat inkwell rested above it. In another life, this might have been a hotel registry. Signatures, round and large, small and cramped, covered the first pages like inky spiders. *Jim Allardice. Bob Buck. Pete Donoff. Henry Larmon. Carolyn Banks.*

One of the waiters had just handed Barbara Addams a single long-stemmed white lily. "Why do you sign yourself *Chas*, Charles?" She posed with the petals held to her cheek like a fan, her fair skin nearly as pale, her thick hair as black as jet. "It seems an affectation."

"I've told you," he said sharply, handing the fountain pen to his other half. "It looks better."

"And saves time," Alma Hitchcock offered, adding her name below the Addamses'.

"It's a sound aesthetic decision," Hitchcock agreed. He signed his name, then drew a little silhouette of a man, a series of swift strokes and, voila, he was in two places: trapped on the page and alive at the party.

"And it saves time," Alma repeated. Everyone looked at her. "Milliseconds add up," she said, waving her own lily like a baton. "Every editor knows that."

Hitchcock beamed at his spouse, then turned to the cartoonist. "Why, you've probably saved a month with that frugality, Charles. What will you do with the eons your simplified signature has gained you?"

"Attend to the needs of *me*," Barbara purred, tickling Charles's nose with the flower, then linking her arm in his and pulling him into the throng.

"Attend silly parties," Addams mumbled over his shoulder.

Chas Addams
Barbara Addams
Alma R. Hitchcock
Alfred Hitchcock

Alma linked arm in arm with her husband and shook her head. "I don't think it's a silly party, dear," she whispered. "Those two have forgotten how to have fun."

And off they went into the belly of the house, like children following a path into the woods.

13

PETE HOVERED BETWEEN DAN Wilcox, the point man on the Bristol-Myers account, and The Duck, and waited for an introduction to the guest of honor. Could Hitchcock be guest and host? Sure, Pete decided. Carolyn stood loyally behind him, on the watch for any impromptu apparitions. His chest was tight. Geez Louise, what *had* happened that afternoon? It couldn't have been real. But Carolyn saw it, too, and she had *spoken* with it. It? *Her*. A girl ghost. Could she have been some shared mirage?

The famous figure turned toward them.

With all the times he'd seen the man in films, on television, Pete expected seeing him in person would be old hat, as if they'd already met. But it was unnerving to see the director as the real deal, not a rumor. The man had a presence, even at a distance. Jolly, but not quite benign. No wonder Jim Allardice's lines worked so well. He caught Hitch's essence in a punchline, a sort of frozen concentrate of Hitchcock. When the director beamed at the group, his smile had the same swift potency. Mrs. Hitchcock stood by his side, smoking a long cigarette in a longer black filter, seeming simultaneously detached and amused, her attention moving from the guests to the details of the house, the flickering candles and the somber portraits.

"This is exactly what I was looking for, gentlemen. Bravo. When your research team hinted there were no more haunted houses here, I knew it was preposterous. Exorcised by modern architecture? Bosh." It was such a rarity to witness The Duck getting chastised, Pete didn't know whether to laugh or wince, but the bosses all kept grinning. And Hitchcock kept going. "I know the streets of your fair city are *terribly* haunted . . . by advertising men and actresses. All of you." He waved an arm to include them, a magician holding a hat and producing the infamous rabbit.

"I don't doubt that." Wilcox ignored the director's disdain. He was jubilant. "We're everywhere."

Hitchcock glanced at the flight between floors, the banister spindles casting striated shadows on the wall. "This is perfect. Oh, I do love a good staircase."

"We knew that, sir," Wilcox said, with a nod to The Duck, who nudged Pete.

The Duck stepped forward after his introduction. "And this is the man who brought it all together, Mr. Hitchcock," he said. "Pete Donoff. He led the team that secured this place."

Pete felt a wild surge of pride at the praise, as if The Duck had handed him an Academy Award. He couldn't stare at his boss or blurt *thank you, thank you*, so he took Hitchcock's surprisingly soft hand and gave him his best thousand-watt grin. Then the director's grip turned firm and the Englishman nodded. Pete's mouth hurt, giddy from looking Hitchcock square in his searing eyes. His gut roiled with the day's overindulgence of coffee. His brain buzzed. He should have had Postum. Mr. Coffee Nerves was lurking over his shoulder again, giving his best to mess this up. Hitchcock glowed next to Pete, but whether he was a warm hearth or bomb about to go off, Pete couldn't guess.

"You've seen some of my films?" Hitchcock's cheeks rose with his smile.

"Of course! I mean, everyone has, haven't they?" Pete kept himself from swinging his arm in an attaboy curve, like Mickey Rooney bragging to Judy Garland. *You betcha, we're putting on a show!*

"Not quite everyone. But I'm working on that." Hitchcock paused. "Can you work on something for me?"

Pete leaned in. "Sir?"

Hitchcock inched closer. "A cocktail would be divine. One of those ghoulish delights I read on the menu."

The waiter named Igor materialized as stealthily as a leopard, his face pale with powder, his eyes rimmed with kohl. "I can get that for you, Mr. Hitchcock," he said solemnly. He was really feeling the role. No emotion, no smile. Pete was impressed. Hitchcock seemed amused. Wilcox smirked at the trio.

"Dead Granddad, if he's available," Hitchcock said.

"I'll have one as well," Wilcox seconded. Hitchcock could have ordered actual arsenic and Wilcox would have accompanied him, sip for sip. "And you, Pete?"

"Sure, make it three." When in Rome, drink as the emperor, right? But he'd keep a tally. Tonight was not a night to tie one on.

The Duck and Mrs. Hitchcock were in an animated but hushed conversation and the waiter was reluctant to interrupt them. Instead, he stood in front of Carolyn. Hitchcock seemed to notice her for the first time and raised an appreciative eyebrow, taking in her slender figure, her shining green dress and high heels. "And who are you, my dear?"

She held out her hand. "Carolyn Banks, Mr. Hitchcock. It's a pleasure to meet you." She was cooler than Pete had been. Later, she would admit to feeling like a bobby-soxer meeting a ballplayer, but now she held it together by concentrating on his wife, who was watching them both. Hers was a friendlier gaze, less like a grocer assessing the lettuce.

"Enchanté," he said. "Are you an actress, Miss Banks? I feel like I've seen you before."

"Oh, no, sir. I've never had the theater bug."

"Or cinema?" he countered. "Never caught a bug at the movies?"

"Thankfully, no," she said, with dramatic relief. "I've remained fever-free."

Somehow she had charmed him in seconds. Boy, she was an asset. Pete tried to imagine throwing this party without her and suddenly he couldn't. How did that happen so quickly?

"It's Miss Banks's family who owns this place," Pete explained. "It was her aunts who lived here."

"*Grand*aunts," Carolyn said. "My father's aunts."

"And where are the *grand*aunts now"—Mr. Hitchcock glanced about—"to be so generous to lend us their home?"

"They've both passed away, sir. That's why the house was empty."

"Oh, dear," he said. "I hope they haven't gone far."

"Perhaps we could conjure one this evening," Wilcox interjected, "with a séance?"

Oh heck no. Pete shot a glance at Carolyn. She looked like a canape was lodged in her throat. Who knew what a séance would raise? She swallowed and gave him a nearly imperceptible shake of her head, a tiny jerk, her lips tight. He knew the translation: *stay cool*. He tried for a bemused smile but felt like the poster boy for panic.

"Don't give Alfred ideas," Alma said, then glanced away and blew smoke in the opposite direction.

"They weren't much for parties, I'm afraid," Carolyn apologized. "No actual ghosts here tonight."

Pete was impressed with her acting. She *should* take a screen test.

"Tonight? But other days?" Hitchcock joshed.

"Who's to say? I'm only here for a brief stay and then the house will be sold. It's going to be made into apartments."

"Of course," Hitchcock said sadly. "A tragedy. But that's the modern way. Take big old places filled with character and chop them up into bland, easily digested portions. It could happen to me, too, you know? I'm a perfect candidate, just like this place. Too big, too old, terribly inconvenient, not modern at all. Television has shown that the modern way is smaller, less impressive. I feel fondly for this place, and I've only been here a minute. Are you certain it has no ghosts? No chance I can chat with one of the grand dames?"

"I wouldn't want to promise you anything I couldn't deliver," Carolyn said. Pete admired her calm. "I've learned that working in sales. Customers get so frustrated."

"I shan't complain. The decor is charming, even if the ectoplasm is from props and not the Great Beyond. What is it that you sell, Miss Banks?"

"Table settings. Silver. China to brides."

"Ah, you know the nerves and demands of the engaged. Rather like actresses, I'm afraid."

Alma rolled her eyes.

"I expect so," Carolyn agreed.

"A dear friend of mine is getting married shortly. Perhaps you've heard of her? Grace Kelly? She lives just up the street, you know, on the corner. By the museum."

Carolyn smiled. "I think that bride is a bit out of my league. We've never outfitted a palace."

Hitchcock scoffed. "Princes and princesses aren't so different from we mortals. We all dine on the same matter, sleep the same way. They simply have more complications."

"And money," Carolyn said.

He chortled. "Yes! And a most serious complication it is." He sipped at his cocktail. "I thought perhaps she might appear tonight, but, alas, only in our conversations. She could have walked here, but she's not in the city this evening. She's in California, then off to Monaco to prepare the festivities." He waved his arm. "But look at the fun she misses!" His eyes sparked like firecrackers. "She made a poor trade, I'd say." A flicker of annoyance crossed his face, then he brightened and studied Carolyn again. "You've really never acted, Miss Banks? Shame. You have the looks for it. I can tell right off you have the poise. Perhaps you'll read for me one day."

Pete watched her cool expression. He would bet she was photogenic, but he didn't even have a picture of her. And he wouldn't, unless one of the photographers took one tonight. It was a shame. She'd go home and he'd never see her pretty smile again. He missed her already and she was standing right there.

"I would be honored, Mr. Hitchcock," Carolyn said, surprising Pete. Then she stepped on her agreeable beginning: "Though I'm afraid you'll discover I haven't a jot of talent."

"Let me be the judge of that," the director said.

"He always is," Alma said.

"Trust the Duchess," he nodded. "I am an excellent judge. And I've only sentenced a very few actresses to beheadings. I'm celebrated for my leniency."

"Like the Red Queen," Alma said.

"Leniency?" a tall man snorted. Even stooping, his dark hair had brushed the high doorjamb. "Is that what they're calling it these days?"

"Ah, Charlie," Hitchcock said. "Let me introduce you to my new friends. Gentlemen," he addressed Pete and Buck, "and lady," he winked at Carolyn—oh, she'd have something to say about that later—"this is Mr. Addams, Charles Addams, of *New Yorker* fame. He draws appalling little illustrations and makes a lot of money."

This was the father of those creepy cartoons? Pete stifled a surprised laugh.

"Not much money," Addams scoffed. "Not as much as you."

"My pictures move, yours don't. I'm paid by the frame."

"I believe it," Addams laughed.

"You shouldn't," Hitchcock confessed. "Not a word. Not tonight." He gave each of them a challenging stare. "Don't believe a thing out of me tonight." He rose on the toes of his well-shined shoes. "That's an order." Pete could tell he liked giving edicts. This was the director at work.

Pete wanted to give the guests the same kind of direction. Don't believe a thing you see tonight. Not one thing. It's all pretend, folks. Only pretend.

Igor Imagines THE HUSBAND'S LAMENT, a screenplay

INT. An alcove off the busy kitchen. ALFRED HITCHCOCK stoops over a dessert table, eyeing every sweet like an admiral inspecting his fleet. CHARLES ADDAMS paces by his side. Neither of them notices a server standing silently in the shadows.

> CHARLES
> Have you ever heard of such a thing—
> a wife taking a hundred-thousand-
> dollar policy out on her husband?

> ALFRED
> Yes, yes, I believe I have. Isn't it
> in *Double Indemnity*?

He puts a finger to his chin in a thoughtful pose.

> ALFRED (cont'd)
> You should really see *Dial M for
> Murder* and not just because it's mine.
> There's a hubby in it, perfectly
> willing to off the wife for her money.

Charles's eyes widen and he blinks twice.

> ALFRED (cont'd)
> If you're asking whether you can trust
> your wife not to kill you for an
> insurance claim, I'd say you already
> know the answer.

Alfred glances to his left, then his right, then left again, like a child crossing a busy London street. No sign of his wife, so he steals a ladyfinger off a platter and pops it between his fleshy lips like a clever fox. He groans, a voluptuous appreciation.

CHARLES
With your waistline, Hitch, those'll
kill you faster than Babs could do
me in.

ALFRED
But could she kill you so delectably?

He licks crumbs from his lips.

ALFRED (cont'd)
Here's a better question. What keeps
young Chas alive? Living on the
precipice of death is exhilarating.
Think of it as a gift.

Charles pulls the director closer, tugging at his lapels.

CHARLES
Listen, Hitch, I love Babs—I really
do—but I love living more. I don't
want the precipice. You don't really
think she's simply out to kill me for
some dough, do you?

A waiter comes from the kitchen with the pièce de résistance—a cake in the shape of a haunted house, its yard decorated with fondant tombstones. The men pause as the waiter makes space on the table for this masterpiece and then exits. The director seems mesmerized, reaches out to touch the house's sugary roof, then stops himself. He turns to his companion.

ALFRED
I see the world through a morbid
camera. Of course she's out to get
you. Everyone is out to get everyone
else.

He cocks his head to listen to a distant screech, one of the sound effects drifting about the house. Charles watches the plastic eyeball bob in his martini. As if for vengeance, he plucks it from the drink, sets it on the nearest tabletop, and takes a triumphant sip. A castaway in its little puddle of gin, the eyeball tilts to watch him from its new perch.

>CHARLES
>Maybe all wives are out to get us.

He turns the eyeball in the opposite direction, so it stares at a crowded mantel above a cold fireplace.

>ALFRED
>Oh, Alma wants me to live forever. She wants to keep me going, nourished by nothing but gruel and water, for as long as she can.

>CHARLES
>It's better than conking you over the head for a windfall.

>ALFRED
>You shouldn't think so narrowly. There are so many ways she could kill you.

The pristine cake nags at Alfred. He picks at the frosting, one bit at the tip of his thumb and index finger. He inspects it like a detective, then places it with reverence on his tongue.

>CHARLES (his voice forlorn)
>I need another divorce.

>   ALFRED
> I can't counsel you on that. I'm a
> believer in the Church of Rome.
>
>   CHARLES
> Oh, priests. What do they know?
> They've never married.
>
>   ALFRED
> You underestimate imaginative reach.
> One doesn't need direct experience
> of a thing to become an expert. I've
> never murdered anyone in my life,
> but I understand full well what it
> takes to become adept at homicide.
> One needn't marry to understand its
> special circumstances.

CAROLYN BANKS strolls to the cake table and pauses before it, an empty plate in her hand. The men nod at her. She cuts a small slice of the front yard. Alfred does a little jig. Oh, thank goodness, his dance seems to say. There was no reason to preserve its sanctity and now he could eat. He elbows Charles.

>   ALFRED
> Look! That headstone.

The girl considers the cake, too—the little church, the graveyard, the tiny black fence enclosing the plots.

>   ALFRED (cont'd)
> It's like the one in your living room.

The girl had been pretending not to listen, but grins as she turns to them.

>   CAROLYN
> Excuse me. You have a *headstone* in
> your living room?
>
>   CHARLES
> Doesn't everyone?

The director steps to her side.

>   ALFRED
> I can vouch I've known others who
> collect them, dear. But his would be
> the only one functioning as a coffee
> table.
>
>   CAROLYN
> You have a headstone for a coffee
> table in your living room? In
> Manhattan?
>
>   CHARLES
> Correct. But the dearly departed isn't
> here. She's in New Hampshire. I have
> her grave marker, not her corpse.
> She's been dead a long time.
>
>   ALFRED
> Little Sarah.

His fingers melodramatically trace letters in the air. Age Three.

Carolyn shudders. Charles moves to her other side.

>   CHARLES
> She expired in the wilds of the
> Granite State, oh, three-quarters of
> a century ago. Maybe more. The dates
> are worn, eighteen something-something
> to eighteen something-something else.

> I was visiting friends who lived near her family plot. It was in disrepair. The locals were bulldozing, the headstones askew. Little Sarah spoke to me.

Carolyn flinches, covers her mouth. Alfred chuckles.

> ALFRED
> A talent I wished I possessed. It would make writing scripts so much easier if the dead could speak.

> CHARLES
> That was a figure of speech.

The men speak around her like animated bookends. Alfred touches Charles's arm.

> ALFRED
> So, it ended up in your trunk and you drove it here, liberating it from the obscurity of a Yankee wasteland, thus, freeing her spirit once more.

> CHARLES
> Something like that. Little Sarah has been a loyal companion ever since. I mean, she's never appeared to me, but I'm sure she's happier in my digs than she was in New Hampshire.

> CAROLYN
> That's ghoulish, but not without sweetness.

> ALFRED
> Like the cake.

                    CHARLES
          She was only a child. Even a savage
          like me can see the waste. Little
          Sarah lived so briefly while hordes of
          us thrive for decades here—

                    ALFRED
          Or California.

                    CHARLES
          California, especially. Horrible
          state.

                    ALFRED
          Disturbingly so. Who would live
          there? Little Sarah, even were she to
          come back as a spirit, would be less
          terrifying than countless things I
          encounter in Los Angeles.

                    CAROLYN
          Actresses?

                    ALFRED
          Agents.

Charles glances across the hall. Carolyn and Alfred follow his gaze to where the second Mrs. Addams dazzles amid a throng of men with microphones and cameras; even in black, she's a bird-of-paradise, a shocking bloom against a habitat of muted suits.

                    CHARLES
          Wives.

He plucks the eyeball from the tabletop, contemplates it the way a boy might contemplate a baseball, and pockets it.

ALFRED
And you, Miss Banks, what sort of wife are you planning to be?

CAROLYN
I have no idea. Perhaps none at all. It's a forward question, Mr. Hitchcock. I'm sure I can't answer.

ALFRED
Here's an answer: a pretty one.

He gives a little bow.

ALFRED (cont'd)
And a lively one.

CAROLYN
I do plan on being an *alive* one.

ALFRED
The best sort.

CAROLYN
Gentlemen.

She dips her head in a farewell and marches back into the crowd. Alfred nudges Charles.

ALFRED
Did you see my show on Sunday night? It's apropos. A man buries his wife in the cellar, but he couldn't keep a good woman down.

CHARLES
Hitch, you're not helping.

He exits and Alfred watches him go. He glances to make sure no one is observing and runs his finger along the edge of the cake. He admires the dollop and then makes it disappear with a smack behind his Cheshire cat grin.

14

BARBARA ADDAMS STOOD BY the staircase like an Erté statuette: one slim arm extended, her painted nails blood-red, fingers tapping the ornate banister. A pair of eerie green footprints stuck to the faded wallpaper glowing above her head. Alfred imagined a bird's-eye shot, peering from the top floor, down and down and down, to her gleaming black hair, her white hand waiting, or rather, from below, lens lingering on her long stockinged legs, her dark dress, her parted lips, the winding steps.

His fondness for staircases was no secret, a staple of his films for years going back before the talkies. Stairs take effort to ascend, hurt us if we fall, sometimes curve and take us places we don't expect and certainly can't predict. In his loathing of physical exertion, Alfred sometimes looked at a flight (or worse, two) with revulsion. Sweat gathered at his neck just imagining a climb.

But this old staircase, narrow to fit the absurd space, snaked from gallery to dining room to bedrooms and more bedrooms to rooftop aerie. It was sublime.

Barbara Addams wasn't bad either. She looked like one of her husband's sketches, the brooding wife from the *New Yorker* cartoons, sensuous in a pen-and-ink illustration, even more so in the flesh. Charlie had, of course, created the wife years before he'd ever met the second Mrs. Addams, back when she was still the singularly euphonious Barbara Barb. Charlie's first wife—also named Barbara—had been the same type, sallow and shadowy and curvy, but not as much as the second Madame Addams, La Deuxième, this set of bones covered in well-tempered and tempting flesh. Alfred felt pulled to her in the same manner as some of his starlets, but few actresses had such cold and calculating eyes. Actresses were women merely practicing a theatrical craft. Bad Barbara (everyone thought of his first wife as Good Barbara) was a practicing attorney. He had heard of Bad Barbara's likely conniving to get hold of Charlie's wealth, both current and future, via crafty contracts and now this talk of an insurance policy. It was in poor taste to discuss such matters, but would it be in even poorer taste to let Charlie suffer mariticide?

There was the rub, as the Danish prince would say. And the Prince of Leytonstone? What did Alfred think? A grocer's son could always spot a fruit that seemed delectable on the surface but rotten at its stone. Yet telling a friend his spouse was a poisoned peach was never an enviable task. He tried to let Alma do that sort of heavy work, but she didn't really care for either American and if Bad Barbara knocked off Charlie and stole his every nickel, Alfred doubted his wife would mind one whit.

Dorothy Kilgallen, the reporter, and her phalanx of radio engineers were gathering by the staircase, but Bad Barbara wouldn't move. She struck a resistant pose so glamorous she glowed. Charlie had wandered away and missed her luminosity.

No, it wasn't Babs who cast a light, it was something else, a figure farther up the stairs. He squinted and refocused. An afterglow from the phosphorescent feet glued to the walls, contrasting with Barbara's deathly white skin? No. No, there had been something there.

But what?

A different sort of girl.

These props fellows were outdoing themselves. Alfred was a difficult man to impress and the night was young, but his appetite was piqued. He'd hired the right team to capture the mood he'd envisioned. Eyeballs in drinks and graveyards in cake! Glowing girls on staircases! Marvelous, oh, hearty men of Young & Rubicam. Good show!

15

THIS WAS THE KING holding court: Hitchcock ringed by reporters and sycophants at the edge of the gallery, the second Mrs. Addams leaning on his every proclamation. Carolyn watched the scene as she sipped champagne from a spot across the room. She had misplaced her whiskey. It was going to be a night of abandoned drinks and half-smoked cigarettes, followed by well-intentioned fresh starts. Her brain was having a hard time holding anything amid the chatter and distraction and her brief bursts of anxiety. Snug could suddenly waft through a wall or lounge on a davenport. She'd had a fleeting desire to tell Hitchcock: *Yes, this house is haunted! There are real ghosts right here!*

It was a bad idea.

"I've always been interested in spontaneous combustion," Hitchcock dramatically confessed into a Mutual Broadcasting System microphone, and Dorothy Kilgallen was smitten.

The on-site broadcast was The Duck's idea. *Breakfast with Dorothy and Dick* had huge ratings on WOR and Kilgallen was a master of patter. She had told the crowd she was here to store up mad Englishman stories for her usual morning broadcasts. So much gossip, so little space! Her husband was back home on East Sixty-Eighth, waiting to get the full scoop; scads to chat about tomorrow over coffee with their usual listeners and there were a few thousand folks eavesdropping right now! Of course, this wasn't her first meeting with the main man; they'd been on *What's My Line?* a year before and she told everyone that he was charming, if a little strange. But that's where the fun was!

"In Dickens's day," Hitchcock began, "my countrymen routinely exploded. It seems since we no longer believe in it, no one ever does it. We need a revival . . . like flagpole sitting or dance marathons—trends we abandoned because they no longer amused. Too brutal. There's nothing wrong with a little brutality. Spontaneous combustion needs a renaissance. I highly encourage it."

Hitchcock's eyes twinkled, actually twinkled. Carolyn was reminded of St. Nicholas in *The Night Before Christmas*. A bowl full of jelly and a side of menacing mirth. Happy Christmas, indeed, and to all a good night.

The crowd chuckled as a chorus.

"Americans are always appreciative of a Dickens reference. If he lived now, besides being preternaturally old, I believe he would be an American. I became an American citizen myself last year." There was brief, skittering applause. "I considered it very seriously, and not only for the advantageous taxes. What was stopping me?" He put a finger on his chin, mock pondering. "You haven't a decent cup of tea on the entire continent—unless Alma brews her magic—" he glanced around the crowded room for a sign of his wife but plowed on when she wasn't revealed, "and some of you are boors. Present company excluded. Yet America seems to have taken to me. It's impolite to ignore the love of the masses even though I don't quite fit in. Audiences are like eggs. I need them, but I must put up with some repellent features." He looked at Kilgallen conspiratorially. "I loathe yolks. Disgusting little yellow sacs. Foul. But we need eggs for so many marvelous concoctions. Cakes and brioche. So, I choose to pretend they don't exist. Not in an egg cup, not on my plate. But I accept them as a necessary evil. And I believe the feeling is mutual."

Carolyn smiled, but it was all a schtick. What doesn't start with an egg?

"You haven't really taken to *all* of me, not every inch of my corpulence. Americans may love my films, the program you tune in to every Sunday night, but I have no delusion. You can't trust an Englishman. There's no cowboy in me. Yet—" he dipped his chin to a comely redhead two yards from him, smiling on the arm of an adman, "—you are entertained. And you," he nodded at her date, "you pay me, so why wouldn't I want to stay?"

This time the crowd roared. He gave a shallow bow and disappeared into the shadows down the hall.

Carolyn followed his exit and watched the guests break into shifting cliques, quartets and trios, a smattering of couples, shoulder to shoulder, all in a gauze of smoke. She scanned the room for Pete, but he wasn't there. She needed a report from her partner on Ghost Patrol. A man she didn't know gave her the eye. These men were used to making pitches. Even here, everyone was buying or selling something. She skirted his advances by ducking behind a passing waiter.

Then Hitchcock was back, leaning on the banister, and peering up the first flight. For a moment, she imagined him spotting Snug. If he had an inkling of what he could find in this house, it would be disastrous. The man was P. T. Barnum. He would capture her, somehow, and turn her into a bit for his show. A freak in a circus. If anyone could make Snug into something terrible—and profitable—it was the men in this house tonight.

Pete materialized by her elbow, sweat on his forehead. "I need a favor." He hustled her toward the stairs and there was the director.

"Sir," Pete said, turning the word into an apology.

Hitchcock gave them a nod of recognition and waved them up the stairs like a concierge. Carolyn felt her feet rising even as she turned to look back at him, her fingers brushing the banister. He gave her a paternal smile, then marched himself back into the party as she ascended the steps on autopilot.

16

PETE PEEKED INTO THE dimly lit library, saw that it was empty, and pulled Carolyn along. She smelled like a garden. It made him want to kiss her. (*What? Now? Eyes on the ball.*) They sat at a cumbersome table, heavy-legged and medieval, and he leaned toward her, arms across his knees. His gaze was intent. "Okay, hear me out. If we can summon Snug, we can ask her *not* to crash the party." His smile was tight, but he couldn't loosen his lips. His face was a size too small.

She pulled back and frowned. "That's a terrible idea."

He took a deep breath. "If we summon her, we can ask nicely. That's the polite thing to do."

"*Summon* her? Stop with that word. She's not a demon."

"She's not a human."

"She was!"

"Well, she's not anymore. That's about the only thing we can be certain of if she's floating around years after her death." He stood, agitated. "Plus, she's blue."

Carolyn crossed her arms. "She's still human."

"A long-dead human."

"That seems . . . unkind."

Carolyn stewed while he took in the room, from crown molding to dark corners. The crowds assembled on the floor below. Laughter and more introductions. He needed to get back. "We need to do *something*. Do we tap? Once for yes, twice for no? Once for come out and play, twice for stay put?"

"I don't know," Carolyn said, an edge to her voice.

Pete rolled his shoulders, tried to relax. He scooted a chair closer to her and sat again. "Hey, Carolyn, don't be mad."

"I'm not mad."

"You said your aunt had spoken with her? Loads of times?"

"I don't know how many 'loads' is. She had moments with her. But I think it's just, she just shows up. Aunt Bella didn't tell me, but I don't think we *call* for her."

"Not even a yoo-hoo? Anybody home?" Pete snapped his fingers. "Let's call Bella and ask. She'd be game to help, right?"

Carolyn sighed. "She was hesitant to tell me in the first place. When I went back to change, she wasn't even there. I think she's pretending tonight isn't happening." She moaned. "If she knew I told you—"

"You *didn't* tell me. What did your other aunts do about her? The ones who lived here."

"I don't know that they saw her."

Pete stood and stretched, arms up to the high ceiling. "I was thinking I could tap, just a little, and maybe call her up?" He collapsed. "Except I'm too short."

"What are you talking about?"

"I don't know. I'd heard you could call a ghost tapping on a ceiling? Maybe it was a wall."

"Where'd you hear that?"

Pete scowled. "My grandfather." He put his hands over his face.

Carolyn nudged him. "My sisters had a Ouija board when I was a kid."

"Such an obvious prop and I didn't even consider it. Got one in your purse?"

"It never worked."

They looked at each other and laughed, laughed so hard his mouth hurt from grinning and her eyes watered.

The Duck's voice rose above the downstairs burble and Pete was back to his task.

"Did Snug tell you anything? When you were alone?"

Carolyn studied the chandelier.

He followed her gaze. He touched her arm. "You don't have to tell me everything. I mean, if some stuff is personal. It's *your* family ghost."

She looked at him slowly. "That takes the prize as the strangest thing anyone has ever said to me. And the sweetest." There was a circular glass ashtray on the table. She spun it, a small wheel of fortune. "No, she didn't say anything. But I felt things. Her feelings. Sadness. Loneliness. Pete, I don't want to insult her or treat her like a freak."

"All I want is a favor—not to scare anybody. Just ask her to let us be here for one night. That's all." Pete opened his palms in a minor plea.

Carolyn nodded. "That isn't much." She looked around the room. She took his hands. "I think someone else may be able to help."

✦ ✧ ✦

They stood in the doorway of the third-floor master bedroom.

"Um, Carolyn," he said, looking around, "there's no one here."

The mannequin corpse was where they'd set him hours before. A long, lean lump in the bed, his gray head poking from the top, sheets undisturbed—

Then: *there*. The outline of something wavered by one of the bookcases. The figure dimmed, like a neon sign on the fritz. It firmed up, briefly, and faded again, an irregular current. The figure shuffled, looked at its feet, then shuffled another step. He was an old man. No, the ghost of an old man.

Pete heard Carolyn's quick intake of breath. He grabbed her arm. "Another one?"

This one's shade was a washed-out gray. He wore a short dressing robe and slacks, slippers dangling where he floated, toes pointed south, glasses perched on his head, as if he'd forgotten they were there.

"Did you know about him?" Pete hissed.

"I thought I saw something earlier."

"And you didn't tell me?"

She gave him a weak smile. "I didn't think you'd believe me. It was before we met Snug."

They watched the man move about the room, his attention high on the empty bookcases, then lower, under the furniture. He avoided the bed and its fake sleeper. "I bet it's Dr. Satterthwaite," Carolyn whispered. "Isabella's husband."

Dr. Satterthwaite float-slipper-stepped toward the door, as if he'd seen them, though his face registered neither surprise nor regret and he seemed to forget why he was moving. He bent to look under the bed. Empty-handed, he stood again, puzzled.

"What's he doing?" Pete touched Carolyn's elbow. Her skin was warm in the cool room.

"Looking for something to read? One of those books? They always talked about him like that. Nose in his papers."

Dr. Satterthwaite reached out and patted the empty shelves, a man on a mission.

"He died here, too?"

"Yes, in thirty-three."

The ghost grimaced. And then vanished, as if someone had flicked a switch.

"Oh boy," Pete said. "I need to sit down."

He perched on the edge of the mattress. The mannequin shifted. Pete glared at it.

The old ghost flicked back on, hovering above Pete's head. Pete scuttled off and fell *plop* to the floor. Carolyn hurried to him and knelt.

"Holy moly!" he panted.

The doctor floated lower, lower, until he was face-to-face with the prop. Ghost face to plastic face.

"I don't think he likes that decoration," Carolyn mumbled.

"Understandable," Pete gulped.

Dr. Satterthwaite stroked the mannequin's skull and a tuft of gray hair shifted, blown by a light breeze.

"He can *move* stuff," Carolyn said.

"Uh-huh," Pete croaked.

The ghost swung around and briefly his silhouette grew brighter.

"What—is—he—doing—in—my—bed?" His voice was rusty, a door that hadn't opened in a long time.

Pete froze. Carolyn spoke gently: "He's just a prop, Dr. Satterthwaite."

"What is he doing in my bed?" There was more force and steadiness in his timbre.

"Goldilocks," Pete whispered. He gave a tremulous little *ha*.

Carolyn ignored him and directly addressed the ghost. "It's a party," she soothed. "Just for tonight."

"I don't like it," the spirit murmured. "I don't like it at all."

He was gone again, a pale gray buzz, an afterthought in the air. The plastic corpse rocked a tad, then stilled.

Pete stared at the space above the bed. "Ah, hell."

"What did you expect when you advertised for a haunted house?" Her voice was brittle.

"Make-believe." He looked at her, eyes wide. "I expected make-believe."

She pulled the sheet up to the mannequin's chin and smoothed out the wrinkles. Pete bet she looked like that tucking in her nephews. Except her nephews were rosy-cheeked toddlers.

She patted the mannequin's head. "What do young men become if they're lucky? Not like my brother." Her voice was so low when she turned to him. "They become *old* men. But then old men end up corpses." She turned back to the mannequin and poked it.

"And what we just saw?" Pete was having a hard time swallowing.

"Something beyond corpses. But *real*. This party"—she held out her arms—"all of this stuff you're doing, we're doing—*that's* make-believe."

Pete shivered, then stood, trying to shake it off. "We didn't even get to ask him to talk to Snug."

He reached out to her and Carolyn took his hand. Together they hustled out of the room, leaving the pretend corpse in the bed to sleep on without them.

17

MALCOLM TOWER HAD COME to get his girl.

His face stung from a sloppy shave in a men's room of Grand Central and his hair was thick with too much pomade. He wasn't going to crash a party with a five-o'clock shadow and smelling of the train. His cheeks felt wet, but that was the damp Manhattan night as much as nerves. He had walked from the subway stop on Seventy-Seventh and settled across the street from the address he'd written on the back of a torn envelope, copied from the *Herald Tribune*. When a party gets coverage in a newspaper, it's a big deal.

He'd scrawled another address below the party's locale: *10 Gracie Square*, Carolyn's aunt's place, but he hadn't the gall to drop in on her unannounced. A lecture about proper dating etiquette wasn't his goal—and that wasn't where Carolyn was anyway. She was here. He felt it.

Cars parked up Eightieth, taxis arriving every other minute, dropping off men in pressed suits and women in cocktail dresses. Malcolm didn't recognize anyone in the brief walk between curb and door, but that meant nothing. Movie and TV people registered only faintly with him. Theaters had always made him restless, sitting in the dark, looking at projections.

How had he gotten himself perched behind this skinny tree watching them like a stupid hoodlum, a cat burglar casing the joint? Who wouldn't notice the bulky paper bag at his feet?

The black metal 7 on the limestone front, he liked that. It had class. The wrought iron gate in front of the glass-windowed door said *not only are we fancy, but we've got stuff to protect*. Carolyn told him her aunts were a pair of old biddies living together on the Upper East Side; she didn't say they were loaded. She hadn't been telling him much of anything lately.

The telegram, avoiding his phone calls, her complete radio silence. It gave him a queasy sense about his proposal. His pitch was moldering on a store shelf and the longer it stayed there, the less likely she'd go for it. He didn't need to be in sales to understand that.

But he hadn't really *asked* Carolyn. She hadn't let him finish. And then she ran away—for a breather, he thought—but maybe for something more. Maybe it was too late already. She should have fallen for him by now, it had been over a year, and they'd had good times—dinners and day trips, walks and movies. Movies again. Maybe she'd fall in love with some television star tonight.

There were sallow men in tailcoats greeting the guests at the front door, beckoning them, handing each a long-stemmed lily. The doorman had greasy black hair and an unhealthy pallor. The guys were in greasepaint. Every article called it a haunted party, a morbid shindig, and they weren't fooling. But he hadn't seen anyone else in costume. Had she lied? He nudged the bag at his feet. He'd look ridiculous. Malcolm assessed his suit, his polished shoes—he'd had them shined at the terminal. Maybe he'd jettison his plan. Could he get in pretending he was a producer's son? An executive working on some campaign? Was there anybody Carolyn mentioned he could use to wing this? It would be so much easier to go in his costume.

He'd lugged it all the way on the train, the outfit pilfered from the locker room at Superior's Catholic high school. The Knights. It wasn't difficult to nab it, visiting after the school day was over, gabbing with a boyhood chum who was coaching basketball. Malcolm had gone in with only a vague idea, remembering the mascot from a football game last autumn, but when he saw the visored helmet on the shelf, the shiny silver gauntlets, the plan appeared like an arrow out of the dark. It was perfect. But the goal was to blend in—and if there were no others in costume, he'd stick out and Carolyn would see him before he was ready.

And then, as if in answer to his plea, a man in armor appeared from out of the twilight, heading down Eightieth with a lumbering gait. His visor was lowered, his breastplate slick with condensation from the threat of rain. His outfit was sturdier than Malcolm's, but it wasn't a contest. Was this guy headed to the party? A jaunty feather flopped along the top of his helmet. Malcolm watched the knight's cumbersome procession, but then his view was blocked by yet another limousine. The car slowed to the curb and Malcolm lost him. Had he gone in? He must have ducked into the shadows. Or the house. But he hadn't seemed that quick.

A black sedan swooped to the curb and a tall man stepped out. A clutch of reporters hailed him. One of the gloomy doormen met him at the entrance and presented a flower. The man posed at the front door, his sleek black suit, his gleaming white teeth. He waved at a pair of photographers, a man and woman, who had been lingering by the entrance. "Hank!" the man called. A reporter yelled, "Mr. Fonda!" Greetings and pleasantries. Malcolm squinted. Fonda. Henry Fonda. How could he pull off being Carolyn's knight in shining armor with matinee idols in every room?

And there she was: stepping out of the basement-level door, laughing and batting the arm of some young guy. The guy smiled. They shared a cigarette and slipped back inside. Malcolm watched and all the time fought a pain tucked below his ribs, as if he'd been jabbed with a lance.

He could rush across the street right now, shout to her, call her out, demand she give him an answer. The fellas with the cameras might eat that up, even if he wasn't a celebrity.

But that wasn't Malcolm's style. He didn't go off half-cocked. He was going to crash this party; he had a plan and he'd stick to it. Hide in plain sight. Don't worry about the other knight. There was more than one gallant at the Round Table and he'd be the hero. The other guy might be a useful decoy, and he doubted Carolyn was interested in him. No. It was the guy in the suit he worried about. This was chain mail versus Brooks Brothers.

18

THE WAITERS PROPPED OPEN the rooftop door for a cigarette break. There were four of them working the party, but only Renfro and Igor smoked. The boss, Angelo, older and all business, was allowed to use his real name (by decree of Mr. Buck), because he was full-time, accustomed to these gigs, and like a good general, threw himself onto the front lines and didn't ask the others to do anything he wasn't willing to do himself. Angelo got his apron dirty and let the others steal breaks whenever he could. Hyde, the fourth waiter, was a little younger than Renfro and Igor and kept to himself. He wasn't an actor, but a poet, and while he seemed nice enough, the others hadn't gotten him to smile the whole day. He was a natural at playing the somber butler. If he had been an actor, it would be impressive Method work.

Igor and Renfro stamped their feet by the edge of the roof. Up here, the wind was strong and night had turned the mild day into a brisk evening. Gray clouds and the scent of rain weighed on the breeze, hinting at something to come.

"Have you had a chance to chat with *him* yet?" Igor's blue eyes danced in contrast to his grim getup. "He's something else."

"Him? Him who?" Renfro smirked.

"Capital H. El Hitch. Hitchcock."

Renfro lit a cigarette and offered the pack to Igor. "And you're already on nickname terms with him?"

"If they can call me Igor," he said, striking a match, "I can call him anything I want."

"Fair enough. Aliases all around. But if you're asking did he see me, immediately recognize my silver screen potential, and schedule an audition? No. He did ask for an extra cocktail napkin. And when his wife wasn't looking, a second round."

The sky was purple-gray and a pair of silhouettes—night birds or bats—flitted above them. Igor pointed to them. "We're being watched."

Renfro admired the pair as they winged their way east. "Spies," he said, and swiped at a fallen strand of greasy hair. "Brylcreem. I can't stand this stuff. It smells like my old man."

Igor smoothed back his own hair. "I'm partial to this look. Like a Lon Chaney movie. Dressing vampire feels right."

"Too bad El Hitch doesn't do monster movies. We might have an in on the casting for that kinda flick." Renfro took a long draw. "Where you from?"

"Minnesota. You?"

"Montana." Renfro picked a loose bit of tobacco from his tongue and flicked it into the dark.

"We're practically neighbors."

"At least in the alphabet."

"How'd you wind up here?" Igor sat on the tar roof.

"Here? This party? Or here, this city? Or here, this life?"

"All three." Igor pointed out the bats again. "They're back."

"Hired because I've worked parties for Angelo before and I'm between shows. In the city, because I'm like you—"

"Maybe?" Igor smiled.

"I played too much pretend as a kid and decided it would be a good career. This life? Are actors born? Not made? Heck, if I weren't here, I'd be on a farm."

"Same here. It was this or drive a tractor. But honestly, acting isn't really the goal. What I really want is to *direct*."

Renfro sat next to him. "Then I've met the right man. So you can cast me!"

"To a couple of temporarily greasy artists." Igor raised his cigarette like a champagne flute.

Renfro followed suit. "Or always greasy, temporarily employed waiters. Hail to thee, oh runaways from M states."

A siren wailed in the distance. They listened.

"Henry Fonda's here," Igor said. "You seen him yet?"

"He's a tall drink of water," Renfro said. "Maybe *he* can give us the big break."

"I doubt he wants the competition," Igor said.

"I doubt we're big enough to be competition. Mice on a battlefield. Thrive by staying beneath the line of fire."

"Ah, sometimes I *want* to poke my head above the breach."

They worked on their cigarettes.

"How old are you?" Igor spoke through smoke.

"Twenty-six."

Igor laughed. "We really were separated at birth. December baby?"

"January. Just missed ya."

"I don't think so. Just right."

Renfro looked at Igor. Igor looked at Renfro.

"Okay," Renfro said.

"Okay," Igor returned.

Their Camels had burned to ash.

"We better get back," Renfro said. "I don't want to abuse Angelo's kindness."

They stood and tidied their morning coats. Igor crushed his still-smoldering butt beneath his heel. "Want to grab a beer after this thing dies?"

"Will it ever die?"

"Every party ends."

"I meant your cigarette. It's out. Now you're just abusing it." Igor laughed and Renfro nodded. "Yes," he said. "When it's over, let's find the right bar."

"Just gotta get through the rest of it," Igor said. A drop of rain hit his hand. Then another. By the time they'd strolled back toward the rooftop door, whatever drizzle had begun was gone.

Igor froze and Renfro walked smack into his back. "Oh!"

"Did you see that?"

"That? What?"

"That girl. Right there!" Igor pointed in front of them, by the brown door, its paint chipped and peeling. "She was there and—she was gone."

Renfro followed his finger, then glanced around. "The light is weird up here. A shadow?"

"No, she looked *real*." Igor shivered, then tried to shake it off. "And blue. Maybe those ad guys did it."

"Yeah," Renfro said. "A gag."

Igor shook his head. "I don't think they're that smart. A few mannequins and a barrel of fake cobwebs doesn't make it seem like they went out of their way."

"Any visions the guests have are the result of *our* bartending." Renfro tapped his chest.

"Yeah, right," Igor said. The tension eased. "I do like the dame in Jell-O."

"She's a nice touch. I wouldn't want to really touch her, but she's the best thing they got."

"Maybe I just got a preview of whatever they have downstairs. Projections or something, you know?" Igor turned back to the roof ledge and saw the bats in their circuit. They swooped once, then twice over the spot the waiters had just left, a companionable pair of night friends.

Then the rain began in earnest and they ran for the door, hands over their heads to protect the thick face paint.

When they descended all five floors, they found the kitchen empty. Angelo and Hyde were making rounds with the canapes. The sideboard was filling with smeared plates. "There's gonna be a heckuva lot of dishes tonight." Renfro grabbed a clean stack of cake plates.

Igor was silent. He absently held a sheaf of forks.

"You okay?" Renfro touched his arm.

"She hovered, right over the door. She hovered, man. I think something was really there."

"She hovered?"

"Like a balloon. And then she was gone."

"You sure you haven't been hitting the Dead Granddad?"

Igor joined Renfro at the sink. Then the tap handle turned. *It turned.* On its own. A thin stream ran into the sink. "That's a sign." Igor pointed. "She's here. It's a sign. I didn't do that."

Renfro followed his gaze. "She works for the utility company?"

"She's *here.*"

Renfro was about to respond when Angelo marched in. "Why you two standing around?"

"You leave the water on, Mr. Angelo?" Renfro leaned past Igor and twisted the tap off.

Angelo glanced at the sink. "No! Why? One of you try to cause a flood."

"Hyde was in here?"

"Hyde is tending the second-floor bar." Angelo huffed. "Working. Which is what you two should be doing."

Igor shook his head, then grabbed Renfro's arm. "A sign. She did it as a sign."

"Yeah, she's a mermaid." Renfro smiled.

Igor let his arms drop, defeated. "I don't know, man. Maybe I'm dreaming."

Angelo shooed them out of the kitchen. "The guests are waiting," he said like an anxious hen, "hungry and parched!"

"And see-through," Igor muttered.

Renfro nudged his arm. "Maybe all three," he joked, and pulled him through the doorway.

Igor Imagines A KNIGHT'S QUEST, a screenplay

INT. The Library. Guests stand along a broad table, too primed with alcohol and attention to sit. ALFRED HITCHCOCK and ALMA HITCHCOCK banter. CHARLES ADDAMS twists a cocktail parasol and fiddles with a petite plate of mixed cheeses. CAROLYN watches the HITCHCOCKS' verbal volleys, a tennis set between equally matched competitors. BARBARA ADDAMS admires her own reflection in a dark window. The lights—candles on the table, dim bulbs in wall sconces—cast odd shadows as the guests move warily. The waiter in the corner is a sphinx.

        ALMA
Alfred won't readily admit it, but I'll tell you—years ago he made a pilgrimage to Charles's house in Connecticut and knocked on his front door. A knight-errant on an errand—to praise the artist of the macabre. This was after the perfume ads, wasn't it, dear?

        ALFRED
Yes, the Angelique illustrations. Gold Satin. Red Satin. Of course, I already knew the cartoons. You've moved on to hawking typewriters, I see.

        CHARLES
Yes. Remingtons. Like the rifles.

        ALFRED
What a combination. They should be my sponsor.

Barbara strokes Charles's chin with one graceful hand, though he shivers as if she were tracing a line for an executioner's axe.

BARBARA
I'm wearing Gold Satin tonight.

ALMA
You seem more like Shalimar.

BARBARA
I wouldn't want to be typecast.

Everyone leans forward to take a sniff.

ALFRED
Not all the rewards of art are remunerative. (*Aside to Carolyn*) I began my work as an illustrator. Making credits and title cards. I have great admiration for those who still put pen to paper.

ALMA
Alfred is not accustomed to feeling so struck by someone else's imagination. (*Aside to Carolyn*) When you're a genius, it's difficult. He just *had* to meet him.

CHARLES
On my front porch. He asked to see me in my natural state.

CAROLYN (with a smile)
Connecticut?

ALFRED
Alive. I thought for a moment he was going to leave me on the stoop, just shut the door and pretend I never appeared.

                    ALMA
          It's always an option.

                    ALFRED
          You speak from experience, Duchess,
          yet you've always let me back in the
          house.

                    ALMA
          Always, Alfred. I can't imagine our
          house without you in it.

She blows a smoke ring and smiles as it floats above them. Everyone watches as it sails, and then, all at once—pop!—it disappears.

The waiter notes this tableau: the Hitchcocks exchange a loving gaze; Charles Addams lost in a thousand-yard stare; Barbara leans toward him, one hand still at his neck; Carolyn has gone pale, as if she's seen a ghost.

Before anyone can speak, Carolyn breaks the spell and hustles out of the room.

19

CAROLYN FLED TO THE dining room and paused to catch her breath between the dumbwaiter's door and a half-empty dessert cart pushed along the far wall. Why had that smoke ring panicked her? It had seemed in that moment so like . . . Snug. It was ridiculous. To calm herself, she observed a pair of young couples like an ornithologist watching courting robins. Then the flirting annoyed her, so she idly opened the door to the dumbwaiter and found, to her surprise, something glinting in the dark. She stuck her hand in before she weighed any drawbacks—spiders, for instance—and felt a sharp, hard edge. She withdrew a metal whistle, the kind policemen blew on busy corners.

"My wife," said a man from behind her, "really is a lovely woman."

She turned. Charles Addams had followed her. He nodded to the distance. Barbara posed by the staircase, a sort of Scarlett O'Hara waiting for her beaux. "She is," Carolyn said. She pointed the whistle at him. "Is she after your money?"

"I didn't think I had enough to be after." His face drooped like a basset hound.

"But if you are worth more dead than alive?" Carolyn wagged the whistle at him, then stuck it between her teeth. The metal was cold against her lips. She almost blew it before she considered the commotion it would cause and quickly shoved it back into the dumbwaiter. She didn't need the temptation.

"Death makes it a different condition," he agreed.

"Yes," Carolyn said. "For her and for you."

A canned scream, a woman's cry, echoed from above. For a second she thought it was the whistle, then realized it was one of Johnny's sound effects.

Addams's face blanched. He blinked. He put his hand out to the wall and faltered, the door of the dumbwaiter moving unexpectedly beneath his weight. He jumped back, startled, and shivered. "Excuse me," he said. "I need some fresh air."

Carolyn watched him go, his gait unsteady, as he wove through the room. He could have been traversing a crowded train station, men in dark suits, women with red lips. *Petals on a wet, black bough.* A gray face appeared in black lace. Carolyn's stomach dropped. Aunt Mariah? Then time sped up and this woman was just another piece of pretend, a costumed player, dressed as an old-fashioned widow, grotesque and arresting in her black crepe. Why hadn't Pete said anything about this act? Bella wanted her to stop them from stealing the furniture, right? What of their aunts' dignity? Her stomach revolted again, a quick flip.

The dumbwaiter demanded her attention: the black handle, worn bald by a hundred thousand journeys that began with a yank, its burnished wood grain a mesmerizing whorl made beautiful by a century of tasks. She could blow the whistle and stop the whole appalling performance. Carolyn put her palm to the spiral, a gold-brown-black galaxy trapped in the confines of a single square, and let her fingers cover the universe.

She'd leave the whistle be, but it was good to have options.

Her nerves calmed, though a seed of anger remained.

20

PETE WAS CORRALLED BY Dan Wilcox into restocking the second-floor bar, but they hadn't found the extra upstairs booze. Elbow to elbow, they searched the butler's closet off the dining room. How many weird closets did this place have? Pete didn't see any stash of whiskey, but he wasn't going to argue with a big shot. A squat red extinguisher, its FIRE CHIEF label long faded, sat on the windowsill above a short shelf crowded with dusty plates and saucers. A brown glass medicine bottle next to it, its prescription smudged and unreadable. Left behind by one of the aunts? A long-ago maid? He gave a gentle shake and it rattled like a baby's toy.

Wilcox read over his shoulder. "Harmless little guys or killers?"

"Can't tell." Pete handed it to him. "This may be the scariest thing on the property."

"This crowd will only care if it's from the competition." Wilcox pulled a clear Bufferin bottle from inside his suit coat. He put the familiar bottle with the blue label in the spot where the dusty old bottle had left a clear ring. He slipped the brown bottle into his suit pocket. "Even Steven. Last thing we need is an OD tonight. *Actual* death would be bad publicity."

Pete clicked his tongue. "Actual death would be bad in a lot of ways."

Wilcox pulled the brown bottle out again. "I can't decipher a thing. Suppose a pharmacist could tell us what they are."

"Are there any actual pharmacists here?" Pete was skeptical.

"The Bristol-Myers boys are all salesmen. They leave the scientists back in the lab."

Carolyn arrived and touched Pete's arm. Her eyes were tense and her posture stiff. Something was bugging her. And the room was stuffy. Two was crowded, three a sardine can. Pete wanted to ask her what was up. Wilcox peered into another cupboard.

"Mr. Wilcox," she said. Oh, she wasn't here for Pete. "Who's the old woman in mourning clothes?"

Pete stared at her. "What . . . old woman?" What had he missed?

"The one on the couch." She bobbed her head in the direction of the parlor.

"Which couch?" Wilcox said, still kneeling to the lowest shelf. Pete had already checked there: nothing but an empty mousetrap and more dust, the real stuff. "This is the House of Couches."

"Yes," Carolyn agreed, "but there's only one old woman."

Wilcox stood and brushed off his trousers. "Ah, you mean the actress."

"What actress?" Pete said. "We never hired an actress."

"We did. It was Larmon's idea. An actress to play an old dame who used to live here."

"That *old dame*," Carolyn said, her irritation sparked, "would be one of my aunts."

"She's your aunt? Then why are you asking me?"

"No," Carolyn said. "Not the actress. The woman who used to live here. The women. They were my aunts."

Wilcox was defensive. "We could only budget for one."

"I don't think that's the problem," Pete spoke up.

Wilcox's face soured. "She's a lousy actress?"

Pete stood straighter and gave it another shot. He looked at Carolyn while he chose each word like he was checking fresh eggs for cracked shells. "Carolyn here is simply concerned that hiring someone to portray her aunt might be in poor taste."

"We don't want to offend *anyone*," Carolyn said.

In that instant, Pete understood. Let's not offend *anyone*, anyone being Snug. Carolyn gave him a tight smile. He needed to fix this, but Wilcox barreled on.

"You're part of the family that owns this place?"

"I am." Her voice was steely.

Wilcox considered her from heels to hair.

The Timex on Pete's wrist ticked like Big Ben. His every nerve widened in the moment.

Wilcox shrugged. "I'm sorry if it's in poor taste, but what's done is done. I'm not going to fire the lady. This entire evening is in questionable taste. And your family's taking the money, right? So, it's ours for tonight." Carolyn opened her mouth, but Wilcox kept on, hand raised. "Remember this: It's not your aunt. She's just a prop, a bit of décor. She's like Miss Havisham, you know? That's what Bob Buck called her. You let us drape the place with cobwebs. Think of her as a big cobweb."

Carolyn weighed Wilcox's words. She was biting her tongue.

"It's good to have an explanation," Pete offered. She frowned, unconvinced.

Wilcox patted Pete on the shoulder. "Buck has been saying great things about your work here." He squeezed around Pete and Carolyn, then strolled into the hall.

Pete reached out to Carolyn. "I had no idea."

"It's fine, Pete. It's not sacrilege. It's just . . ."

"Snug?"

"I don't think we want her angry. How would you feel if someone pretended to be your mother?"

"No one wants to be my mother," he said, trying to make light.

Carolyn relaxed, her shoulders dropping a little. "Could we maybe keep Snug from seeing her?"

"I don't know how," Pete said. "Snug can see everything, right?"

Carolyn laughed. "She's not Santa."

"Maybe Miss Havisham will charm her. Get on the Nice list."

A middle-aged man in a striped suit stepped into the cramped space. He glanced at Carolyn and Pete as if he were looking for someone else. A Y&R colleague? A Bristol-Myers guy? Pete tried to place him.

"Gentleman," the man said. "And lady." He leered at Carolyn.

Pete moved closer to her side.

The man opened his mouth, then closed it when he spied the Bufferin bottle. He strode to the spot Wilcox had occupied moments before and plucked it from the cabinet. "This stuff works, you know," he said, shaking the pills with vigor. "It's not just hyperbole. We might pitch it hard, but it's no joke. No quackery, you know? You've got a headache, this is the stuff."

"I may need it sooner than I thought," Pete said to Carolyn. Pete pointed to the door and started out. Carolyn began to follow, but the stranger had drawn closer to her.

Pete held up when she wasn't right behind. Even he could smell the heavy wave of aftershave and a pungent sidenote of bourbon. Carolyn was in his cloudy midst.

"You know my wife is out of town," the man whispered to Carolyn.

"Lucky her," Carolyn said, and she strode past Pete and into the hall.

The man scowled. "What the—"

"Take some pills," Carolyn called back. "You'll feel better. I'm sure."

Don Juan skulked away, like the realtor's son had the first time he'd met Carolyn. She must handle a dozen jerks like that a day. Exhausting to fight them. Yet when Pete turned to catch up to Carolyn's lead, she was already halfway down the hall and ready for another round.

21

DOROTHY KILGALLEN NODDED TO the lean actor as he squeezed by her in the narrow passage. "Hank." She held her drink above her bosom, careful not to spill.

"Dorothy." Henry Fonda tipped his head.

She'd seen him doff a hat to enough cowboys on the big screen to recognize the gesture. It was more sincere on film. She knew he hated her, was certain he had since the morning five years earlier when she'd tattled in her column on the collapse of his second marriage because he was hot to trot with a girl half his age. Maybe he had reason to despise her, but it didn't mean he hadn't treated women badly for years. The public had a right to know the solemn do-gooder in the theater wasn't the man he was in real life. Though who would remember that now with all his success? The second Mrs. Fonda was just another dead woman, and he was the toast of Broadway. He was going to be the star of Hitchcock's next film, that was why he was in New York. His latest divorce papers (from Mrs. Fonda Number Three, the child bride) were sitting in his lawyer's office and there was buzz about his current fling, an Italian princess—baroness—something. She had departed Manhattan after Christmas, bored with Hank's latest project. That was the scuttlebutt. The lack of nightlife was killing her. Fonda liked a party, but at heart he was driven to work. No one could call him indolent, that was certain. They could call him all sorts of other things, behind his back, even to his face, but not that.

Fonda strode down the hall and left her alone with one of the radio boys. He'd rolled his eyes at the actor's departure and kept coiling a spool of thick gray wire. When he spoke, he spoke around a toothpick. "The house down the street, the Brokaw house, didn't Fonda's wife live there?"

Dorothy raised a precisely plucked brow, arched in feigned surprise.

"Oh, we won't mention Frances tonight. That would be impolite."

The man snickered. "Weren't you the one to tell the world about Hank's dumping her?"

Someone did remember. Dorothy looked over her shoulder. She was tickled. Furtively, she stage-whispered, "Frances herself told me what he was doing with the girl. It was before her great fall. After he took up with Susan, well, Frances simply collapsed." Dorothy remembered those days: as the press followed him, the pile-up of photographs of his new girl with their children, closer in age to the daughter than the father. She knew Frances would be crushed. She hadn't thought Frances would go so far as to kill herself, but then again, one can never be certain what someone is capable of when they are in despair.

She really did feel terrible about the whole ordeal.

"He married the girl, didn't he?"

She blinked herself back into the hall—oh, memory, what a trap—and nodded. "He did. And now they're done, too. Kaput. There's a new love, a Sophia Loren type. Dark and hot-blooded. How long will she stick with stuffy old Hank?"

"Stuffy? I wouldn't call him that. He likes his cocktails. And the Stork Club."

"That's not saying much," Dorothy scoffed. "Everyone likes the Stork Club."

The reporter and the radioman watched Fonda, in the distance, leer at a comely young woman in a shiny green dress. The woman had the good sense to duck into another room, so the actor joined a circle of smoking men. Dorothy kept her gaze on Fonda and imagined gathering above them a storm cloud of Valkyries—his poor girl bride and the Italian countess, and at the apex, Frances, grim Frances, seeking vengeance on these men who leave wretched women like her every day, everywhere, in their stupid, careless wake.

22

CAROLYN SLIPPED INTO THE small powder room off the hall and shut the door. She needed quiet. The world was too much with her and this seemed the only safe place to hide. She wouldn't stay long. Hiding wasn't her style, but if she didn't have a moment to herself after her dealings with Bufferin man she might scream. And she hadn't been the one hired to do that sort of thing. Clearly, there were sound effects and actresses for that.

She flipped down the toilet seat and sat on the lid. She would have put her chin on her fist, à la *The Thinker*—there was a replica in her father's office—but her hands were full with the alembic. Why had she plucked it from the gallery and carried it like contraband into this tiny bathroom? Had she seen steam rising from its spout? Had it really felt warm when she swiped it from among the other decorations?

What was she thinking? What did she want? Right this second?

To talk with Pete. No. To have a drink? No. To find Snug. Not really. She had questions, but no one could answer them. Who could? Not Bella. Not her father. Well, someone could have, but she wasn't there.

The voice in the Flame had been real. The voice that brought her here, tonight, this city, this house, this bathroom. She rubbed the alembic like a genie's lamp and wondered how she became such a hypocrite: She wouldn't summon Snug, but she'd certainly try for another.

"Mother?" Carolyn said aloud to the air above her hair, to the mirror over the small porcelain sink, to the faded wallpaper, dim flowers and vines, like a forgotten garden.

"Mother, if you're here, talk to me."

She waited, palms pressed to the pot. Her breath came like she'd run a block. Then it hitched, her heart and lungs ready to cry. She wouldn't cry. That would ruin her makeup and she'd look ridiculous and call attention to herself, and she had no desire for anyone to look at her again tonight. Not now.

"Mother, what am I doing here? And what are you doing *not* here? Why not you?" She groaned. "There are ghosts in this world. Who would have guessed? Not me. And they're not you, evidently. I'm not getting the ghost I need, Mother."

She lay her forehead against the alembic, but she didn't weep. No, she wouldn't do that.

"Come on," she whispered. "Please. One word. Just one. I *know* you can do that."

The revelry beyond the door continued. Johnny's canned creaks. Ripples of laughter. Water in the pipes. Passing footsteps, hustling waiters. Blithe spirits all around, and not one with her in this room, not even if she begged.

She waited. She waited. She waited some more.

There was a knock at the door and a woman's voice. "Anyone in there?"

"Just me," Carolyn said. "Be right out!"

"Hurry," the woman pleaded, then giggled.

Carolyn looked at the dumb thing in her lap. It was nothing special. Did she think she was Aladdin? Foolish. She tucked the alembic in a shadowy corner on the tiled floor, stood, and nodded at her reflection. Hair tidy, cheeks flushed, but nothing out of place. She looked fine. She smiled at the girl in the mirror, just a girl waiting for her dead mother to appear. Nothing strange at all.

23

DAN WILCOX COULDN'T STOP sneezing. His eyes were watery and swollen. His nose ran. The elegant woman on his arm—not his wife—gave him a sympathetic squeeze. He was holding the problem: Oscar the cat.

"Get it out of my sight," he hissed at The Duck and stormed off down the second-floor hall, his footsteps punctuated by curses. He parted the small crowd like a bitter, besuited Moses.

The Duck took the cat to Pete, who had been pretending he wasn't watching from a yard away.

"Get it out of my sight." He turned to chase after Wilcox, then pivoted to Pete. "Dan can't see it again. Not once more. Do whatever needs to be done—but remember, I have to return it to my sister in the morning. Don't lose him." He started and stopped again. "And tell me if anyone else starts wheezing."

The Duck scurried off and Carolyn appeared at Pete's side to take Oscar from his arms.

"Mean men," she said, snuggling the cat. "You're the best boy here."

"What about me?" Pete said it before he could stop himself. Did he really want an answer? And why did he care?

Carolyn stuck out her chin. "Only the night will tell."

That was as good as he was going to get.

She bent and gently pushed Oscar into the closest bedroom. Pete shut the door with a *thunk* and leaned his back against it.

"He'll need water," Carolyn said.

By the time they'd returned with a small bowl supplied by Igor, Hitchcock was assembling another hallway audience.

Oscar howled from behind the closed door. There was thumping. There was scratching. He sounded more like a horde than a solo act. The director rubbed his hands in glee and his eyes sparkled. A semicircle of a half dozen guests watched him, a guard at the palace gate.

"Goodness," he said, "whatever's on the other side is a killer." In a grand mime, he put his ear to the wood and held up one hand for silence. Dorothy Kilgallen gave a dramatic shudder and two men behind her elbowed each other. It was a charade.

"Unfortunately, sir, what's on the other side of that door," said Pete from behind the crowd, "is a cat."

The Duck stepped up. "I have to admit, this one's on me." He hung his head, playacting at remorse, feeling out how much fun the director was having, versus having to admit a genuine mistake. "We rented a feline and forgot about . . . allergies."

Hitchcock tapped The Duck's arm knowingly. "Allergies kill more Americans than murderers, Mr. Buck. Every year. Terrible traps. Sneezing and wheezing until you're blue in the face . . . and then you go." He bent toward Buck. "There's a reason cats are known as witches' familiars. They are familiar with death." He paused for effect. "And watery eyes."

The crowd was jovial, eating up the act while Pete leaned against a wall, arms crossed. He enjoyed the scene like a play, one he helped put in motion. Maybe this was what it felt like to direct. The cat screeched, then a paw appeared beneath the door, patting this way, patting that. Hitchcock quaked, as if threatened by a beast, and Kilgallen widened her eyes like a silent-movie heroine in peril.

Carolyn pressed against Pete's arm. "This is a great gag," she whispered. "It's like you planned all along to put the cat behind closed doors. You're always this lucky?"

"Not until you came around," he said, grinning at her. He meant it.

"Maybe the cat's your lucky charm," she deflected.

They both watched as Hitchcock and Kilgallen continued to feign terror to the delight of the crowd. The Duck was right there, too. Then the cat went quiet as if on cue and Alma took her husband's hand and that was that. Time to move on. Alma strolled back to the parlor. The audience drifted to the bar tables and food, out of the hall and up the stairs.

"My aunts hated cats," Carolyn said, still holding the bowl of water. "Thought they were inbred and evil."

Pete nodded. "They weren't wrong."

They crossed to the closed door, sneaking like children looking for hidden presents, and stepped into the bedroom lit only by a lamp on the far side. Pete closed the door behind them, then crouched and whispered, "Here, kitty, kitty."

Carolyn bent, too, and set the water at the foot of the bed. "He's probably under here."

Pete went to his knees to peer under the ruffle and a trail of blue smoke snaked from the dark between the floor and the bedsprings and he skittered like a panicked crab, his arms and legs gyrating. The cloud twisted and dipped into the silhouette of Snug, who grew more defined each second.

The ghost was gleeful. "He's under the bed and he's a beauty! He's under the bed and he sees me! He sees me!"

Carolyn stopped crawling at the edge of a settee. Pete tried to shake off his astonishment, but he couldn't stop staring at Snug, undulating and iridescent, like a sea creature in midair.

"What's his name?" Snug was ecstatic. "What's his name?"

"Oscar," Pete said, his voice only a little quavery.

"Here, kitty, kitty! Here Oscar!"

Snug held out her hand and they heard her snap her fingers; her see-through fingers flicked again and *snick!* another snap.

Oscar slunk from under the bed. He slithered to Snug, his purr rumbling as he drew nearer. She stroked the cat's back and it arched. "I've always loved cats, but mother wouldn't let me have one. Then we moved here and Aunt Isabella said they were vile. Diseased. Untrustworthy. But Dr. Satterthwaite believed they were useful for killing pests. There was a mouser, a handsome boy. They told me to stay away from him, but I thought he was delightful." As if in agreement, Oscar pulled himself up in self-admiration, an Egyptian statue. They all watched. Then he tired of the attention, licked his outstretched leg, bent farther, and lapped at his belly. It was undignified.

"He's gotten the petting he wanted, and now he's only interested in himself," Carolyn said. "So like a man."

"That's unfair." Pete frowned. He didn't want to be lumped with the cat.

"Only a bit," she teased.

Pete and Carolyn watched the girl kneel by the cat. He cleared his throat. "Hey, Snug?"

The girl's attention remained on Oscar. He sat on his haunches and batted at her hand as if it were a toy. Snug wiggled her fingers and the cat pounced. He went right through her hand and she giggled. He landed and spun, his small brain grappling with the surprise.

"Can you avoid the guests tonight?" Pete spoke tentatively, a man tiptoeing across ice. "Try not to terrify them?"

She kept her attention on the cat and answered without concern. "I've never been terrifying."

Pete laughed pleasantly and said, "I want to keep it that way."

Her head snapped to face him. "I can play with the cat whenever I want?"

"That would be great. Perfect, in fact." He clapped his hands, two quick beats. "Just not the people." He bit his lip. "And could you tell your uncle to stay low, too?" He glanced at Carolyn. She was holding her breath, he could tell.

Snug was thoughtful. "Okay." She ran her hand over the cat's head. Oscar shivered, then bolted. "Kitty," she called and then they were both gone—the cat back under the furniture and Snug to wherever she went when she wasn't with them.

Carolyn exhaled. "That went well."

"We got a promise!" Not that she'd vanish or never come back. Just keep to herself. The key to success, Pete believed, was moderating his expectations.

"Easy-peasy," she said.

Pete cocked his head. "That phrase always comes back to haunt me."

Carolyn gave a short nervous burst. "All sorts of things are haunting you tonight."

The cat peeked out from under the bed, its eyes glinting, then slinked back into the shadows.

24

MR. ADDAMS LOOKED GREEN. One of the other photographers turned to Orlando and wondered aloud if perhaps the cartoonist hadn't overindulged. Too much booze?

"Too much wife," Orlando nodded, his voice low. She laughed, secured her camera, and tripped off to follow Henry Fonda, who was posing with his lily in the next room. The waiters had made a valiant effort with the flowers, but few held on to them for long. Wilted blooms were scattered everywhere, on chair seats and tabletops. Their white heads drooped, their green stems bent, they looked like drowsy orphans.

Orlando knew he was being indiscreet, but what had he overheard by the cake? A hundred-thousand-dollar life insurance policy out on the man, his wife the sole beneficiary? And Addams hadn't known about it? That wasn't a marriage, that was a setup for homicide. If Orlando had heard his wife doing something like that—well, first off, his wife would never do such a thing because she adored him and he adored her, and second because she was a devout Catholic and he knew she didn't want to end up in hell. But if he were Addams, he'd have been on the first train as far from her as possible. Was Mrs. Addams good-looking? Oh yeah. He'd snapped her a few times tonight just for the fun of looking into his viewfinder. But was beauty worth the risk of not waking up some morning? Not a chance. No wonder the man had a strange tint. He was contemplating his demise with every sip.

"Smile, gentlemen," Orlando called as he set up the shot. Neither the director nor the cartoonist complied, but he steadied the camera and focused on two too-somber-to-be-at-a-party fellows. It looked like a put-on. Maybe it was.

Pop went the flash and the pair relaxed.

"I won't show up in that photograph," Hitchcock said. "I've borrowed skills from my friends the vampires this evening. I won't show up in mirrors either." He smiled. "Only Mr. Addams will be in that picture, looking as if he's posing with a bit of air. A very little bit of air, as I'm sure I don't take up much more space than that."

"So, it'll look like I'm posing with a ghost," Addams said. "That won't hurt my career. It will strengthen the belief that most of my friends are of the non-breathing sort."

"I don't know how they can think such unkind things of you, Charlie," Hitchcock said. "You're a peach."

"Don't worry, Hitch. They say worse about you."

"That's ridiculous. I'm a peach, too. If I were any sweeter, I'd be toxic."

Addams nodded at the crowd. "You've got a houseful of admen here and a fair number of journalists. Who's to say you won't be eaten? Guest of honor, main course. Six of one . . ."

"I'm under the impression that none of them are fair. And a correction: I am the host, not the guest of honor. That distinction should go to the cast of my upcoming film, but only Mr. Fonda is here this evening and he's too thin to make a meal. Miss Miles is delectable, but absent. She was previously committed to spending time with Tarzan."

"Tarzan?"

"Her beau. Now there's a man who would look right turning on a spit."

"That appetizing?"

"No, that inconvenient. He's distracting her from the marvelous opportunities I've offered. The ape-man has her rattled. Serving him up tonight would have solved myriad problems."

Addams snickered. "I'd rather eat the cake. When does Miss Miles arrive?"

"Tomorrow morning. Our driver is shuttling me out to New Jersey to greet her plane. Alma thinks it's unnecessary, but I don't want the little girl wandering lost in the city."

Addams raised an eyebrow. "Or you want time alone with her in the car?"

Hitchcock tucked his head into his substantial neck. "Are you suggesting I'd do anything untoward? Not a chance, Mr. Addams. I'm explaining the film to her, that's all. I'm not a beast."

"No, you're a peach. An angel, really."

Hitchcock posed like a saint. "A peach and an angel. A combination I hadn't considered." He touched his nose. "But I couldn't think of a more fitting still life to describe me."

The pair looked at Orlando, who quickly feigned cleaning a lens. He was so wrapped up in eavesdropping, he'd started to watch them like a TV show. He smiled and tried the shot again. This time when the flash went off, he knew he had a winner. Ah, victory. He'd call this one, *A Peach and an Angel.*

25

CHARLES ADDAMS STEPPED INTO the WC on the first floor, right off the main gallery, desperate to wash his face. He felt flushed; he'd killed a pair of Bloody Marys, but booze never sank him. His constitution was sturdy. Only women got to him like this. Barbara got to him like this. A quick splash and a clean towel and he'd feel brand new.

He hit the switch and closed the door, but the tiny room stayed dark until the power met the bulb. In the gap, there was a blue glow before him and when he blinked to focus his vision there was a girl clearly hovering by the sink. Well, the outline of a girl. And she looked . . . surprised? Gazing through her, he saw his own face looking faintly aghast in the age-mottled mirror. Which of them had stepped into the wrong room? Who was supposed to say *excuse me*? She gave a little bob, *so sorry*, and disappeared through the wall.

The light burned brighter. What a marvelous trick, he decided. His mouth was open, working at nothing, like a gasping fish—he'd never had his jaw drop in surprise before, but there he was, a tall fellow, a little tipsy, carp-mouthed and wide-eyed, wondering what he'd just seen. A girl? A ghost? A gimmick?

What the hell. Real-deal flesh-and-blood women—how often were they all three of those things to him anyway? This was nothing new.

His face was damp, a reflection like one from his boyhood when he'd locked himself in a black bathroom and chanted (raise the dead, they'd said) *Bloody Mary, Bloody Mary*, half a dozen times in a mirror and she'll talk to you. Come on, Chill, you can do it. (Once upon a time, his nickname had been Chill. So unflappable was he, so cool. Not tonight.)

She never came. (It still scared the bejesus out of him.) Nobody came because Bloody Mary was dead—right, Chill?—and who'd want to be at the beck and call of every boy with a mirror and an unnatural interest in the morbid?

The girl was nothing.

His fears were nothing.

Sober up. Or get some sleep. (That won't come until the party ends, Chill. And where will you and Barbara be at night's end?) There was no girl, he mumbled into the running tap, another palmful dripping off his face, down his neck and under his collar. No phantom, no specter, nothing summoned by a woman's name.

He rested his forehead on the cool glass and let his breath fog the reflection. He was in the dark, alone, and that, at the end of it, was nothing new.

26

THE GUEST BOOK ENTRIES had swollen to a dozen pages, an autograph hunter's treasure: *Jay Kanter. Judy Balaban, Frank Gifford, Henry Fonda.* Someone had drawn a caret between Bob Buck's first and last names and added *Lucky*, then another scrawl went further and a full arrow pointed to *THE DUCK* with a small cartoon of a duck (bill, tail feathers, cigar—very Groucho Marx). Beyond that, the entries devolved.

Edith Head sends her regards.
Edith isn't here? A shame.
Is lovely the word for this evening? Charming, rather. Or charmed.
Bewitching!
I expect to chat with my long-dead Uncle Rudy this evening, old boy.
Oh, Rudy, we hardly knew you.
Murder can be fun.
Murder tonight!
When is call time?
When is last call?
Elvis Presley is in New York. Why didn't you invite him, Hitch?
Grace sends her regards.
If only Vera were here-a.
Anybody need an aspirin?
That's spelled B-U-F-F-E-R-I-N.
Kilroy was here.
The Duck was here.
(Another drawing, another duck.)
And so it went.

27

HENRY FONDA, TO CHARLES Addams's surprise, didn't want to hear about the girl in the bathroom, whatever she was, ghost or gimmick. It was strange comfort, watching the movie star squirm. Saying it out loud, Addams discovered, made it a lark. Hitch smirked, his hands folded in front of his stomach, as if he were waiting for a bus and chatting about the chance of drizzle. He rocked gently on his heels. Perhaps they both enjoyed Fonda's discomfort a little too much. Still, Addams wouldn't relent, not when the actor's lean face went white, white as the waiters in their makeup, the furrows between his blue eyes prominent as little ditches.

"I don't think much of the idea of spirits," Fonda said.

"Not merely the *idea*, Mr. Fonda," Addams said, delighted how his greater height threw the actor off-balance. The man wasn't used to looking up. "The *reality* of them. Ideas don't appear. This . . . did. It did. I saw her."

"A ghost appeared here? Tonight?" Fonda laughed, but even his acting chops couldn't hide his nerves. "You two are pulling my leg."

"You have ample leg to pull," Hitch said, "but rest easy, Henry. I am not, as of now, a believer. I do believe Messrs. Buck and Wilcox have gone into cahoots with someone else in our esteemed industry to give the *impression* that this house is, indeed, haunted."

Bad Barbara appeared behind her husband and stroked his cheek. "You're always seeing a girl, honey. What's new about that?"

Addams wanted to object but instead took a sip of yet another Bloody Mary.

Alma turned to her husband. "It is what you wanted, Alfred," she said. "Real or not, correct?"

"It is. But I hate to accept the brilliance of a rival. It galls me. Disney is clearly behind this."

"Walt Disney?" Fonda scoffed. "What does he have to do with this?"

"Have you heard of his creation in Anaheim?"

"The park? Yeah, I've heard of it. He's building Cinderella's castle."

"Sleeping Beauty's," Hitch corrected. "An understandable error. A princess is a princess is a princess. Like actresses, they are interchangeable."

Alma snorted. "Are we talking about Grace again, dear?"

Hitch plowed on. "It isn't only a castle Disney's constructing. It's an entire *land* . . . a marvel, really. Rides and tricks and shows. He's building robots, you know."

"Robots?" Fonda's eyes hardened. "Why?"

"Metal men to look like humans." Hitch's eyes went steely. "To replace us."

"I don't like that idea. First thing they'll get rid of are actors."

The director grinned. "I hadn't considered that. You needn't worry, Hank. They'd never replace a profile like yours. And these phantasms tonight. They've got nothing on you."

"I don't know, Hitch," Addams said, remembering the scent of the girl in the bathroom, salty and sweet and sharp. The veins in his neck throbbed. "She wasn't solid, but she wasn't like a projection."

"Then the Mouse King is using vapor and contraptions. His boys are brilliant." Hitch shook his head. "This is Disney's one-upmanship. It's his pleasant Californian way of telling me I'm not the best."

"I wouldn't worry about that, dear." Alma patted his arm. "You aren't playing the same game."

"Of course we're playing the same game, Duchess. The game is *storytelling*." He glanced longingly at the sweets on the table, then at the bar. "Don't misunderstand me, Henry. There are cinematic ghosts, as we have here tonight, *and* there are real hauntings, too. We all have someone or something ready to come back to us at any moment. I can't be the only one." He shrugged. "But maybe I assume too much."

Fonda's face was stern. "Assumptions are dangerous."

"You have someone trailing you, Hank?" Addams pressed, relishing the flicker that passed over Fonda's face. "Someone eager to lurk around your life?"

The actor kept so still, Addams thought he was frozen. "No," Fonda said curtly. "No one in particular. I'm just not partial to the afterlife." He rattled the ice in his empty glass. "We do what we do here and we're done." He bowed and walked away, glancing in both directions like a man crossing a street.

"He looks a sturdy fellow," Hitch said, "but something in his eyes tells me he's already seen a specter. But how will we ever know?"

28

THE BLUE GIRL WAS back, and Pete had to find another way to mollify her. She was tired of the cat. So, he gave her a pen.

It was a ballpoint he'd picked up at Gimbels. Years earlier, his uncle had shown Pete his first one—something Salvatore picked up from an RAF pilot during the war. The flyers used them because they didn't spill. An Italian invention, his uncle had said proudly. Pete had coveted it, that little ink machine. The first time he saw them at a department store he was speechless.

He was sure they would be ubiquitous one day *if* the price ever came down. Maybe they weren't built for calligraphy, but for day-to-day chores they were perfect. He envisioned everyone from the biggest boss to the lowliest mail boy having them, and he had an idea to throw at Buck and the guys above: what about putting a client's name on the side of the barrel, sure, tiny print, but legible. If it could be done—and cheaply enough—he imagined a world where ballpoints were cherished advertising spots. YOUNG & RUBICAM printed on the side of a sleek silver cylinder. Every time anyone picked it up, there would be the little billboard.

The one he gave Snug was unblemished, nothing on the side of it but his fingerprints. Would she leave fingerprints? He'd check later. He watched her hold it as if she were wielding Excalibur. She raised it to the chandelier's light and turned it in her faint hands. The strangeness of it all renewed. This girl made of light could *hold* things.

"Do you have any paper?" Snug asked Carolyn.

Sitting on the edge of the bed, Carolyn shook her head. "I didn't bring my purse."

"I do," Pete said, reaching into his suit coat and pulling out a folded sheet of letterhead. "Here." Maybe this would win her over? She'd behave if she trusted him. It felt cynical, and Pete, at heart, wasn't manipulative. At least, he didn't think so.

The girl took it and scurry-floated to the desk. She laid it flat, pressing on the creases. He marveled watching her. She hunched and brought the tip to the paper. "Ooh," she whispered. "Miraculous!"

She had written a large cursive:

$$\mathcal{cl}$$

The ink was smooth and blue. "No smudges," she said. "And my hand!" She raised it and turned it, palm this way, palm that. "No stains."

"Can you get dirty?" Pete blurted.

"That's rude," Carolyn scolded.

Snug giggled. "I *can* get dirty. You need to visit me in the cellar! There's a coal chute there. And a furnace the size of a woolly mammoth. I can get *filthy* there. And then I'm not." She waved her arm. "Whoosh. It doesn't last long."

"Do you see where it goes, the dirt?"

"No. It just isn't there any longer."

Pete whistled. "That's a trick as good as floating." Carolyn scowled. "Think about it. Self-cleaning? Imagine if we could all do that. Or all our stuff. A car!" He thought, finger to his chin, dramatically. "No, wait. Something that gets really disgusting. An oven! A self-cleaning oven. Just wrinkle your nose, snap your finger, and poof!"

"A million mothers would thank you." Carolyn went dreamy for a moment. "We should go into business."

Snug ignored them and bent over the paper again, squinting in concentration, then glancing at Pete. "Do you mind terribly? If I write more? Will you lend me the paper and the pen for now? I promise to give it back. The pen, I mean. The paper would be a gift." Snug turned the paper over. "It says Young and Rubicon—"

"Rubicam," Pete corrected.

"Rubi*cam*. Here on the top. It's embossed, like my father's stationery. It must be important."

"I'm sure I don't need it," he insisted.

"And then it says *stipulations*."

"That's it?" He leaned to read it.

She held it up. One potent word. How long had that been in his pocket?

"Go ahead." He laughed. "Use it."

"Thank you," she said, then turned to pick up Oscar.

She handed the cat to Pete as the door to the bedroom rattled. Carolyn hustled to bolt it, but Pete turned to see Dan Wilcox cross the threshold—just as Snug faded into nothing, the pen and the paper gone with her.

That was close.

Instead of greeting Pete, Wilcox sneezed. "It's still here?" he spat.

What was the right answer? "Uh," Pete said. "Yes." Wilcox glared. "And it was *my* idea, sir," Pete lied. "Not Mr. Buck's. I apologize."

Wilcox stared at Pete a second, then nodded once, curtly. "Thank you for the honesty. It wasn't your best work."

"No, sir," Pete said, still holding Oscar.

Wilcox closed the door harder than he needed, then swung it open and poked his head back in. "Remember: that cat stays in this room." He slammed the door again.

Pete dropped the cat and it hustled back under the bed.

Carolyn pursed her lips. "Why'd you tell him it was your idea? I thought it was The Duck's."

"The Duck likes a sacrifice." He plopped next to her. "Taking the heat now can only help me later, right?"

Snug abruptly popped in front of them. This time neither of them jumped. "I'll watch Oscar!" she cried. "I promise, I promise!" For a moment, she seemed more than happy, more than enthusiastic, she seemed—the word pulsed in his brain—*alive*. This was what Snug was like in the before, before whatever it was that killed her. Pete didn't want to think about that.

"I promise!" she repeated.

"Okay, okay," he said. "That would help a lot." Carolyn clutched his hand. He squeezed it back.

Snug flew under the bed. Pete waited for the yowl, but nothing came. Then she returned with a docile Oscar in her arms, purring and levitating.

"Thank you," Carolyn said. "Really, we appreciate it, Snug."

The ghost floated off to the corner, still snuggling with Oscar. They watched the space she left behind.

"If that's all this party has left to keep it smooth," Pete said boldly, "we can do it."

"Here's to keeping the cat in the bag." She raised a coupe.

He was still holding her other hand and was reluctant to let go, but he did and grabbed his mostly empty glass from the nightstand. Pete looked into her blue eyes. Carolyn looked back into his brown.

They toasted; the rims made a sweet high chime and it tasted good, maybe the first real taste he'd had all night.

29

THE SIGNATURES CONTINUED. A late addition: *Isabella Taylor.* And then, after that, another, the last, in the same fresh ink, in the same flowing hand, but bolder:

Snug.

30

HITCHCOCK WAS TRACKING THE blue light. He'd seen the glowing girl once more. She'd drifted toward the second-floor stairs, then zoomed right up them, as if carried in a stiff breeze. How was this possible? He followed her lead, pausing to peer behind some drapes. A projector? Not there. Disney was a magician. Perhaps hidden behind one of the paintings? A cutout in a face, a peering eye through which the image was cast? He shuffled away from the stairs, then stopped. The chattering cliques were too thick, too difficult to maneuver. A plate of cake balanced in one hand, his brain afire with speculation, his was a tippy ship traversing a rocky bay. He shied away, tiptoed to study a chandelier, cobwebbed by design. Did they bury a device in the false strands? He was too short to inspect it thoroughly—he'd need a stepladder and he could hardly ask for one now.

His attention returned to the staircase: no sign of the girl.

No, he had to stop thinking of her. She was a trick. He *knew* tricks.

Yet she had seemed more than vapor, more corporeal than a misty film. What West Coast innovation had Walt mastered so old Hitch would look ridiculous at his own party? He knew Disney was up to something. Pulling a practical joke on the king prankster, wouldn't he feel triumphant?

Shockingly, no one was collaring him, tugging at his elbow, stealing the opportunity to fawn. He was impatient with obsequious admen, preening would-be stars, yet buoyed by their sycophancy, too, if he were honest. He hustled as well as he could, given his frame and the plate of cake he held with both hands, and jostled his way through the crowd and up another flight. She was hiding in one of the rooms of this spidery mansion, he was certain. The house was a maze of musty chambers—a library here, a study there, and bedroom after bedroom after bedroom. He'd had the tour. When he saw every nook busy with partygoers, he kept going, up another flight, then another. His heart raced and his chest tightened. He felt drawn, following a fairy, Tinkerbell, oh, Tinkerbell, where did you go?

With every heavy step and every groan of old wood under new weight, there was Alma's hushed voice inside his head. How many girls did he have to hunt to find the one who could replace Grace? How many incarnations would there be, Hitch?

One hand grasped at the banister, the other steadied the plate of cake. A blue silhouette burned just beyond his reach. A trick or a treat, he would find her!

31

ALMA PLOPPED ON THE couch. She needed a respite amidst the cacophony. Alfred hadn't followed her—he was still in vaudevillian mode. The old woman dressed like Miss Havisham rested on the opposite end, in formal mourning—layers of black crepe and bombazine, pearl drop earrings, a lace veil, and, shockingly, lipstick a shade too red for her years, a tip-off that this was no genuine widow. She was exquisite, Alma thought. A beautiful vision from a crypt. Central casting knew what they were doing. The old woman had been conversing with some of the men from NBC and another man Alma recognized from the advertising agency, one of the crew who helped with Alfred's quips. She checked again to see if the crowd had dissipated by the cat door. Ah, no one there and Alfred nowhere in sight. Perhaps he'd drifted into the kitchen to ogle the hors d'oeuvres again. Perhaps he'd drifted upstairs to eye something else; there was no shortage of men with attractive dates. There were two young women in particular, one brunette, one blonde, both of whom would catch Alfred's attention—though the brunette would always be at a distinct disadvantage.

Alfred much preferred blondes. Evidence in point: Grace. Evidence in point: Vera. Evidence in point: Doris. Thank God none of them were here. Alma was exhausted talking starlets down after some collision with her husband, patting knees and telling them not to fret, talking *him* down after another day on set. Soothing egos all around. *Of course, Alfred, they will listen to your counsel.* Yes, they trusted his direction, not that he ever thought much about an actress's opinion. He told them what to do, what to think, and they either followed his lead or weren't invited back into the fold.

Actors were cows, he said, yet he wanted the cows to love him and some of the cows, oh, he thought they were beauties. Does the farmer love the beast? Does the beast love the farmer?

Alfred wandered to observe sights but never strayed. He wasn't faithful because Alma was the be-all and end-all of womanhood, far from it. He had never fully strayed from the Church and still held on to certain tenets of his Roman Catholic boyhood—specifically, the existence of Hell. Alfred didn't want to go *there*, that was certain, so other women remained theoretical or, if more than theory, then at arm's length. Besides, Alfred was a germaphobe. The human body, even an attractive feminine one, was covered in the pestilence of everyday existence. Alfred never forgot that. The closest he got to coarseness was a bathroom and bathrooms were temples to rid the body of its ever-present, mundane disgusts.

Miss Havisham had scooted nearer. When did the woman move so close? She'd done it in a wink. The couch cushion sank with their shared weight.

"Your husband is following the light," the old woman whispered.

Alma flinched. "What did you say?"

"He's following the light," she said, brushing Alma's hand. Her touch was cold, surprisingly, in the warm room. Too many bodies, too much hot breath, too much radiated heat. Yet the elderly fingers were icy. Alma didn't back away, as her instincts insisted, but turned to face the old woman more fully, twisting from her hips. Her wine lapped a bit over the side of her glass and a drop dripped onto her skirt. The rest sloshed back in place, the tiny tidal wave slowing to a stop.

"Are you telling me he's dying?"

"Not at all." The old woman bent closer. "The girl glowed. I thought only I saw her, then I noticed your husband drawn to her."

Alma harrumphed. She didn't mean to do that. Where did that terrible noise originate? "That's just a gimmick, I'm afraid."

"No," the old woman insisted. "I'm a gimmick. She was a girl. Faint and blue, but something true." Miss Havisham nodded, more to herself than Alma, and then gestured to the stairs. "If you want to find him, follow her."

"This is all just for fun," Alma said. "Nothing uncanny."

Miss Havisham downed the rest of her drink. "Honestly, I'd prefer that." She shuddered and set her glass on the coffee table in front of the couch. The rim had a lipstick stain. "I'm not sure I'm up for too much of this funny business." Then she stood, surprisingly spry, with more speed and agility than Alma would have anticipated. Tidying the front of her dress, brushing it off as if she had breadcrumbs on her lap, and fluffing her mantilla to let in a breeze, she set off with a drooping long-stemmed lily cradled in her arms like a dying child, her own little floral Pietà. She waddled to the far side of the room and disappeared into the bathroom. Ah, the loos. So important for the party. No restrooms, no go, Alfred had insisted, and he wasn't wrong. The man knew the devil was in the details and the details always included functioning facilities.

Alma minded the stairs. It wouldn't be the first time she ventured to retrieve a starlet-struck Alfred, but it would be the first time she'd been told to do so by a Victorian crone.

32

CAROLYN HAD LEFT PETE with Oscar and a promise to bring him back a plate, then wandered past the crowded bar in the dining room. Renfro handed her a fresh glass of champagne and she drifted into the parlor. There was the gaunt old actress, weaving through the crowd and into the small bathroom, a slim slice of light glowing under the closed door. That black mantilla, a mourning veil—the woman had seemed to float in the wispy clothes. Carolyn could imagine Aunt Isabella praying over Dr. Satterthwaite's coffin in this room, twenty-three years ago. What if the doctor caught sight of her? He hadn't liked the man in the bed, what would he think of an actress playing at being his wife?

No one at the party knew anything about the people who had lived here. Not even Carolyn. Not really. She was embarrassed and annoyed, at all of them, cavorting in a house that must have once held so much more than this.

Except Pete *had* taken the time to ask, to listen to her stories. He'd taken the time, after his initial shock, to speak with Snug. He was a decent guy. If Hitchcock or Addams or anyone else here ever saw Snug could they be as decent? Could anyone here really handle the history of the house? Not without turning it into a gimmick to sell something. Aspirin, cars, refrigerators. They'd make the undead hawk anything, given the right deal, the right script. Everything was staging. Smoke and mirrors have their reputation for a reason. And smoke and mirrors filled the house tonight.

She wasn't blaming Pete, and she wasn't blaming Johnny. They had jobs to do.

Carolyn closed her eyes and imagined an inventory of the room, like so many in the house tonight: candles, candelabra, dripping wax, squat pillars, tapers, votives in shimmering glass, snaking tendrils of smoke reflected in dark windows, gilded mirrors dancing with the flames of a dozen different sources. All the cigarettes: Viceroy, L&M, Pall Mall, Lucky Strike. A Zippo on this desk or that table. A pack of matches by the cake. There were at least two men smoking pipes and another waving a cigar. Only the old woman was spared this vice. Good thing—her veil would go up like a curtain of gas. Carolyn opened her eyes and watched wisps linger by the ceiling, then drift to the doorjambs where the human to-and-fro created little eddies.

For a moment, she was in the Flame, it was snowing, right there in the restaurant, and Malcolm was waiting at the table, still waiting for her. He needed an answer.

She needed air.

But every gulp tasted of cologne, hair oil, perfume, and sweat. Brylcreem and Chanel. Every clear thought drowned in dust and dollar bills. Then as fast as it had descended, her gloom dissipated because there was Pete, walking her way. It made her momentarily lightheaded, but not ill. His grin sparked a flitting giddiness she hadn't felt since middle school. Carolyn was not a giggly schoolgirl. This felt buzzy and awkward and entirely welcome. Maybe it was the champagne.

The wall sconces were draped with sheer black cloth, like floating versions of the costumed woman. Pete pointed at them.

"Amazing nothing has caught fire," he said.

"Yet," Carolyn added. "Filmmaker Flambé?"

The Duck sauntered over and slapped Pete on the back, a jovial one-of-the-boys gesture. Pete coughed into his hand, recovered, smiled.

Carolyn winced, but shared his rush of pride, how he welcomed the jolt of bowling team camaraderie.

"Nice work, kid," The Duck bellowed, his voice loose with glee and whiskey. "Hitch is on cloud nine, or to wherever Englishmen ascend. Larmon and Allardice are impressed. The Bufferin boys are—well, drunk—and drunk means they're happy. They're happy, *I'm* happy. You pulled it off."

"Is Mr. Hitchcock really happy?" Pete wanted that reassurance.

The Duck looked around for the director; when he couldn't find him, he turned back to Pete. "I spoke with him just minutes ago. He raved. Said the party was *divine*—his word—and he's had the pleasure of both *a marvelous aperitif* and *a marvelous apparition*."

Carolyn felt her chest tighten and she reached out for Pete's hand. She waited on her exhale until The Duck's next words.

"I definitely think," he said, "the director's had his share of the sauce."

"No doubt," Pete readily agreed. "Apparitions. Ha ha." He squeezed Carolyn's hand and she could breathe again, a relief, despite the tobacco and the bay rum and the general ballyhoo.

The Duck gave Pete one more violent bit of brotherhood, a sock to the shoulder that Carolyn knew would be black and blue in the morning, but Pete was beyond pain. Bufferin and Larmon and Allardice were impressed. Hitchcock was happy. There would be more copy opportunities. More clients. All the dreams he'd told her about. When he held Carolyn's hand, a beckoning gentleness to his affection, she felt a hot rush to her face. She wasn't a blusher, but the party was exactly what Pete wanted and she had helped.

"Thank you," he said. He squeezed once more, then let go to rub his upper arm.

"For not punching you, too?"

He laughed. "Yes. And for helping me out. You were on my side."

"Of course."

She watched him look around the smoky room, the paintings and the out-of-date décor. "Your family doesn't want to keep this place?" She followed his gaze and knew he felt her fondness for it, the whole cobwebby mess. "You could live in New York. We could go into business selling self-cleaning ovens."

She swayed. "Honestly, when Aunt Bella first told me about the party, I thought it was ridiculous. And a little heretical. But if this were a beloved family home, we wouldn't let it go to market and allow strangers to chop it into apartments, would we?" She sighed. "I don't have the wherewithal to fix it. Aunt Bella has oodles of money, but her own place—"

"A very fine place," he said.

"Yes, very fine. She's not leaving *that* anytime soon, and none of the rest of the family want to come back to Manhattan. They're living their own lives. This is Number Seven's last hurrah and I'm square with it." She waved an arm. "And who wouldn't be a little impressed? The Master of Suspense himself says my ancient aunts have the right stuff for a haunting."

"Little does he know," Pete said, eyeing the others as if they could hear him sotto voce.

"Little does he know," Carolyn repeated, and clinked Pete's tumbler. "And we've kept it like that. Good on you."

"Good on us," he said. "Here's to Snug and the good doctor. May the articles in his eternal journals be always to his liking. And to Aunt Isabella and Aunt Mariah, wherever they may be. Here's to the whole lot of them." He paused. "But not a whole *lot* of them," he amended. "Two's my limit."

"Two drinks?"

"Two ghosts. I draw the line."

"Ah," she acknowledged. "We'd need *five* for a full house."

"We have a full house as it is," he said, surveying the chattering crowd.

"Indeed we do, Mr. Donoff. Here's to your full house, filled with bosses impressed and ready to give you the go-ahead on your next important project."

"And here's to you, Miss Banks, and our full house. I couldn't have done it without your help." A *full house* had never sounded so appealing. She drank it in, the heady scent of a party at full steam and everyone having a gay old time. This wasn't the Flame: this was something strange and new and altogether magic.

Then a woman screamed, long and rattling. It wasn't one of Johnny's tapes. The crowd hushed. Pete swiveled.

Carolyn followed the sound to the powder room down the hall.

When the old actress stepped out into the light, she looked frenzied. She raised her arm, a preacher's gesture, and cried, "I have seen a spirit!" Every guest turned to watch, and she collapsed in a black heap like a fallen swan. Her back curved, her arms splayed, she was as still as a photo. She gave a little convulsive hiccup and then was still again. The hushed room was frozen.

"Good lord," a man's voice cut through the din.

Carolyn glanced at Pete. Was this one of The Duck's surprises? Pete, scowling, shook his head, as if answering her silent question and started moving toward the body. There was a gasp. Then a titter. A man chortled and the dread-filled silence cracked, like ice smacked with a hammer. The crowd burst into applause, not slow and gathering, but simultaneous and abrupt. *Bang, bang, bang* their hands went. "Brava," a woman called. And then they stopped applauding, turned back to their conversations, and the thrum of chatter resumed.

Pete was hustling through the throng before Carolyn could catch her breath. Had the woman really seen someone? Snug? The doctor? She'd come from the bathroom where Carolyn had sensed nothing. But had this woman? Had this actress seen her mother?

Carolyn's anger was swift and surprising, a jolt of bitterness that left her ashamed of her response. Why wasn't she helping this stranger? And why wouldn't this house let the dead rest?

There was a swirl of dark suits gathered around Miss Havisham, who still lay unmoving on the floor. Igor and Renfro and Charles Addams—that was a surprise!—were already at her side. Yet Carolyn felt someone watching from above. Across the room, Carolyn spied Alma Hitchcock on the stairs, studying them all with an inscrutable Mona Lisa smile.

The man wore a gray wool suit, freshly polished shoes. He carried a Homburg in his hands. The back of his skull was missing, the bullet from the service revolver having crashed through the roof of his mouth. It was efficient and messy and didn't leave him handsome.

Handsome was for days far in the past. This was Walter now, as is, and ever shall be. Mrs. Albrechtsen, the maid, had found him still breathing, but not much more, and soon he wasn't even that. On that day, long ago, he'd left letters on the kitchen table of his apartment on Twenty-Third Street (to his brother, his doctor, his accountant, and the police). He covered the bases and made sure everyone who should know did know and then the deed was done. Martha, his second wife, was already dead. He would see her soon, he hoped, though he didn't expect a fond welcome. Mariah, his first wife, had been living with their son, on Walter's money, some fifty blocks north of his blood-spattered bedroom. She was dead now, too.

He remained most sorry for Mrs. Albrechtsen. She heard the shot and found the macabre scene, but that's what being a servant sometimes entails.

He had expected to be done, discovered he wasn't, and, God, it's all he wanted, to be finished, but he never was, and that's how it had been for as long as he had wandered, and he didn't see any reason to believe it would ever be otherwise, this drudgery of trudging over the island with his filthy clothes and his once-fine hat and his distracted mind, or what was left of it. Searching for what? He didn't know.

And then, tonight, he was drawn here, to this address, to this threshold he had not crossed in many decades.

He never fraternized with the living. It would be a different way to spend an evening.

33

HITCHCOCK STOOD ON THE fourth floor at the threshold of a child's room—a single narrow bed, a chest of drawers, a dim table lamp—and gaped at the blue girl before him. This was no fairy. She vibrated while he circled her and spun to see him cross behind, a cat chasing its tail, and tangled in her own footwork. No, not footwork, but what to call it? She reminded him of dry snow blowing into piles on a windy winter day. She gathered, then dissipated, then gathered again.

He waved at her, one shy hand up. She waved back. He smiled. She smiled. He reached out and lifted his palm to touch her, then thought better of it. She raised her corresponding hand, then he paused, and suddenly leaned forward and swiped his hand and arm through her. It passed into her blue-gray light and out the other side. He gasped.

She shuddered. "You didn't have to do that."

She disappeared.

Alfred was left alone, still holding the plate of cake, his mouth gaping. He'd never been so surprised or giddy in all his life. Whether a dream or a device, did it matter?

Then he was stabbed with remorse. She was gone. He'd never see her again.

He didn't need to fear. She returned.

He jolted. "You're back," he said. "Who *are* you?"

She held out her hand, her fingertip gleaming blue.

"You—" she said.

"I," he said slowly. "I am—"

"You," she repeated. She cocked her head. "You have cake." The fire behind her eyes shifted. Hitchcock recognized desire when he saw it.

He held out the dessert like he was coaxing a songbird with seed, and a gentle current ran through the length of his arm when she took the plate in her diaphanous hands.

Such a perfect exchange! Both the girl and Alfred were delighted.

34

PETE SURVEYED THE CROWD, looking for the glint of Carolyn's golden hair. There was a preponderance of brunettes; she was a diamond among bobby pins. So where was she? Ten minutes ago he'd left her in the back garden where they'd carried the old woman to get some fresh air. Miss Havisham wasn't dead after all. He couldn't dwell on what would have happened if she *had* croaked. Fate would have run roughshod over any of his great expectations. He'd taken high school English Lit.

Don't despair. No one was dead *yet*, said a grim voice in his head. Maybe not even *the dead.*

A better perch, halfway up the staircase, and he'd find her. Unless she'd gone upstairs on another interruption from Snug. A further tug at the back of his brain: Then who was with the cat?

Addams scurried toward him. "Did you see that?" The tall man pointed to the staircase, as if he'd read Pete's thoughts.

"The old woman will be all right," Pete said.

"Not her," Addams said. "Hitch. He waddled up the stairs, eyes to the ceiling, like Joan of Arc talking to angels."

"The party is up there, too," Pete cheerfully insisted, despite a case of creeping dread.

"He was looking *at* something. The strangest expression on his face. Apostle-like. Hitch never follows anyone's lead."

Pete's dread quickened. "He's just looking for more friends."

"I don't know." Sweat beaded on Addams's forehead. "Maybe it was a girl."

Pete tried to keep his voice cool. "Really?"

Addams wiped at his brow. "Hitch thinks *you* are up to something. Hiring the old actress in the parlor, the floaty girl in the bathroom. Something to scare him or make him a fool. He's convinced Disney's behind it."

Floaty girl? Pete's dread galloped. "Behind what? He thinks we want to humiliate him?"

"He's used to being in charge. Your tricks put him off-balance." Addams's eyes popped. "Something just flew down the staircase and then back up it! Explain that!"

Pete's tongue was stuck against his teeth. Where did the words go? He coughed. "A trick of the chandeliers, Mr. Addams."

Addams scrutinized him. "You are up to something. You *want* us to think the place is haunted. It's a dangerous game. It'll kill Hitch if you aren't careful. He's got an iffy ticker, you know." He shuddered. "We've got to find him."

Pete watched him stride up the stairs, spider legs taking two at a time. Snug had promised to stay with the cat. She'd *promised*. They could convince Addams he'd hallucinated, or it *was* all a trick. But Hitchcock? It was no-go in either direction.

Pete trailed in Addams's wake, hustling to keep up.

35

SNUG DEVOURED THE ENTIRE piece. She didn't use the fork, still clutched in the round man's hand. He had backed up to the open window, steadying himself on a carved-edge, tilt-top table. He watched her eat with unabashed awe.

That scent, that scent. It was so familiar. Her head felt ready to explode with such sweetness. It was sugar! Oh, sugar, how she'd missed it! She hadn't tasted a dessert in years. When was the last time she touched cake? Or candy? Cotton candy. Spun floss, a web of pink crystals. The memory melted on her tongue like snow. She wasn't sure if she would weep real tears tonight. Everything was different. Old things were new. Even if just for the length of this ridiculous party, Snug would have it. She was Cinderella and she would have it all. She wasn't above lunging at the food, and she did, like a wild dog. The plate was heavier in her hands than she expected as she lowered her chin and lapped at the crumbs. Bits of frosting stuck to the corners of her mouth. It was the most delicious thing she'd ever tasted.

The man held his palms open to show they were empty, a gesture to a dog: *No more here, no more here, good girl.* He thought she was a beast. Snug smiled at the idea and stopped herself from barking. That would make the fat man jump.

"Are you going to start vomiting pins and needles? My mother told me of bewitched little girls in Ireland who spewed such things. Perhaps even nails and knives." His hands wavered upward, readying to protect his face. If she had said *boo*, he would have flung himself to the floor, arms over his balding head. *Boo!* or *Arf!* Even just *Ha!*

She lowered the plate and pulled up her spine, dancing class posture, a string extended from the top of her head. She tried to make herself flat-footed, firmly rooted, but that was something she still couldn't do. Floating was her nature now; she willed herself to the floor, pointed her toes south to touch something, anything, but always she rose. Even at best, she was an inch or two above landing, never on solid ground. It infuriated her, this unwilled undulation.

She looked directly at him.

Sugar lingered on her tongue, but was fading quickly, almost gone, only a remnant of sweetness past. Nothing sticky clung to her fingers. They were as clean as if she'd licked them, which she hadn't. Nothing ever stuck, especially the things she wanted to stay. She set the plate on the table, her fingertips nearly brushing his.

"I'm a ghost, not possessed. And I'm not little." She snorted. "But if you get me more of that cake, I could promise to vomit frosting. I haven't been sick on a full stomach in—"

She flashed to the brief, passing nausea of the Witching Waves, which had so quickly turned to joy. She hadn't been sick then; she wasn't going to succumb now. This *was* the first time she'd eaten in decades. Maybe the cake was too rich, maybe the sugar would make her ill . . . but kill her? Reduce her to even less than she already was? She had nothing to lose.

His posture loosened and he laughed with her. His belly shook, like St. Nick and his bowl full of jelly. Oh, she'd forgotten jelly! She'd scoop up whole handfuls of it if she could, no dignity at all, raspberries and blueberries and strawberries. Oh, marmalade, her mother's favorite, the bitter rind and the sweet fruit, glistening yellow and orange on the dining room table.

"Take some," her mother had urged. It was the first morning after they'd moved into No. 7. Father was gone. Curzon was asleep, only a child, but Snug was old enough to understand her father had done the unpardonable. He had turned sour to her, her mother had gone rancid, all the sweetness of their former life gone, and the three of them were like sailors shipwrecked in a place that offered safety, maybe even comfort, but would never feel like home. Not that morning, not over that cold toast with the opaque orange sheen.

She remembered that tart bite. This was better, so much better.

"I can get you whatever you want, child," the fat man said. He had an English accent.

"I'm not a child," she said, anger flicking at the edge of every word.

"You were someone's child," he said. He gazed at her face, too much like a botanist inspecting new foliage. "Though you are far older than you appear and you're no one's fool. But neither am I." He pushed out his arm, as if it were an unwilling participant, and then flicked his fingers through her again.

"Stop that," she warned.

He jumped, a cautious old rabbit, he was. He cocked his head, trying to figure out where the fox had run. "Or perhaps you aren't what I hoped." He jerked his attention left, then right, up and down, checking for traffic this way, then that. "Where's the projector? How's he doing it? You're Disney's. You're his doing."

"I'm no one's *doing*," Snug sniffed. "Who is Disney?"

His eyes narrowed. "Who is Disney?" He touched one thumb to his mouth, privy to a private joke. "And who, I suppose, is Mickey Mouse?"

Snug giggled. "That's someone's name? Mickey Mouse?" Her quaver grew and she shimmied.

He held out his hand again.

"You make a breeze," he whispered. "How can you make a breeze with no fan?"

He dropped heavily on the divan and put his chin in his hands, his elbows on his knees. She could feel his thoughts like water seeping through cheesecloth. She didn't have to ask. What a wonder! That had never happened before. Her brain swam with an onslaught of questions, notions, more questions. Then a pause: He recalled a scolding he gave his daughter, a few weeks earlier. Or perhaps it had been years before. Snug couldn't gauge anyone's time now, not hers, not his. He had attempted to extract a confession from her regarding a pilfered plate of cookies. The daughter was not the culprit, it was the terrier, but his demeanor had been this: kind, yet stern. Weary.

She had something for him, he believed. She possessed an answer.

Snug shook her head, snapping away from his thoughts. She did not have anything for him, not for this man.

"If you are not made by the Mouse King," he said, musing aloud, "then you are real." He leaned forward, a flash of the boy hidden in the man. "Do you have a message for me? From my mother?" His breath was staggered, as if he'd run a race. "Or my father. I can't imagine he would have anything to say to me." His bald head was slick with sweat.

"I don't know your mother. Or your father."

"They are dead."

The downstairs party was the faint rumble of a distant city.

"I can't know *all* the dead," Snug scoffed. "That would be . . . vast. I'm only one soul. If that's the right word."

"I don't expect you to know everyone. But you are here and I am here. I expect you are here for a reason."

Oh, he was vain. "And the reason is you?"

The man was silent. He hadn't considered he *wouldn't* be the reason.

He was always the reason. His hands were in his lap, his fingers laced. One thumb over the other. They reversed. The quiet shift seemed tremendous in the otherwise still room.

She couldn't help but smile, even as she continued her relentless undulation, always a gently moving pool. "You are an important man?"

"Yes," he answered without a thought, but with a hint of suspicion. "I am important."

She touched one hand to her chin. "Not to me."

"But to these people here." This was a defensive schoolboy talking to a teacher. "To people in Los Angeles and London, I am. To people in New York. This party is mine."

"And this is my home," Snug stated. He stared as her silhouette stuttered, then returned brighter. She could see her own hands flicker. "My aunt's house, and uncle's. My mother and my brother's. You are not important to them."

"No, I suppose not."

"But you came here. You came for me. Not the other way around." She gathered herself straight, improved her posture.

"In that sense, you are right. I sought ghosts and look what I have discovered."

"Discovered?" She laughed. "But I have no message for you."

"In tales, ghosts lead to gold. They have apologies and confessions. They have secrets."

"I have no gold," she insisted.

"But you have secrets," he prodded. "You know what it is to be dead."

"Do I? Or do I merely know what it is to not be alive?"

He was vexed. His thumbs reversed again. Snug didn't need breath, but she needed him to breathe. She considered reaching out to his shoulder, to push him, to get him to inhale.

Then he spoke: "There is a difference?"

She wished she could give him more than her narrow knowledge. "There is a chasm between them," she said. "At least in my experience. But I don't know what's on the other side any more than you."

She couldn't stay in the room any longer, not with him, not with his fears, not with his memories, and she willed herself to leave. Yet in the last moment of her presence in the bedroom, she heard, distinctly, not the whimper of a terrified man or a cry of pain, but a note she did not expect: a laugh, a clear and hearty laugh bouncing about the walls and following her through the ether like a puppy on her heels, a quick and buoyant peal.

36

THE WAITER CALLED RENFRO stood in front of Pete, holding an empty platter to his chest. "We've lost Mr. Hitchcock." His voice was tight.

"What?" Pete craned around him, but Addams was gone, up the stairs and out of view.

Renfro grimaced. "Mr. Buck told me to tell you." He bit his lip. "And Mr. Larmon. And Mr. Allardice."

Addams hadn't been exaggerating.

Pete looked at Renfro—his slicked-back hair, the makeup bags beneath his eyes, his dramatic pallor—yet under the getup was just a guy who thought he'd made a job-losing goof-up. Except this was a one-night gig and Renfro didn't really have to worry about that as much as Pete, who could see tomorrow's headline: Famous Director Disappears at Ghoulish Party.

That would cost somebody his job. Goodbye, Young & Rubicam.

"Where'd you see him last?" He worked to suppress his panic. Everything was fine. Yep.

The waiter pondered. "The first-floor cake table. He likes that. But maybe he went farther up the house? He wouldn't be . . . speedy."

Pete thanked him, then hustled across the rest of the room, hitting the stairs and leaving the bustle of the party behind him. This was the staircase between the second-floor parlor and the third floor, which had mostly bedrooms—the doctor's bedroom, in particular—and the library. If he could find Carolyn, they could come up with a plan. Split up the house in quadrants and find the fool. Oh, that was unkind. Find the . . . guest of honor.

Pete peeked into the library. No Snug. No Satterthwaite. But there was Henry Fonda collapsed in one of the reading chairs. Passed out? No, his eyes were open, his attention upward. Pete had a fleeting thought of the mannequin in the bedroom, right down the hall. This was not how he pictured the leading man.

Footsteps loud in the quiet room, he approached the actor as he would approach a lounging lion. Fonda acknowledged him with a dip of his chin but kept his gaze on the ornate ceiling and beyond, a few mere stories of wood and brick between him and the starry sky all but obliterated by the million burning bulbs of New York. The actor was more incandescent than the actual stars. In the badly lit room, reclined in his terrible posture, he still had an aura. Pete slunk into the adjacent seat and leaned toward the actor. "Mr. Fonda," Pete ventured, "have you seen Mr. Hitchcock?"

"I think I've been drunk for about a week now, and I figured it might sober me up to sit in a library," Fonda said in a voice Pete recognized. It was disconcerting to spend the night with men he'd never met, yet felt he had known for years, simply because of their celebrity.

"Has it?" Pete watched Fonda's profile, the actor's eyes still focused north.

"A little bit, I think. I can't tell yet. Did I tell you about the books? They're real." He waved to the walls crowded with volumes. "Medical texts. Stoddard's *Lectures*. Encyclopedias."

"You thought they'd be fake?" A sole heavy volume lay open on the large oak table that occupied the center of the room, its legs like thick trunks under the broad top.

"The whole place looks like a set," Fonda said. "Facades. Spines with nothing behind them." He brought his cocktail to his lips, a nearly spent Bloody Mary with a sad stalk of celery listing against the rim like a seasick sailor. "I was wrong," he said over the rim, his voice muffled. He drank.

Pete stood and walked to the table and leaned over the book. It was enormous, the pages yellowed, the font ornate. The words were German. He couldn't read it but admired the illuminated letters at the top of each page. It was a Bible. He didn't remember Carolyn mentioning her aunts being particularly religious. Pete turned back and was unsettled by the actor's gaze. "I'll leave you to your thoughts," he said and moved to the door.

As Pete passed, Fonda caught his wrist, his grip tight. "The stuff in this house is real, isn't it?"

The quaver in the actor's voice made Pete jerk his arm away. Maybe he shouldn't have done that; Fonda was a big deal. Would he complain? But the fire in his blue eyes was too much. It gave Pete the willies.

"I don't know what you mean," Pete said. "The house is real. Real is real. But what's fake is fake, you know?"

"I don't know," Fonda said, his voice dropping. "That's my problem. I don't know."

Pete needed to leave the library. Hitchcock wasn't here. That was the task at hand. Stay focused. He focused on the light from the hall as a beacon.

"I don't appreciate the getup—" Fonda said.

Pete stopped and turned. "I'm sorry?"

"On the woman in the bedroom." He waved his hand. "It's in poor taste."

"What woman?"

"The one with the blood." Fonda shuddered, a genuine revulsion. He took another sip and shook his head. "Too much for a party, don't you think? No matter what Hitch wants."

Pete steadied himself on the doorjamb. The ship was swaying. Sweat gathered at the back of his neck, between his white collar and his undershirt. His tie was constricting, a tie he'd bought just for this event, blue diamonds on a maroon field. It felt like a noose.

"I'll make sure she tones it down," he said.

Whoever she was. Wilcox hadn't hired any second actress as far as he knew, and nobody was *bloody*. The dummy in the bed was a man, the corpse on the dining room table was clearly a mannequin, too, and unblemished. Snug wasn't bloody—transparent, yes, but not bloody. The old actress. Perhaps she was a little bloody. A scratch on her head after she fell. But she was outside.

Pete walked, dazed, into the hallway and paused. He forced his head to clear, like a man waking up in the middle of a crosswalk, terrified of traffic, but standing in an empty street. The hall was deserted, and he'd left the movie star alone in the library, staring at nothing but air.

37

THE BROKAW MANSION ON Fifth Avenue was no place to work alone on a gloomy March evening, yet Seymour Barnes bivouacked on the second floor, in a large room crowded with tables, stacked with transformers and receivers, black wires coiling like snakes over the parquet. In another life, it had served as the late Mrs. Brokaw's parlor. The intricate woodwork was gleaming even a decade after the Institute of Radio Engineers bought the mansion, years with irregular moppings and a lot less buffing. Few families wanted the upkeep of this sort of behemoth, not in the modern era. A French chateau on the Upper East Side didn't look right anymore, if it ever did, and selling it to the Institute for a laboratory was no stranger than the rest of its story.

Hired fresh out of Columbia University nearly a decade prior, Seymour Barnes had worked his way from junior assistant to mid-management by being the first in and the last to leave every day. Hunting spirits didn't pay the bills, engineering did, but use of the equipment after hours was the real reason he worked so diligently. He applied it to the *other* institute in his life, the American Psychical Research Institute. Tonight was extraordinary. Reading about Hitchcock's haunted party in the *Times* on his subway ride that morning, he analyzed his meeting with the admen a few weeks earlier. He'd told them what he felt was the truth, what his research had pointed to, but all day he felt a buzz, anticipation hooked on him like burrs, a dozen little prickles he couldn't shake off. Despite the odds, he sensed they'd found the right place—and it was right in his neighborhood.

Heat gathering under his bulky headphones, a clear voice cut through the storm of static crowding Seymour's airwaves, jolting the machine of his own concoction, his as-yet-unpatented psychic receptor. A woman, not young, but not old either, who spoke with an educated accent, perhaps English, perhaps American of a certain class, had something to tell someone. A someone named Hank.

"Well, all right, Hank." That was it. Pretty simple.

Heard once, it was a curiosity; heard twice, it was a shock. Heard a dozen times and it was an unnerving circuit; heard a hundred and it was among the spookiest things Seymour had experienced. This wasn't the first time he'd picked up disembodied voices. Ham radio operators, overseas broadcasts, French Canadians and Mexicans, across their respective borders and blabbing away in their different Romance languages, crossed over. But this wasn't like that. Seymour bent farther over the hulking receiver, gunmetal gray, spotted with buttons and arrayed in plastic-coated wires. He tried to quiet his stumbling pulse. He was terrified and delighted.

"Well, all right, Hank," the woman agreed—surrendered—capitulated again and again.

"Well, all right, Hank," she said. Seymour felt it was anything but. Her voice feigned steadiness, but the timbre was unpleasantly taut. His grandmother would have noticed it right away, whatever ailed this woman, and fixed up one of her old New England potions. It was she who'd convinced Seymour of the spirit world, despite the protestations of his parents. They had been pragmatists, a pharmacist and a high school biology teacher. Seymour followed suit, as a scientist, but never forgot his grandmother. This lab gave him tools. He knew someday he'd encounter such a phenomenon, but he didn't expect her palpable grief. This woman was pretending, pretending very hard to be okay.

There was more static, a spin of a celestial dial, and then a new tone, soft and slow.

"Snug," a man's voice whispered. "Snug, are you still here?"

Seymour snatched the headphones off as if they'd seared his ears. He tossed them across the desk. They skittered, careened into a short stack of reports, and landed on the floor with a thud in a brief shower of graph paper. It wasn't like him to mistreat his equipment. He normally mothered, nestling them in padded cloth when they weren't in use. But the distress of the woman's voice, the shock of hearing the man's, it was too much like claustrophobia.

The cord torn from the headset dangled uselessly off the operator's board, a broken leash.

He hustled down the impressive staircase, glanced at the dark carved wood of the landing. Crown moldings, wainscotting, stained glass, and all of it felt dipped in amber. Seymour's people in Maine hadn't cared for vain trappings. He was always a little embarrassed by the extravagance, but now he was frightened by it. He caught his breath in the marble-floored foyer and waited for the woman's refrain to catch up to him and chase him out of the house like a lick of fire hunting paper.

He stepped onto the sidewalk, patting his pockets for a cigarette. He knew what was going on around the block, on Eightieth, a line of double-parked limos and a Mutual Broadcasting truck. He took a few steps, drawn to the commotion. Seymour didn't really like crowds up close. He liked things at a distance. That's why he loved radio. But there were other engineers at the party, fellas he would know in the tall house. As he approached, he saw every window lit up like a Christmas tree. He did a double take at a man in a suit of armor walking toward him, then crossing the street. What was happening there?

He shivered again, this time because it was chillier than he'd expected. He should go back and grab his jacket. The carousing in the town house clashed with the morose castle behind him. His workplace looked more welcoming to ghosts than the party. What had happened to Mrs. Brokaw, after she wasn't Mrs. Brokaw any longer? She married famous. An actor. Henry Fonda, that was it. Ended up divorced. Was she dead? Is that what Seymour had been told? He couldn't pinpoint it, other than that he'd read about her in the society pages, years ago, and his mother had made a comment about how wealth couldn't protect anyone from mundane tragedies. Dead daughters and unfaithful spouses, things like that.

He ground the butt of his spent cigarette on the cement and vowed to go back to the castle, tidy up the gear, and go home. Go have a quiet night outside the lab.

That was a lie. The voices were making him itchy. He had to investigate.

"Well, all right, Hank."

Nothing was *all right* or *well* about it. Seymour felt it in his bones. He steeled himself and turned back to the mansion, surprised how far he'd wandered, and ran to the front door. He sprinted up every floor, flipped off the lights, and made rounds like a zookeeper closing up shop. Goodnight to the monkeys and lions. Goodnight to the transmitters and receivers, to the circuit breakers and the wax and the metal that made the tumult of the radios run. To the coolants and the hot new ideas. To his colleagues and the pleasure of solitary work, even on a gloomy Wednesday evening in March.

He would go up Eightieth and stroll by the party, keep to the other side of the street, and maybe he would spot somebody famous. Everyone knew Grace Kelly lived practically next door.

Maybe he would see Hitchcock.

Seymour locked the front door and swore the woman's refrain rode the breeze, one last time, even with all his machines upstairs dark and still. "Well, all right, Hank." He shook it off, a fleeting rancid scent. "Well, all right, Hank." Seymour walked off into the shadows, a hint of rain about to fall, moisture clinging in unpredictable eddies to the New York air.

Maybe he would see that young guy from Young & Rubicam.

Maybe Seymour would tell him that he had been wrong.

There *were* spirits in Manhattan, and Seymour had a good idea right where he could find them.

38

ON THE QUIET FOURTH floor Carolyn bumped into Charles Addams spiraling into panic. Then Pete appeared, looking as jittery as the artist, dark lines settling between his brows. She sensed he was about to ask her a question when, as if by magic, Barbara Addams materialized, her red lipstick freshly applied—Fire & Ice, of course—and her dress as tight as a mummy's wrappings. Carolyn wondered how she appeared so silently, but Charles whisked into the nearest bedroom with a loudly whispered "Alfred! Alfred!" as if he were interrupting the mighty director cracking a safe. When he didn't find him, Addams swooped out of that bedroom and into the next. Pete shot Carolyn a tense glance and they jogged to keep up; Bad Barbara didn't even try. She waltzed down the corridor sipping her drink, her lean face gleaming, her smile sly. "Darling," she said in a languid voice, "I'm sure Hitch is just fine."

Addams popped over the threshold shaking his head. "He's not in this one." He loped down the narrow hall and knocked on a bathroom door. They listened to him whisper-hiss-cajole "Alfred! Alfred!" again and he flung open the door. His shoulders slumped. "Empty."

Barbara snickered.

The parade careened into the third bedroom. It was dim, but clearly unoccupied. Still, Charles raced to the far side, peeked behind the curtains—too narrow to hide Hitch's girth if they'd been sewed three times their size—and even dropped to peer under the bed. The musty air was a mix of stale dust and faint perfume. A breeze behind Barbara had propelled her scent before her, a servant strewing garlands at the feet of the forthcoming queen.

"I need to get back to Miss Havisham. Can you come?" Carolyn whispered. "I feel like we're hunting a Heffalump."

Pete let out a muffled snort.

"What's so funny?" Addams asked. "What could possibly be funny now?"

"You, dear," Barbara said. "You're a crack-up." She sipped her martini. "Or cracking up." She turned her cat's eyes to Pete.

"There's nothing funny about a man missing—under strange circumstances—at his own party," Addams snapped.

"I wasn't laughing at you, Mr. Addams," Pete explained. "Or Mr. Hitchcock. It was Carolyn's face. She didn't like the stuffy air in here. Am I right, Carolyn?"

"So stuffy," she said.

Addams heaved a sigh and hurried from the room, and they followed him, reluctant ducklings, to the fourth, even smaller, bedroom. It was lit by a frail table lamp near the door, but streetlight spilled through a window on the far side. The shade was half-raised and the space above the sill revealed a screenless gap. To Carolyn, it looked like a wound. She thrust aside the image and scolded herself for being absurd. Noises from the sidewalk below carried to them. A siren in the distance. Conversations at the curb ebbed, then grew again. She linked her arm with Pete's and gently tugged.

"There's nothing here," Carolyn whispered, turning to the hallway.

"Well, that's what we thought," Pete said, hesitation in his tone, "*before*, too."

"Before what?" Barbara blurted.

Addams ignored them and crossed swiftly to the open window. "Oh, dear lord," he gasped, "what's that?"

Pete and Carolyn, frozen at the threshold, watched him throw a hand over his mouth. Addams pointed to the sill. "That." They hurried to the window; Barbara slunk to his other side. She tilted her head and squinted.

A splattering of something wet, like a thin splash of faintly blue paint, covered the wood frame. A small splotch made a cloud like a Rorschach test along the bottom of the glass. It glistened, whatever it was. Addams took a tentative step closer and held out his shaking index finger, then he ran it along the ledge like a butler testing for dust. He held the tip under the pale light and shuddered. "It's still warm." It didn't run down his hand; it was thicker than milk. He swallowed. "Hitch . . . he . . . *combusted*."

Barbara guffawed. "Combusted?" Her sly smile returned.

Addams swiveled to his wife, his tainted finger held high. "Yes," he hissed. "Exploded."

Carolyn stood in an expectant hush. Pete was petrified beside her.

"That," Barbara said, "is ridiculous."

Addams waggled his glistening finger. "He was flaunting his belief in it earlier. I think he had a premonition!"

She shook her head. "You've lost your mind."

"This is all that's left of him!" Addams insisted, holding the proof in front of her face.

And then Barbara leaned in and licked his finger like a Popsicle. Carolyn gasped. Pete choked. Addams's eyes grew three times their size.

Barbara ran her tongue along her Revloned lips and smiled. "Just what I thought."

Addams stared at his now clean finger and back at his wife, then back to his finger. His cheeks had lost their color.

"It's not Hitch, honey," she said. "It's frosting."

Pete pushed around them both and went to the sill. He knelt and smelled the wood—one of the stranger things Carolyn had ever seen a man do—and nodded.

"Someone was eating *cake* here," he said.

Barbara tapped playfully at her husband's arm. "That's not death," she said. "It's sugar."

Carolyn laughed. "Mr. Addams may not be right about Hitchcock blowing up, but I think we can guess he's been here." They all turned to her. "Who else would hide out and eat dessert far from the sight of witnesses?"

Addams's shoulders slumped in relief. "I really thought he was gone," he mumbled.

"You really thought he was *goo*." Barbara marched out of the room and Addams tagged behind, glancing one last time at the sill, perhaps still not entirely convinced Hitch hadn't burst over the sidewalk in a shower of gastrointestinal brilliance.

"What a drawing it would make," Addams said. Carolyn sensed his spirit lift. "Hitch will be fine." He went on, inspired and defensive: They'd never been concerned, only he cared about his friend, but what a concept he had now—a spontaneous combustion panel for his wicked little family. *The New Yorker* would love it. He wasn't the same man who'd entered the room. He was joyous.

The Addamses strolled away, oblivious the younger couple hadn't followed.

Pete was staring at the wallpaper, faded flowers, but Carolyn doubted he was inspecting the pattern. "You okay?"

"It's nothing." But he anxiously ran his hand over his hair. "No, it's Henry Fonda. I saw him earlier. Can't get it out of my head."

She raised an eyebrow.

"Long story," he said. "Weird guy."

"We're surrounded by them," Carolyn said, trying to make light of it. He gave a wan smile. "Have you heard anything about Miss Havisham?" She was whispering, as if they were discussing state secrets. Ridiculous.

"No," Pete admitted.

Her patience was unraveling. Hitchcock sneaks off for cake and everyone dissolves. A woman actually collapses and these men hardly bat an eye. She couldn't shake a fuzzy and familiar sense of nearing disaster. Her mother's descent at the hospital, cloudy eyes and tousled gray hair. Agnes's frail touch and her whispered condolences the last time she visited the bank.

A gust of burning wicks and cigarettes drifted up the stairs, mingled with the house's miasma of dust and worn wood. Sick women on her brain, Carolyn tried to shake them out, but all she gained was a rattle in her skull, not an answer.

Frances Ford Seymour, when she had been Mrs. George Brokaw, lived off and on for seven years in the terrible castle on the corner of Fifth Avenue and Seventy-Ninth Street. She never imagined she would return to the neighborhood. George and his booze spoiled so much, even the Upper East Side of Manhattan. He had drowned long ago. Their daughter, Pan, was grown and married. And Frances, well, Frances—lastly, Frances Fonda—was dead. She hadn't imagined any of these endless moments after her death either, this afterlife of pointless floating, weightless, buoyed in any warm current that might catch her. Her spirit, if that's what she called it, was cooler than the rest of the world, than all the matter of the living—even Hank, and he was a cold, cold man.

After she slit her throat, Frances expected relief.

She didn't get it.

And what had called her back tonight? And why this place around the corner from the castle? It meant nothing to her while she was alive. Had she strolled this block? Certainly. Had she gazed at the limestone house and wondered about its occupants, the doctor and his wife, childless and old-fashioned? The sad sister-in-law and the news of her husband's sordid affairs and his ludicrous ending, more ludicrous for its parallel to her own. She knew who lived here; they had been a part of the neighborhood as steady and unremarkable as the trees and the curbs.

And regarding sordid stories, who was she to talk? Her husband had his women. The one from Imperial Valley with the babe in her arms, Hank's child if anyone believed the girl (and Frances did). Of course, Frances had her own men and her own anger. Trapped with the children while Hank worked and worked, any excuse to escape them. Their daughter was aloof, but their son acted out, with matches and guns and hijinks that nannies might excuse as nothing more than ruffian play, but Frances knew better. When the pastures at Tigertail burned, those California acres with the citrus trees that Hank had planted with his own strong hands, crooked and charred by his boy's errant match, the salty Pacific breeze wafting over the murdered fields, she wished she'd struck the flame herself. Peter may have been merely thoughtless, but Frances longed for premeditation.

Then there was Greenwich, Connecticut, and the drafty old house he'd put them up in while he played on Broadway. The Count Palenclar Estate, it was christened, all shadowy angles and grim corners. Frances was reduced again, just another wife in an attic, trapped and going mad, while her man played king of the castle.

She stole the razor from that house when they'd let her out of the sanitarium for a weekend. It seemed fitting, the blade had once rested in the drawer of the bathroom she and Hank had shared.

Not long before that time, he sat her down, spoke in his most reasonable voice, the one all America considered stalwart, and asked her for a divorce. She had answered him with equanimity, "Well, all right, Hank."

She was forty-two and he was marrying a woman half her age. Damn him.

Before the blade did its work and the blood came to pool, she wrote notes. To her doctor. To the nurse. To Peter and Jane, apologizing, trying to explain. But to Hank? Absolutely nothing. She had taken care of him. Cut him out of her will. Struck him off the list of people to whom she owed any rationale or kindness. She would die and he could live with whatever guilt he might muster, which she knew would be sparse. He was a pragmatist, a man from the Middle West who understood that to travel swiftly meant packing lightly and guilt was simply another weight in a bag. Jettison that useless drag as soon as you can.

Now he was done with the last one, Susan, and was on to the Italian girl.

Tonight, Frances had a message. *Remember me, Hank. I'm all right after all, but don't let me catch you crying. Crying is disgusting—as you said, any number of times.*

George might have hit her, drunk until the rage came, but he was always repentant. Hank never believed he'd sinned. He was simply doing his job, pretending. Pretending: cowboy, soldier, lover, husband.

All right, Hank, everything's all right after all.

Igor Imagines *THE COVER-UP*, A Screenplay

EXT. The Courtyard. The OLD ACTRESS lay awake but corpse-still on a chaise lounge. The rest of the furniture—a pair of chairs, another lounger, a short table—is covered by heavy off-white tarps. The tarp that had been on the exposed chaise lounge is tossed to the side, a huddled bundle like a distraught baby elephant. The private garden is enclosed by ivy-covered brick walls, more tendril than leaf. PETE, BOB BUCK, DAN WILCOX, a TRIO of other Young & Rubicam managers, and ORLANDO, the photographer, gather in a semicircle ten feet from the woman.

>BUCK
>No ambulance. We don't want that sort of publicity. The Bufferin Boys already nixed that.

>PETE
>And if the old woman dies? That'll be worse.

>BUCK
>Don't speak of it.

He hushes them all with a glare and wave of his hand, like a pirate slicing air with a cutlass.

>BUCK (cont'd)
>Don't you dare even think it.

>ORLANDO
>Mayhem's always a bit of fun.

They all look at him. He shrugs.

>ORLANDO (cont'd)
>Good for business.

                    WILCOX
               Maybe yours.

He turns to Buck.

                    WILCOX (cont'd)
               We'll tell guests it was a stunt.
               They'll want to believe it's a stunt.

                    BUCK
               But only if Hitch is directing. *Buck
               turns to Pete.* Nobody wants undirected
               mayhem. We need everyone to believe
               he's behind it.

                    PETE
               And Hitchcock?

                    BUCK
               He needs to believe we're *not* behind
               it. Blame somebody else.

*All the men turn to look at Pete. Pete puts his
hand over the lens of Orlando's camera, as if
covering a microphone, too.*

                    PETE
               He's already paranoid about somebody
               pulling one over on him.

                    BUCK and WILCOX
               Who?

                    PETE
               Disney.

The men stare at him.

                    WILCOX
               Walt? M-I-C—

                    BUCK
               K-E-Y Disney?

                    PETE
               Uh-huh. He thinks you might be in
               cahoots.

Wilcox turns to Buck.

                    WILCOX
               Make it work for us.

Buck turns to Pete.

                    BUCK
               Make it work for us.

                    PETE
               I'm your man, sir.

CAROLYN arrives and kneels by the old woman's side. Buck, Wilcox, and the other admen disperse like startled flies. Pete remains. The photographer steps to his side.

                    ORLANDO
               Let your conscience be your guide!

He laughs and exits, singing "When You Wish Upon a Star." PETE glances at CAROLYN, then follows the other men into the house. The waiter stands by the draped furniture and tousled baby elephant, simply another aspect of the silent, shrouded décor.

39

MISS HAVISHAM RESTED IN the narrow, brick-enclosed courtyard. Carolyn, perched on an upside-down flowerpot, held her hand. The old woman's skin was paper thin and fragile, tiny bird bones and veins, just as Carolyn's mother's had been in her last days. The actress studied the young woman with her misty but fierce blue eyes squinted into an accusation. "You," she whispered, "you know the other girl, the glowing girl."

Carolyn straightened. "What are you talking about?" She withdrew her hand. "What girl?"

"The glowing girl," the old woman said with drill-bit eyes and a curt nod.

Carolyn's heart jumped like she'd touched a hot stove. She had no idea the old woman had spotted her among the guests, let alone spotted her with Snug. The panic in her pulse was unwelcome and erratic. She felt her eyes widen to the size of dinner plates and turned to check on the men across the courtyard. Wilcox was browbeating an underling. It wasn't a good sign.

Carolyn neatened the crepe sleeve of the woman's mourning dress. She had difficulty speaking around the lump in her throat. "I don't know what you mean—"

One of Johnny's tinkling piano riffs floated over the humid night air, then dissipated like mist. A werewolf's howl was next, a cry from across rooms.

"The girl who glows," the old woman insisted. "You saw her, too."

"She speaks," spoke a familiar voice from behind Carolyn's back, "of Grace, of course."

Carolyn turned to see Hitchcock behind her, his fingers laced and resting over his round belly, a sparkle in his eye, as if he were playing a clever trick. He hadn't combusted. And he was giving Carolyn cover? He was up to something, but she couldn't very well accuse him when he was helping her.

"You can't meet her now," he said, looking directly at the old woman, a gentle but condescending lilt to his voice. "She's shortly setting sail for Monaco."

Miss Havisham pushed against the pillow tucked behind her back and tried to sit up. "That's not what I was—"

"Fans," Hitchcock continued, barreling over her correction. He spoke conspiratorially to Carolyn but clearly wanted Havisham to hear. "The things fans will say—and do—to get a closer look."

"I don't want a closer look," the woman said, rising on her elbows. "I don't need a movie star. I want to know what I saw—what she saw, too!"

Carolyn flushed. She hated what she was about to do, the gaslighting she was about to commit. "I didn't see anything. I'm sorry." She knelt by the woman's side, like kneeling in a confessional. "I really don't know what else to say to you."

"Tell me I'm not hallucinating," the old woman said. "I was hired to be morose, not crazy."

"You're not crazy," Carolyn said, remembering what she'd said to Bella a day earlier. It felt like months ago. There had to be some comfort she could give without endangering Snug.

Was it Snug she was protecting? Or Pete? Herself? The party? She wasn't certain anymore.

"Even if you can't have Grace—" offered Hitchcock, stepping closer, his hand briefly on Carolyn's shoulder. It was a light pressure, then lifted, as if it had never been there, a strange absence. "—I have hopes," he said, "there will always be another."

Carolyn watched his mouth twitch, hardly a perceptible flinch. Here was a man trying to convince himself, as much as he spoke to the bewildered old woman, that one glowing girl was interchangeable with any other.

Grace, she imagined in his brain. Snug, she imagined in her own. Then: her mother. There will never be another you.

"You're not hallucinating," Carolyn told the woman, but made sure Hitch would hear. "It just may not be what you think it was."

The old woman lay back on the faded blue cushion. "It was terrifying." She closed her eyes and shut them out.

Carolyn's stomach twisted; she hated lying to the old woman. It was like lying to her mother, to Bella. To every woman who'd ever been told she wasn't seeing what was clearly in front of her face. But if she told this woman the truth about Snug, where would it leave them, all of them?

Hitchcock took a step back, nodded to Carolyn, and retreated into a growing crowd attracted by distraction and chittering like a murder of crows.

She watched him go, the familiar waddle, and fought the impulse to chase after him the way Addams had flung himself from room to room and ask him what to do. He was the director, after all. Everybody wanted answers from the Great Man, to know what he knew, to let him guide the moment, and not even Carolyn, she was dismayed to discover, was immune to his sway.

Walter Taylor trembled at the front door of the blazing limestone, every window lit up for guests. He remembered a long-ago trip to Canada to marry Martha, formerly Mrs. Martha Leavitt Morgan—oh, what a mouthful. The other Mrs. Taylor. The cold of that September morning. The welcome comfort of the sleeping berths. She was gay on the passage north. He had told her his former wife was seething but had reluctantly allowed for the divorce—which was true, he simply had yet to make it finalized. Divorce, to the first Mrs. Taylor, his Mariah, was a deeply shameful wound, and Walter's betrayal had left her in an enduring rage. Walter vowed Martha would never see Mariah's disgust. When the justice of the peace in Montreal had them fill out the forms that afternoon, Walter froze, the nib of his pen hovering above the paper. "Widowed," he scrawled on the form. "Widowed."

The justice didn't need to know his life, he needed to give Walter and Martha his blessing. Rather, his seal of approval. Walter didn't care about blessings. Those were a younger man's concerns, a first marriage's concerns.

It wasn't all a lie. Mrs. Martha Leavitt Morgan really was a widow—John Hewitt Morgan, her husband, once his friend at the brokerage—had died several years earlier. That's how they had met; she was simply the handsome wife of a colleague. In moments of rare honesty, at least to himself, he knew they should have remained no more intimate than that.

A week after their elopement, one mundane morning, a man from the *Times* came calling to his Wall Street office. *Is it true you eloped with Mrs. John Morgan? But were you divorced, Mr. Taylor? Do you know bigamy is illegal in this country? Why have you kept this secret, Mr. Taylor? Tell our readers: Does your first wife know you married another woman, Mr. Taylor?*

"We've done nothing wrong. We've gone through all the proper channels, though it's none of your damn business!" he had spat, then closed the door, but not before the reporter lodged his scuffed boot against the jamb. Walter wished he'd pushed harder, made the fellow scream, but instead the man had grinned.

"You called yourself a widower on the marriage license, sir. Is that a translation error? Perhaps there's a French word for a man who marries twice but forgets to divorce the first wife?"

Walter dislodged the reporter's foot, then slammed the door with enough vigor to make the office shake.

The man kept at it, cackling and knocking. Eventually he grew bored and left.

Walter sat at his desk and tapped his fingers on the leather blotter.

Mariah would never forgive him. She would make him pay in every way possible.

He and Mrs. Morgan lived together for the next seven years, then she died. Alone, after the turbulence of his choices, did he have regrets? Perhaps.

Alas, he would never outlive Mariah.

And all the while the lawyers battled. How much did he owe her? A few thousand dollars? A hundred thousand? Two hundred thousand? The settlement was worth more than his seat on the Exchange. $284,485.59, to be exact. He had marveled at the amount. Who hadn't? And again the newspaper men crowded at his door. *Did you promise her money when you left, Mr. Taylor? Do you care about your child, Mr. Taylor?*

Another headline in the *Times*.

It had been *children* when he deserted her. We had two, he thought. But poor Snug. Thank God, she didn't live to see all of this. She saw enough. He did regret living with Mrs. Morgan and her children, and all but ignoring Snug and Curzon, back with their mother on Eightieth Street, living under the protection of Mariah's terrifying sister, Isabella, and her supercilious husband, the doctor. Satterthwaite! A do-gooder. An intellectual. Surgeons were baloney. Hacks. They dealt in impossibilities. You can't make a body right again. Just delaying the inevitable. And then acting like they were miracle-makers. Snug didn't benefit from living with a doctor when the Spanish flu came. A hearty girl, prime of life, and she was gone in a weekend. Walter never said goodbye. There was no opportunity.

That was a lie. There had been time and world enough. He left

Mariah in 1911. Snug passed in 1919. Eight years of avoiding the girl, Walter. There's your truth. And what's the word for a man who abandons his children, in any language? Who is widowed now, sir?

A walk in the park cleared his mind, set his resolve. The gun in his apartment, a service revolver, though he never served, not in that way, waited in a bureau drawer. He'd sent Mrs. Albrechtsen on an errand. Tea, was it? A loaf of bread he'd never eat and doubted she would either. But then she returned before he had a chance to do it. He heard her in the pantry.

He supposed she would hear the shots. He pulled twice. He didn't think he'd have to do that.

He was still alive when she stepped into his bedroom, though missing a good piece of his skull.

His last letters play in his dreams like a quartet. He could have left a fifth, a letter to Mariah. He considered it. No, that would be poor taste. And why would she have cared?

He was sorry to have it end this way. Life hadn't been all bad.

And then it didn't end.

He continued. Despite his efforts, he wasn't *gone* at all.

He waited at the front door. Should he ring the bell? Should he make a grand entrance. Should he even enter?

He gripped the hat in his hands. He wasn't dressed for the occasion, though at least he had worn his best suit. Once upon a time, it had been a very fine suit. Very fine.

The wind swirled and he felt it on his cheeks, yes, sensed its cold, a welcome sting though instinctively he sought warmth. He stepped through the door without opening it and wondered who he might meet on the other side.

40

ON THE THRESHOLD OF the French doors between the courtyard and the hallway to the gallery, Charles Addams clutched Alfred Hitchcock like the prodigal son. "So good to see you," he mumbled over Hitch's head, "so good." The affection was smothering, but fortunately brief. "Thank goodness you're in one piece, Hitch."

"I do better that way." Hitchcock retreated, but was still within Addams's long reach.

"You just don't realize what we—" Addams gushed, but his attention snagged on movement across the courtyard. "Oh. New York's Finest."

Hitchcock swiveled to follow Addams's attention. A clutch of police officers clustered around Miss Havisham. He felt a breeze of fear cross his face, his childhood mistrust of men in uniform, then banished it under bogus bonhomie. "We should welcome them!"

Addams withdrew to the other side of the panes and sniffed. "They look like the Keystone Cops." The men in blue shuffled forward, then back. None of the Y&R boys intervened. The men in blue reordered themselves, three to the left, two to the right, then reversed, all the while taking notes and nattering. A pair branched off and then collided as they inspected a narrow passage at the side of the yard.

Hitchcock chortled, as if he were watching a pantomime. "Goodness. They haven't learned basic physics. Objects can't share the same space."

Addams shook his head. "I can't watch. These men have guns."

Hitchcock folded his hands, like Friar Tuck on Savile Row. "The American police system has always bamboozled me. Our bobbies aren't armed. They have nightsticks, but no way to shoot the average Englishman, be he criminally inclined or not. They might beat you about the legs now and then, but nothing fatal. Here, it seems the authorities are allowed, even encouraged, to shoot the citizenry. And they call my films frightening. Your countrymen don't see horror when it's staring them in the face. Say, at a traffic stop. Or unannounced at their front door."

Addams followed Hitch as they strolled back inside, two gentlemen of means touring an estate, eager to leave the hubbub behind.

"Americans *adore* horror," Addams said. "Take my macabre little family. Grim jokes and bloody implications. But nothing real. Actual tragedy? We pretend that doesn't exist. Americans are Victorians at heart, sharply dressed prudes who insist nothing is amiss in our own houses, but everyone else's is stuffed with malice."

"I quibble with 'sharply dressed' to describe any American. And everyone's house *is* more sinister than mine—what makes it terrifying is exactly its difference from my own. How can one be anything other than a stranger in a strange land in another's house? You have to look outside for true terror. If I had spooks in my house in Los Angeles, I wouldn't have needed to find them here. Of course, I have no spooks because I am a gentleman. I have Sealyham terriers. There are no *spectral* oddities on Bellagio Road."

"Hell is other people," Addams said, an eyebrow raised, a smile on the corners of his mouth. "I wish I'd said that first."

"Hell is other people's houses," Hitchcock amended. "I can't wait to leave this one, just to get back to my own and relish how delightfully normal it all is. That's the point of a party, isn't it?"

"Of course," Addams said. "*We* are always the normal ones."

They surveyed the room for their wives. Or for dessert. Or for simply a safe place to sit in someone else's home.

41

HENRY FONDA GLANCED AT his wristwatch. It was later than he'd thought. Why was he back in the library?

Called by a voice, no, voices, he had drifted upstairs, a beckoning. But whose voice was it? Susan? Jane? They were both in California. His mother? No, she was long dead. Something—someone—had coaxed him down the hall, a man lured by a siren, but a spectrum only he could hear. He stepped over the threshold and into yet another sitting room. Good god, there was one on every floor, so many divans, so many overstuffed chairs, all of them squatting sullen and dusty and there she was, the bloody woman. He bolted, then stumbled into the library. She hadn't followed him.

But here the bloody broad was back.

The young man from the ad agency had left and she had slipped in, as if to prove that *real was real*. This time Fonda got a clear look at her. She wasn't just any woman. He hadn't expected to see this lean face ever again, not this side of the cemetery: Frances, the mother of his children.

He felt his hand wobble and tried to steady the tremble. The ice in his glass clattered, the sound bouncing around the room. But the pale gray figure stayed still. Frances hovered a foot above the floor, the toes of her slim silk slippers skimming the Persian rug. The slippers he recognized from the days she'd spent entirely in her pajamas, a brocaded pair he'd given her one birthday. She was trying to speak, her lips moving, but she was a silent movie with no title cards. The ends of the scarf around her neck wafted and in the instant of recognition, Fonda knew she would take off the wrapping and he would never forget what he'd been avoiding for years.

They had been married, she had been alive, both of those states no longer true.

He watched her, but couldn't speak, his tongue anchored. *Oh, Frances, what do you want me to do? Frances, what did you do to yourself?* The ghost stared at him as if reading his thoughts.

She was Jacob Marley unwinding the cloth from around his head, his mouth falling open like a black chasm. But the chasm would be at her throat, slit ear-to-ear, that fatal, self-inflicted slash.

"Frances," Fonda muttered. "Frances, what the hell are you doing here?"

Down the hall, a woman's scream sliced through the party's din. Was it his own silent anguish manifest in someone else's cry?

The ghost didn't waver. She blinked. Once, twice. Then, like a bolt of lightning, she lit up ten times her brightness and flashed. He dropped his vodka and pulled the crook of his arm to his face. He fell to his knees, the rug slick and damp with booze and ice. The heavy glass didn't shatter, but rolled away from him, toward the ghost. There was a tilt to the old floor and gravity bent to where the dead woman floated.

Fonda pulled his face from his elbow and glanced to where she'd been. She was a dull shimmer, her hand raised to the end of her scarf. She tugged at it, a magician yanking a never-ending handkerchief from a hat. She pulled and pulled and the scarf unwound and then it drifted away, out of her hand. It should have dropped to the ground, but it didn't. It stayed in the air and Fonda watched as the woman turned her head and exposed the gash he knew would be there. She had drawn the razor across her neck and opened an artery; now it was nothing but an echo of her silent, open mouth, a dark maw where her throat should have been.

"Frances, you didn't have to do that," Fonda whimpered. "Nobody asked you to do that. Nobody. Not that. Not me."

She pointed at him. He felt the accusation thrust beneath his rib cage, a fiery ball of guilt, and was knocked to the floor. He curled into himself and felt his teeth grind. Then a gale blew across the room. Another girl flew across his vision: this one a different tone, a different temperature, her energy lighter, more pale blue than gray, and Frances sparked and darted and disappeared. Fonda felt her absence like a crater. In Frances's place was the girl, younger by decades. She floated to him, stretched out her arm, and he felt a touch on the top of his head, some benediction—but how could he feel it, when the girl was as thin as a cloud of steam?

She touched him and he felt calm. His legs quit shaking and his blood steadied.

And then she vanished, too.

42

CAROLYN WATCHED A HARRIED man in a rumpled suit stumble from the foyer into the gallery, his face a shade too pale to call healthy, a wilted lily in his hand. In his other, he sloshed a clear cocktail. The ice shimmied as he pointed backward with the drink. "I just saw someone walk through a wall," he stammered. "Just . . . went right through it."

Moments earlier, Charles Addams had accused his wife of upsetting the party, upsetting Hitchcock, upsetting everyone. She was the culprit, Carolyn learned, for most of the ills in Addams's world, inflation and auto problems included. The Hitchcocks had listened dispassionately, a pair waiting at a bus stop for all the distress they revealed.

"Oh, wonderful," Barbara said with relief, steadying the stranger before he fell on his nose. "A different suspect!"

"I really saw it," the man insisted. "One minute he's there in the room with me, the next, pfft, gone!"

Carolyn felt sorry for him. She *could* tell him, tell them all here right now, that Uncle Thomas meant no harm, and that might relieve them. Or might get her tossed in a padded cell.

Then Pete seemingly appeared from the ether and hustled to the newcomer's elbow, like a hospital orderly. "Maybe we should get you some fresh air."

The man studied him, then nodded. "Yeah, okay, sure." Befuddled, he patted his suit coat, looking for something important: car keys, a wallet, a map of Manhattan, a map of the night? She knew Pete was doing this to protect the party, keep things on an even keel, but there was gentleness in his approach as he and the man strolled to the courtyard. Fresh air for everyone who saw a spirit, as if the cold could clear brains of alcohol and phantoms.

Hitchcock hummed approvingly. "Your young man is doing that man a kindness."

Oh, he sounded like Aunt Bella! "He's not my young man," she protested.

"But he is kind," Alma said, moving to her side. "Never a quality to discount."

For a moment they had let their towering personas disappear. Carolyn understood how these two spoke to their daughter, imagined the conversations, the advice. She imagined her own mother would echo them. Kindness was not to be discounted.

"Was he drunk? Really?" Addams said, breaking her mood. "I'm not so sure. There's something going on here. I sense it. I think we all do. Come on, Hitch. What are you up to?"

Hitchcock's façade returned. "About the middle of your torso," he quipped.

"That's deflection. What's your gimmick?"

The director's posture stiffened; his next pronouncement was not going to be a joke.

"I don't need gimmicks, Charles," he said, insulted. "I'm better than that. If these were *my* ghosts, you'd all be running into the street. If I *really* wanted to scare you, of course I could. This isn't my weak tea. Maybe it's Disney's, maybe it's an adman's idea of a prank on the King of Pranks. It's not my *gimmick*."

"No offense meant, Hitch." Addams looked like a scolded boy.

Hitchcock flicked an invisible fly from his shoulder and tidied the knot of his tie. He forced his smile to return, a small uptick of his lips. "None taken," he said, but it sounded like deliberately bad acting. There *was* an offense. But the director was declaring the conversation over.

Pete returned and pulled on Carolyn's arm, his mouth bunched in a grimace. The patience she'd seen in him a minute before was gone. She tried to keep up as he led her by the elbow, as he'd done with the drunk guest, to the first-floor stairs.

"We have to get rid of her," he hissed.

"I agree. She needs to see a doctor." Carolyn gave a feeble smile to a couple who passed on the way to the gallery.

Pete waited for them to walk out of earshot. "No, not the old woman." His hand gripped the banister like the rail of a wave-tossed ship. "I mean Snug. She can't keep coming out and rattling the guests. We need her gone."

"She promised to stay out of our way."

He bent nearer, so close she could smell his aftershave. "Well, she lied."

"No," Carolyn said. "I wouldn't be so sure. That man said he saw a *he*. It could have been the doctor. And anyway, it's their house."

"Not tonight it isn't."

Carolyn stiffened. "I don't think she understands the idea of *renting* it for a night."

"Make her!" He was too loud. She took a step back.

"As if I have any control over what she does."

Pete bit his thumb. "It's just," he lowered his voice again, "she's going to mess it all up. They're already mad about Miss Havisham and the cops *somebody* called—" Mr. Buck was marching toward them. Pete gave her a pleading look. "This is so strange. I know you can't control her. I wish—this is so beyond anything I planned."

"Pete," she said, "it's not—"

And there was The Duck looming behind them. Pete sensed it and turned, intercepted him, and pulled his boss in the opposite direction. Carolyn was flummoxed. And furious. Fine. She could be helpful. She'd try to *summon* Snug, as if finding a ghost in this house when she wanted one was so easy. It wasn't like picking up the phone.

She was disappointed in Pete. The Hitchcocks would be disappointed in him! It made her want to laugh out loud, a bitter little bark. Her kind young man indeed.

She hopped up the narrow steps, a pair of flights, then dipped into the first bedroom she saw on the third floor. The only guest who seemed to notice her stealth was Oscar, the cat, who padded at her heels like a witch's familiar and slunk into the room right after her. He was supposed to be under guard.

Pete was right; Snug *had* broken her promise.

Something clinked across the room and Oscar lowered to a stalking crouch. Mice? Carolyn hated them. Or maybe it was a cockroach, a fleet of them. This was New York. Even the best places had bugs and rodents. Carolyn followed the cat to a mirrored armoire on the far wall. She hesitated, then opened the double doors and felt a twinge of sadness. How many outfits had it held in distant years? A few empty hangers hung in an otherwise barren space. A dentist peering into an old man's mouth would have recognized the view, a place once crowded now wrecked with age and absence. Oscar lost interest at patting under the wardrobe, then meowed at the air above them. The overhead light was off, but a Tiffany lamp burned on a small desk in the corner and its shade cast a shadow on the ceiling.

She could beckon Snug here. Perhaps she had found her bedroom, maybe Snug had spent hours here, not reading her uncle's research, but novels, stories from magazines. Carolyn knew she had a kinship with her, if only they had met in life—an impossibility, of course. But what was impossible once you met a ghost? Nothing. Anything can happen once you converse with a girl dead long before your birth.

"Snug," Carolyn whispered. "Snug, come back. I want to talk."

Oscar murmured, a question with a rolling "Err?"

She felt its sleek torso brush her ankles. "You want to find her, too?" Carolyn smiled. "Oscar misses you."

Claws clicked on the parquet. The cat crept carefully toward the farthest wall, more shadowed than the rest of the room. A step further and she'd lose him in darkness.

"Snug? It's me." Why was Carolyn whispering? Despite the party burbling below, the room demanded quiet.

The cat stopped and his back arched. A figure began to shimmer above it.

Carolyn crouched to soothe him. "Don't worry, boy, it's just Snug."

But it wasn't Snug. It was larger. Uncle Thomas, surely. He probably spent more time here than anyone.

Less blue than Snug, grayer, and older, with a heavy mustache and poor posture, it was as if the man had weights laid across his shoulders. He clutched a hat and when he tried to move toward her, he revolved, spinning slowly like an autumn leaf aloft on a branch. Carolyn caught her breath. The back of his head was gone and the wound—hair and skull and something else—glowed iridescent, glistening and messy. How light could look wet, Carolyn couldn't put into words. She wanted to scream, but she didn't. He spun again and his mouth opened, but nothing came out. This certainly wasn't Snug. And he wasn't Uncle Thomas.

This man was miserable. His eyes burned and looked right at her. Something snagged between them, a thread on a nail, a sort of recognition, and he lurched in her direction.

Carolyn's breath hitched and the room spun, and her legs twisted in an awkward jitterbug. She sank to all fours on a thin rug, threadbare beneath her palms and knees. The cat bolted around her arms and she felt the weight of his legs spring across her calves. She heard screaming. Johnny's sound effects? Or was it her own voice? Her lungs were ragged and at the side of the room something dark darted through the door. If only she could move that fast. She struggled to get to her feet, palms on the floor, then tucked back on her heels, arms over her head, like a soldier under a barrage. The room *pop-popped* again and everything went dark.

J ames Lenox had lived a long life, nearly eighty years, and gathered more riches than anyone would ever need. When he died, one of the wealthiest men in Manhattan, he left it to his youngest sister to decide where his money would do the most good; he trusted Henrietta. She was, as was he, spouseless and childless, with little interest in supporting excess in the habits of nephews and nieces. Thousands of dollars went to the church, thousands to homes for the aged and the infirm and the inebriated, more went to the upkeep of the Lenox Library—his crowning achievement, and the only thing on earth he was sorry to lose when he departed this life.

He didn't like to consider his philanthropy as driven by guilt, but while alive, he had spent an embarrassing sum on collecting books, scores of manuscripts, religious treatises and Shakespeare's plays, Donne's poetry, maps by explorers of the New World. Paintings and statues and miscellanies. Milton's drafts. Turner's oil of Fingal's Cave. A suit of armor.

That empty metal had stood in the entrance hall of his home on Fifth Avenue, many blocks south of where he stood now. That home was gone. The library was gone, too, the great stone building torn down to make a mansion for the arrogant Mr. Frick, the books consolidated with Astor and Tilden's into the city's public library, guarded by a pair of stone lions, Patience and Fortitude.

Patience and fortitude, indeed.

For decades the suit of armor had gathered dust in the basement of the Metropolitan Museum, until this evening, when roused from his regular months of serene slumber, his spirit felt compelled to a night of recollecting. Literally, re-collecting his collection.

He had flown to the museum and donned the armor. Decades of existence after death had taught him how to move things with ease, muscles and gravity no longer a question of how much to bear. It was simply a matter of mind. Perhaps not *mind*, but something like it. The armor weighed no more than feathers to his phantom form. It would have crushed his once corporeal body.

He kept the visor down. What would a living human see if the helmet was off? A pale grayish light. The silhouette of his stern face in shapely mist. The glee in his eyes as he rummaged through the stacks of the dark library, haunted the halls of the empty museum, traversed the grand park, over the trees, a folio of *Macbeth* in one arm, a family portrait by Gilbert Stuart in the other.

The rain that had threatened to erupt all night had yet to arrive. There was drizzle, intermittently, which he avoided when hauling his treasures, but didn't bother him otherwise in the least. Weather passed through him without trouble, unless he wanted to catch drops in the cup of his glowing palm, and then, if he put his will to it, he could hold a small puddle or an ocean.

In the armor, there was a pleasant *tap-tap* on the metal shell and he watched moisture bead and ripple down his breastplate.

It was amusing, a sensuous memory stirred by soft *pings*.

What was he doing? He had no idea. But it was a joyful noise, this gathering of his lifetime of riches.

Yet why was he hoarding them in a house he had never entered while breathing, why was he summoned to *this* place? This house was new to him. He felt like an explorer in a recently discovered yet clearly inhabited land. Inhabited, he knew, by a relative or two.

He drifted silently up the stairs on the floors above the living guests, their chatter and their laughter masking any bumps and thumps he made as he dropped books in the library, art in the master bedroom, a pair of Roman statues in the maids' cramped bathroom. He was stashing his riches haphazardly like an industrious squirrel, this dormant instinct stirred by a cosmic call beyond his comprehension.

James Lenox, dead lo these three-quarters of a century, sat, not winded, but resting, at the library table, in a dull but no longer dusty suit of Spanish armor once worn by a conquistador expired even longer than himself. The Spaniard certainly didn't need his outfit any longer. Honestly, neither did Lenox. He hadn't needed it in his life as a merchant either, or after he was done with that wretched business, when he spent the second half of his life as an eccentric millionaire, committed bachelor, a hermit holed up in his mansion sending others to do his bidding. Henry Stevens, his broker in Europe, was commissioned to bid on any rare volume Lenox desired, correspondence between the two crossing the Atlantic at a swift pace. One man roamed the stalls of antiquarian booksellers and the other spent his day cataloging the latest acquisitions. It was an ongoing scavenger hunt. Items came to port every day. Boys from the harbor rang the Lenox bell, handed servants wrapped packages or unloaded valuables buffered by straw in heavy wooden crates.

This evening, the armor was mere disguise. Lenox had never attended a costume ball as a living man. Parties were for other people; he was always more comfortable with silent companions. Words on vellum, oil on canvas. Henrietta, his one soulmate, and their companionable silences.

He hadn't seen Henrietta since her death, though he watched her in the intervening years between his ghosthood and the end of her human existence. Once she made the Great Change, she was gone to him. He knew not where she was.

He knew there were dead like him, still earthbound, but he kept to himself, as he did in life, the habits of hermits difficult to amend.

Until this evening, he had been happy to wake on rare days and wander the places he'd built or loved or pined over. The Presbyterian Church on Fifth Avenue and its stained glass. The home for widows. The land of Five Mile Stone, once his father's farm, now teeming with tall buildings. The hospital on the hill.

Why begin an afterlife of crime? He knew he was stealing. These things, they were not his any longer. Why touch them, take them, carry them, tonight?

Forearms across his thighs, he bent forward and wondered.

There were others in the house.

The girl and the damaged man. The angry woman. The elderly couple, older even than he had been when they expired. They made him look spry.

He *was* spry. He felt twenty years old.

James Lenox was expected at this party, he simply had no idea who sent the invitation.

Igor Imagines *THE CAPTION*, a screenplay

INT. The first-floor gallery crowded with party guests. At the back of the room is a makeshift bar where A SAD MAN hunches, trying gamely to stay out of the throng. A WAITER mixes cocktails. The man's attempt at innocuousness is thwarted by his costume: a breastplate of flimsy tin, gray chain mail of woven cotton. His oversized gloves are clean and white. His helmet is open-faced and his deep frown nearly clownish. A SECOND MAN strides toward him. This man wears a full suit of armor, gleaming in the candlelight. His visor is down and the plume on the top of his helmet waves. The visored knight slaps the man on the back with a gauntleted hand.

          PLUMED KNIGHT
   Hale, good sir. Fellow gallant!

The sad knight looks at the man with suspicion.

          SAD KNIGHT
   Oh. You. Great. My Bobbsey Twin.

          PLUMED KNIGHT
   And I thought I'd be the only
   chivalrous one in the crowd.

          SAD KNIGHT
   Chivalrous! That's good. You would
   think she'd like a chivalrous guy like
   me, but nah.

He drinks from a martini glass.

          PLUMED KNIGHT
   A fair one weighs heavy on your mind?

                    SAD KNIGHT
          Fair? She's strung me along for weeks.
          But I came to show her. She has no
          idea what she's missing.

CHARLES and BARBARA ADDAMS arrive. A moody cloud hovers over him. She is breezy.

                    BARBARA
          Look, Charles! Men prepared to die for
          their women!

                    CHARLES
          Of course that's what you see.

He studies the two.

                    CHARLES (cont'd)
          This is the embodiment of a *New Yorker*
          cartoon. Two knights walk into a bar.

                    PLUMED KNIGHT
          What is that?

                    CHARLES
          It's a living.

                    BARBARA
          Oh, more than that, dear.

To the knights.

                    BARBARA (cont'd)
          He's going to make me millions.

                    CHARLES
          I am?

He is distracted.

CHARLES (cont'd)
But what's the caption?

Barbara turns to the sad knight.

BARBARA
Why so blue, chum?

PLUMED KNIGHT
"O what can ail thee, knight-at-arms,
alone and palely loitering?"

SAD KNIGHT
You haven't seen a girl here?

CHARLES
Can you be more specific?

SAD KNIGHT
Pretty. Big smile. From Wisconsin.

BARBARA
The girl from Wisconsin is upstairs.

SAD KNIGHT
Really?

He stands straighter. Pulls back his shoulders.

SAD KNIGHT (cont'd)
I've come a long way for her!

BARBARA
Look for her in the throng of madmen.

PLUMED KNIGHT
Mad men? What's this?

SAD KNIGHT
They don't stand a chance against me.

He thumps his chest with a fist.

> PLUMED KNIGHT
> Gather your wits, lad. Go find your damsel!

The Sad Knight charges from the gallery.

> CHARLES
> Those hands! He has the hands of Mickey Mouse! Hitch is *right*.

> BARBARA
> What's that, dear?

He turns to speak to the Plumed Knight, but he is gone. He taps the waiter.

> CHARLES
> Did you see the knight? Just now?

> THE WAITER
> I've seen a lot of things tonight.

> BARBARA
> How much *have* you had to drink, Charles?

Charles lifts a napkin from a short stack and flattens it neatly on the bartop. He whips a pen from his pocket and it flashes like a little wand. He hunches and begins to draw. Barbara taps her empty highball and the waiter slides her a fresh one. They both crane over the artist's shoulder. Charles ignores them. On paper, they are there in duplicate, only much smaller: two knights at a bar, a waiter, a husband and wife watching from nearby.

43

NITRATE. DUMBWAITER. WHISTLE. EYEBALL. *Nitrate, dumbwaiter, whistle, eyeball.*

Carolyn's mantra to stay calm.

But, no, that wasn't right. It wasn't *eyeball*, it was *highball*. A drink. All the drinks had eyes. A glance at the cocktail in your hand and it was glancing back at you. Carolyn had helped Pete unload the boxes and boxes of plastic eyeballs and stacked them in the narrow kitchen that afternoon. Was it really only hours ago? It felt like a lifetime. Maybe several lifetimes. Hers, Snug's, Aunt Isabella's. The Doctor's. And now this? Who was this guy? Half-eaten or half-digested or just a lot worse for wear given however many years he'd been dead? And why was he here?

Carolyn had scuttled across the room and huddled in an empty closet, trying to find whatever would keep her calm: The light at the bottom of the door. The warm air around her face. The rhythm of words like a poem or prayer. She wasn't much on the "Blessed Be Thy Name"s and hymns of her Presbyterian youth. She was really a believer of the Church of the Woods, as her brother had called it, venturing out into the birch forests and letting the birds and the sky and water tell you what's sacred. Oh, Andy. Had his skull looked like that as he lay on some French shore? She felt her stomach tighten and every appetizer she'd eaten threatened to come up. She grappled to focus on something else, not Andy, not this new ghoul.

Lake Superior, jack pines in Solon Springs, the boys' camp, big-city boys playing for the summer. Flashes of death kept intruding—Snug, she was dead, and so was the old doctor, so was this latest vision. Then she'd turn to her mantra again: *nitrate, dumbwaiter, whistle, highball*. That was it. That was the verse.

Nitrate. The stuff of film—not actors and costumes and sets and scripts. Chemicals on a plastic strip. It burned, it melted, like the man's skull. Maybe he was made of nitrate, a mere projection of his former self? Isn't that what ghosts were? Projections. No, she answered herself. They were more real than that. More real than any movie. Movies were just one still picture after another, sped up for the illusion of motion, but a ghost was something real. Not flesh, but still there. There was no *there* there with movies. It was collective delusion, nothing more than illuminated cave paintings. And they didn't last forever. Stack them, reel on reel in their metal cannisters, and they still went up in smoke, and the smoke didn't tell you anything about what the movie once was. *Gone with the Wind* would burn as easily as any Bob Hope road movie. Bette Davis would burn as readily as Lillian Gish.

The thing about ghosts is they used to be alive.

Hitchcock had been complaining about the lifespan of his early work, silent movies made in England that no longer existed. What was that, thirty years ago? Forty? Pictures much older than Carolyn. The ghosts were older and more resilient, too. Resilient as the dumbwaiter, right there. No one had dumbwaiters built into homes anymore and yet there it remained.

Carolyn had always loved the dumbwaiter. She imagined if she'd grown up here she wouldn't have been able to resist the urge to send a dolly, a teddy bear, a toy, from one floor to the next and then run up the stairs to fling open the door and find it, as if she had nothing to do with its journey at all. Imagine everything the dumbwaiters had once carried: tea and coffee and cakes and sandwiches. Did they use it to send books? Sweaters? What would Snug have done? Carolyn imagined the girl sending notes to Curzon, playing games with clues. That's what she would have done.

Dumbwaiter. Whistle.

The whistle was in the dumbwaiter. If Carolyn crept out of her spot and tiptoed over? The whistle would scream. Someone would come running. And what would she say? *There are ghosts in the house! There's a nightmare loose in the halls!* They would find it a grand lark. After the laughter, after the condescending *yes, yes* and *of course there are*, might come *what have you been drinking, young lady?* and still worse: *Who invited her?* Pete would arrive and her mortification would be complete.

She could crawl into the dumbwaiter herself. If only she found a potion labeled *Drink This*. And shrunk. And if she got stuck? The men would guffaw. *Look, pal, what Hitch had them put in here! Ha ha, that's a stitch. He doesn't miss a thing, this guy. That's why he's the master.*

There was silence. Her father's office at the bank could be this silent. The tick of a mantel clock, the buzz from an incandescent light. What would her father say if he saw her? This is not what he meant by a trip to his sister's. A life in Superior, the wife-life, wouldn't lead to this. Dumbwaiter, dumb girl. Silent girl. Silent girl, like Snug.

And what was that light from beneath the door, the light that once burned yellow from the hallway and now glimmered blue?

The blue girl was back.

✦ ✧ ✦

Carolyn turned the knob, slowly, slowly, and opened the door a careful inch. She pressed her face to the crack and looked. There was her flickering cousin again, her blue hand reaching out across the room, but her finger crooked at Carolyn. *Come out, come out, there you are.* Carolyn pushed the door wider and stepped into the room. What do you know? Snug grinned. Carolyn felt her breath release, her chest lighten. She smiled in return.

You are safe, safe now, Snug's eyes seemed to say. And then her attention turned to the hallway and her face contorted. Carolyn followed her gaze and there was the maimed man, blocking the exit, backlit like an ogre under a bridge.

"Snug," the man spoke. "Snug, you are here."

Snug shimmered between Carolyn and the man, then hardened her form, burned a more vibrant shade, her edges firming like batter on a griddle. She spoke, her voice stronger than before, older. Carolyn trembled, her hand still on the knob, ready to bolt back in the closet at the slightest prevarication. But she didn't. Mesmerized, she watched the insubstantial girl take shape. She was, simply, more present, much more present than before.

"I've always been here, Father," Snug said. "Always." She groaned, a ragged shudder, yet her silhouette stayed rigid. "It was *you* who went away."

The man drifted forward, then lowered, the soles of his shoes nearly to the hard wood. The party noises slipped miles away, as if they'd been transported across town, and each of his staggered steps seemed as if it should boom, but he was still treading air. Step. Step. Step. His gait was awkward, his face tormented. Why couldn't he fly? He drew closer to Snug. Closer. When he was near enough to touch her, she shot across the room, her colors vivid, turning blue to bluer, then silver, then white, then blue again. She spun and zipped back, a furious cloud of dust and girl.

"But you," she hissed, "should not be."

Carolyn clenched from her toes to the top of her skull. Snug flitted and zagged, veered around the ceiling, a hand here, a foot there, disappeared into the wall, then returned. She flew lower, right through the couch and stopped, spun back to face her father, and glowered.

"Mother can't see you." Her voice was acid. "That would not be kind."

The man was crying, phantom tears running down his phantom face, snuffling like a toddler, his shoulders shaking. Carolyn had never seen a grown man cry like this. He was more than grown. He was disintegrating. Shadows bounced around the room as he wept. "Is she here?" He swiveled. Carolyn saw more of the back of his skull than she wanted. He looked up and down, as if Aunt Mariah would descend from the sky or rise from the floor. Maybe she would? Carolyn wasn't sure of the rules.

"Of course she's here! Mother never left."

Mother. The word, a wish, if only . . . but Mariah! Mariah was here. A rush of blood and heat flushed Carolyn's cheeks. Her brain swam.

The man moved forward. His name, his name. Carolyn almost had it. He was the one who caused such a scandal. Running off with another woman, claiming to be a widower when his wife and children were inconveniently alive and well. The alimony. He was the man who made headlines with his divorce settlement. How many thousands had he owed Aunt Mariah? It was staggering, even now, and that had been decades ago. The 1920s. But what happened to him? No one ever said. Looking at him now, Carolyn could guess.

"I never meant to hurt you, child," he mumbled through hiccups.

"Do not dissemble," Snug warned.

"I was a fool." He shrunk under her stern gaze.

"Was? Was?" She zoomed to his broken face, a hurtling force, then stopped and hovered over him. "*Was* isn't over, Daddy." He shook his bowed head. She rose higher, then tilted, her feet above her hair, her boots disappearing into the ceiling, her face right to his nose. "*Was* is *forever*," she rasped. "You should know that by now."

She flew through him and up, up, into the ceiling, and she was gone.

Carolyn watched Walter—that was his name, Walter!—sagging, weeping, and she wondered, what was the right thing to do now?

What was the proper etiquette to soothe a guilty, grieving ghost?

Before she could decide he disappeared, and Carolyn was alone in the room. She stepped out of the closet and the cooler air washed over her. She looked around the room, empty and silent and nothing out of place.

Oscar mewed at her feet.

She glanced at the couch. It was perfectly reasonable to sit and remain and avoid the rest of the evening in this room, which now seemed a safer place to be than anywhere else in the house. Wasn't that odd? A minute ago she was watching two spirits and now the room had the serenity of a chapel.

She couldn't hide here. She had to buck up, take a deep breath. Find Pete and tell him what she'd witnessed. But what had she seen? Could Bella know *this*?

She sat and let her stomach settle. In the aftermath of whatever it was she just saw, there was a stillness. The party sounded so far off. It was all so . . . distant.

By the time she stepped into the hallway, she was working on fresh explanations. What was she thinking, believing in Snug, in ghosts of any sort? No, it wasn't what she thought she'd seen. Nothing but a bit of undigested beef, Ebenezer Scrooge would have said. A hallucination from the Ghoulish Goulash. She had never had a suggestible imagination, never one to suffer bad dreams after a night of campfire stories. Maybe someone had spiked the drinks! Was that possible? She'd read about absinthe. The Green Fairy! Maybe her blue girl was nothing but a drunken vision. But this wasn't Paris. And she wasn't that drunk. Why was she acting like a gullible child? There was nothing in this house but admen and a few vain stars.

Blame New York, the bustle of the big city wearing on her nerves. Pete's pressure to make a perfect party. Aunt Bella and her paintings. She had a bridge to sell Carolyn and it was right there outside Gracie Square. Ships in the river, ships in the river, so many men moving and hauling and leering and shouting. None of it was real. She felt her legs wobble as if she were on water. She needed a bridge.

Nitrate and eyeballs and—

But, no, no, there was the cobalt silhouette of Snug down the hall, a flare of her violet scent, and the desperate groan of a man from an adjacent room. A groan of grief or pain. Someone needed help.

Carolyn willed herself to walk to the sound.

—dumbwaiter. Whistle. Eyeball. Nitrate, dumbwaiter, whistle, eyeball.

The heat, Mariah Taylor remembered, was the sense she dwelt on years later, her daughter's face agreeably warm, there at the beginning of the end, deceptive comfort as the frigid March winds blew. Then Snug's cheeks burned, sweat soaked her hair, her beautiful brown hair. When it was all over, she was frigid, a cold Mariah was damned never to forget.

The evening of that prior Friday had been unseasonably pleasant, chilly yet comfortable enough for people to stir, to get out and gather. They'd been cooped up all winter, at once terrified and bored, but the influenza seemed to have abated. Eager to mingle in a city of restless spirits, crowds gathered again after months of isolation.

Mariah hadn't wanted Snug to leave that evening. Meredith and Phoebe, the Woolworth girls from down the block, were going to a movie house; where they went, others followed. Of course it was safe, Mama, Snug insisted—no, promised, it had been a promise—of course we'll be careful.

Promising to stay out of the worst throngs, certain she could stay away from any danger.

Promising to stay healthy.

When she returned that night, she was flushed from the novelty of entertainment, from the excitement of resuming friendships, from seeing young men, and showing off her new shoes. Chattering in the family parlor, Snug tucked her hair behind her ear, again and again, as it fell out of its chignon, a little frantic with youthful enthusiasm. That was all. A little frenzied storytelling.

The wheezing started in earnest the next morning. The light fever, then damp skin and lips parted with labored breathing.

By Sunday, she turned blue, shockingly so, and Mariah relied on Thomas, her brother-in-law. He would know what to do, or know other men who had handled it, during the worst of the pandemic. He summoned them to the house.

Oh, God. Her only daughter.

Thomas wanted neither Mariah nor Isabella to go into Snug's room. She couldn't stay away. What sort of mother would that make her? They sent Curzon to friends in the Bronx. He didn't want to go, sweet boy. He did love his sister so.

By the end of the week, he was back, for her funeral. She wasn't a threat after she was dead.

They gathered in the parlor, the same one where mere nights earlier she had told her mother of her evening out, the laughter in the cinema, anise candy on her breath.

Walter didn't come. Mariah wouldn't have let him in the house if he had tried. Later, at Woodlawn, he could pay his respects, though how a disreputable man had respects to pay was beyond her understanding.

He believed she was out to make him a pauper, as if that were her plan. He *would* lose it all, the way he had taken everything from her.

She took his every penny. (But that was years later. Then she could hardly spend it, it made her stomach turn. It moldered in a bank account she tried to ignore.)

Her girl was gone. Where? Was there the heaven they sang for every Sunday? What came next? Mariah couldn't fathom it, regardless of her professed faith. What had become of her darling daughter?

Would she ever see dear sweet Snug again?

In the language of the books Mariah loved, the novels she and Snug had read aloud to each other, she found an answer.

Dear reader, in case you haven't heard, she did.

44

CHARLES ADDAMS WAS ALONE again in the WC. The same bathroom where he'd seen the glowing girl. He waited by the sink, hands on the cool porcelain. Nothing was out of place. (Clean hand towels. Seashell soap in small dishes.) Nothing felt wrong. (Though there was an antique tucked in the corner. A pair of pots? A tortured spittoon? It didn't make sense.)

Then:

The faint outline of a child stood at his knee. His legs shook as if he were straining under a great weight. There was a dainty chair beside the tub. He'd sit, that was a plan. This was a hallucination. He would sit and she would disappear. He dropped onto the seat. How many hours had he spent sitting in his lifetime, years, he imagined, and never once had his thighs quaked like this. If he let himself go, if he didn't fight it, his knees would have banged together like loose shutters on an old house. But she remained. The outline grew bolder, more defined, a little girl, not much more than a toddler, in a simple dress and a cotton cap, strings dangling by her chin. She was plump and smiling.

This was not the same girl he'd seen before.

"Mr. Charles," she said. There was something adult in her voice, the aural equivalent of those Renaissance paintings whose babies seemed ancient.

It had followed him here. Not *it*. That wasn't fair. *Her*.

He knew who she was, had considered her life too many times over the years not to have a keen sense of her. He had perhaps even imagined a meeting such as this. Yes, he had. She had found him. How was that possible? That's what he meant to ask. He coughed and instead said, "How are you?"

"I am well," she replied. "How are you?"

"Fine, thank you," he answered by rote, a flash to his boyhood response to elders. The little girl was his elder. She was owed some deference. "No, I am perhaps unwell. I am seeing you." He closed, then opened, his eyes. (Nope, still there.) "Do I know you?"

She giggled. "You know me. You've known me for years!"

"I make it a habit not to know any children," he denied. A flash of flush-cheeked W. C. Fields flew across his mind. What was the joke? *—How do you like children? —Well done.* "I try my damnedest not to know any."

She frowned.

"Excuse my language. Darnedest."

She smiled. "You know me."

"No," he insisted. "I don't."

"But you do." She leaned closer and whispered in his ear. "My name is Sarah."

Charles jolted upright, as if he'd jammed a wet finger into the outlet behind him. He sat primly for a moment and studied her. "You are Little Sarah?" His voice softened, warmer than he'd thought possible in a moment of dread. "Little Sarah, Aged Three."

" 'Tis I," she nodded.

"What are you doing here? How are you here?"

"I don't know. I've not been anywhere like this before." She patted his knee, but he felt only a cold stirring at the fabric of his trousers.

"Where are you usually on a Wednesday night?"

"Is it Wednesday? Where am I? Nowhere. Perchance by the trees at Mama and Papa's farm. Sometimes I'm where you live, but not for very long. Mostly, I'm not anywhere at all. I nap. When I was little, I hated taking naps, but now I like them."

"You're not little anymore?" He held up his hand to measure the top of her head. "You look little to me."

She giggled again, then grew solemn. "No one stays a child forever."

"You seem evidence to the contrary," he said.

A couple tittered in the hallway, footsteps receding.

She glanced about, freshly uncomfortable with her surroundings. "I don't know." Once more, her hand went to his knee.

He wanted to flee, but he couldn't make his muscles work. If he stood, he would fall, so he kept sitting with the tiny phantom by his side. He put his hand on top of hers and all he felt was his patella.

"But why are you here now?"

"Many people are here," she said.

"Yes," he said. "It's a party."

"I don't mean them," she said. "I mean people like me."

There was a drip in the sink. Water in pipes flowed to the floors above.

"They live here," she added. "And they invited me. I don't know why. I simply knew to come here tonight. I *need* to tell you something."

"Tell me what?"

Her sweet face collapsed into a terrible frown. She pointed beyond the closed door. She leaned closer to him again, the same feathery brush against his ear. "Get away from her."

"Her?"

"The woman in black." She hugged his leg, an affectionate child, the act of a niece to a beloved uncle. They were neither and it broke his heart. "She doesn't want you anymore."

With that, Little Sarah vanished in a gentle breeze. He gripped the lip of the sink for balance.

Formidable silence rushed to fill her abrupt absence, then the burble of the party popped it, a swell of volume.

Charles gulped, a hard catch in his throat, a sharp bit of stone like a polished barb.

45

FONDA HEARD STEPS AT the library door but kept his eyes closed. Maybe he didn't have the heart to witness what was next. He would feign sleep, collapsed in a wingback chair again, but imagined a scarecrow on a hay bale. Bookshelves loomed like fortress walls, but little protection they'd been before.

"She doesn't mean any harm," a woman said. "She isn't out to scare you."

He opened his eyes and blinked, bringing her into focus. Carolyn Banks stood in the doorway. He always remembered names. Even distraught, he tallied the dark blond hair with its streaks of gold, the shapely legs silhouetted by the hallway light.

"Whatever you saw just now," she continued, as if to a jittery horse. "It wasn't meant to terrify you."

"Who was that?" His lips had difficulty forming the words. He swallowed. He never had hitches in his speech. He was an actor, for God's sake. His throat felt stuffed with dirt and dry leaves. "Just now."

"A cousin of mine. Someone from long ago. She can't hurt you." Carolyn took a step closer.

"But how does she know my wife?"

She stopped. "Your wife? Your wife is at the party?" She looked back at the low rumble of chatter, the high-pitched sporadic laughter.

"I'm divorced now. From a different woman. I mean"—he rubbed the back of his neck—"my former ex-wife." He tried to line up the arithmetic. "My late wife. She was here. Before the other one, before your aunt."

"Cousin," Carolyn said. "But that's impossible. Your wife's not relat—it's impossible."

"It's *all* impossible. Ghosts. Flying girls. But Frances was here." He pointed at the floor, meaning the room. "Here."

Carolyn felt sweat at her temple and pushed away her hair.

His chin trembled and, for a moment, she saw the little boy he must have been decades earlier. This man was not heroic or stoic, not the courageous but reticent hero she'd seen in half a dozen movies at the cinema in Duluth. She was disappointed and unsurprised: another man who wasn't what he seemed.

"Did she have any connection to this home? Had she ever been here before?"

"What? No. I've never been here before. I don't know if Frances had, but I doubt it. No, why would she know the girl?" She followed his attention to the floor, to an empty glass in a puddle of melting ice and booze. Something had surprised him enough to waste his drink. He cocked his chin. "She did live up here, around the corner, with her first husband. In the castle on Fifth Avenue."

"A castle." Carolyn hummed. "This is new. All the other . . . spirits have a connection." She sat in an armchair. "If your late wife is showing up, then this is more than my family reunion."

"She was *my* family. She's the mother of my children." His hand went to his chest, as if his heart clenched. His blue eyes were bloodshot. "Wait. Did you say spirits? *Others?*"

Carolyn ignored his question. "And she's dead?"

"Yes." He nodded and checked the room as if for spies. "A suicide."

"Like Walter," she mused.

"Who?" Fonda said. "Disney?" He stared at her, but not accusatorily. Not menacing. He was simply confused. Too many Bloody Marys. Too little sleep. Too many wives. "Hitch is right?"

"No, no," she said, "not that Walt."

Too many Walters.

Henry couldn't keep up and he prided himself on being a man who could always keep up.

"Not that Walt."

A riotous chorus from the parlor below rolled beneath them, carried on invisible waves. And how was that so different from this, Fonda thought, this talk of ghosts floating in and out of rooms, through walls and up staircases. They moved like sound.

His raw voice cracked. "She killed herself after we were divorced. I think she blamed me."

"Did she have a reason?" Carolyn blurted. She knew it wasn't polite, but it seemed the only question possible. Her grasp of appropriate manners was unraveling with each hour.

He didn't flinch or tell her to apologize. He shrugged. "Don't they all?"

The sound effects tape clicked on; Carolyn recognized the tiniest shudder in the moment before whatever was in store rumbled from one of the hidden speakers. This time it was a single piano, echoey, as if Johnny had recorded it in a subway tunnel, notes in a minor key, carefully off-kilter, just enough to jangle nerves. She was certain it was Johnny playing, but . . . all those nights at the lake. He was a human jukebox. Those boisterous singalongs. That's what a party was supposed to feel like, not these jarring interludes with the dead. Not this discordant lullaby. This was no fun at all.

The piano stopped and there was the lament of a loon, one that sent her back to the Northwoods, that forlorn cry.

And the movie star stood trembling before her, shaken by his vision of a self-destructive spouse and her long-dead cousin. Come to rescue them all? Torment them? Maybe a little of both.

Carolyn didn't know what to do with that. The man before her seemed to shrink, so much smaller than he'd ever appeared in a dark movie theater. Here the shadows were swallowing him up in despair and shock, and Carolyn watched with no sense of how to offer solace. Who would believe movie stars needed consolation?

Her mother's slow wearing away, yes, that was a trek. The news of her brother's death was the swift blow of a telegram. *We regret to inform you.* Grueling or swift, she should know some comforting words. Grief was the oldest thing on earth and yet it seemed to gleam with sharp new facets every time she faced it. He sank into the chair and closed his eyes, and she knew it was easier to abandon him than try to heal him. She slipped out of the room. She had to find Pete.

She always felt like an amateur in the company of mourning.

T he paper was folded in half, ready for an envelope, but the page was blank and missing its top third, where it had read *Young & Rubicam*. Snug loved the company name, chanted it under her breath. She was once *young*, was still in many ways, yet older than anyone she knew. Older even than the Doctor or her mother or her aunt. She'd been dead the longest and that gave her something like wisdom. Or, if not wisdom, it certainly didn't make her young.

Rubicam was surely someone's last name, but it sounded to her like Rubicon, a river she'd crossed long ago. There was no going back. She wasn't convinced there was any going forward. Perhaps she was knee-deep in the Rubicon and didn't even know it. Rubicam, Rubicon. *Am* or *on*, verb or preposition, it didn't make a difference. She was on this side of the water, whatever one called it.

She held Pete's pen in her hand, forcing herself to support it. To grip the smooth handle—yes, she could feel smooth—and drew the ballpoint over the paper, the ink spilling out in luxurious curves. This was a D. Here was an r, lowercase. Here was another D. *Dear Daddy*. No, too young. She put a vivid line through Daddy and wrote Father. *Dear Father*. A much better beginning.

The writing looked like waves across the page. Witching waves.

She continued, bent like the studious girl she'd once been, learning French verbs and Plato's *Republic*. *Je suis, tu es, il est. Elle est*. She is— what? *Incroyable. Impossible. Elle est* . . . what was the word for *forever*? She couldn't recall. Was it *maintenant*? It looked so much like maintenance. It took maintenance to maintain . . . No, that wasn't it. That was *now*. This was exhausting.

Dear Father.
You were a terrible fool. I hated you—
—I missed you so much. I wanted to forgive you.

And now, I don't know how, you and I have become the same—thing—it is

She held up the half-formed sentence, mired in bewilderment. What did she want to compose? A demand. An apology. A curse or an olive branch. Who could compose a letter to contain all things? She was Mr. Whitman, she contained multitudes, she was Miss Dickinson, she was grief and wonder, but all it created was cacophony.

She *would* send him on his way; he would stay away from Mother.

The skittering of cat claws on the polished floor pulled her from her muddy rut.

"Oh, Oscar," she cried. She knelt and gathered him in her arms, the breeze of her catching the paper on the desk. It fluttered to the floor like a moth. The pen rolled away and she sprawled to catch it. Above her outstretched hand, another spirit hovered. She craned to look up.

Uncle Thomas floated above her, quiet as the cat, pale as thin milk. "Isabella," he said. "It is time for us to talk."

46

THERE WAS ANOTHER ECHOED screech in the dark hallway, lit only by a pair of weak sconces.

The cry called again to Carolyn's mind the loons at Lake Nebagamon, their eerie call, the hazy spill of the Milky Way above her, and the wishes she made on shooting stars when she was still a girl. There were midnight wooded walks with Andrew, Carolyn not even ten, her brother in his middle teens. Together, he would lamp the way to the pier and they'd step gingerly into one of their father's red canoes. Paddling to the center of the lake, stars reflected in the black water, the sound of his stroke a steady splash, punctuated by the occasional plop of a muskie's rise and the distant birds' lament. The tree-line silhouette of the far shores, pines rigid against the paler sky, made a ghostly horizon. Where her brother led, there was magic. When she made the trek back after his death, a competent woodsman on her own, it was a deliberate act of remembrance. The loon call was a keening, the water glittering with empty vows. The rest of the universe was a million miles away, not within the stroke of a paddle.

There were no visible stars over Manhattan, not that she could see beyond the city's bright lights. And recorded screams weren't the birds of her youth. They were pretend. What wasn't a performance here? Death seemed an arbitrary state, not an end, not a beginning, and everyone else was playacting parts that didn't make sense.

Carolyn stood in the center of the hall and let the shadows fall behind her, the doorways loom ahead. She was caught in the middle and something needed to push her this way or that.

The tape stopped and she felt a presence behind her.

It was Johnny, his dark hair disheveled like a Bowery Boy and the knees of his chinos dirty. He'd been crawling in his mob of wires. His lopsided grin made her gloom go away.

"Oh, thank God, it's you," she exclaimed, and took his hand.

"I don't hear that often."

She peppered him with questions as they walked down the hall—how was it going? What did he think of the guests? Had he seen Hitchcock? Anything to keep him talking and her mind distracted.

He stopped her. "How long were you in the room with Fonda?" She was going to deny it when he smirked. "I was checking a tape deck running in a closet down that hall. I couldn't help but hear."

"That's eavesdropping!"

"Not much. I mean, I couldn't hear much. Though he did sound pretty broken up. Life on the silver screen not all it's cracked up to be?"

"Is anything all it's cracked up to be?"

He was about to answer when a woman's scream curdled the air.

"That's a bit much, don't you think?" Carolyn flinched.

"It didn't sound that bad when I put it on the reel."

The hall was quiet again, the party noises an uneven murmur, a faint battle on some far plain. She glanced into another dimly lit bedroom. Leaning against the wall was a small painting, something she remembered. But not from here. It hadn't been here before. A tiger, nearly a cartoon. Johnny followed behind her and he gasped. A man had stepped from the dark side of the room, a man in a suit of armor.

"I never owned it." He held a helmet under one arm and when he stepped closer, Carolyn realized he was entirely silver. Not buzzing blue, like Snug. Not a pulsating shimmer of gray like the doctor. This man was silver.

She recognized his face from other paintings, bigger than the tiger, nearly as old, in gilded frames.

"Hello, Uncle James," she whispered. Snug was a shock; Dr. Satterthwaite was a hunch. Walter was a horror. This was awe.

The man didn't seem to hear her, but Johnny did. Huddled by her shoulder, he whispered, "Uncle James?"

"The problem is . . . I've stolen it," the silver man confessed. "I was honest, if a rich man can be entirely honest, my whole life long. Certainly not a thief. Tonight, in a matter of hours, I've stolen with impunity. Most of it I owned in my prior—no, not prior—*earlier* life. But this. And this"—he withdrew a small blue statue of a hippo from behind his back and held it with both hands in front of his gleaming chest plate, an offering—"these marvels, I never owned."

"Why did you take them?" Carolyn's voice was calm. It wasn't fright, not quite. Was she growing accustomed to spirits? Or was it because he wasn't missing half his head? He seemed intact. Johnny was gulping heavily, as if he'd run up and down the staircase. She understood his panic, had felt it herself, but this was different. Why did she want Uncle James to linger? Shouldn't she shoo him away like an old crow?

"The Blake watercolor I've admired for years. I didn't know about it when I was alive. I could have, I suppose. But his work was not in my ken. Years of wandering the museum—"

"Are you a ghost?" Johnny blurted, stepping forward, reaching out. The knight didn't budge.

"I believe," he said, "I am."

Johnny groaned like he had a gut ache.

"You've been haunting," Carolyn spoke deliberately, "the Metropolitan Museum?"

"Only recently," Lenox said.

Johnny choked a little, gave a cat-with-a-hairball cough. Carolyn felt him waver beside her, just like Pete had on seeing Snug. She took his elbow and they both sat on the edge of a tall bed, shrouded in canvas cloth. No mannequin on this mattress. The ghost in front of them glittered like a tinseled Christmas tree caught in a tin can. Lenox kept talking—to them, to himself. Carolyn glanced around the room, a stack of books, a framed map. No, two. And who knew what a ghost could see? Perhaps he was lecturing to some invisible gallery.

"I didn't have the wherewithal for the first years," he testified. "I was like any new eidolon, limited in mobility. Now I'm the most accomplished ghost I know. I can go where I want, for what it's worth, pick up what I want, again, a previously pointless power. What did I desire? Nothing, until recently. Then, suddenly, tonight, *everything*."

Johnny's grip was clammy on her bare arm. Short, quick breaths punctuated his soft moans. He was sickly green in the dim light, but Lenox kept going.

"In my earlier incarnation I went nowhere. I wandered the halls of my home and sent Stevens to Europe. Scavengers and antiquarians! I let him buy the books I needed to complete my collection, scour for manuscripts and paintings, compete with princes and captains of industry haggling for the right price. I spent obscenely on my books, all those words on paper, on parchment, and bought solace by donating enormous sums. Charity, charity, and more charity, anonymous and stealthy. I yearned for neither fame nor power." He laughed. "I didn't want that." He waved at his spoils. "I wanted these."

Johnny laughed, too, a little giddy echo, then his face soured. "Carolyn, I don't feel so hot."

"You should lie down," she said, standing, gently nudging Johnny's shoulders. She turned her back on Lenox. He was noise, a television no one was watching. His volume grew.

"They begged me to run for governor and I rebuffed them. Why would anyone of sane mind enter politics? Bureaucracy is a sort of asylum, the sort for lunatics, not refugees. I was always seeking refuge from the world and the work I pursued I adored, doting on my catalogue. It was the core of my existence. I never married, never fathered a child, had no passion but my library. Oh, the library, my love." He paused and took a breath. Carolyn cocked her head. *Took a breath?*

"I'm seeing stuff, Carolyn," Johnny mumbled. "I must've eaten something bad." He rubbed his neck, like he'd slept on it wrong, and she realized he was trying not to look at the knight. "Do you see him, too?" he whispered.

She could lie. Johnny would believe this a nightmare brought on by bourbon and canapes. He was no different from Miss Havisham. Lying could become habit, another strange thing to which she'd grow accustomed.

Lenox was speaking faster. "And my sister Henrietta. I loved Henrietta. No sister was so loved by a brother. What a mind she possessed! In another world, she would have rivaled our father with her head for figures. A compassionate accountant, she was, exactly what a man of means needed when I had no place to spend my money other than sending it overseas for manuscripts. Shakespeare's quartos, Milton's epic, the Bible in every shape and form, many times over. You've seen the jewel of my collection, the Gutenberg?"

The book on the table, the tome in front of Fonda. "Yes," Carolyn said to Lenox. Then, turning to Johnny, "Yes." He was sweating, his lips parted like a gasping fish, but he smiled.

"You do? I'm not going crazy, Banks?"

"You're not crazy. He's here."

The flood of words from Lenox stopped like a dammed river. "Miss—"

"Banks," she said.

Lenox tucked his chin and gave her an evaluating gaze. "You are kin to my sister Isabella? She married a man named Banks."

"Yes," Carolyn said. "That's right."

"Astonishing," he said.

She watched the light of his face glint like a jewel. "That's the word," she said.

"Astonishing," Johnny muttered, and Carolyn watched his eyes roll up and back as he passed out like she'd once seen a girl do in the church choir. Johnny's had a cartoonish quality. All he needed were swirling birdies. She touched his damp face. He was out and already snoring. Behind her there was a pop and Uncle James was gone with the speed of a blown lightbulb, dropping the room into sudden darkness.

The only company left was Johnny's steady breath and the tick and wheeze of a surprised radiator called into work on a spring night.

47

RAPID FOOTSTEPS CLICKED IN the hall. Carolyn looked around the bedroom as if it were a crime scene. On the surface it was all surprisingly normal. Uncle James had disappeared; playing hide-and-seek it seemed was a game for all ghosts. Johnny was passed out on a musty gray duvet, but that was easily explained—he didn't know his limits. When Alma Hitchcock strode across the threshold, polka-dotted dress swinging, a long-stemmed lily in her grasp, Carolyn wasn't sure if this was a best- or worst-case scenario.

Alma scowled at Johnny's gentle snoring. "Well, that's one man we don't have to worry about." She waved the flower like a wand. "Have you seen my husband lately? He seems to have disappeared again."

"People have a way of doing that tonight," Carolyn said.

Alma smiled, lips together. "Alfred's the only one I care about. As long as I find him, the others will have to find themselves."

Carolyn's mood leapt at her words. She wanted to cheer *hear, hear!* Let the others find themselves. She was done wrangling restless spirits. Then she considered the one man she did want to see. "I'm looking for someone, too," Carolyn said. "The fellow with the agency. Pete Donoff?"

Alma spied around Carolyn at prone Johnny, then flashed her a knowing glance. "The kind one. Your young man."

Carolyn blushed. "He's not my—"

Alma waved the lily again. "Of course he isn't. Always deny. You must have seen Grace's pictures. Denial is potent." She spun, her skirts flaring briefly like a pinwheel. "If I find him first, I'll tell him there's a pretty girl on the lookout. Do the same if you find my Man Who."

Alma in heels disappeared as swiftly as Uncle James on air.

Carolyn checked on Johnny once more—no more nervous sweat, sleeping off whatever sick-making jitters the ghost gave him—but she'd hunt down a bottle of Bufferin and a glass of cold water. She'd find Pete and warn him about Lenox. She'd check on the old woman in the garden. That was a plan. If she saw Hitchcock, she'd relay Alma's message. Treading the stairs, hands brushing the banister, the descent felt freeing. Those upper rooms had been an exercise in claustrophobia. With every step down, she felt the air grow more humid yet more human and her spirits, surprisingly, lift.

There was a buzz to the conversations as Carolyn wove her way through the gallery to the courtyard. *Had she heard?* The police were on the premises, not for the collapsed woman, but to investigate a burglary. *No, not in the house*, the whispers hissed. *In the neighborhood! A rash of them, tonight!* By the time she stepped outside, Carolyn saw she had been preceded. There he was: a knight at the edge of the brick wall. No one else seemed to have noticed. Policemen huddled over the old woman (prone, but still breathing, thank goodness). How could they miss the metal, the feather? Maybe she was the only one who could see him? Ghosts were only apparent to some people, right? She'd learned that somewhere, *Topper* or Noël Coward. But Johnny had seen Uncle James, that was certain.

She tiptoed up behind him, a stray copy of *LIFE* rolled in her grasp—maybe the very issue Vincent Valiano had used as a baton on the tour of the house a few days (a century?) ago. Was she exorcising a phantom or swatting a fly? She just didn't have the right equipment, physically or temperamentally. She wasn't a priest. But maybe if she knocked him hard enough, shook up his ectoplasm, he'd simply plop into a gelatinous puddle, like the frosting upstairs? That would make Charles Addams happy. If she made a ghost's existence quaver, might it send him out of their time and back into his? Or were these some sort of planes of existence, like dirty plates stacked in a sink, time on time on time. Whatever it was, there he was, garish and gleaming, and here was Carolyn, crouched like her father hunting pheasant. She pulled her arm back, happy for a few summers' worth of tennis lessons, and gave a healthy swing.

At best, she expected a clang, a Hollywood jousting sound effect; at worst, she'd make a breeze, a pathetic *whoosh*. But what she got was a sorry thud and a muffled "Hey!" The helmet swiveled in her direction.

"Carolyn!" the knight cried.

That voice! She pushed up the visor with more than enough strength. It clunked against his forehead. There was Malcolm, red-faced and sweating. She hadn't seen him since the Flame. He was out of breath and out of place.

"What—are—you—doing—here?" Carolyn's tone was machete-sharp. She stared at him, his expression tenuous below the raised visor, the plumes on his crest fallen like a wounded bird on the hood of a car. "And why are you wearing—that?"

"It's a costume party?" He took off his helmet and wiped his forehead. "You said! I thought I'd fit in."

Oh, he had seen Uncle James! "With . . . whom?"

"Lots of people were made up! The guys in tails with the eye makeup."

"Those are the waiters, Malcolm."

"The lady in the long dress."

Please be Miss Havisham and not Snug. She tried to keep the panic out of her voice. "That lady?" She pointed.

"Yeah, her. She's in costume!"

Whew: Miss Havisham. "She's an actress. A professional. Are you a professional actor? Were you hired for this party?"

"Well, no." He had the decency to look chagrined. "What about those guys?" He pointed a gloved finger. She followed it to the clutch of cops.

"No, Malcolm, those are actual police officers. There's been a robbery." She huffed. "Robberies. All over the neighborhood." She poked at his breastplate. "And a man in armor probably looks suspect."

"Not me!" His dark, damp hair was plastered to his forehead. She had an urge to brush it away, to fix him up. She reached out, but he slid down and plopped himself on the courtyard stones in an awkward heap, his back against the wall. He gripped his helmet to his stomach, his legs splayed, like a boy worn out from an afternoon of play. He was a vision from a cover of *The Saturday Evening Post*. Call him "The Weary Pretender." It was difficult to curse at him when he looked all of ten. She sat next to him.

"Why are you here?"

"I wanted to see you."

"You were going to see me in a few days back home."

"I thought you might forget me, hobnobbing with movie stars."

She snorted. "Have I ever said I wanted to hobnob with movie stars?"

He pouted. "Not in so many words."

"Not in *any* words. Ever."

"You love the city. You always talk about what life would be like here."

"I do?" Carolyn didn't remember ever telling Malcolm about New York, well, except for the night at the Flame. Had he been listening before then?

"Yeah. You do. I thought you might not come back."

She tidied her dress across her lap. This position was only ladylike if she were at a picnic and the memory of Pete at lunch made her blush. How could that have been only today? Time was stretching like taffy. She stiffened her spine and tucked her legs under her, then rearranged the fabric. It wasn't perfect. Was anything ever perfect?

"I do love it here," she admitted, to herself more than Malcolm. "I would love to live in Manhattan. But this isn't where my life is."

"You mean, your life with me?"

Carolyn tensed. "I'm not sure if that's what I do mean, Malcolm. I mean—" She weighed the next sentence. "I mean—I *had* no desire to leave Superior. Not you, not the shop, not my family. But I'm also not sure if I want to make anything forever either."

"Is that a no?" He picked at the chipped paint on his helmet. "No, wait, it's another *you need more time*," he sneered, his volume growing.

She felt people looking, as if their sitting on the ground didn't call enough attention to them, as if a knight in the courtyard wasn't spectacle enough. "Yes," Carolyn nodded. "Which is what I told you before I came here. Yet here you are."

He crossed his arms, a gesture she recognized. Petulance. In gray flannel, in armor, he was the same man. "I thought you'd be happy to see me and you'd realize you should say *yes*." He paused. "Aren't you happy to see me?"

"No," she said, her honesty a surprise. "It's rude." She gave him a hard stare, then felt her resolve slacken.

"It's not really a surprise. I was fishing for an invitation. The telegram?"

"It would have been different if you were already here. I would have invited you then. Probably."

"Probably?"

"Maybe. Probably. Maybe. That's all you're getting."

Malcolm frowned. "I guess it's better than you hate me."

She stood and held out her hand. "Let's skedaddle before you have to answer to the boys in blue." He took it, his gloves rough against her fingers, and she helped hoist him to his feet. He clanked like a knapsack filled with soup cans. "Where did you get"—she flicked his fake chain mail—"this?"

He glanced at his torso as if seeing it for the first time. "Cathedral High's mascot. I *borrowed* it." She guffawed. "I know," he plucked at the silver tunic, "it's not quite up to the Great White Way."

"Nobody wants knights on Broadway."

He fixed the helmet over his head and flipped up the visor. "You know I did see another guy in armor and thought I'd blend in."

"You saw another man in armor?" For a few minutes, she'd forgotten about Uncle James. And Snug. Imagine that. "Where?"

"When I was outside. Hours ago. Then he was by the bar? Why?"

"Long story. I'll tell you sometime."

"Sooner rather than later."

"Maybe," Carolyn hedged.

"He's probably still here," Malcolm said.

Carolyn shook her head and said ruefully, "I hope not."

"You know him?"

She stopped and considered this mild request. Could Malcolm handle the truth? Perhaps this was a test. "My great-great-great uncle."

Malcolm whistled. "He must be ancient. And tromping around in that armor? Healthy bugger."

"I'm not sure that's the word."

"Then what is?"

"Haunted."

"He believes in ghosts?"

"I'm sure he does." Carolyn considered spilling it all: the ghosts, the grief, the thievery. What would Malcolm do? She imagined his eyes popping like a *Looney Tunes* character. He started to speak, but she bopped the visor, and it dropped with a louder clank than she'd intended. At least she didn't have to see his big brows stuck up on his forehead like twin arcs of black ink.

"Why?" It was alarming how the visor muffled him. Here was a man two feet from her who sounded a million miles away.

"He's superstitious." Carolyn slapped his back like an old chum. "That's all."

48

PETE SMACKED HIS SHIN bone twice, tripping over statuary as he crossed the library yet again. He'd come looking for Carolyn and ended up among this—so many little figures. Not decorations his team put in place, but a new gaggle of angels and nymphs and bearded busts that weren't in the house before. And books. Books out of nowhere, books everywhere. Expensive leather-bound, gilt-edge spines. Stacks of manuscripts and yellowed maps. A framed portrait of George Washington. He couldn't find Carolyn, but corralled Johnny Kander in the hallway. The musician looked dazed and unwell, like he'd just woken from a lousy nap. Pete pulled him onto the stairs leading further upward. To the nursery? Maids' quarters? The roof? The house felt as if it were growing, beanstalk-style, ogre at the top and all.

"There's a portrait of a Founding Father back there," Pete laid out.

"Uh-huh," said Johnny. He chewed his lip.

"And a manuscript that says it was written by Shakespeare next to the sleeping dummy in the master bedroom—"

"Yep," said Johnny, rocking on the heels of his sneakers.

"—and the book on the table in the library, I saw it before. It's important, it's a Bible—"

"It's a Gutenberg," Johnny said.

"How do you know that?"

Johnny's eyes darted. "I'm not sure?" The musician spoke like he was surprised by his own knowledge. "People think it's one of a kind, but there are actually a bunch still floating around." He gave a chagrined smile. "That probably doesn't make it any less special."

Pete sighed. "I would like to know where all this stuff, this very valuable stuff, is coming from." He eyed Johnny. "And why you already know."

Johnny cleared his throat. "You need to ask Carolyn about that."

Pete held his arm. "What does Carolyn have to do with this?"

Someone was upstairs, thumping like a man with a wooden leg. *Buh-bump. Buh-bump.* Johnny leaned and whispered, "Her uncle. Her uncle the—"

Pete held up a hand. "Don't say it."

"—the ghost."

"You know about the ghosts?"

Johnny went pale. "You, too?"

"The old man? In the bedroom."

Johnny nodded, reluctantly.

"Snug's uncle."

Johnny bristled. "Who's Snug?"

"The girl."

"There's a girl? A girl ghost? I saw a fella in armor."

"Armor? What are you talking about?"

"Armor. Knights in shining—that stuff."

"The uncle is a doctor. He's in a nightshirt."

"The uncle is insane. And metal plated."

"Nope, nope." Pete felt sick. "Two. Now three. How many ghosts are there?"

"There's more than one?" Johnny plopped on the stairs. Pete collapsed next to him.

"A girl and a tired old man."

"A *second* old man? The one I saw has energy. Uncle James, she called him. A great-great-something uncle. He's strong." He marveled. "He can carry things."

"Hello, Uncle James," Pete whispered.

"That's what she said!"

"Oh, Carolyn," Pete snapped. "I don't get her."

Johnny bumped his shoulder. "Well, she gets you," he snorted.

Pete wanted to believe this skinny guy with his hair tousled and droopy eyes. But maybe he was drunk. Or suffering post-ghost after-effects, his head addled. Pete wanted to believe him, more than he was willing to admit.

"I've known Banks forever," Johnny said. "I can tell when she likes a guy. And it doesn't happen often." He absently studied the ceiling. "All the guys liked her but . . . you're the lucky one."

Pete's nervousness broke like a fever—because Carolyn liked him? That seemed juvenile. Was he a teenager again? Enough. "The uncle's holding a flea market?"

"No." Johnny spoke as if remembering a dream, grasping for faint images. "He's recovering . . . valuables he once owned. He had a big collection when he was alive. Like a Collyer brothers problem, piles all over his mansion." Johnny tapped a statue tucked in the shadows of the step. Pete hadn't noticed it before. It was a small blue hippo. Next to it was the alembic from downstairs. Or a different one? No, it was the same one. He recognized its dents.

Art on the staircase? Where wasn't this stuff accumulating? He touched the cold marble. It was smooth and hard and real.

Johnny plowed on. "A bunch of it's from the public library. And the Metropolitan Museum. He's sick of his belongings scattered all over the island."

"Of course." Pete slumped. "I'm sure that makes it better. It's hardly like theft at all! No one will ask us a question about how it ended up in the house we're renting for a single night. That's not one bit suspicious."

Johnny leaned back and closed his eyes. "This makes me so tired."

Pete stared at him. "How can you be—"

But the musician was already out, right there on the stairs. Was this the brain fog Seymour Barnes had warned of? He remembered The Duck getting confused simply talking about ghosts. They didn't seem to bother Carolyn at all and even Pete felt okay. Uptight, sure, but not loopy. Not like Johnny.

He stood, brushed the wrinkles from his trousers, straightened his tie, and buttoned his suit coat. This was a mission. He would find Snug. He would chase away every single one of these . . . these apparitions. He'd be damned if he was going to lose his job because Hitch happened to rent the wrong house the night Great-Great Grand-Uncle Larcenous decided to go on a crime spree.

49

THE POLICEMEN CAME IN a pair: one was shiny, portly, and bald, the buttons on his uniform straining at his belly. He looked like a drawing from a children's book, Carolyn mused. The other was tall and thin with a prominent Adam's apple that bobbed like a cork on a river.

"We had reports of a man in a suit of armor exiting the museum this evening," said the round one. "And we have a rather expensive theft. We're pretty certain the sighting and the crime are linked. Have you been in the Metropolitan Museum this evening, sir?"

"No, Officer, I haven't," Malcolm answered with Boy Scout sincerity.

"Are you sure?" said the tall one, training a beady eye on him.

Accosted before they could make their escape, this little quiz was out of the way, in a corner of the courtyard. Miss Havisham was dozing on a chaise. Small pockets of guests smoked and chatted. The light from inside was the only light left, the hurricane lamps all run down. A dozen dots of orange glowed from cigarette tips.

"It doesn't seem like something that would slip my mind." Malcolm scratched his forehead with a gloved finger.

The round cop glanced up from his notebook. "You being a smart aleck?"

"No, sir."

"Nobody likes a smart aleck," said the tall one, still squinting.

"No, sir. I agree. I mean, yes, sir. Nobody likes a smart aleck. Not even me. Especially not me."

The round one cleared his throat. "You done?" Carolyn was shifting her weight from one heel to the other. Malcolm was usually more debonair.

"Um, yes, sir. I'm done."

"A confession?" asked the tall one.

"No," Malcolm snapped. "Continue."

"Oh," said the round one. "Thank you for giving us permission to do our job. We appreciate it."

Carolyn stepped between them. "He didn't mean it that way." And now she was Perry Mason.

"I'm sure he didn't," said the tall one, smiling at her. He turned to glare at Malcolm. "Continue," he said, waving his open palm as if welcoming his partner through an open door.

"What's with the getup?" the bald man asked Malcolm.

"I thought this was a costume party, sir."

"You didn't notice nobody else was wearing a costume."

"I thought there were costumes. Or they were changing inside."

"He's not very bright, is he, miss?" The tall one nudged Carolyn.

"Oh, no, Malcolm is quite bright. Or can be! He's a banker."

"And that's supposed to sway me? Stupid is as stupid does, my ma always said."

Carolyn shrugged. "She wasn't wrong."

"You steal a Bible tonight?" The tall one stepped closer to Malcolm. "From the library?"

"What?" Malcolm backed up, arms waving to catch his balance like the Tin Man. He steadied. "No! That seems a particularly weird thing to steal."

"If by weird, you mean stupid, yes, I agree. It's pretty stupid to steal a Bible."

"There is one in every hotel room." Carolyn chirped. "Why steal one when the Gideons have us covered?"

"This was no hotel Bible," the short one said, waving a finger. "No, no, no. It was a Gutenberg."

The tall one whistled. "A Gutenberg."

"I couldn't do that!" Malcolm pleaded.

"You had help, then?"

"I didn't say that."

"You did it alone, then?"

"I didn't do it at all!"

The short one glanced at his notebook. Carolyn wondered how he could read in the dark. "You know anything about a little blue hippo statue?"

Malcolm shook his head. "No offense, sir. That seems a non sequitur."

"Just tell me what you know about the little blue hippo."

"It's little. And it's blue."

The tall cop frowned.

"It's a hippo?" Malcolm offered.

"How do you know that?"

"Because you just told me!"

Carolyn tugged at Malcolm's arm. "Dear," she said.

"*Am* I your dear?" He looked forlorn. "Am I?" He turned from Carolyn back to the cops. "I really have no idea what you're talking about."

"Likewise, buddy," the short one said. "I have no idea what you're talking about."

"He wants an answer to his proposal," Carolyn explained.

The short one jolted. "He proposed to you tonight?"

"No," Malcolm and Carolyn said in unison.

"It was a few weeks ago," Malcolm continued.

"You made him wait that long?" The tall one looked as if he'd just seen an ugly bug on Carolyn's shoulder.

"It wasn't really a proposal," Carolyn said.

"He's either in the game or he's not," the short one said.

Malcolm turned to Carolyn. His armor rustled. "He has a point. Am I in the game?"

The trio of men stared at her. She sucked in a great draft of cool air. There was rain in it, hanging there like a damp coat. It was going to storm. After the party was over. After everyone had left. Goodness, one more thing to stave off.

They were still looking at her. Waiting.

"I don't think it's a game, Malcolm," she said.

"You treat it—" he began.

She turned to the policemen. "He didn't steal anything. A Bible or a hippo. He's the wrong man. He's here to find out if I'll marry him." She turned to Malcolm. "I'm sorry, Malcolm. I'm not going to marry you. It wouldn't be fair."

"Fair," Malcolm sneered. "Don't act like you're doing me a favor." He turned away, then swung back, nearly stumbling with the momentum. "No, wait—you *are* doing me a favor. I dodged a bullet here."

"A bullet would go right through that costume," the tall cop snorted.

"Not that kind of bullet." Malcolm yanked off one glove, then got hung up trying to pull off the other. "I know there's a guy here. I saw you two on the stairwell."

"What?" Carolyn shook her head. "It's not like that."

"That Valentino in the maroon tie sure has ideas," Malcolm spat, finally freeing the second gauntlet. "I wonder why?" He glared at Carolyn.

"Don't be like that." She didn't want this confrontation. This was the moment she'd dreaded since the Flame. She felt as if she might cry, and she didn't want to do that in front of this trio. She would not cry in front of these men. "We're just not right together."

"You're right about that," Malcolm said, shaking the gloves at her. "*I am* fine. You're the wrong one."

She nodded, her mouth pinched. If she spoke a word further, she'd start sobbing in the garden, so she turned and ran toward the house, her shoes clattering against the paving stones.

She heard the police say "Get outta here" to Malcolm as she stepped through the back door. "Get outta here. She's right. You're not the guy we're looking for. You're the wrong man."

The wrong man.

In her rush inside, she landed in a huddle of waiters, who hustled to either side of her like canoes around a rock. Carolyn offered an apologetic smile, a nod, and kept moving. The bustle of the kitchen muffled and the chattering from the party grew, like a great dial had been twisted left, then spun right to a volume she couldn't stand. She was headed to the heart of things. Again. She darted, in search of a powder room, to cry quietly where no one would find her, where she'd mourn the choice she'd known she would have to make without any prodding from fathers or lovers, policemen or ghosts.

50

COULD THE SCENT OF old coal float this far? At the top of the stairs leading to the dank basement, Pete's nose twitched. Mildew, ancient dust, the fire of a furnace. What else would he find? Rat dung. A bust of Cicero. The bones of Andrew Carnegie? How about a loose cannon of a phantom, one ready to disrupt this entire affair and drag Pete's career lower than this cellar.

If Carolyn couldn't call her cousin into line—and you would think asking a small favor from family couldn't hurt, blood and water and all that—then Pete would do it. He was sick of this. The odor of decay wouldn't put him off if it meant keeping this party on course and The Duck on his side.

He flicked a yellowed switch and a bulb buzzed below, a burn of weak wattage and iffy wiring, then the skitter of tiny rodent feet. He hesitated to glance back, as if he were under some mythic curse, but chanced it and saw a fleeting glimpse of Igor with yet another tray of hors d'oeuvres. The food, at least, was a success. He took some comfort in that.

Each step creaked as he went deeper into the house. The floor at the bottom of the steps was pockmarked brick and the walls shed their filthy once-white paint like molting snakes. Calling this the bowels of the house would be kind. Here was another closed door and it swung open only after a hard push with Pete's shoulder. His legs shook when he crossed the threshold. One more glance up the stairs before stepping further and at the top of the flight was the silhouette of a man, broad-shouldered, thick-armed. Wearing a hat with a plume? Pete blinked and the silhouette was gone.

An enormous furnace rumbled in the center of the room. An overhead light hung bare on a thin cord. His mother always told him to hum when he was frightened and what came across his brain? Sammy Davis Jr. and "That Old Black Magic." He struggled for a verse and made his way into the shadows.

"Snug," he sang. "I have a favor to ask. I don't have the cat, so no bribes." He quit the rambling melody. "No complaints," he lied. "Just a favor." At least that was the truth.

When the light went out, Pete spun back to the door in time to see the same broad shoulders and the thick arms, the ponderous stance . . . of a knight in armor? Then there was the slamming door and a clatter as someone lumbered up the steps and, again, the sharp slap of another door slammed.

Uncle James. Just like Johnny had said.

Pete was proud he didn't scream, no matter how reasonable a response: a very reasonable response to a very dark basement. He swore once, then found his way to the first door, fingers bumping over the crumbling plaster. He imagined it swinging open and saw himself rushing up the steps like a mountain goat. The door at the top of the steps would let out into the hall and the light and all the guests. Here is the church, here is the steeple, open the door and—

He grabbed the cold handle and it wouldn't turn. He shook it. It resisted, the sturdiest thing in the entire place. This stupid rickety house had a door like Fort Knox.

He shook it again. No dice.

Behind him resumed the tip-tap of clawed feet.

He hollered and banged, but knew full well his wailing wouldn't break through the commotion upstairs. Pete gulped the stifling air. Coal dust caked his tongue, his throat ragged from the shouting. He rested his damp forehead against the grimy door, solid as a safe, and surrendered to the silence and whatever hovered in the dark around him.

A screaming man was just another sound effect.

51

BEFORE CAROLYN COULD ESCAPE into the bathroom, she was accosted by the Addamses and the Hitchcocks clucking in the first-floor gallery.

"I found mine," Alma said, snagging her by the arm. "You find yours?"

Carolyn tried to speak but her tongue refused to budge.

Alma gave Carolyn's red eyes a knowing glance. "Have you considered this is like the house from *Cluedo*," she announced to the others. "Rooms full of props and menace."

Carolyn knew Alma was directing the conversation and she welcomed it.

"*Cluedo*?" Barbara turned from inspecting the mantel. She posed there as if she were Joan Crawford.

"*Clue*," Hitchcock corrected his wife. "It's called *Clue* in America." He turned to Barbara. "The board game. The one about death." He relished the last word.

"Oh yes! How fun! Proper people running around an old house, murdering each other, and in the lead is an Englishman." Barbara brushed her husband's lapel with an elegant hand.

"No one is *actually* murdering anyone," Addams said. "Right?"

"Not yet anyway," Barbara cooed.

He took a step back, while Hitchcock meandered toward the stairs. Everyone followed. Carolyn sensed this was not a conscious decision, but the wandering of a mesmerized herd.

"As marvelous as whodunits are," Hitchcock said, "I leave them to Mrs. Christie." He rested his hand on the newel post. "Those to the manor born really don't spend their time scampering about trying to vivisect one another. They're far too dull for that. Besides, *whydunits* are so much more revealing. Why would Mrs. Addams, for instance, bump off anyone in the kitchen? There are only two reasons for murder: lust or money. Which is it, Mrs. Addams?"

Henry Fonda, sallow-skinned, stumbled into the gallery behind them.

He gave Carolyn a careful nod, sized up the others, and collapsed on a love seat. When he spoke, his voice was back to its camera-ready steadiness. "The most offensive thing I've seen tonight is the fawning over that halfback from the Giants."

Carolyn was staring at him, then made herself look away. Even drunk and drained, he was an excellent actor.

"Was that a play on words, Henry?" Hitchcock grinned. "*Offense*? It was nearly witty."

"A giant?" Alma laughed. "How did I miss him?"

"Not a giant-giant, Mrs. Hitchcock," Carolyn said. "A football player."

"*American* football," Hitchcock said. "Not one of our fellows. They introduced me to him earlier. Grace's agent thinks he's popular with the public and pretty enough to be in pictures. Wants to send him to Hollywood when his playing days are through."

"Who knows what his face will look like by then," Addams said. "Might end up with a mug like mine."

"Jocks turn to acting," Fonda said while he picked at a tray of cheese and crackers. "It's not impossible." The stray slices were mouse-worn and Fonda wasn't helping. He wasn't eating, he was dismantling.

"Indeed," Hitchcock agreed. "This fellow might be a Shakespearian in the bud. He's certainly strapping. I've had my share of working with hunks. All actors are pieces of meat. Athletes are simply a different cut."

Fonda glared. "That's putting it directly to your leading man."

"No offense meant, Henry."

"No offense taken, Hitch." For the first time that evening, Carolyn saw Fonda smile. It was impressive. Sour most moments, not entirely handsome, too craggy, too stony, but when he smiled, his charm increased tenfold. She'd seen girls do this, particular beauties, but never a man, not even those boys with perfect teeth at the Flame, not even Malcolm. This was Fonda's secret weapon, like he'd taken off a pair of ugly glasses, and, *bam*, he was Superman. She had a difficult time not smiling in return, despite herself. She'd never trusted Clark Kent.

"Vera isn't here tonight because she's run off to marry Tarzan," Hitchcock said.

"That really gets your goat," Addams poked.

"Johnny Weissmuller?" Fonda said.

"No, we're two Tarzans beyond him," Hitchcock said with disdain. "Gordon Monkeycall or something."

"Maybe the Giant can be next," Alma added.

"Oh, perhaps. Now that Vera has stripped the jungle of the last man, she'll have to move on to other terrain."

"A giant of the jungle," Alma said.

"King Kong, I guess," Hitchcock offered. "There's a film I still admire. Such a perfect tale, like *Beauty and the Beast*. Maybe Vera and her new husband would be willing to star." He turned to Carolyn. "Or you and this athlete from across town? I could find the right project for you." He summed her up for the second time that evening, his eyes lingering from her shoes to the top of her head. She didn't want him to know it annoyed and embarrassed her, so she stuck up her chin.

"I told you," Carolyn said, "I'm not an actress." Though maybe she was, more than she'd admit. Surely holding back tears for a quarter of an hour was a performance.

"Good girl," said Alma.

"Perhaps not," Hitchcock said. "But you really are quite fetching."

"It's kind of you to say." Carolyn fought the urge to curtsy, the old habit so ingrained from her youth. What an unwelcome tic to resurrect.

"Humility is also attractive," Hitchcock observed, still judging Carolyn. "I suppose I should try it." He studied her some more. She felt as if she were strung behind the counter at a butcher's shop. "It makes me want to put you in pictures all the more."

Fonda was still fondling the cheese tray and giving Carolyn nervous glances, back to his Clark Kentness. Addams grimaced at his oblivious wife, who had returned to the knickknacks on the mantel, picking them up and putting them down as if pricing items at a bazaar.

"Stay away, Carolyn," Alma whispered, with genuine warmth and a fleeting touch on her arm. "This business isn't for nice girls."

"You seem a nice girl," Carolyn said.

"I haven't been a girl for a very long time," Alma laughed. "Or for that matter, ever very nice."

52

TRAPPED IN THE BASEMENT, Pete would come to understand the house was the ghosts' realm, not his, not Carolyn's, not The Duck's, but first he had to wonder where was Snug when he wanted her? She was supposed to stay low, had promised, but not so low he couldn't find her. Carolyn had seemed as clueless as he was, but he suspected she knew about all of this. Why didn't she help him after the week they'd had? Maybe that was unfair, but she had disappeared just like Hitchcock, down hidden passages, lost chambers, rabbit holes he hadn't considered. Was there a secret tunnel? If he could venture with a candle, he could find his way out, but, no, he was here, on the floor, in the basement, in the dark.

"Snug!" Pete called. "Snug! I need to talk with you!" He wanted to raise his voice, scream to the ceilings, but he was all screamed out. He leaned against the grimy wall and willed himself steady, hands pressed to the sides of his head.

At least his hair was still neat.

What was it, a half hour since the door locked? An hour? He couldn't gauge the passing minutes. A ghost in the afternoon, unwanted, a ghost now—ten o'clock, eleven?—sought and unfound. "Snug! Come here!" he hissed. Snug didn't have ears, not the kind with canals and drums. How could she hear anything? And yet she did. Pete could speak or whisper, maybe even merely *think* loudly. So that's what he did: he thought. He pinpointed his mind's gaze to a single idea: Snug floating by the light of the furnace. He squeezed his eyes tight, really squeezed, and concentrated. Snug would appear before him, taking shape like a cloud in a blue sky. Not a horse or a winged bird, but a dead girl from decades ago.

He felt a buzz in the room and opened one lid. There she was, outlined in electric blue, blazing like a billboard in Times Square.

"You rang?" she said, not annoyed, maybe even pleased.

Pete tried to speak, coughed unexpectedly, caught his breath, and held up a hand. There was dust down his throat. "Yes," he croaked. He wanted to ask her to free him, but that's not what came out. "And now you need to go. And leave us the party. Take your uncle, too." He saw the hurt flash across her face like lightning, but he couldn't care. "All of them."

"This is *my* house," Snug said curtly. "This is *our* house."

"Not tonight, Snug."

She flew right to his nose, a chilly wind with a pinched expression. "I thought you'd want me to open the door, let you out. I would have done that. I might even have given you two more wishes. I was going to be your genie, you stupid man."

She swung around him, went through the wall, and there was silence. Then she flew back into the room, up to his face again. "You are rude. Another rude man in *my* house." She flew around the furnace, a blue cyclone, went through the wall again, and returned.

"Too bad you can't do that or you wouldn't need me. I'm good at opening doors." Then she was at the furnace, opening its maw, pointing to the fire. "It's burning tonight because we have guests. Wouldn't want them uncomfortable." She shut the furnace again, but her hand lingered on the long handle. Then she was back at his nose, so, so angry. "Or is that what I *do* want? To make the guests uncomfortable."

Then she was gone.

Pete realized three things: 1) Never anger a ghost, 2) Snug was beautiful, her mouth and her eyes and—oh, she looked like Carolyn, and 3) This *was* her house, not his. Not The Duck's or Hitchcock's.

Three more stipulations, but too late.

It was too late to apologize. Left alone in his moment of contrition, the air she'd disturbed pooled around him like a pond returned to stillness. She had flown like a great predator, an owl hunting in a thick wood. Beware, groundlings. And he was a mouse.

He understood, or thought he did. Pete hadn't appreciated Snug's place in the house, her family's place, their history, not even with Carolyn by his side. He couldn't just storm in for a single night and change everything. That wasn't his right. He'd tell Snug that if she were here.

But she was off to do some damage.

His timing stank.

53

CAROLYN HURRIED PAST THE kitchen, alive with Angelo's labor, and snuck out the side exit. A pair of reporters were smoking by the servants' door and stepped politely out of her way.

"Don't mind me," she said. "I just need a little air."

The shorter, dark-haired one said, "I say that, then light up one of these." He offered his pack and she thanked him.

The taller thrust a folded newspaper at his companion. "Your rag says there's no ghosts in the house."

The short smoker laughed. "Watch what you call a rag!" He bent to read by the light cast from an uncurtained window. "Hmmph." He looked at Carolyn. "You seen any?" He pointed to a column above the fold:

> Architect Curzon Taylor heard telling a friend: "Read about the haunted house at 7 East Eightieth where Alfred Hitchcock is throwing a party (tonight by the way)? I lived in that place for twenty years. Never saw a ghost."

Snug's brother. So she hadn't shown herself to him or he was protecting her. Wouldn't a loyal brother keep his sister's spirit a secret? If her brother Andrew returned, Carolyn wouldn't tell the press. She'd keep it hidden for as long as it meant protecting him. Andrew. Her mother. If only Carolyn had that secret to keep. She could be like Bella, keep it quiet for decades.

"Not a one," Carolyn said. Despite the evening's practice, she was certain they could see the lie scrawled across her flushed cheeks. "Would either of you know where the closest telephone is? The house doesn't have a line. Not anymore."

They both turned to the curb. "See that big truck with the WNBC logo?" the taller one said. "If you ask nice, they'll hook you up."

Carolyn stared at him. "Really? You can make a telephone call from a truck?"

"And more," the shorter one added. He crushed the end of the cigarette with his heel. "Did you hear there's a transatlantic cable going under the ocean right now? By the end of the year, we can call Europe on the cheap."

"She don't want to call Europe." The taller one turned to Carolyn. "Right?" She nodded. "Take her over to the boys, Orlando. Tell them to be helpful."

Carolyn looked at Orlando. He shrugged. "Worth a shot."

There was a slender man standing at the truck's open back doors. Another fellow hunched on a short stool inside the packed cavern, huddled among wires and metal consoles and blinking lights. The capsule of a flying saucer couldn't be busier.

"Lady wants to make a call," Orlando said. "You boys spare a line?"

The seated man wore a headset and a scowl. "Do I look like Ma Bell?" He plugged a heavy black cord into a port. "Seymour here just asked the same."

"He charged me fifteen cents," Seymour said with a smile.

"Oh, I don't have my purse." Carolyn looked back at the house. From this distance, the party was muted and seemed much farther away than possible.

"The network doesn't need your money," Orlando insisted.

"Got a free line to Radio City," the headset man offered.

"I don't need a Rockette." Carolyn smiled.

"Now he'll charge you a quarter," said Seymour.

"Nah, it's free," the headset man said. He lingered on Carolyn's face and his eyes narrowed. "As long as I don't get caught."

"I won't tell a soul." She pointed at the headset. "Do I need to use that?"

"We're not that nifty." He turned to his buddy. "Barnes, grab that field phone again. Unless you want to take her to the castle."

Orlando hummed. "You an engineer?"

"Sometimes," Seymour answered. He turned to the headset guy. "But I'm not going back tonight." He shivered and crossed his arms.

"You look like the place is haunted," Orlando joked. He tapped Carolyn's shoulder with the rolled paper. "Maybe Hitch rented the wrong place."

"I doubt that," Seymour said.

Carolyn studied him. "There's a castle?"

"Just around the corner," he said. "We have telephones, but I'd rather not."

"How far away is it?" Carolyn glanced back at her aunts' house again. She had to return to the party but felt a pull to investigate. Fonda had said something about a castle.

"Up to the corner and half block around."

For a moment, she felt the weight of another decision.

"Just let her use the field phone," Orlando said. "I gotta get back."

"So do I," she said. "I won't be long."

"Better not be," headset man mumbled. He spun to Carolyn. "Who you gonna call?"

"Isabella Markell. It's Regent 7-2911."

Seymour standing beside her giggled and she felt his chill lift. His arms opened wide. "Oh, you don't need to do that!"

Carolyn cocked her head. "Excuse me?"

He patted her shoulder and gave her the widest smile she'd seen all evening. "I already did."

Thomas Satterthwaite shimmered with a pulsing current, unmoved by the wind atop the roof. Snug had taken him from his usual spots in the house. Strangers were everywhere, threatening the familiar. The night was skewed, but he had weighed what the girl should do and he would plead Walter's case.

"I have spoken with your father, Snug. He wants to apologize. He was wrong—wrong to run off. Wrong to wound Mariah so. But we only have one life and he can't undo his choices. He's done the worst and desires to say he is sorry. Walter was clever with numbers, a bright boy in school, at the office, and a dunderhead at home, with women."

He watched bats wing between buildings. She waited.

"Walter couldn't make amends, not in the end, not after all that water under the bridge. Nothing could save poor Walter. No boat could keep him afloat. I saw him, flayed and walking. He was always exhausted, a man who spent too many days at the mercy of his stupid whims. And that was before his death. I can only imagine his condition decades later."

Uncle Thomas was a gentle man and a gentler spirit. And nothing like her father. An hour ago, she wasn't ready. But she discovered, to her own surprise, after coming from the cellar, she was prepared. This was the way to end something—the dismay that began the morning her father left. If Uncle Thomas believed her father wanted to apologize, then she was committed to listening. She was ready to be done.

And later, if she so desired, she would give him the letter.

54

HER NIECE MET HER at the front door and whisked her up the stairs, away from the hullabaloo. She didn't expect Carolyn at the door—after all, Seymour had called her—and though she knew it was a party, she didn't expect the guests. So many! Isabella and Mariah would have had the maids shoo them out with a broom. "Are you trying to hide me from the host?" Bella said. She felt she was bellowing but the racket below was a din, so alien in the otherwise familiar house. It had never sounded like this before.

"No, Aunt Bella," Carolyn assured. "Not you."

Bella knew the place well, despite not having been in it for years. The gallery. The parlor. The library, where her niece opened the door and slunk inside as if they were spies. They sat at the heavy round table and Carolyn took her hands. "Snug is here," she said.

"I know," Bella said. That was not news.

"And there are others."

She inhaled. This wasn't exactly news either. "Seymour said as much."

Carolyn leaned closer. "Who *is* Seymour and why does he know *that*?"

Bella had prepared an explanation, but she was distracted by a thick book on the table between them. "What is this?" The words were German in that Gothic font that made everything stern. She turned an illuminated page, recognized the numbers.

"It's a Bible," Carolyn answered.

"Yes," Bella said, "but not any Bible."

There was a distinct change in the room, barometric pressure, or scent, a shift that told Bella things were not the same. She turned in her chair to follow Carolyn's gaze.

At the other side of the room was the hazy border of a man. Through him, she could still spy shelves. Each moment he grew more substantial, yet still translucent, a stack of books balanced in his arms and a plume on his King Arthur helmet. Its pointy visor raised, his silver face lit the interior with a faint luminescence, like a child's night-light. Bella recognized him, no question, though she'd seen him only in faded photographs and painted portraits. Without a word, she stood and approached the figure, greeting him as she would a dignitary from a foreign land.

"James Lenox," she said, "why are you wearing a suit of armor?" It was not the question she'd intended.

"It's mine." He patted the shining breastplate. "It was in my collection," he said, eager to educate them. "I couldn't wear it then—it was far too heavy for my mortal self. But I can wear it now as easily as cloth. You'd be surprised what I can hoist. Simply put my mind to it and use a little air, and whoosh, I can lift most anything."

"Even a priceless book carried blocks from where it's supposed to be," Bella accused.

"It is supposed to be where I am. I am here, hence it is here. It's mine, you know."

"*Was* yours, Uncle James," Bella added. "Was." She spoke to Carolyn. "Henrietta Lenox left everything to the library," Bella said. She turned to the ghost. "That's what you wanted."

"Yes, when I was alive. Now I'm here. I want it back."

"You're going to keep bringing stuff out of the library and into this house, tonight, while the house is filled with strangers?" Carolyn's voice was incredulous.

"I hadn't thought it quite so plainly, but now that you say it aloud, yes, yes, that is my intention. And I will continue to do so, whether there are festivities or not. I can restore all my favorite belongings here and no one will be the wiser."

In her living room, twenty minutes ago, Bella had a bit of Dubonnet in a crystal glass on a side table by her favorite armchair. That had been peaceful. Here, she was bickering with the dead.

"Folderol!" scoffed Bella. She studied his opaque eyes. "Those are not the actions of an honorable man." She knew what would stir this fellow, sure as she knew her own code. He would consider himself above reproach. "You had a reputation for wisdom. Now you're being impossible. You can't store anything here—not books, not paintings, not statues or armor. Not even yourself."

Carolyn stood by her side. "This house is for sale. You all have to go." Bella considered how many *all* might number in that statement, but Carolyn barreled on. "You, especially, but Aunt Isabella and Aunt Mariah, and Uncle

Thomas and Uncle Walter and even Snug, who it seems to me has the greatest stake in this house, she's been here the longest—"

"I've been dead considerably longer than she—"

"Yes, but she's been *here* the longest. This has been her home, and the doctor's, for decades, and even they'll see that they have to leave. You must go and return all your belongings. They aren't even your belongings anymore." Carolyn stamped her foot. "They belong to the New York City Public Library! To the Metropolitan Museum!"

Bella tabulated souls. Six. *Six!* She sat on the nearest chair. It was a Hitchcock. Not *that* Hitchcock.

Uncle James walked to the Bible, closed it, then rested his hand on the cover. "Henrietta," he whispered. "Oh, Henrietta."

He took off the helmet and wiped his brow. He tucked it under his arm and raised his chin. "You are correct. I have been selfish and greedy. This is not how I wish to be known."

"My boyfriend was questioned by the police because of *your* stealing," Carolyn said. Bella gave her a quizzical look and Carolyn faced her aunt. "Yes, he's here. And we broke up." She turned back to Lenox. "My ex-boyfriend," she corrected. "Even so, I'd hate to see him end up sitting in a precinct house."

"I can resolve that, my niece." Lenox paused. "And your young man in the cellar? Not my fellow cavalier. The other boy, the one who works here."

Carolyn put both hands on the edge of the table. "What do you mean *the cellar?*"

He gave a little shrug. "I mean the lowest level. That's typically a cellar."

"I'm sure she's familiar with the concept," Bella said from her perch.

Uncle James scowled at her. "Sarcasm does not become you." He turned to Carolyn. "Go to the basement. The girl is not helping him."

"What girl?"

"The maiden of the house."

Carolyn shot Bella a nervous glance. "I have to go," she said and scurried out of the room.

Uncle James hovered by Bella's seat. She drew her finger along the top of the heavy book. It was weathered and sturdy. She felt a kinship with it.

"Do you know long it took me to obtain it?" He spoke as if he'd read her mind. "How many resources I had to expend to bring that book to the New World? And yet, I never really enjoyed it. Not the way I should have. There was always another volume to discover, another quest. I spent a king's ransom and more on my bibliomania. It was a madness. And I let that madness take hold tonight." He patted her knee, a strange swift pressure, *one, two*. Then he floated to the door. "I will not let our family suffer for my transgressions. You can be assured of that."

Helmet fixed on his head, he flipped the visor closed with a dramatic flourish, hoisted the Bible with precision and care to the crook of his elbow, and flew out of the library.

"There," said Bella, admiration in her voice, but speaking to an empty room, "goes a ghost I believe we can trust."

55

THE STAIRS TO THE basement squealed with a whining cat's cry. Carolyn gripped the railing and let her eyes adjust to the dark, despite the candelabra in her grip. *Cree, cree,* the wood winced, as she set her weight down tenuously with each step. The air was dry, a mix of dirt and coal and stale time, grit that caught in her throat. She coughed.

There was a closed door in front of her. The knob resisted, so she tried again. It wouldn't budge. There was a tap on her shoulder and she twisted to see Snug hovering behind her.

"What are—"

"You can't go in there," Snug said.

Carolyn grabbed the knob again. A whoosh of air ran between her and the door, a brief and direct wind, and she plopped back on the steps. Half the candles blew out. "Stop it!" she yelled at Snug, who was grinning like a naughty child. Carolyn pushed off the stairs and lunged at the handle, and this time the lock popped like the give of a loose tooth and the door swung open. She fumbled for the light switch and the buzzing of a frail bulb was her reward.

"Fine," Snug whined and disappeared.

It was difficult to align this room—the peeling cement walls, the stained floor—with the elegance of the stories above. Clearly, few people ever ventured here. The party was a brook of bobbing conversation, accompanied by the house itself: the air currents, the whisper of radiators, the steady churn of the furnace in the next room. She followed its heartbeat and found the old cast-iron furnace with its thick ducts curving upward into the ceiling. To the left, by the light of her three flickering wicks, was the coal room. Its walls were stained with angled patterns. Angels or demons? Oh, she was thinking like Hitchcock. That had to stop.

Something glowed beyond the doorframe.

Blue light. Dark shadows. Blue light again. The motes of suspended dirt glowed like neon snow, just for a moment, then were gone.

A voice spoke in the dark: "I'm glad someone came to get me."

There was Pete, brushing his knees, like he'd just gotten off the floor, and his eyes too wide. Unruly hair fell over his forehead and he swiped at it impatiently.

"What are you doing down here?"

"Looking for wine." His laugh cracked. "Amontillado, anyone?"

She didn't laugh back. "Snug is still on the loose."

"I know. I tried to get her to cooperate—"

"That was my intention—"

"—and she didn't find me persuasive. I probably made things worse." His breathing was loud in the otherwise hushed room. "Thanks for rescuing me. You're my knight"—his smile returned and she knew, without a doubt, he saw her smiling, too—"in shining—"

She balked. "I've had enough of those for one evening."

"I know what you mean." He was putting on a brave front. How long had he been trapped down here? With an infuriated Snug?

They stood facing each other by the light of the furnace and candle flame.

"Honestly," he repeated. "Thanks."

Carolyn didn't speak but the room lost all its gloom. Pete was okay. Worse for wear, but okay. She had a plan and she had Bella above. Taking his hand, she led him through the battered door and up the stairs before her dead cousin had second thoughts and locked them both in the basement for good.

It was early in the influenza and Snug remembered her mother hadn't wanted to go to the opera house that night. There was so much talk about illness, but Aunt Isabella and Uncle Thomas had given the tickets as a present for Mariah's fifty-third birthday. When a doctor tells you the theater is permissible, it seems odd to object. Fifty-three had sounded so old to Snug at the time and now it didn't seem old at all. Curzon had no interest in the arts, though he did love the building, so he spent the evening gazing at the golden walls and the ornate scrollwork. Mariah and Snug went for the drama on the stage and the elegance in the crowd. The audience was exactly as they'd imagined, the gowns and the gloves and the hats, but the mood was strange. Dozens of people wore scarves over their faces, others had cloth masks. Something was lurking in the air and it wasn't all gas from the stage lights. The bill was a trio of one acts by Giacomo Puccini, and Mariah loved them each but the third one, *Gianni Schicchi*, was the one she recalled, again and again. It was marvelous. An English woman sang an aria, "O mio babbino caro," so beautifully, Snug had wept.

Her mother had touched her arm, a warning not to make a scene, to keep her emotions in control, but Snug wasn't alone. The stranger next to her was sniffling. A woman in the row in front of them—in a burgundy gown revealing her bare shoulders, even in the dead of winter—cried quietly. Snug had watched her shake gently as the last note floated to the top of the high ceiling. The crowd was silent for a second, then roared for an encore. Mama whispered that the singer wouldn't do it. There was a rule against encores. Snug couldn't understand. Why would anyone forbid a second chance to experience rapture? They all wanted her to sing it again. She could have listened to it all night. They clapped and the men shouted and the soprano reappeared, her cheeks flushed. She sang it all over. It was as heartbreaking the second time as it had been the first.

The rule against encores tilted against her thoughts, a jousting spear. It seemed to bury itself in her brain and jabbed at the oddest times. There was a rule against encores, the sharp sting said. No one gets to plead for a second chance.

What if you didn't ask for it, but the song simply started again? The violins, the cellos, the French horns—they all began. You couldn't leave them playing along without joining in, that wouldn't be right, would it?

But we shouldn't do the same thing twice, even if it's beautiful. That was cheating.

If something was thrilling once, though, what's the harm in doing it again?

Especially if you didn't ask for it.

Oh, Papa, the girl in the opera pleaded, *have pity*. The soprano only wanted to love a boy and if she couldn't, she would die. *At last, I want to die*, she told her father at the end of the song. *I want to die.*

We made her sing it twice and we cried both times.

Snug could say that to her father and mean it, but it wouldn't be about romance. She had never loved, not like that. If she had lived, would she have married? Had children? She didn't know. Sometimes she thought not, but what would she have done to fill her days instead? Live like her mother, or her aunt, or her cousin? Bella had lived, why hadn't she? Snug had all this *extra* time and what had she done with it? She had waited, and watched Mama live, and waited some more, then watched Mama die, and watched Aunt Isabella live, and then watched her die, too. And waited.

She was caught in the audience, watching everyone else's drama.

Why was she still here tonight? Watching these strangers live. And if she saw her father again tonight, what would she say? Forgiveness, yes, but in return? Whatever Papa could or couldn't give her, she was more than ready, well past time, to say, at last, *she* wanted to die.

She thought they should all be there, wherever *there* was, Mama and Aunt Isabella and Uncle Thomas and Father. That other angry woman. The old man and his precious collection.

All the servants were gone now and no one left alive but Curzon and he'd never come back.

None of them caught even a cold that night. They read the review in the *Tribune* that weekend. The reporter had loved the performance as much as Mariah and Snug. The show went on to a long run, so many people wanted to hear the English woman sing that love song again and again and again.

Encores were outlawed, but that didn't mean they didn't happen.

Igor Imagines A STRANGER COMES TO TOWN, a screenplay

INT. The Gallery. The party continues. A NEW MAN enters, dressed in a windbreaker and chinos. He is raw-boned, but not unhealthy. He holds a drooping lily, but he bounces with enthusiasm. His eyes burn brighter than any candle in the room. A lock of curly brown hair spills over his tall forehead. No one notices him, except a single WAITER. He warily approaches the newcomer.

        IGOR
May I help you?

The man takes a quick look at Igor but can't keep his attention from darting from one end of the room to the other.

        THE MAN
Oh, this is wonderful! I've never seen anything like this before!

        IGOR
And you are?

        THE MAN
Delighted! This is such good news. I feel like it's my birthday. What a gift! What a relief!

        IGOR
And this relief belongs to?

        THE MAN
Me! Seymour Barnes. I haven't felt this in, well, ever.

Igor watches Seymour Barnes with caution, as if he might leap like a leopard or sing like a diva at *any second. He glances around for help, but RENFRO is nowhere in sight.*

> IGOR
> Have you had a lot to drink, sir?

> SEYMOUR
> Not a drop. Oh, I'm rude.

Seymour extends his hand.

> SEYMOUR (cont'd)
> Pleased to meet you.

> IGOR
> I'm Joe—no, wait—I'm Igor. Tonight, I'm Igor.

> SEYMOUR
> I'm still Seymour.

His attention is drawn to the ceiling, his mouth a happy bow. Igor stares up, unsure of what he'll see. The air above them is empty. Igor wonders what he expected.

> SEYMOUR
> There's so much going on here!

He strides from the waiter and heads boldly into the next room but is stopped. There is movement in the crowd and a hurried series of excuse me, excuse me. CAROLYN rushes into the gallery, followed by PETE, his suit rumpled, his eyes adjusting to the light like a mole pulled from his hole. She glances around, looking for someone, then leaves. Pete begins after her, then freezes.

> PETE
> Mr. Barnes? Mr. Barnes!

Seymour skids to a stop, bobs his bird head, and gives Pete a fond glance.

> SEYMOUR
> Hello again, Mr. D'Onofrio!

> PETE
> Donoff.

Seymour is still looking for something, side to side, up and down. He takes Pete by the elbow and leans in to him, whispering animatedly. He leads him out of the gallery, holding him by the arm.

Carolyn returns from the other direction.

Igor looks at Carolyn. Carolyn looks at Igor. He gives a they-went-that-a-way nod. She smiles and follows them.

The lone waiter watches her go. He holds an empty tray. He considers where to put it, then tucks it under his arm and follows the others, leaving the gallery to the rest of the guests.

56

SUDDENLY SEEING SEYMOUR SEEMED a disaster in proportion with spotting another specter.

"I didn't think," Pete said, "we'd see you here." They shook hands—Seymour's grip aggressive yet cheerful—and Pete put his other hand on Seymour's arm to steady him. "Manhattan's a dud," he said, overacting in his most dispirited tone, "a bust, isn't it, Mr. Barnes?"

"Wrong!" Seymour exclaimed, his head jerking like an excited chicken, his arms free and waving the lily. "And I'm so happy to be wrong. The spectral energy here, tonight, is unlike anything I've ever gauged."

A pair of buzzed admen turned from their conversation and stared.

"There's *something* going on here," one man said. "Heavenly bodies." He nudged his companion and wagged his head at Carolyn. His companion chortled. She rolled her eyes and walked off.

"Wait," Pete called.

"I said spectral," Seymour corrected. "Not heavenly. Spectral has no body at all! Just air, wisps, but nothing we'd think of as physical!" And he was gone, hustling off in the opposite direction, hunting after—Pete didn't want to imagine what. The night had somehow become more complicated. Had Snug summoned Seymour?

"Well, that's a shame," the man sneered. Pete turned to tell the guy to take a hike when Carolyn reappeared in the far doorway, Mrs. Markell beside her in a deep blue dress. The artist parted the seas as the women strode toward him. Men made a show of stepping out of her way, as if the Queen had arrived. They weren't wrong.

"Mrs. Markell!" Pete gave a little bow. "I didn't know you were coming."

"I wasn't," she said, taking his hand in a gentler fashion than Seymour. "Then I received an urgent phone call. I would have arrived before, but it took our doorman longer to hail a cab than the drive itself. Even at my age, I could have walked it faster."

He turned to Carolyn. "You called her?" There was commotion and Seymour Barnes called "Shoot!" from the hallway.

"We're in over our heads," Carolyn said. "A lot over our heads."

Seymour Barnes was back, smiling and sweating like a man who'd just played tennis. The letch and his buddy from before were watching. Pete retreated and gently pulled Carolyn along. Seymour and Mrs. Markell followed. They were out of earshot from the rest of the crowd.

"Mrs. Markell," Seymour said, catching his breath and settling next to Pete.

"Mr. Barnes," Bella said. They nodded, like business associates. "Thank you for calling."

"He called you?" Pete blurted. He swiveled to Seymour. "You know each other?"

"Everyone knows Bella," Seymour said. "From the docks to Gracie Mansion."

"And everyone knows Seymour," added Bella, "from the living to the dead."

"You exaggerate," Seymour said, shaking his head, cheeks flushing even more.

"This is about the ghosts," Pete said, stating the obvious. He felt them staring. Why was he the only person bailing water from this leaky boat? Why were they all just watching, doing nothing? "You need to help us direct them to the right place."

"Certainly not!" Seymour resisted. "They can't go anywhere, Mr. D'Onofrio."

"Donoff," Pete snapped. He hadn't chosen the stupid name, it was his father who erased the past, but here he was left defending it. Seymour Barnes recognized Pete's albatross. Tomorrow, if Pete made it through the party still employed, it was time Mr. D'Onofrio went to the office. No more Donoff. It seemed an easier fix than every other problem tonight. "Can't you get them where they need to go?"

"Unthinkable. They can't leave! Not until I've fully documented them." Seymour had a pen in one hand and a notebook in the other.

It was Pete's pen, the one he'd given to Snug. "Where did you get that?"

"Excuse me," Bella interrupted. "This is their home." Her voice was firm. "They will do as they please. We are merely guests, and we do not get to order them to do anything." She stared at the men and Pete felt her gaze reduce the chatter of the party to background static. Carolyn stood beside her aunt, arms crossed in defiance. "They may not be alive," Bella said, "but they *live* here."

Pete blinked and Hitchcock appeared next to Carolyn, as if he'd been dropped from the rafters. "*Live* seems a stretch," he intoned.

Bella turned and gave him a once-over. "Mr. Hitchcock," she said with a chilly nod. "You know what we're discussing?" Her voice was firm; a lesser guest would have wavered. Hitchcock responded to her strength with vigor.

"I do, madam. I have had"—he searched for a word—"a *visitation*. A charming young girl. Oh, neither young nor girl any longer, I grant. But charming nonetheless."

"Snug," Bella said. "You've seen Snug."

"More than seen," he said. He bent conspiratorially: "We spoke."

"What?" Carolyn said.

Bella huffed. "I haven't spoken with Snug in decades." Her eyes clouded. Pete feared for a moment she would cry, but Bella shook it off and recaptured her poise. "Will you tell?" She gestured at the other partygoers. "Reveal them to these people? To the media?"

"I won't tell a soul." He crossed his heart. "I promise, Mrs.—"

"Markell," Bella said.

"—Mrs. Markell. Not a soul about the souls." He tapped his nose. "I'm not entirely convinced Disney hasn't put you all up to it to make me look foolish."

"Disney?" Bella sounded incredulous.

"Surely you have heard of him?"

"What's he got to do with—"

Hitchcock waved his hand irritably. "He only looks kindly. His hands are in everything, including, I suspect, these apparitions." The director turned to Carolyn. "So, no, I won't tell because I won't look a fool. If Disney is doing this, it's his brilliance."

Hitchcock's voice, for the first time that evening, didn't sound like a put-on.

"And if she is real—and perhaps I would like her to be, fiercely so—if she is real, I would hardly want my competitors to know about her. I will save her for myself."

Carolyn touched his sleeve. "No one can know about her," she insisted.

The showman returned: he mimed zipping his lips. "Nobody does."

Bella held Pete's elbow and ushered them all into a tight semicircle. Even Hitchcock deferred to her authority. "But to make the party more manageable for our young man," she smiled at Pete, "we could reason with her, for her sake as well as our own." She surveyed the crowded gallery. "But not in the midst of this. Let's go to the library."

"A library?" Seymour marveled. "Oh, splendid! Do you know how to get there?"

"Yes," she said with a glance at Carolyn. "I am quite familiar with it."

They trailed behind her like such obedient ducklings. They even picked up Mrs. Hitchcock, like a straggler, at the end of the line. If they'd wound up in Boston, Pete wouldn't have been surprised. Instead, they only ventured to the third floor, to the library, which seemed dimmer, lit with a single green-shaded lamp on the conspicuously clear table. That big Bible was gone.

57

"OH, THIS IS STUPENDOUS," Seymour Barnes sang, taking in the room like a child at a circus. "So inviting! The aura, the temptations. How could she resist? It isn't tacky at all. I thought it would be ridiculous. It's not."

"Thank you?" said Carolyn.

"This room, it's like a delectable treat to the denizens of the Other World."

"Denizens?" Pete coughed.

"Ah, yes, we're inviting them to a kind of banquet," Hitchcock said gleefully.

"You are, in a way. It's not dissimilar," Seymour lectured. "Would you go to an environment that wasn't enticing? They don't want a sterile area. That wouldn't speak to them. Think of ghosts as memories energized into a kind of matter, though a matter we can't dissect. We can't explain it, we can only lure it into the open with the sort of time-dense goodies that appear here. This house is stuffed—"

"Indeed." Hitchcock eyed a taxidermied owl perched on a high ledge over the doorway. "I quite like that one."

"That owl *might* have been my aunts'," Carolyn said. "It certainly looks fierce."

"Like our aunts." Bella squeezed Carolyn's shoulder.

"Stuffed with cerebral—no, celestial—delicacies," Seymour Barnes praised.

"That's unappetizing," Pete said.

They stood, like a group of tourists led to a holy site who found themselves with nothing else to do.

Reflected in the window overlooking Eightieth Street, Hitchcock observed, "I'd be more impressed if someone could conjure Grace here this evening rather than welcoming the underworld."

"Nooo," Seymour murmured. "They haven't been to the underworld. I don't think they've ever left New York."

The director sighed. "My Grace is definitely more cosmopolitan than that."

Pete looked askance at Seymour. "Wait, why didn't *you* know about them?"

"Our research team is understaffed."

Carolyn had an inkling. "How many people are on your research team?"

Seymour looked sheepish. "*C'est moi. Moi seulement.*"

Hitchcock smirked. "French always makes a difficult admission more palatable."

Seymour flinched. "I did the best I could. Don't consider this revelation a flaw—it's a happy discovery. I'm thrilled to be wrong!"

Carolyn turned to Pete. "It's not often a man says that."

Pete said, "I—"

"I'll say!" said Alma Hitchcock, formerly silent beside her husband. She raised her champagne coupe and gave Carolyn an approving bow. Carolyn felt her cheeks flush.

Hitchcock pretended offense. "I'd admit I was wrong . . . if ever I were."

Alma pecked his cheek and the tension defused. And that's when the blue girl appeared, blazing in the midst of their circle, as if they'd conjured her with a spell. Alma's hand went to her chest, Hitchcock gave a short, snorty laugh. Pete reached for Carolyn's hand. Snug buzzed and floated across the ceiling, dipping at each figure to snare their attention like a mesmerist, then returned to the center and froze.

Pete's impulse to run was still strong—he pictured them all watching him bolt across the room, Seymour shouting, "Mr. D'Onofrio!"—so instead he locked his knees. Carolyn was staring at Bella staring at Snug. And Seymour, well, Seymour was smitten.

Snug vanished.

"It's the oddest thing," Seymour spoke, breaking the silence, his voice dreamy. "I wanted to bottle her. Like a butterfly in a jar."

"You would need a very large jar," Hitchcock said. He jabbed at Pete's chest. "It's you, isn't it?"

Pete covered his torso with a defensive arm. "No. No."

The director gave him a withering stare. "Did your agency come up with this?" It wasn't a joke for Hitchcock. He wanted answers.

"I wish we could take credit," Pete said, "but, alas, I can't."

"You're starting to speak like him," Carolyn whispered.

Pete winced. "He's contagious."

Heavy steps made the group turn as a chorus and there was Charles Addams striding toward them. He broke into the circle and grabbed Carolyn by the arm. "I need your ghost girl to help me. To send Little Sarah back."

"Little Sarah?" Carolyn said. "The dead girl in New England?" She heard the incredulity in her own voice.

Pete jumped. "Someone died?" He was about to say more when Igor rushed from the hall and waylaid him. The waiter led Pete by the arm, out of earshot, to the rear of the room.

Addams whined, "She *was* in New England. But tonight, she's been . . . here."

"Here?" Carolyn pointed to the floor. "Here-here?"

Addams pulled her away from the others. "Yes." He was trying to tamp down his volume, but it wasn't working. "Here-here."

Pete was nose-to-nose with Igor, deep in conversation, a mirror of Carolyn and Addams. So much whisper-whisper, so many secrets. It felt more like a CIA meeting than a cocktail party—not that she'd ever been a spy.

Bad Barbara appeared in the doorway behind them on a perfume-laden breeze. "I need to get rid of her," she mimicked her husband's desperation. "I thought you tried to keep all the girls."

"It's not like . . ." protested Addams, then stopped. "What did you hear?"

She blew a thin trail of smoke from her pursed lips. "Enough. I do live with you. I know what's been happening."

"You do?"

"This marriage has been a train wreck for a while, Charlie. We can admit that much."

Charlie blinked, then everyone sensed his relief. "Yes," he said, smiling, obliging Barbara and happy to have switched the conversation. "On that we agree."

Barbara's white teeth shone wolf-sharp and glinted in the candlelight. "Also, you think you're being visited by a dead girl. I doubt that. But once you have a morbid thought in your head, no one can jimmy it out."

"I've been jimmying morbid thoughts out of my brain my entire life," he said.

"Hear, hear." Barbara spoke to the crowd like the lawyer she was. "He wants to use one ghost to scare away another. Even if ghosts existed, which they do not, why would they be scared of each other? It's illogical."

"She doesn't have to scare her away," Addams said. "Reason with her. Explain the situation."

"Ghost counsel," Barbara snickered.

Carolyn had heard enough. "This is fascinating, but I have no interest in using my family to heal your poor judgment, Mr. Addams. Little Sarah is yours to deal with, not ours. And clearly, I have my hands full right now. Honestly, I'm trying to make sure the rest of the guests don't see anything unnerving. You believe in Snug—"

"Who is Snug?" Barbara's eyes flashed.

"Snug is our cousin," Bella said sharply, as she came to Carolyn's side. Pete followed behind her. "She is not a tool or an opportunity or a courier service. She's a girl. A dead girl. And she doesn't have to do our bidding."

Carolyn stepped up. "Or any of yours." She waved her arm to include them all. She pointed at Addams: "She can't be your mediator." She glanced at Pete, then Hitchcock. "She can't be your party favor. She's not Disney's next cinematic trick. Leave her alone. Let her be. She doesn't do stunts. Or have answers. It's not her job."

"Precisely." Aunt Bella gave Carolyn a supportive pat. "It's her own afterlife."

"Now and forever," Alma piped up. "Amen."

A faint blue glow began above them, then formed into a fully lit girl.

Bad Barbara's eyes bulged.

"Mrs. Addams," said Carolyn. "*This* is my cousin."

Snug gave them a startled glance, then flitted from the room.

Seymour Barnes cried "Wait!" and waved as if for a runaway cab. Everyone followed. He chased after her and with his spindly fingers caught the hem of a diaphanous gray shroud draped from one of the hallway chandeliers. It wavered more ghostly than the actual ghost, then edged a flickering candelabra and *whoosh*, Carolyn watched as the flame zoomed up the material faster than a hummingbird's flutter. The fire fed itself across the length of the shroud and she instinctively tossed her drink at it, forgetting it was mostly gin. The flame engorged with a menacing *pop* and she ducked behind her raised arms. Seymour was a tableau, frozen in incompetence. Pete had the presence of mind to crouch behind a heavy brown curtain and come out with a metal pail in his hands, a one-man bucket brigade. He heaved the sand into the air, a dry wave. One side of the thick cloud of yellow brown dirt came down and smothered the fire, the other stuck to the faint outline of the buzzing blue girl, revealed in a silhouette of sand.

The fire sputtered on the remains of the charred cloth, an ugly scent wafting up from the pile. Seymour sighed. Bella squeaked, a small cry of astonishment.

The girl remained above them, a human bird, crusted as if she'd been to the shore, but backlit by sconces.

Hitchcock smiled beatifically, as if in the presence of angels, and Alma let loose a surprised bark.

"There she is," Seymour murmured, "the lady of the hour."

Snug grimaced and spread her arms like wings and the sand fell away from her figure. She shook her head gently and the granules cascaded from her shoulders, past her feet. She was an hourglass in motion. The sand gathered on a Persian rug, a lattice of red and gold and green.

Carolyn held her breath.

Snug winked and gave a little wiggle.

Bad Barbara held her husband's arm, her mouth a red lipstick O. "A trick," she muttered. "That has to be a trick."

"She's not a trick," Bella insisted. "She's the most genuine among us."

The blue girl turned to Carolyn and put a finger to her lips, then disappeared in a blink.

The smoldering shroud fell to the carpet amid clumps of sand puddled at their feet.

Walter stood before Mariah. She considered him from her armchair, mouth tight, spine rigid. There was an ear trumpet on the end table and he wondered how long she'd needed it. Impatient with his silence, she flattened her skirt and folded her hands in her lap.

"Mariah," he whispered. His voice was rough-edged but gentle.

"Mr. Taylor."

Her expression was dyspeptic, her full hair iron gray, her middle thicker, so much older than when he last saw her. He had hardly changed since 1928.

"Will you let me talk with you?"

"Have you put away the gun?"

"I've put away the gun." He held one hand palm open, battered hat in the other, and offered them as proof. "I carried it for years, but somehow, I could let go of it tonight. I've left it behind." He looked directly at her. "Not in this house. It isn't on the premises."

"It was a foolish thing you did." She talked as if he were a boy.

"Yes, I know. I know."

"You've come looking for your skull, I suppose."

"No, it's not that. I've got of my head what I can get." He gave a wry smile.

"Then why are you here? What have you come to say?"

"It's been a long time, Mariah. I've hung about this city for I don't know how many years. I couldn't stay in my building. They tore it down. I couldn't stay in the park. I mean, I did, for many nights, but it's dark and I don't care for the animals. I roamed all the places I used to go. Wall Street. The Exchange. Mrs. Morgan's house."

Mariah flinched at the mention of the other woman, then regained her composure.

"It's gone now. Razed. I don't know when." He swallowed, or made the motion of swallowing, though he had no throat, no lungs, no gut, not in the normal way. Walter didn't understand how he could exist without them. Both in life and death, Walter realized he didn't understand many things. "Then I came up here, finally. I spent time in George Brokaw's old place. No one lives in it anymore; it's a place for science. Astonishing. Then, tonight, something called me here, took me around the corner and down Eightieth. I was compelled. Something wouldn't let me go. Then there was Snug. And you. Tonight—" He shook his head. His entire body, the outline of his gray figure, trembled.

"Yes, Mr. Taylor?" Her expression remained firm.

"Call me Walter. You called me Walter once."

"Many times more than once."

"Then once upon a time."

She almost smiled, then stopped herself. "Once it was like a storybook. Not anymore." She inhaled, her chest rising, then let it out slowly. "What is it you need to say, Walter?"

"I am sorry, Mariah. Sorry for everything that I've done." He pushed forward. "Everything I did."

He was spent. Perhaps that was it and he could fade away, a reprieve from his wandering.

She didn't speak. The mantel clock ticked. The party noises continued to wind their way through walls, up chutes, chatter and more chatter, that terrible music and the recorded screams, the rattling of dishes and ice in glasses and the bustle of waiters. Something brushed her legs, something hidden by the folds of her skirt. A cat. Snug's kitty, the mouser. She felt it lean against her legs and press, heard its purr, the warmth of its vibration.

"There is nothing I can do to fix it," Walter said flatly. "Not anymore."

"Not anymore," she repeated, "You are correct."

He shifted his weight, raised his hat to cover his half-head, then paused. His image was flickering steadily. Off and on, off and on, an alternating current.

"But thank you, Mr. Taylor," she said, her voice louder and clearer than she expected. "Walter."

He lowered his hat.

"What's done is done, Walter," Mariah said.

"Yes, that's true," he said. "Still. I am sorry."

They stood in the dark, his outline unsteady, hers burning brightly.

"It's time for me to go, then," he said.

"Soon enough it will be for all of us," she said in camaraderie. "I feel it."

"Yes. But sooner for me."

"I feel that, too."

"Goodbye, Mariah."

"Goodbye, Walter."

He went to leave, then turned.

"Our Isabella, our Curzon—"

"Somebody could get hurt again with all of this, Walter."

"Our girl," he said, and lo, surprised her, surprised himself. He began to weep, his shoulders shaking, his fingers latched on his hat like a man holding a life buoy. His hair, what was left of it, fell across his eyes, and he felt there were tears. She had never seen Walter cry in life. He knew it was a pitiable sight, an uncomfortable vision, for a grown man to let himself go. But, oh, he wasn't wrong to weep, was he? There was so much—so many reasons to mourn.

"Snug," he mumbled. "Do you know where she is now? May I talk to her?"

He watched her close her eyes, then open them, her vision raised, up and up.

Inhale.

Exhale.

Mariah considered the ceiling, its outline faint. She felt it widen, knew she could fly right then, high and out of the house. She could leave No. 7 forever and abandon Walter and his insignificant misery, his tardy repentance, as surely as he had abandoned them. She could zoom across the East Side, over all of Manhattan and be gone.

She remembered her mother's house on the Hudson, she remembered Newport.

There was no one left to visit there, no promise to find other family than the ones right here.

Lord, enough with Walter's grief. He didn't deserve her time, no matter how much time she seemed to have acquired, so unexpectedly, after her demise. She felt a twinge of spring in her heel. She could turn into Wendy Darling and fly off to Neverland. She wriggled her toes inside her boots. She glanced at the ear trumpet, waiting for her, more detritus from a past life she could leave behind.

"I know she's in this house. I've seen her. I didn't expect it." He began to cry again. "She was so angry. Where is she now?"

The tilt of his damaged head deflated her escape.

"You expected otherwise? She has always been in this house. Always been angry. For as long as she has been dead. If you had ever come to visit, you would have known it, felt it, felt her here."

"It wasn't my home, Mariah. It never was. It wasn't my place to come back to, not then. Not in the years after she died. I couldn't. I would come up to the museum and stand there looking down the street and wonder what I could say. And then I didn't come. And then I did. That was tonight. That is now."

"Well, go to her, then."

Walter wiped at his face with one faint sleeve. "And what do I say? She won't forgive me. She was revolted by me before."

Mariah crossed her arms. "You've had decades to consider how to apologize, Walter. I'm not going to tell you what you rightly know. Start with what you told me. And then say it again. You owe her more than even me."

"I know," Walter said, his voice low again. "I was a terrible father. A terrible husband. A terrible man."

"I won't argue about a thing there. But all that was then. Then is the past. We, of all people—if that's what we are—we, of all creation, know the difference between then and now. Speak to her tonight. If you don't, you're a greater fool than decades of repentance should have allowed."

Walter gave a weak smile. "You still have a wit to you, Mariah."

"I'm dead, Mr. Taylor," she said. "Not dim."

He began to float backward, turned, then turned again, to face her, the dance steps of a doomed man, his gaping wound forever apparent, a hole that would never heal. So it would be Walter, not Mariah, to leave this place. She wouldn't have to flee.

"I didn't come looking—" he faltered. "I didn't come for my head." He reached out to her. "I came for my heart."

She lifted and nearly went to him, then willed her spirit to stay put. *Stay*. Like an obedient dog, stay. She did. "That is not for me to save," she said. "Whatever comes of that, it is your doing." She paused. "It always has been."

"My doing," he whispered. "I know."

He vanished in an instant, blown away in a zephyr, not a wisp left to linger.

He was gone for good, absent as always, and she felt, at last, free. She was done with Walter Taylor for eternity.

58

SEYMOUR BARNES WAS FIRST to kneel at the smoking cloth. He held it to his face, in grief or longing, Carolyn couldn't tell. Perhaps he was a hound dog seeking the scent to follow Snug? She remembered her father's Labradors, dogs trained for the carcasses of birds.

"She'll come back?" His eyes pleaded with Bella. "I will find her. I must."

She hadn't misjudged Seymour Barnes one whit.

"That's very dramatic talk," Bella said, unimpressed. "If she doesn't want you to find her, you won't."

Still clutching the shroud, he stood and shook it like victor's spoils. "I will. She is the proof my theories have not been wild. She's the most substantial spirit we've had in Manhattan in years. Years!"

He grabbed Pete's shoulders. "You must come with me. To find her. To—"

"No," Pete said.

"You must!"

"That's not my job." He looked at Carolyn. "That's not my place."

Seymour swayed, nodded, and threw back his shoulders. "Then I'll go back to the castle."

"Good idea." Pete pointed him to the staircase. Seymour surveyed the mess one last time and hustled away.

Carolyn moved to Pete's side. "Thank you."

Their arms brushed. "You're welcome."

The Hitchcocks and Addamses were tucked together in a neat quartet, their faces harmonizing for a single bright chord: Charles's note was fear, Barbara's was confusion, Alma's was surprise, and Alfred's was (wasn't it always?) amusement.

"A grand show," he said, slapping Pete on the shoulder. "Pity it was so fleeting. And poorly timed. That should have happened hours ago, before the crowd dwindled. Seems a pity to waste it on so few." He scanned the room. "Duchess, I'm famished. Let's find some more of that cake."

Alma took his arm and they followed the path cut by Seymour a minute before. The Addamses had found a shadowed davenport and sat in silence.

Bella turned to Carolyn.

"Like Mr. Barnes—though for far different reasons—I feel I must see Snug again. Is there a place we might find her?"

Carolyn had a hunch.

59

THE ELEGANT ARTIST AND the blue girl stood nearly toe to toe. The bedroom was empty, save for the mannequin still tucked under the blankets, and he wasn't listening. Carolyn had left them to each other moments before.

"You live," said Snug, floating in the dark and quiet.

"I do," Bella answered. She wanted to reach out and touch her cousin, but her hands were frozen at her sides. Snug circled her.

"You live. You were able to do all those things I was denied." She faced Bella again and shook her head, like shaking away a fly, then stopped and considered the older woman. "You married?"

"Yes," Bella said, her eyes downcast.

"You had children?" Bella didn't answer. She could count her own heartbeat. She felt the blood speeding through her chest, her arms, her legs. Snug was insistent: "You had children?"

"Yes," said Bella.

"How many?"

"Three."

Snug's mouth opened, laboring on the next word, then closed and opened again. "You worked?"

"I painted."

"Like our great grandfather?"

"He was a sculptor." Bella chuckled. "You remember the figures?"

"He was an artist. He made things. Like you do. You made a family, you made life, you made art." Snug's light dimmed, her current fading. "I am nothing."

Bella stared into Snug's eyes and moved to take her hand, then stopped. She knew she would pass right through. "That's not true. You, you are a *wonder*."

Snug backed away. "I'm nothing no other dead girl couldn't become. And

I don't even know why it's *me*. This family. My aunt and my mother. My uncle. Why us? We aren't special."

Bella followed her. "But you are."

"We aren't," Snug moaned. "We're just dead. And that's something that happens to everyone."

Their hands mirrored one another, dancers with a scrim between them.

"I am sorry, Snug," said Bella.

"No," Snug answered. "There's no need to apologize. This isn't your fault. This isn't anyone's fault." Snug looked at her cousin and for a brief moment Bella felt their fingers graze. "I loved life. And I loved you. And I loved Mama. Isn't that wonder enough?"

Then there was only Bella.

Carolyn stepped from the doorway and walked to her aunt.

And Bella wept.

60

HITCHCOCK DIDN'T LIKE THE state of his leading man at all. Fonda looked like hell. His hair—neatly groomed when he'd arrived—fell over his forehead in a sad, lank mess. Dark circles hollowed his eyes. Even his tuxedo looked tired. Then again, the role did call for a certain exhaustion. This could work to everyone's benefit.

"Are you going to be ready to shoot, Henry? You look unwell."

Fonda shook his head. "I'll be fine, Hitch. This place. A day away from this place, I'll be ready. I'm always ready."

"This place?" Hitchcock asked, his arms wide. "This domestic treasure?"

"Gives me the heebie-jeebies."

"I didn't expect you to be the sensitive type."

"That one actress was out of line, Hitch. Too much. All too much. Too gruesome for a cocktail party. Throat slit? Blood all down her dress? That's a sick stunt. Glowing stickers and a tombstone cake are fun and games. But she was disgusting."

The drama before, while it was well-played at the time, seemed both overdone and insubstantial, a too-sweet dessert with no real taste. He could hardly recall the scene, yet there had been . . . ghosts. An old woman. A girl? Fonda was overreacting, but he didn't really want his guests to leave undone by the décor. "I'll tell the young man from Young and Rubicam he went too far. Your concerns are duly noted."

"Thanks, Hitch. I'll see you on Friday."

"A day off will do you well, Henry. Get some rest."

Fonda stepped out of the front foyer and into the March dark. The man from the agency—Wilton? Wilby?—came up behind the director, his shadow over the departing actor. Hitchcock was startled and he worked at never being startled. He hadn't expected the adman to loom so large. Fonda, he was strapping. This fellow? He found the honchos at the agency interchangeable.

"He looked worse for wear," the man observed. (Wilshire? Willoughby?) "Something pulling on him?"

"Guilt, I'd say. But specifically: He didn't like the actress upstairs. The one in the library. Too shocking for his delicate system."

The man scratched his chin. "We didn't hire a performer for upstairs."

Someone screamed—in delight, not fright, Hitchcock noted—followed by guffaws.

"Then who was the bloody girl he was going on about?"

The man shrugged. "Party crasher?"

"They do come in all shapes and sizes," Hitchcock said. "But perhaps it is we who are the crashers here after all."

T he house around the corner was filled with machines, radios, and wires, all of it a mystery to Frances. When she had lived here with George, despite his anger, despite the alcohol and the ranting, or worse, bitter pouting, the house had been filled with art. The house itself—the filigreed banisters, the gleaming mantels, the stained-glass windows, the parquet floors—was glorious, as had been the paintings and the sculptures and the tapestries. The art, the art, the art.

None of it was here. None of it mattered.

Frances drifted, quiet, her rage at Hank abated, down the familiar halls, her memory already clearing of No. 7, the party quickly receding. In the castle, she visited a more distant past yet somehow felt more present.

Also, she had nowhere else to go. She had confronted Hank and discovered he was nothing, nothing worth scaring or caring about. She had no need to go elsewhere. She was now truly done.

One of the machines squawked, then settled into a staticky hum, its dials glowing green in the dim light, the room formerly only lit by streetlamps. She hadn't turned it on. Did the place have ghosts?

The idea made her laugh.

This was no room to linger in. The world was no place to linger. She was ready.

She would find a way to leave forever. There was nothing left for her here, in this house, or that house, this island, or this earth.

She would find a way to leave and feel thankful for it.

It's all right, she would say to anyone who cared. Tonight, it was really all right.

61

BELLA MARKELL STOOD ON Eightieth Street waiting for a cab, half a block down from the party so as not to catch her niece's attention. She was slinking off quietly, the way she liked to leave gatherings, no hullabaloo in the goodbyes, a French exit. She wasn't alone for long: a gleaming knight appeared beside her. He cradled a pair of books in the crook of his arm and balanced an ancient alembic on top, its separate pieces fragile, the last of his goods to return.

"Every life is hapax legomenon," James Lenox said, as if resuming a conversation interrupted by a passing train. He did not acknowledge that she was a woman suddenly accompanied by a spirit. Bella responded blandly to his appearance, but it took some effort. She didn't want him to see her startled. And, honestly, she enjoyed his abrupt company. Lenox was cheerfully oblivious. "Only once," he continued, "never repeated, so this is not a second life, as much as a continuation. A strange and unexpected continuation."

"Hapax legomenon," Bella recited, tongue treading carefully around consonants. Her cheeks felt cold in the damp night, but she was giddy with a little girlish flush she hadn't felt in ages. "Hapax legomenon." She smacked her lips. "Like phenomenon."

"It's a concept that comes from studying texts," he continued. "A phrase repeated once in a large manuscript, a word used singularly, that's hapax legomenon. An outlier, an outcast—"

"A one-off," she offered.

"If that means unique," he said, "yes. We are all hapax legomenon, truly. Even those of us with epilogues."

"Are there," she began. She bit her tongue. "Are there many more of you? Those of you who are living . . . epilogues."

He seemed to study the house across the way. "I don't know the numbers. Perhaps we are rare. Perhaps there are dozens or hundreds or thousands across the globe."

"You've met others?"

He put his attention firmly on her. "Not before recently. Snug. Her people."

"Our people," Bella said.

"Our people," he agreed.

"No one at the museum?"

"No one from a sarcophagus, you mean? A pharaoh or a habti with a soul? No." He was wistful. "I desire to find my sister—my youngest sister, Henrietta. We had a special bond. But I have not."

"She died before you?"

"No. She was alive when I met my end, if not my Maker. She outlived me by several years. I have seen her headstone. I sense she is on the other side, across the veil, however one puts it. She is not here."

"I am sorry," Bella said. She had a fleeting thought of the people she would like to see behind the veil. Her mother. Her father. Her husband. Oh, too many to consider.

"As am I," Lenox whispered. "It is time for me to leave. Perhaps, if I am very fortunate, there is still another place where I will meet her again. I was a devout man in my breathing years; I have not lost faith, despite this odd venture on an undiscovered road. I may yet return to the path I had imagined."

"Heaven," she said.

"Or something very much like it."

A yellow cab pulled to the curb. She had to leave Lenox. It felt drastic, sudden. But why? She didn't know the man, if man is what he was. The action, simply sitting in a car, seemed monumental. She tried to put a hand on his arm but it slipped right through him. But the armor? It should have been real. He had already returned the actual suit. Maybe this was simply his envisioned ideal. She knew then that the driver would think she was talking to herself. There was no one else on the street able to see James Lenox.

"You won't be back to tell us," she stated.

"It seems unlikely, madame." He smiled and touched her hand. She felt a brief chill. "But I would never say impossible."

She turned and stepped into the cab and watched through smudged glass as it pulled away from an empty curb.

62

THE MIDDLE-AGED COUPLES STOOD at the black gated door of No. 7, as if this had been a conventional double date. They shared an unspoken vow to avoid any specifics about the evening. "A *unique* experience, Hitch," Charlie said, shaking his friend's hand. "Thank you for inviting us. Me. Us."

"I didn't want you stuck at home on another Wednesday night," Hitchcock admitted.

"It *would* have been just another Wednesday for the Addams family." Charlie stopped and pondered, like Keats's stout Cortez. "Wednesday. I've never noticed how beautiful that word is. Arresting, isn't it, Hitch?"

"Mellifluous," Hitch said.

"Wednesday's child," Alma said, "is full of woe."

"Full of woe?" Hitchcock exclaimed. "Goodness, no. We *celebrate* the midweek. Saturdays can be banal and Sundays are for heaven."

"Says you," Charlie huffed. His wife was distant, staring into the dark.

"But Wednesday, ah, that's the girl for me," Hitchcock rhapsodized. "A little cold, a bit unpredictable. You never know about Wednesday."

"Should you ever have a daughter," Alma said, "it would make a lovely name."

Barbara twitched.

"Should I ever have a daughter," Charlie said, "declare me legally insane." He shook Hitchcock's hand again and gave a little bow. "We better end the evening or we'll turn into poets. And no one wants that." He turned to Alma. "Thank you. You've been a marvelous hostess."

"It was all Alfred."

"It's never *all* Alfred," Charlie said, smiling. "But we'll keep that our little secret."

Alma offered a benign smile and stroked her husband. "He thinks it's a secret."

"It's my experience that humans are very bad at keeping secrets." Hitchcock turned to Barbara, still silent at her husband's elbow. "Tell me, Mrs. Addams, did you learn any secrets tonight that you would like to divulge prior to your exit?"

She blinked slowly and her eyes brightened. "I'm not a woman of secrets, Mr. Hitchcock."

"Everything is right out in the open." Hitchcock made a point of glancing at her cleavage. Alma rolled her eyes.

"Not everything, honey," Barbara said. Her husband snorted. Bad Barbara was back to her old self and gave them a wiggle as she walked away. "Catch up, Charlie," she called over her shoulder.

"My wife," Charlie said, "is provoking you, Hitch. Don't take the bait."

"I never fall for the simple ruse," Hitchcock said. "That's how I survive."

"So far," Alma said. "So far, dear."

Addams jogged to catch up and the couple disappeared, obscured by trees and parked cars. Alma squeezed his forearm in affection.

"They're doomed," she said.

"Only as a couple," he said. "Better people apart."

"Not like us," she said.

He kissed her hand. "Never like us, Duchess. Never like us."

Igor Imagines *ROOFTOP FANTASIA*, a screenplay

EXT. Night. A rooftop on the Upper East Side. A PAIR OF MEN, both dressed in black suits and faded stage makeup, stand and gaze out over the edge of a town house. The drizzle has ended, the clouds are breaking up. The men gawk at the street below. There is laughter and cries of goodbye. Yet there is still work to do when they return to the kitchen. Pack up the food. Put away the bottles. Clean the dishes, so, so many dishes. Take out the garbage.

>IGOR
>I'm not sure my driver will get here in time.

>RENFRO
>You have a driver?

>IGOR
>You don't?

>RENFRO
>I took the subway.

Igor grins. Renfro shrugs.

>IGOR
>So did I. But I like to pretend.

>RENFRO
>Oh, in that case, my limo will never make it through the crush. Look at that line.

>IGOR
>It's difficult to hire good help these days.

There is a companionable silence.

          RENFRO
Did you ever talk to Hitchcock?

          IGOR
Yes. He was . . . exactly as I expected.

          RENFRO
He's very good at playing the part.

          IGOR
He's typecast as Himself.

          RENFRO
He is what he is.

Renfro offers Igor a cigarette from his pack. Igor accepts one and dips his chin to Renfro's lighter. He stands straight and exhales.

          IGOR
Are any of us that simple?

          RENFRO
Or honest? This is a party full of admen. Everyone expects a façade. Maybe the cleverest façade is no façade at all.

          IGOR
Hail, philosopher.

          RENFRO
Philosophy major. Well, a dropout, but I'm still deep.

                IGOR
        Always been partial to Heraclitus
        myself.

                RENFRO
        You can't step in the same river
        twice.

                IGOR
        No, you can't. It's a new river.

                RENFRO
        Water's always going. New water.

                IGOR
        And voila, a new you.

A melody drifts across the neighborhood. Distant orchestra, a floating sort of tune.

                RENFRO
        Do you hear that? I know that music.

Igor cocks his head.

                RENFRO
        Fantasia.

                IGOR
        I would have said Tchaikovsky.

                RENFRO
        Ta-may-to, ta-mah-to.

                IGOR
        You are a man of nuance. And
        philosophy.

> RENFRO
> New water. New waiter. What a difference a letter makes.

> IGOR
> When the letter is I. That's a pretty big one. Without I, the waiter is water.

> RENFRO
> We've come full circle.

> IGOR
> The river flows in a circle.

> RENFRO
> Rivers can't do that.

> IGOR
> But I can.

He holds out his hand.

> IGOR (cont'd)
> Care to dance?

Renfro looks both ways, like crossing a street. Looks up, looks down, like stepping into a spaceship. After deliberation, he takes the other man's hand. They begin a tentative waltz.

> RENFRO
> What if someone sees us?

> IGOR
> Up here? In the dark?

> RENFRO
> It is dark.

They waltz away from the edge.

>				IGOR
>	So, will you get an audition?

>				RENFRO
>	I'm sure he'll be calling my agent—
>	I brought him a dessert. Or three.

>				IGOR
>	He does need extras for a movie out in
>	Queens. We should definitely do that.

>				RENFRO
>	Yes.

They make another square about the roof.

>				IGOR
>	We seem to be alone.

Renfro curtails their box step.

>				RENFRO
>	Seem to?

>				IGOR
>	You never know. There are things we
>	cannot see.

>				RENFRO
>	Ghosts?

>				IGOR
>	And more.

They resume swaying in the silence.

>				RENFRO
>	There's no music.

                    IGOR
            Does it matter?

Renfro shrugs and they continue, unseen stars glittering above them as the clouds dissipate. More fare-thee-wells and laughter below.

                    RENFRO
            My driver won't get here in time.

                    IGOR
            Are you in a rush to leave?

Renfro shakes his head.

                    RENFRO
            Not at all.

He laughs.

                    RENFRO (cont'd)
            And I'm walking anyhow.

                    IGOR
            Walk with me?

                    RENFRO
            Wherever you want to go.

They nod and dance and the stars shimmer in the cloudless black sky.

63

PETE WAS TREADING THE fourth floor, seeking Carolyn. Instead—in the back bedroom where they'd investigated the remains of Hitchcock's cake—he found Snug, drifting like seaweed in a tide pool. *Now* he could summon her? There was an irony he didn't appreciate, and he stepped back stealthily, so as not to attract attention. It didn't work. She pivoted. Pete held his breath.

"You don't need to go." Her voice was empty.

"I do," Pete said, but stayed where he was.

"I know we aren't friends."

"You did lock me in the basement."

"I didn't. The shoddy knight did. I simply left you there."

"That's a fine line."

This conversation felt normal, but the girl was opaque. And floating. Pete rubbed his temples. All these ghosts were giving him a hangover.

"You're free now," she said—trying to comfort him?—and drew closer. The air wavered, a fresh coldness cut through the room's dusty stillness. She hesitated. Every time she appeared, his chest tightened. Allergies? No. Terror. Yes. Even though she didn't seem all that ghastly.

She shimmered, her light gentle, and held out a folded sheet of paper. "Take this. I don't want to see him again, but he needs to know. Take it." She tucked the paper into his hand, folding his fingers around it. He let his hand relax, though the sensation was bizarre: dry snow with the force of rushing water. He recognized the paper he'd given her earlier. Two days ago, it had come from his office. Now this weird girl version of Mr. Coffee Nerves was giving it back. On the outside of the fold there was her black cursive initial, followed by a dot: *I*.

"Who are you talking about?" he stuttered.

"My father. You've seen him."

"No, no, I haven't." His nerves started up again. "I've seen a lot of things tonight, but not him."

A glowing gray figure emerged from the darkest corner of the room. Snug bolted past Pete and zipped to the ceiling.

"Wait!" cried the spirit. He pulsed, his arms out like a supplicant. "I'm so sorry," the man begged. "I didn't mean to hurt you."

Pete trembled. The man's head was a wreck, glowing and gory.

Snug looked at her father with scorn. "I don't like it when people surprise me." Her current pulsed. She focused on Pete. "Just give it to him," she said, and then she turned and flew through a wall. Every time she did that, Pete wondered if it hurt. But the girl hurt all over. Maybe going through a wall was nothing.

Walter shimmered before him. Pete held out the paper, then staggered, nauseous, to the doorway. The ghost bowed his head, read the note, and stayed that way, like a stuck frame in a reel of film. Pete moved farther away.

Walter's shoulders shook, his head still bent.

Snug appeared between them, facing her father.

Pete was at the threshold, wanted to run, but couldn't. They didn't need him, but he was captured by a duty to witness this. But for who's sake? Not his. Then it came to him: for Snug. She needed him to remain.

Snug waited. Walter raised his face and gazed at her. He nodded. She nodded. The paper burned in his hand and turned to ash. His eyes glistened, sparkled, then dimmed. He held out his fingers. She brushed him.

He was gone.

Pete said, "Criminy."

Snug glanced at him and zoomed through the ceiling. No falling plaster, no gaping hole. Nothing to reveal the girl or the gleaming man had ever been there.

Pete was sweating like he'd run ten blocks, his collar wet, his wingtips heavy as lead. He couldn't fathom what had happened, this hush after the storm, but maybe it was what peace felt like for ghosts. Maybe it was the true sound of the afterlife, this tremendous silence.

64

THE PARLOR WAS EMPTY of guests, the stragglers gathered in the gallery a floor below. Carolyn spied Pete across the room. Between them danced the spirits of the household.

The living guests had arrived at No. 7 with no intention of doing anything more strenuous than hoisting highballs. But upstairs there was this: a long-married couple, separated for more than twenty years, waltzing gracefully across the open floor. Dr. Satterthwaite was frail, his arms thin, his steps tremulous. Mrs. Satterthwaite was more robust, but only a tad so. Thomas held Isabella in a tender embrace, though she was the strength behind each step.

From the far side of the room, Mariah Taylor watched, alone, her demeanor proud. For a moment, Carolyn wondered if Walter would appear, a gruesome apparition with perhaps his hand extended in invitation? What would Mariah do? As if Carolyn conjured it, there was static and shimmer, though the spirit that came was not Walter, but Snug, who glowed gently by her mother's side. Snug seemed older. Mariah relaxed. They entwined their fingers.

The Satterthwaites took center stage and as they twirled, they seemed to grow . . . younger. Isabella was no more than twenty as she stepped and spun in her husband's arms. Snug led her mother to a love seat, and they perched, backs straight, knees together, and watched attentively like satisfied cats. Mariah, too, seemed younger. What an impossible vision! To see this generation in their youth, from a time before Carolyn ever arrived, wasn't this what some people called paradise?

If there was a celebration in No. 7 that night, it was this. Yes, the power of Hollywood was alluring, the money behind Madison Avenue intoxicating, but it was nothing compared to this collision of time and space and love.

And it was so brief.

Carolyn and Pete watched as years reversed and then played out again like a Rodgers and Hammerstein dream. The Satterthwaites shifted from frail and tentative to young and confident, then to elderly again. They were careful once more in their steps. To the side. To the side. Back, back.

Every little sway a step beyond the ordinary.

There was no music, but they stayed in time to a melody the living couldn't hear.

Mariah smiled at Snug. Snug put her head on her mother's shoulder.

And then the ghosts were gone and Carolyn and Pete remained in an empty room a minute longer. Silently they crossed to each other and descended the narrow stairs to bid the last of the guests goodbye.

65

THE REMAINING REPORTERS CLUSTERED in the front hall and spilled out onto Eightieth Street. WOR was still there with a tired Dorothy Kilgallen trying her best for a final interview with Hitchcock. Alma was tugging at his arm and he followed her lead. But Dorothy persisted. She touched the director on the shoulder. "Are you disappointed you had no special visitors this evening?"

"Who says I didn't?"

Carolyn watched from the stairs, Pete behind her, her brain busy casting a spell or a prayer: *Don't tell. Don't tell. Don't tell.*

Dorothy's eyes widened. "You did?"

He glanced around the foyer dramatically. "The house was stuffed with special visitors this fine evening. What else could I call this crowd? Even you, Dorothy," he flirted, "are something special."

She laughed. "That's not what I meant, Hitch. I meant specters."

"And I mean spectators. What's a few letters between friends?"

"So, no disappointments?"

"Only with the living," he said, his smile fading. "Never with the dead. They can't disappoint me anymore."

"But was the evening everything you'd hoped it would be?"

Carolyn wondered how she'd answer the question herself.

"Things should never be exactly what you imagine," Hitchcock said. "Our imaginations are so paltry, so underfed. Well, most people's. Not necessarily mine. Or yours. Or hers."

Here he picked Carolyn out of the intimate crowd. A few hours earlier, she might have blushed. At this point, she merely nodded. It was nearly one and she'd been busy since early morning. That was yesterday. Then there would be tomorrow. And tomorrow. Shakespeare was right. Today is followed by an endless series of tomorrows, at least for a while. And maybe occasionally for a while longer. Snug's endless tomorrows had lasted nearly forty years past her death. Uncle James? Nearly eighty. Were they done? Carolyn hoped so.

Carolyn had lost the thread of Hitchcock's pontificating.

"I'm certain there were specters here this evening. My sponsors would never disappoint me like that. Who thinks this is an empty house? This grand manse isn't just sizzle; it's steak. I spoke with a young spirit myself."

Kilgallen did a double take, but this was a radio spot, so no one would see that at home. "Really?" She tried for nonchalance, but it came out in a croak.

"Oh, certainly. There were darling young spirits all over the place. I tried to lure one to the wicked business of making movies, but she's reluctant. Others, well, they just flitted away, as spirits are wont. They really can't be directed, as much as I'd like to try. Actors are simply good children who listen and do as they are told. Ghosts are another matter. They have a certain insolence and they've earned it. Can you imagine dying, believing you're off the hook, finished with this miserable planet, only to be chained to it for another day, another year, another era? It would be abominable. Condemned to that fate, I would be insufferable and no one wants *that*."

Alma interrupted. "Perhaps there will be no calories in the afterlife, dear. Don't assume it's all dreary. Maybe you could come back as a kitchen apparition, sampling all the finer things again with no consequences?"

"No consequences? Oh, what will that do to storytelling? All of my pictures are about consequences. If you can do something and it has no reverberations, does it really count?"

"A tree falling in the woods," Kilgallen philosophized.

"Exactly!" Hitch pointed at her. "If you eat a pound of marzipan and there are no calories, why, it's like hardly eating at all. There's nothing to it, so why do it at all?"

"Because it tastes good?"

"But will it, if it isn't forbidden? When everything is allowed, nothing will be worth savoring. That's my vision of Hell. You thought I'd be a man to vote for an existence of consequence-less eating, ingesting, stuffing myself with whatever I'd want, but that isn't me, at all. There must be some guilt attached to the pleasurable, or there's nothing to confess, and what's the fun in that?"

"The driver is waiting, Alfred," Alma said.

"Indeed," Kilgallen said, her voice clear for the listeners at home, ready to go to bed. Everyone was flagging. "There goes our Prince of Darkness, himself, Mr. Alfred Hitchcock, with his lovely wife, Alma, at his side. Off to the Berkshire Hotel, I've been told. A home away from home for the Hitchcocks when they travel east. But they'll soon be back in Beverly Hills."

Hitchcock made a dramatic sweep behind him to No. 7. "How can this place not have won my heart? I'm certain everyone who has lived here has wanted to stay. Or maybe it just seems that way. I'll be back. Perhaps not in this lifetime, but another!"

He trudged the few yards from the wrought iron door to the idling hearse, the patient chauffeur holding open the wide back door.

The director gave a little toodle-oo, and for a flash, Carolyn could see the boy in the man: the son of the grocer, an apple-cheeked lad with a grin and a mischievous glint. Who needs ghosts when all our past lives remain within us, the child not just the father of the man, but every age a permanent roommate housed in a single miserable, miraculous body?

Alfred and Alma disappeared into traffic, conveyed by the black sedan like Charon's ferry. The reporters scurried away, like ants retreating from a ravished picnic. The house remained well lit, every room aglow, but emptier.

But not entirely empty. Not yet.

In there, Orlando was putting away his Leica. Johnny was coiling wires, tucking them in crates.

The dishes were piled high, while Igor and Renfro scoured every floor for more, humming Nelson Riddle's "Lisbon Antigua." Someone had to tidy up and they might as well do it dancing.

The police drove off with Miss Havisham, kindly seeing her home, no worse for wear than a bump on the head and some confusion about what she really saw. The back doors of the radio truck gaped like an open mouth, but the headset man wasn't there. A light mist dampened Carolyn's hair. The city had the cold sweats. The sort you get when you've had a fright.

No ghosts left in New York. That's what Pete told her Seymour Barnes's research had said. Why, there were enough ghosts in this one building for the whole city. What about all the other town houses, the battered apartment buildings, the hospitals and the cemeteries? Manhattan was stuffed with spirits. Maybe they needed a reason to come out. Maybe they just needed an invitation.

The waiters hauled a pair of dented garbage cans to the curb. Igor looked to the sky. "Is it gonna rain again?"

Renfro turned his face to the clouds. "Not on our nightcap."

Pete hurried up to them and Carolyn tried to get his attention, but he was single-minded.

"You guys were fantastic," he said. "Truly. We couldn't have done this without you." He applauded.

Renfro and Igor bowed.

Pete handed them each an envelope and a handshake. "You're off the clock. Time to be yourselves!"

The waiters looked at each other. "We can do that," Renfro said.

"Absolutely," Igor said. "Hey!" He socked Renfro. "Call me Joe."

"Hey." Renfro socked him back. "Call me Ray."

Before Carolyn could get to Pete, he scooted back to the house. She started after him, but a voice behind her called, "Did someone say nightcap?"

It was Johnny.

She shook her head. "I've had my share tonight."

He threw an arm around her shoulders. "You sure about that, Banks?"

"It's the one thing I am sure of." She studied his face. What did he think of the night? Was he rationalizing what he'd seen? Was it already a cloud in his brain? "How was your evening, Johnny?"

"Ah, no picnic," he said. "The bosses were uptight. Not enough screams, not enough creaking doors. They wanted more."

Carolyn waited for him to say it. *Hello, Uncle James.* For a moment, his eyes went adrift—and then he was back and brushing his hair off his forehead and grinning. "But it's over."

"It's over!" Igor yelled. "I'm washing off this grease! Being undead is work."

"And then that drink," Renfro said. "To the city that never sleeps!"

Johnny perked up. "That's a decent lyric."

"Write it! An ode to New York," Igor said. "Then get somebody big to sing it."

"Sinatra," Renfro insisted. "You need Sinatra."

Dorothy Kilgallen, with the last of the radio guys behind her, stopped abruptly and the fellow nearly crashed into his boss's back. It was headset man. He gave Carolyn a sheepish grin.

"Did someone say Sinatra?" Dorothy sneered. "Get *anyone* else to sing your song. Get Hitchcock to sing it. Get her to sing it." She nodded at Carolyn and strode off into the dark, a streetlight casting her long shadow.

Carolyn laughed. "Not me!"

Johnny hugged Carolyn's shoulders. "I've heard this girl. That's not gonna work. I love her, but her singing could raise the dead." He turned to Renfro and Igor. "To the bar, gentlemen?"

"To the bar," the waiters agreed.

"You're really off to bed, Banks?"

"Girl's gotta sleep, Johnny." She touched his cheek. "But it was so nice to see you. Don't be a stranger."

He kissed her on the forehead. "You either, kid."

Like a trio of sailors on leave, Igor and Renfro and Johnny kicked up their heels and loped off down the street, arm over arm. She watched them grow smaller down the block. They'd find a place to land. Maybe she should have gone with them. But she couldn't leave the house alone. She promised to be the last one out.

She turned back to No. 7. As if on command, Pete appeared in the doorway, his figure black against the foyer lights. She couldn't see his face, but she saw his arm motioning, beckoning her.

66

THE DUCK WAS READY to leave, holding the cat, duty-bound to return Oscar to his sister's place in Connecticut. It was the most pampered the cat had looked all evening, an Egyptian deity tended by a temple adman. The Duck lugged Oscar to the front door, turned to Pete, and said, "Nice work. You know how to host a glamorous get-together."

"The host was Hitch."

"Nah, he was the *entertainment*. You were the host."

"This means a raise and an office?"

"Don't get ahead of yourself. Getting excitable leads to dead chickens. Nice and easy. You'll get your turn." He idly stroked Oscar's sleek fur once more. Who was the boss, The Duck or the cat? It didn't seem to matter. "Night, son."

"Good night, sir," Pete said. "Good night, Oscar."

The cat's eyes closed in feigned sleep; he wasn't going to deign to give a goodbye. The Duck marched out the door, a man with one last mission.

Miles to go before he sleeps, Pete thought. Miles for us all.

Carolyn sidled past The Duck as she strolled up the walk. She nuzzled Oscar one last time, then met Pete at the door.

"You rang?" she said.

"Not really a ring," he answered. "But I hear you've been offered one?"

She gave him a sideways glance. "What has Aunt Bella told you?"

"She mentioned Malcolm. The one who shut me in the basement."

Carolyn's eyes popped. "Malcolm did that?"

"I saw a knight. And it wasn't Uncle James. There are only so many knights."

She winced. "I'm sorry. I didn't think he'd take it out on you."

"Where is he now?"

"Heading home."

They watched the final party cars drive down the street.

Pete turned to Carolyn. "Is that why you came to New York? Because he asked?"

"I discovered I'm in no rush," she said. She stepped past him and into the quiet hall, cluttered with the remaining debris and a strange new silence. "I'm in no rush for anything except to tidy this place up and take back the key. And—"

"And say goodbye to someone," he said.

"Yes." She picked up a dead lily and sniffed it. "Any idea where to find her?"

"Not a clue." Which was true. And he wasn't going to tell her about Walter and the letter. He wouldn't be a gossip.

Carolyn was collecting empty glasses like a seasoned waitress. "I'll drop these off in the kitchen and we can head up to the parlor. Unless," she paused, "unless you don't want to say goodbye."

"I think Snug and I are done," he said. "The basement deal kind of put me off."

"I get it," she said. "I do." She marched off to the back of the house.

"That's not all—" he began, then faltered. She hadn't heard him. Pete watched her round the corner. It had been a heck of a night for everyone. She needed to chat with her family, the dead and the living. He should let her get back to Aunt Bella. He wondered if he shouldn't just leave the key on the table where the guest book had been. Last he'd seen of that, it was tucked under Alma Hitchcock's elbow.

He could leave the key and slink out quietly as a shadow.

67

AN EMPTY SUIT OF armor stood in the corner of the living room. Crossed swords hung on the wall. Charles noted Barbara's attention on the medieval kitsch as she lounged on the wine-dark couch. He sat stiffly beside her. The cab ride home had been short and chilly. He couldn't help pouting.

"Oh, Charles," she cooed, "I really don't want to kill you. I want you to be happy."

"Do I make you happy?" He absently tapped on the headstone coffee table. Tonight felt like a fever dream. He couldn't read all of *Little Sarah, Aged Three* beneath a coaster and the latest *New Yorker*, but the engraving jolted him. Odd things had occurred. Why couldn't he put his finger on just *what*? So much of the party was a blur. What had been in those drinks?

She traced his hand with one be-ringed finger. "I still like your little drawings."

"My *little drawings* are my life," he said. "To be honest, I'm not happy."

"You still like the way I look," she said, cocking her eyebrow.

"I do," he said. "But is that all there is? Fleeting amusement?"

"The same way I feel when I read the *New Yorker* panels?"

They sipped their nightcaps, a spot of amaretto for her, a port for him.

"Perhaps we should give it up. This endeavor," he said, waving his hands at their home: her plum curtains, his collection of weapons, her closet full of glamorous coats, his headstone table. "This marriage."

"It's for the best." She sat up straighter. "I'm going to Alabama next month. Nevada isn't the only state with quickie divorces, you know."

"I didn't know," he said. "Do both parties need to attend?"

"No. It's paperwork. But you'll give me something in parting? A token?"

He tried to read her dark eyes. "What do I get?"

"Darling, you have so much already." She drew her hand along his arm, wrist to elbow and back. "But we could part . . . amicably."

Addams tried to leer, but his heart wasn't in it. "I guess that's the way the world should work. No strings, no guilt."

She agreed. "It helps that neither of us wanted children."

"Children are only good at a distance. Beyond the theoretical, they get messy."

"Clutter and noise." She shook her head and her thick hair danced. "Wasn't that your problem with saintly Barbara the First?"

Addams took a great breath, let it out slowly. "Yes, it was. She wanted to adopt and I, well, I thought I did. Then I didn't. And then came you. And now, it seems, you'll be gone, too. Where will I be?"

"Here in New York, sketching your nasty family, penciling trysts in your little black book."

Addams squirmed. "Little black—"

"—*everyone* knows about your little black book. Every woman who's in it, and probably every woman you've ever attempted to get in it. It's infamous. Someday they'll put it in the Met. *The Charles Addams Collection of Exhausted Females.*"

"Am I exhausting?"

"In all the best ways and all the worst, dear. I mean it from the bottom of my rotten heart." She tapped his nose. "You know . . . we won't really be done."

"But no longer insured and beneficiary—"

She guffawed. "You are dying to get me off that policy, aren't you?"

"*Not* dying to, Barbara. That's the point."

"You needn't worry. Alabama awaits."

"I will miss you."

"No, you won't," she said in a husky alto. "But that's okay. Because we'll always have a connection, Charlie."

He rested his chin in one hand and studied her. "You've done something," he said. "Sneaky girl, what is it? My next book deal? Have the proceeds deeded to you?"

"Oh, nothing like that. Books aren't where the money is. No, we're talking about *television* rights."

"I don't have any television rights." He glanced at her over the rim of his glass.

"You do now. You always forget I'm part of the bar. All it took was a little lawyering."

"Who would want to see my ghouls on the tube?"

"Who guessed the American people would want to see that fat Englishman every Sunday? There's no accounting for taste. Your day—your nasty family's day—will come and I'll be right there with you."

"Don't hold your breath."

"I won't have to." She pulled herself into his chest and kissed him hard, then leaned back to look him in the eyes. "You know, you're getting something better than a wife. You're getting a business partner." She uncoiled from the couch like a snake from a wicker basket and strutted to the closet. "We're not done. Don't despair!"

"Despair," Addams whispered. "I've never known the word."

She slipped her coat over one arm, then the other. "When we go our separate ways, you'll have charmed another woman in here before the proverbial ink is dry."

"You make it sound like I cast spells."

"No, that's my job." She left with a blown kiss, the hem of her black fur flapping like wings.

The radiator ticked. The heat kicked on. Had they lived three seasons in an evening? Was winter returning? Someone in the apartment above was pacing, someone else was running water. These were the sounds he would hear without her around.

Addams trudged into the kitchen and sat, one sad light spilling over the checkered linoleum.

He imagined himself a figure in one of his cartoons: a single panel, a man sitting solo at a kitchen table, after the party, tie undone, hair askew, a morbidly elegant woman leaving the scene, a pithy caption beneath it. He could have a competition among his friends: Who would come up with the best line? Hitch? Alma? Jim Allardice? The young man from the advertising agency this evening or one of the old guns? That stiff, Fonda? Doubtful. Or maybe Bad Barbara herself, Queen of the Night, her barrister's snare, a quip instead of a full-blown brief.

His family on television and Barbara right there, profiting off his dark imagination.

Boy Meets Ghoul, Boy Loses Ghoul.

He pulled a pen from inside his jacket and started a quick sketch. A line, a black dot, a swirl and a crosshatching. The idea took shape. Swoop, stop, move on, working into the quiet night. The nib scratched against the paper.

He saw himself as if from above, a hovering man.

Always Charlie, always alone, always looking for love.

Why, that's the caption right there, isn't it?

68

CAROLYN DIDN'T HAVE TO look long. Snug was in the parlor, buzzing blue, her little slippers faintly skimming the floor as she skirted around the room.

"I've come—"

"To say goodbye," Snug finished. "As have I."

Carolyn took a step toward her, approaching a skittish colt. "It was wondrous to meet you."

"Everyone called me a wonder tonight. To think, before this, I was simply Snug."

"You are a wonder!" Carolyn said.

"If I am, so are all my family."

"Except your brother. He's not wondrous."

Snug giggled. "No, no, he is. The living are as wondrous as the dead. We're just different."

"He doesn't believe in you."

"He doesn't believe in *ghosts*. He always believed in me. And he will see me again. Not here, but somewhere, I trust."

"I hope so." Carolyn saw her mother walking down the avenue, her brother on the lake. Her father at the bank. He wouldn't be with her forever. Helen and Maud. None of it would last forever. There are only so many nights. Would they see each other again? "I wish I had that trust."

"Nothing is impossible," Snug said.

"Coming from you," Carolyn said, "it doesn't seem an exaggeration." She had one question, but she wasn't certain she had the courage to ask or to face the answer. "Have you seen my mother? Do you know where she is?"

Snug's head tilted to take in Carolyn's expression, the ghost's mouth a grim line, her eyes sympathetic and shining. "I have not. She is not here—in the house—if that's what you mean. She has never come to me. The world is a tremendous place, too large for any one of us, and I sense the afterworld is greater still."

Carolyn had thought she would be devastated by this news, experience the pain of her mother's death in a dreadful encore, but she didn't. A satisfying peace descended upon the room, upon her and Snug. It seeped into Carolyn and spread from the top of her head to the ends of her fingers to the bottom of her soles.

Snug drifted, a flower in a pond, and smiled. "Where is your young man?"

"He's not my young man."

"Ah, who's to say," Snug whispered, "what that means anyway?"

"You?" Carolyn leaned toward her blue light. "You'd be the authority. You are beyond time."

"No," Snug said. "Not anymore. Every party has an end."

Carolyn didn't want to hear it. "I need to leave, get the key back to the realtor."

"They will need it for the next family."

"Yes," Carolyn admitted, as if she were keeping a terrible secret. It was no secret. Everyone who mattered, or who cared about the house, and there were only so many, knew what was next.

"Yes," Snug echoed. "Time for you to depart."

"And you?"

Snug gave a wry smile. "I already have."

Carolyn watched as Snug faded, slowly the wall behind her coming into view, her shape growing softer, clearer. She was disappearing.

"Goodbye, Carolyn," the blue girl said. "It was a pleasure to meet you."

"Goodbye, Snug," Carolyn answered. "It was enchanting."

"Go find your young man."

Carolyn put up a hand.

"Even better," Snug said, "go find yourself."

Then there was the wall and there was nothing between it and Carolyn, nothing but air and dust and the light cast by candlelight, and, beyond that, stars that burned brightly a thousand-thousand years ago, and yet their light was new tonight, new tonight as ever.

69

ALFRED HITCHCOCK ORDERED A gallon of French Vanilla and a pot of black coffee—there was no hope of getting back to sleep tonight—and met room service in the quiet, carpeted hall so as not to awaken Alma resting behind the closed suite door. He pulled a fifty-dollar bill from his silk robe and tipped the boy, then tiptoed as lightly as his wobbling bulk allowed and skulked into the bathroom.

It was unpleasant to mix gastronomic delight with a place for defecation, despite the well-appointed room and its elegant gilt and cream tile. He didn't like to consider what all had gone on there, strangers and their bodily functions, ever the hint of past performances, but he told himself he'd been vigilant at the party earlier, almost abstemious, every opportunity for another piece of dessert or an extra drink denied, thwarted by Alma's arrival, her tut-tutting should he reach for a tidbit, any minor morsel, and her insistence to everyone who would listen about the unfairness of it, how he was so good, so careful, yet the smallest dietary infraction meant a pound on him. Others could indulge without a care; it was an injustice.

He did eat, of course, he was no parsimonious monk, yet he didn't want to make a liar of his beloved, so he behaved in public, even when Charles Addams raved about the Lady Fingers, or when the producer's daughter offered a sip of Grasshopper. Fonda, rail thin, with the strained look of a Puritan, could imbibe bourbon and gobble treats all night, Hitchcock mused, never gain a pound, damn him and his American frontier constitution.

It was four a.m.

He stabbed at the ice cream, jammed the silver spoon into its unbroken center, and dug. He was prone to blinding headaches if he ate too quickly, to stomach cramps that doubled him over as if he'd run a mile, though he hadn't run a mile since his youth in Leytonstone, if, even, then, but he enjoyed the risk, a little pain for a spasm of pleasure, an equation that always fascinated him, that old human story, the willingness to grab a temporary delight for a later, nastier devil—a stupid, even brutal, exchange, repeated and repeated over so much more than sweets.

The sugar on his tongue lit up his eyes and he caught a glimpse of his red cheeks in the perfect mirror, spritzed every day, no doubt, by some girl in a black-and-white uniform; he'd filmed actresses as maids a dozen times and always adored the promise of subservience the clothing, their doting on dust, anticipated. He poked at the carton again and considered Grace, gone to marry a prince. Vera would do, enticing, if untested, but already off to wrestle her own beau. He would never have Vera the way he wanted, but he'd never had Grace either, not in the lascivious way the press imagined, or the far tamer version of his visions. He just wanted to adore and be adored. Was that so difficult?

He was collecting Vera at the airport in the morning, *this* morning, after the sun rose, long after this ice cream was digested, long after he slid back into the bed next to patient Alma. What would he think when the newly married goddess stepped across the tarmac, purse slung over her slender arm?

Which newly married goddess: Tarzan's Vera or Rainier's Grace? Did it matter?

The chill started at the back of his neck and flooded his busy brain, a dark wave under his bald pate. He squinted and tightened his fist on the cardboard carton, the scent of vanilla and Alma's flowery soap thick in the yellow-lit air. He considered the vision he'd had at the party, the incandescent silhouette of a girl, a ghost he'd presumed, standing at the edge of the cake table. He saw her, he swore, in skirts and ribbons, like the pretty darlings of his past, Victorian fashion, and she'd lingered by that ridiculous dessert. She was dying for a bite, but, he'd sensed immediately, she was already dead and, no, she couldn't have any, not a little, not a lick, because she had neither the hands to hold a fork, nor the stomach to hold the crumbs. He recognized the longing in her distant eyes, the flick of her tongue on her tender lips, saw her glance at the men in the dark suits and the women in delicate dresses, and understood her envy.

But had there even been a blue girl?

Had he followed her up the stairs? Had he talked with her? Sat in a room and watched her eat?

It wasn't Disney. It wasn't indigestion. It wasn't a dream.

In his memory, she was as real as ice cream, as real as cake. She so clearly *desired* in a way he understood, *desired* what she couldn't have, couldn't get no matter what she offered in trade. Sometimes you don't get what you want, ever, and wasn't that every story he wanted to tell? Life was just like that, a bad deal. And then you died. And if you were particularly unlucky, you were forced back to a party with strangers, staring at treats meant for other people.

It was five after four.

He held the sweetness in his closed mouth, his tongue still, the spoon stuck like a gravedigger's shovel in a half-dug plot, and listened while Alma shifted between expensive sheets haunted by other lodgers' dreams from a week before. He listened to her sniffle and the room service carts rattle in the hall, then closed his eyes and thought of Grace and all the things he could not get, yet he felt no regret, no grief, for the blue girl had shown him he was alive, he was no mere shade, and though the taste of sugar would linger for only a moment more—yes, right there—and then dissolve, the memory of this night would last much, much longer.

70

CAROLYN MISSED THE PARTY already, Hitchcock and his coterie. A tinge of melancholy hit her as she locked the heavy wooden door and closed the metal guard. A chilly fog crept up Eightieth Street, snaking around streetlights and descending on dark parked cars. In a jiffy, her nose was cold and she longed for the comfortable bed in Aunt Bella's guest room.

Aunt Bella. She had ridden to the rescue like well-heeled, gracious cavalry. Carolyn pictured her in Gracie Square, dreaming or painting or dreaming of painting. She would have to catch a cab to get back to her.

But there was a man in the mist. She hadn't expected to see him again, not after finding the lone key on the table in the foyer.

Pete stood on the sidewalk in front of No. 7. "Share a ride?" he said, an unfamiliar hesitation in his voice.

"Sure," she said. "Absolutely." The house key was heavy in her pocket. In the morning it would lay on Bella's hallway table, the one by the telephone niche, and wait for the realtor to retrieve it. Who would use it next? A plumber come to start ripping out the old pipes in the outdated kitchens? A carpenter ready to yank out the battered windowsills? The place would be gutted, transformed into apartments, she supposed. New, more practical spaces for the living.

"Wait—" She touched his arm. "Where do you live? I can't believe I haven't asked."

"There's a lot you don't know about me. My last name's just a start." He stopped. "Wait, that sounded menacing."

"Mr. D'Onofrio," she smirked, "are you a murderer?"

"Definitely not." He held up a hand to the moist air. "This fog would be too obvious if I were Pete the Ripper. Fire the set decorator. I'd play against type and only make mayhem on sunny days."

"Good to hear." She leaned into him.

"Greenwich Village," he said. "That's where I live."

"So bohemian!" She nudged him.

"So affordable," he retorted. "My ma, my sisters, they still live in Brooklyn, but I couldn't stay there."

"I understand," she said. Her father wouldn't understand or her sisters. How do you explain that to people who are perfectly comfortable in the same spot?

They walked toward the museum, the same direction they'd gone at noon. There would be no hailing a cab on a quiet residential street at this hour, but it wouldn't take long to find one on Fifth Avenue.

When they'd slid into its back seat, Carolyn was surprised by the warmth, the humidity of the interior. A block into the ride the windows had steamed. She rubbed the condensation from the dark glass and met her reflection, Pete's behind her: what a pair of apparitions.

"Don't go back," he blurted. "Stay." He took her hand.

She turned and looked at him, his face dappled with the passing lights. "What would I do?"

"I don't know," he said. "You'd find where you belong."

The cab lurched, then picked up speed. Her stomach did a little flip. "Are there stipulations?"

He laughed. "No, no," he said. "None at all."

It wouldn't be safe. It wouldn't be familiar, at least not much of it. There would be her aunt. There would be this city. The tall buildings would tower like canyon walls. Even now the taxi bobbed like a small boat on a river gorge. It could careen or crash or capsize. She closed her eyes and pressed against the seat to feel its rocking. The pace wasn't steady, but it wasn't scary either. There was a bob and a weave, but they kept moving forward. She strained to hear beyond the engines and the road. She listened. Her nerves quieted.

One word: *Stay*. There it was again: *Stay*, in a voice she hadn't heard all evening, but was speaking to her all along.

Carolyn opened her eyes. Pete was watching her, the curve of his mouth gentle, his kind eyes nervous and hopeful.

"Yes," she said. "Yes, I think I will."

He squeezed her hand.

She squeezed back. "You really suppose there's room for another person on this island?"

"There's always space," Pete said, kissing her fingers, then looking up to her face and kissing her lips gently, "for one more soul in Manhattan."

She kissed him back, surprised at how easily she did so, at how comfortably they fit together, and then she marveled at the passing lights, shimmering reds and yellows. "Of course," she agreed. "What's one more on an island of millions?"

"Not *just* one more," Pete said, still holding her hand, still looking into her eyes. "But you."

Author's Note

THIS IS A WORK of fiction and the events in this novel are products of my imagination, but the party was a real occasion and some of these characters are based (loosely) on ancestors to whom I owe a debt of gratitude.

Isabella "Snug" Taylor lived (and died) at No. 7 East Eightieth Street with her divorced mother, Maria Banks Taylor, and her younger brother, Curzon, after their father scandalously abandoned his family for another woman. The tale of his bigamy and the headline-making alimony payment are real, as is his suicide. The shame the first Mrs. Taylor felt was genuine, too, at least according to my mother, their grand-niece. Carolyn is not real, but my mother served as a model for her, and it was from her that I first learned of her family's history in New York.

Isabella Banks Satterthwaite and Dr. Thomas Satterthwaite and their passion for medical progress (especially in the fields of maternal and infant care) are well-documented. Isabella lived in the town house until 1955, when she died at age ninety-seven.

James Lenox, book collector and philanthropist, was one of the founders of the New York Public Library. (You can wave at his portrait the next time you visit.) He also, famously, rarely left his home on lower Fifth Avenue and would have kept his distance from any liquor-soaked shindig in his living years. I'm not sure what his ghost is up to, but I doubt it's cocktail parties.

Isabella Banks Markell was my grandfather's sister. Her paintings of the East River during the war and her cityscapes of New York and Boston are in museums and art collections across the country.

Alfred and Alma Hitchcock, Charles and Barbara Addams, and Henry Fonda were, of course, real humans and did attend the party. (Well, maybe not Barbara.) But I've invented their dialogue and have used poetic license with the concerns that were (or were not) haunting them that evening. Three biographies I recommend are Peter Ackroyd's *Alfred Hitchcock*, Devin McKinney's

The Man Who Saw a Ghost: The Life and Work of Henry Fonda, and Linda H. Davis's *Charles Addams: A Cartoonist's Life*.

My mother adored Johnny Kander, whom she befriended during those Nebagamon summers. Of course, he went on to a brilliant Broadway career, though I have no evidence they ever spoke after their teen years and his appearance at the party is all my imagination.

The Brokaw Mansion existed. It is long gone.

Oscar, the cat, was not at the party. He was my family's companion for over a decade and recently passed away. I hope he's having an afterlife filled with ample food and warm laps.

Acknowledgments

ALL THANKS TO MARK Gottlieb and Trident Media Group. I'm wildly fortunate to have you as my agent. This novel would still be in my computer if it weren't for your enthusiasm and skill.

To Peter Borland, editor extraordinaire, whose intelligence and wit have made this novel a whole lot better than it was before. Working with you is a master class in writing fiction and I am forever grateful. For the entire team at Atria, especially Libby McGuire, Dana Trocker, Elizabeth Byer, Davina Mock-Maniscalco, Dominick Montalto, Maudee Genao, Gena Lanzi, and Hannah Frankel (who has answers for all my questions).

To my colleagues past and present at SFASU: Bridget Adams, Mark Barringer, Andrew Brininstool, Lauren Burrow, Court Carney, Daryl Farmer, Dean Franks, Michael Given, Ericka Hoagland, Joyce Johnston, M. Dustin Knepp, Eralda Lameborshi, Billie Longino, Jen McClanaghan, Jason McIntosh, Steve Marsden, Aaron Milstead, Heather Olson Beal, Dylan Parkhurst, Sara Parks, Matt Ramsey, Michael Sheehan, Elizabeth Tasker-Davis, Amber Wagnon, Kevin West, Jerry Williams, and especially Mike Martin, who has been talking fiction with me forever and puts up with my wandering into his office.

To the students too many to name, but in particular Chris Allen, Brent Beal, Rachel Blythe, Tim Bryant, Rae Bynum, Charlene Caruthers, Sarah Cisco, James Clark, Joy Clark, David Collins, Amy Collins-Russell, Jason Couch, Kelsey Cox, Mia Criswell, Lisa Fountain, M. Brett Gaffney, Terri Hale, Nicole Hall, Tennessee Hill, Josh Hines, Ryan Hunke, Jamie Ingrassia, Sierra McGee, Timothy Mercer, Mahailey Oliver, Marthaeus Perkins, Ray Peterson, Jade Ramsey, Celia Ranniger, Emily Townsend, and January Williams.

Thanks to Emma Hill for her early reading of the manuscript and marvelous advice.

To Matt Batt, Matt Burgess, Vera Herbert, and Eric Schlich for the early support.

ACKNOWLEDGMENTS

To my teachers: George Makana Clark, John Goulet, Bob Lamb, William J. Palmer, Sheila Roberts, Ron Wallace, and especially Del Lewis.

To Ronnie Craig, Maija Kroeger, Michael S. Manley, Mark Staunton, and Bill and June Stuckey.

To Stephen and Linda Autrey, Kyle and Jane Childress, Katie Parr, and Kelly Young.

To the Writers' League of Texas, especially Becka Oliver. Without their guidance and advice, this book would never have gotten to New York.

To the writers who have inspired and helped me along the way—Michael Cocchiarale, Kafah Haggerty, Matt Hart, Jack Heifner, Ann Hood, Zeke Jarvis, Toni Jensen, Maya Shanbhag Lang, Johannes Lichtman, Susan Mohammed, Stewart O'Nan, Maurice Ruffin, Stacey Swann, James Wade, and Tom Williams.

To Joe R. Lansdale, who has kept the faith in me for twenty years.

To Reed Clark, Jane Lambert, Mark Lien, Dawn Roe, Rick Wilgrubs, Marie Woods-Petitti, and Russell and Maryann Swift.

To my friends back in Wisconsin and beyond: Adam Chaffee, Amy Chaffee, Jennifer Frankey-Moehn, Greg and Kathy Gaie, Paul and Pam Guilbault, Nick Harkin, Brian Kapell, Nate Lee, Rob Rownd, Antonio and Mary Sella, Joe and Lenette Thompson, and Faith Williams.

To John Urban, who has kept the faith for longer than anyone who isn't related to me.

To Blossom Dearie and Sammy Davis, Jr., whose music could always get me to 1956.

To the Butterworth family: Mike, Gina, Ray, and James.

To all the Banks family up north. This story is yours, too.

To my family: my parents James and Cornelia McDermott, my siblings Liz and Steve Thurlow, Jim and Judilynn McDermott, Nell McDermott, Julie and Gerry Whitty, Aaslaug and Jens Bull, and their many beautiful children.

To Audrey, the daughter of our dreams who is so much better in reality.

And to Christine—first editor, best friend, forever love.